Bang!

Bang!

an anthology of modern noir fiction

Edited by Andrew Hook

All stories are original to this collection

Cover art via Getty Stock

ISBN number: 978-1-7398195-9-0

Printed and Bound by 4Edge

Published by:

Head Shot
85 Gertrude Road
Norwich
UK

editorheadshot@gmail.com
www.headshotpress.com

for the lost

Contents

BANG!
BANG!
BANG!

Introduction:

Like A Hole In The Head

In the 1978 Italian made-for-television giallo film *Closed Circuit* (Italian: *Circuito chiuso*, directed by Giuliano Montaldo), an audience member is shot dead in a cinema during a matinée showing of a Spaghetti Western. It takes a while for the police to figure it out, but eventually they realise the shot was fired from a gun held by one of the characters in the movie that the audience were actually watching. The shot came from the cinema screen itself.

When I had the idea for this anthology I was specifically seeking fiction which embraced the noir genre. Stories of cynicism, fatalism, and moral ambiguity. Life is more interesting at the edges. With crime being one of the most popular genres in terms of sales and the number of books published annually, you might think a new anthology of crime fiction is needed like a hole in the head, but whilst the noir genre developed from short fiction published in pulp magazines in year zero, there aren't too many markets for the shorter form nowadays. There's certainly a need for it, though. If not among readers, then certainly amongst writers.

There were one hundred and sixty stories submitted for *Bang!*. Surprisingly – and I say this because from experience I'd expected a lot of chaff amongst the wheat – most were of high quality. Even removing those which didn't fit my personal definition of noir meant I probably could have accepted enough to fill two anthologies. Difficult decisions were made, but once selected I found these stories were the *only* ones I could have taken. They work together. They're grim, gritty, thoughtful, often threaded with black humour, and occasionally leftfield whilst still fitting the noir remit, meaning I believe, there's plenty here for noir afficionados as well as those less familiar with the crime sub-genre.

We have crooks and crooked cops, lost and missing persons, those running and those hiding, femme fatales, avocados, downbeat PIs, deadbeat insurance investigators, hotel detectives and unsavory gangs, those doing wrong and those done wrong by, fated lovers and failed robberies; even Inspector Maigret at the infamous château in Roissy. What more could you ask for?

Ah, so you're questioning the significance of the *Closed Circuit* reference at the beginning of this intro?

Well, you see the guy on the cover?

His gun is loaded.

Bang!

Andew Hook
February, 2023

Bang!

Out Of Town

Tim Lees

Tap tap tap. Heels in the hallway. But I don't call, don't ask the time or when I'm getting out of here.

First lesson in control, as Taylor used to say: *control yourself.*

He liked me with him, liked having a looker on the team. He taught me how to stand and pose and keep my face dead still, focus on him so that everybody'd know he was the one in charge. "It's a trick," he'd say, "an act," and move his hands like he was shuffling cards. "They're watching you, you're watching me. See how it works?"

He bought me clothes, good stuff, designer names. Never tried to touch me but that once, and even then it's more as if he felt he should, like maybe I'd expect it. Living up to some idea, some picture in his head. By then I knew the truth, in any case, that he was still in love with his ex-wife, the kind of storybook romance you'll never hear from anybody else, I'm sure. The tale-tellers, the finger-pointers, they're blind to how he really was. I could have told them: he used to do her gardening, down on his hands and knees, long after she left him. He hurt his back shifting her furniture around. I gave him massages, laid on the couch, easing the aches. Would they believe that? Would they even think it's possible?

BRUTAL GANG BOSS SLAIN.

They showed me all the headlines. Took some pleasure in it, too.

I wouldn't react, I wouldn't cry or curse at them.

I held it in, deep down.

1

"Psycho bitch," they said. "She never even blinked."
He taught me well.

They tell me he was forty-five but I know better. He'd lived a hundred lives before this, maybe more. He told me he had dreams, better than cinema, he said. He'd been a prince in Egypt, centuries ago, and talked about the palm trees and the way the light caught on the river, and how everyone would bow when he went by, row after row of bare, brown backs. Or he'd been a buccaneer, sword in hand, out chasing gold and glory – oh, he loved that one!

"It's in the blood, girl. Piracy!"

He grinned at me.

They only ever saw the rage in him. The force. Never the kindness or compassion. Those were feelings he kept deep, let out just when he needed them.

"What's in you, babe, it's in you for a reason. Learn to use it. As and when, hey?" His eyes were blue, ice-blue, and never seemed to blink. "As and when, hey, babe?"

They took my phone away. They took my watch. They took my shoes, my purse. I get up, pace in stockinged feet. No sound. No sound at all. I want a smoke, a drink. The point is not to shout. Don't lose it. That's what he'd tell me, "Don't lose it, Shugs." He called me Shugs, Shugs for Sugar. He was Taylor. Just Taylor, no first name. I bet even his wife called him that. I never met her, never wanted to. We were like two halves of his life, two sides of a coin, never together, never in the same place, like that just wasn't possible. He was the link and barrier between us, both in one.

Maybe that's changed now. Maybe we'll meet. Maybe we'll find we're sisters, that's my dream. We'll go to lunch, talk over old times. Or we'll meet and there'll be nothing, void, the only link between us gone for good.

I did his rounds with him. Smoke, pills, powders. And the money. Money, most of all.

Those were early days. But even then, he was ambitious. That's why I was there, he said. For class. Building the brand, he called it. He liked me wearing short skirts, crop-tops, stockings. Everyone watching, wanting, no-one with the nerve to try. They all thought I was his. They didn't dare. But Taylor understood, he knew the tricks. "You never want a thing the way you want a thing that you can't have." He could have made it any way he chose, even legit, if he'd have wanted it. But that's a train that drove too slow for him. Taylor was fast track, all the way.

He stopped me drinking. He'd see me with a brandy, reach across and take the glass from out my hand. "Complexion, Shugs." Spring water with a twist, that's what he liked me on. I'd slip a vodka in it when he wasn't looking, just to keep my head. I don't know how I could have coped without. It got me dizzy, sometimes, seeing what was going on, a glimpse of this and that, flashes of a story that I'd never see the start or end of. So I'd drink, but wouldn't let it show. Not once.

Control.

He said he got his class from me. Fact is, it ran both ways. From him, I got my sense of purpose, the sense that I was going someplace, not just drifting anymore. That's why we were together. None of it was accident.

"All this," he said, "all this was laid out years before. It's destiny, babe, that's what. Destiny."

There was a place on 6th street that he called "the Office". There were places all around town by then, some he owned and some belonged to friends or guys who owed him, or wanted favors. All these secret spots where he could disappear, his life locked off in watertight compartments, one here, one there, a half a dozen somewhere else. But at the Office, that's where I met the crew: Lewis, Pinski, Brig, Jamaica Jay, and Pete, who was his bodyguard. It's Pete that I got closest with. We'd flank him, like those animals you see on coats of arms, me one side, Pete the other. Pete was gentle, never mind his size, he didn't drink or drug, just lived to hit the gym each day, work out, his body getting bigger, full of liquid protein and the steroids that he told me he'd stopped taking, though I never did believe him. "Too much, you look like Frankenstein," he said. I watched his body blow up round him like a cancer, like this big, beautiful cancer. He'd ask me to go shopping with him, pick out new clothes, he'd gotten way too big for all the old ones, jackets, shirts, and jeans that squeezed his calves and thighs. He'd bag up last month's fashions, give to charities and thrift stores, scrupulous about his waste. I'd picture some poor homeless guy, struggling into Pete's gigantic clothes, the jacket like a tent on him, pants that could have fit a family. Taylor liked him for the way he looked, but Pete wasn't the mean one. Like me, he did an act.

He did a show.

I went with them. I went with them, because I didn't want to be the kept woman, the woman with the smart clothes, telling everyone, "I didn't know." Because it scared me and it pulled me in, both at once.

And because it was the business. It was what we did. Taylor's business, my business.

I went with him that last time, too.

"You sure you're up for this one, Shugs?"

"Sure I'm sure."

It was excitement. It was a trip out of town, a chance to see some trees and grass again.

He taught me never to react. Never show my feelings.

"But you're good at that," he said.

He'd seen my talent. Seen it, recognized it, brought it out.

Taylor, who was fine showing his feelings, when he chose. Who kept them on a leash, one more asset to be used.

As and when.

"It won't take long," he said, like it was hardly worth me going. Like even then, maybe he knew.

But I said, "I'll come."

We drove. Two cars, up into the hills. Soon there were trees, then rows of wooden houses, and a church, and trees again. It wasn't a big house where we stopped, though it looked big to me, used to living in the city, in rooms and shared apartments and the rest. Some kids were playing soccer on a field across the street. We sat and watched them for a while. No-one spoke. One of them scored and threw his hands up. He tugged his shirt over his head and did a lap of honor.

OUT OF TOWN

Taylor watched him circling the pitch. Then said, "OK." The house was set back. The front lawn was scraggy, high, untended for a year or more. I'd never had a front lawn but I reckoned if I had, then I'd have had the smartest front lawn on the street, smooth and level as a pool table. It bothers me, that kind of stuff. When someone's got something and won't take care of it. It bothers me.

The guy inside was old. Like sixty, maybe, in an old blue cardigan and suit pants. He looked like Bing Crosby. He poured drinks for everyone – Pete had spring water – and when he came to me I said, "I'll have what they're having," and Taylor glanced across but didn't say a word. The place was nice but sort of cold. Big leather couch and armchairs, good rugs, but no ornaments, no pictures on the walls, no magazines. Nothing personal. Like no-one really lived there. I heard a TV in the back room but Jay went through and turned it off. "Sit, sit," said the older guy. No-one did. Taylor spoke. He asked about the guy's family – he had a daughter somewhere, and Taylor, just casually, let it drop he knew the street she lived on. "Nice neighborhood," he said. It sounded very friendly, very intimate. Taylor smiled, that smile he had with no feeling behind it. Then he said, "Sold us short, Bill, last time." Bill, that was his name. Bill. Not Bing. "Last time, and the time before."

Bill said, "Hey. Have another drink." He picked up the bottle, but no-one wanted refills. He said, "You know how these things go."

"No, Bill, I don't." Taylor's voice was smooth, hushed. "How's that? How do they go?"

"Some weeks – "

"Not talking weeks, Bill."

Bill, he said, and I kept thinking, *Bing*. I couldn't help it. *Bing, Bing, Bing*. Just automatic.

They'd all expected Bill to cave. But he kept smiling, keeping up the act. Pete moved in. Not doing anything, just muscling in on Bill's space. Standing over him. Bill said, "Hey!" and moved away but Pete went with him, close. Then someone, I think Jay, said, "Who's upstairs?"

"Whadya mean, upstairs?" Bill got angry fast.

"Upstairs. I heard a noise. Who's up there?"

"No-one's up there!" Bill was talking quickly. "You think I'd try something like that? You're out of your minds! You think I'd do that? You think – "

His voice went high.

Taylor handed me his keys.

"Wait in the car," he said. "Keep it locked. We'll be one minute, OK?"

I took the keys. Folded them in my hand. Walked to the door like it was any normal door in any normal house. Walked down the drive. *Tap tap tap.* Kids still playing in the field across the way, running, diving, colored summer shirts like flags.

I heard the first two shots before I even reached the car. Pistol shots, quick succession. *Bam. Bam.* A pause, like someone taking breath. Then the automatic fire. I stood there. Turned one way, then the other. The kids in the field looked up. I thought, *I should be in the car. I should start the engine.* But I didn't move.

I remember afterwards.

I remember Pete. His body, swollen, beautiful, and what they did to it. So much work, so much effort, gone in moments.

Taylor, from the prince, the buccaneer, to this.

He'd told me he'd be back. In fifty, or a hundred years.

They made me see the bodies. Made me look at them, identify them.

They took my phone away. They took my phone, my purse, my shoes.

I lift my fist to hammer on the door, I lift my head to shout. But I don't do either.

I know the rules.

Whatever's there, inside, you don't show it. You keep it for yourself.

What Taylor said.

He loved having a looker on the team. "Class, Shugs. Pure, pure class."

I tip my head back. Pose. Imagine it's a photoshoot, a fashion spread, there in that cold, locked, empty room.

They said, "Tell us about him."

"Who?" I said.

"John Eric Taylor."

"Dunno no John Eric. Who's that?"

I kept it all inside me, like he said. Voice empty, face a blank. No matter how they raged and shouted, what they promised me or threatened. I wouldn't let them in. Not in my head, under my skin. That's what they wanted. And I kept them out.

"Cold bitch," they said.

Forget what's going on inside. Forget that I could scream his name.

It's an act, a trick.

Control, he called it.

Like doing nothing. But a hundred – no, a thousand times more difficult.

Salamander

Douglas Thompson

The rain kept on down hard in straight lines in the city of São Paulo. Geometric rain in parallel like rays of light from the sun that never meet, never get further apart. Except there was no light, except the artificial kind, the neon and sodium. City night admits no hope, only further compromises, bargains and debts. Silver. Lines of coins and coke. New debts, old debts, debts gone bad. Transactions. They send me to keep track of these things, for reasons best known to themselves, the city fathers. Slim silver rain like spears, like prison bars, like piano keys spilling muted jazz from decayed brick doorways, weathered with peeling paint and old torn posters, the faint aroma of piss. They call me *Caçador*, meaning *Hunter*, a joke nobody laughs at anymore, because it's the name I was born with. We don't notice coincidence when it doesn't happen. People don't notice me anyway, it's part of the job description.

They sent me to track down Salgueiro, a one-time reliable grass, gone rogue, gone off radar, one time part of the Fortaleza gang. But like parallel lines of light, Salgueiro and I might never meet. Only continuously discover that we had been travelling along side to each other, narrowly missing. Wherever I arrived I would find Salgueiro had just left there, had left only the stub of a cigarette, a folded bill, a tooth pick, a burnt match. If the Forteleza knew he had been our deep throat, then how come his heart was still beating, his blood not all over the pavements? Or if they knew and he still walked, did that mean every scrap Salgueiro had ever fed us was counterfeit? That the city fathers had been played for

9

fools, only jailed or killed the strays Forteleza wanted us to, the scraps they had dispensed with?

The longer I walked and tracked and pursued, the more I began to see a third possibility, unlikely though it seemed, that Salgueiro had finally achieved the impossible: some kind of condition of absolute transparency and elusiveness, in which nobody, neither I nor the Fortaleza would ever catch up with him. It seemed personal, but how could it be possible? Could he have some kind of tracker placed on me? I changed my phones regularly. And if he could somehow track my every move towards him in advance then why not try to kill me? Was he amusing himself with me, like a cat with a mouse? But I am no mouse, I told myself, more like a rat, a vampire bat. He'd stumble and make a wrong move in the end, it was inevitable. I just had to keep up my age-old dogged work, follow the sickly trail of sweat that every living thing leaves, in its long panicked flight from *Senhor Morte*, the Hunter.

In the end my break came through an intermediary, a loose canon as it were, a prostitute named Lucia Volo, who I caught up with just after Salgueiro had finished with her. She had the bruises and cuts, more than just smudged lipstick to prove it. She seemed far too beautiful to be a fallen angel in that convent of sadness, the *Blood Moon Club* in Vila Mimosa. She didn't walk across the shabby bar to meet me, so much as she poured, with the grace of a jaguar. Her clothes, her body, seemed like mere vessels, unable to contain, spilling over with, the heady essence of femininity which welled up continuously from within her, like her sighs and tears, her songs she would later sing me. *You want to know about Salgueiro?* she whispered in my ear, -*then buy me a bottle and we'll find a room. It's not safe to talk here in the open.* That seemed simultaneously both understatement and redundancy, given the jaded setting, the death's head tattoos on the barman's biceps, the carved serpents on the hilt of his dagger, the glint of an AK-47 behind the counter.

Do you really expect me to tell you where to find him, even if I knew? -she asked me, as she undressed behind the unlikely modesty of an antique chinoiserie screen in her boudoir.

Probably not, no... I sighed. *That would be like asking for the meaning of life, the hidden face of God, the horseman's word, wouldn't it?*

You're strange... she said, fixing me with a stare like an archer taking aim. -*Even stranger than him. Why do you wear that black pinstripe suit all the time? It makes you look like a time traveller, a hit man from the 1920's. You're hardly undercover, are you?*

Well, have you ever seen me here before? I laughed, loosening my tie.

I don't think so.

And yet I've been here hundreds of time. You see? Or rather you don't. What is he like, Salgueiro?

She shrugged. *All I know is what we do together, the few clues he let's slip. Phrases he comes out with when he's off guard. Let me show you. We mustn't crease that suit of yours now though...*

He has you do that? And that? And this? -I asked over the following half hour, feeling increasingly shocked, reluctantly excited, and gradually depraved.

Why did he betray the Fortaleza? -I asked her at one point, hoping to catch her off guard, guessing she knew more than the little miss ignorant act.

Who says he did? -She mumbled, before she could stop herself *...if he is still true to his people, the grassroots? And who is true, anyway, Hunter, at the end of the day in matters of the heart? You have a wife, yes?* I nodded, reluctantly, sitting up in bed and looking for my scattered clothes. -*And every time from now on when you think of me secretly when you and her porra-porra with each other, won't that be betrayal of the mind? And if of the mind then how long before of the heart?* -She asked, licking her finger and tracing it along the centre of my chest as if planning a surgeon's incision. *Is all interconnected intimately, I think. No?*

By the time I left, as well as some aches and hungers I'd never known before and have done my best to forget since, I had gathered a few scraps, enigmatic phrases Lucio Volo said that Salgueiro sometimes spouted in his lead-up to the extremity of passion. *The falcon cannot hear the falconer... The blood-dimmed tide is loosed... The ceremony of innocence is drowned... with lion body and the head of a man... a gaze blank and pitiless as the sun... the indignant desert birds...* They all sounded vaguely familiar to me. I went back to headquarters and searched through old files, photographs of personal effects we had confiscated on previous arrests and search warrants issued on the safe-houses and hideaways of Salgueiro. The works of William Butler Yeats, translated into Portuguese in 1924, a copy from the Jesuit library attached to the church of Saint Ignatius in the Sumarezinho quarter. I slipped the old faded volume into my pocket and set off to find if any of the keepers of the institution happened to remember their unlikely borrower.

*

In the vestry of Saint Ignatius, I asked a young novice for a glass of water to recover my composure from the hot bustling streets outside. But it was a priest who brought the drink to me after a suspicious pause and a queer smirk on his face. *Fresh from the oven, officer?*

Stale as old socks more like, I answered, grimacing at the aroma of my own armpits. *I wish I lived in the fridge like this.*

Please signor, I work here, only the dead live here... if you get my meaning.

Now I noticed that the drink he handed me was in a silver goblet. My thirst was such that only after the first gulp did I notice it wasn't water. I nearly spat it out. *Hey, what the hell is this merda, holy fucking water?*

Ahh... no need to profane, my son, he chuckled, *it just has the tiniest tincture of creme de menthe in it, a pick me-up good enough for our holy father after all.* I immediately began to feel unsteady on my feet and he took me by the arm to sit down in the empty nave, a congregation of one. I heard his footsteps going away then the sound of heavy bolts closing on the outer door.

To my surprise, Lucia Volo came in and sat down in the pew beside me as my head went on reeling. She ran her hands through my hair, wiped my brow, kissed me lightly on the cheek, like Jesus or Judas I felt reluctant to decide. *Wait here now...* she said. *I've decided to bring him to you.*

W-w-who? I stammered, my hands clutching at the polished wood bench beneath me.

Who do you think? -she winked. *You know the story goes that he cut his own father's heart out and ate it raw, don't you? -Because he'd betrayed his mother. He's not just feared but loved in these streets. It takes a mixture of both to bring him to the glove. Do you know about the phoenix and the salamander? That thing that's loose inside you now is like the mezcal worm, the cleansing fire of God...*

I don't... I d-don't understand what you're talking... about... I gasped, clutching my chest. But she was gone already, hurrying off to bring Salgueiro back I assumed. How sweet. Just when I suddenly felt least disposed to make his acquaintance. A sense of numb dread had spread over me. I felt as if I was losing the use of my limbs, some kind of progressive paralysis taking hold. Where had the priest gone and what on earth had he drugged me with?

As if to answer me I now saw him climb into his pulpit and throw open an enormous bible and begin bawling at me. *Are you ready to receive him, my son? To receive the host?* -I stood up and nearly collapsed but forced myself forward into a half fall, half stagger, hearing the priest's voice continue to bellow after me as I unbolted the door and fell out into the crowded streets. My whole vision was swimming and rotating. The heat and noise after the cool of the church was overwhelming. I ran and ran, bumping into people I could scarcely focus on. I knew I had to try to get the poison out of me, if it wasn't too late. Whisky, rum, the first bar I could stumble into, anything would do, flash my I.D. if I had to. Unusual medication, but needs must in a civil emergency. If I could flush my system out, fight poison with poison then my liver might get the message and live to tell the tale along with its unhappy owner. But I was hallucinating like crazy, members of the crowd I was bouncing off were turning into blue squids, pink octopus, visible musical notes flooding out of their mouths in primary colours like birds of paradise.

*

BANG!

I woke up some time later in an obscure courtyard, on a debris skip, covered in plaintain leaves and sunflower oil. I reached for the cigarettes in my pocket and nearly lit one before I realised I'd have been self-immolating before the first glorious draw. Returning to the police station after an appropriate scrub-up I found that nobody recognised me. Nobody seemed to have calendars on their walls anymore, but when I finally found one I saw to my incredulity that ten years had gone by. Of course I grabbed and shook the first secretary to walk by me, and asked if this was some practical fucking joke or something. Somebody shouted from across the room, suspecting I was an impostor.

Hiding in the toilets I threw more water over my head and examined my face in the mirror and decided that I didn't seem to have aged a day. More than could be said for the city when I crept outside again. Now I realised that cars and buses and trains were quieter, faster, sleeker, clothes and fashions subtly different, but the thickness of pollution and overcrowding hellishly worse. Rashes of fresh high-rise blocks had risen up everywhere like threatening teeth. Beloved slums and dives had been levelled or overhauled in the cause of gentrification. Beautiful plastic people in primary colours danced the night away in districts that I remembered as cement factories and brothels. I felt like the ghost at the feast, Rip Van Winkle, the masque of the red death. Hunter home from the hill.

Returning to what I thought had been my house in my own street, I found a strange family living there, the old woman of which told some twisted and incoherent tale implying that my wife had left there years ago after her husband had suddenly gone missing. It was useless. I was nobody, I had nothing anymore. Displaced in time. Collapsing on the dusty pavement at the end of the street, I pulled my hat down over my eyes to cry myself to sleep. I woke an hour later with a green gecko running across my hands. I picked him up and opened my mouth wide, we looked each other in the eye, but he bit me first and made his getaway.

SALAMANDER

When I caught up with Lucia Volo again, I didn't recognise her at first. What I thought was an aged tramp shuffled up and sat down beside me on a park bench on the Avenida Paulista in the early hours of the morning. *Why didn't you wait for me?* -an unexpectedly familiar voice from within the living pile of rags said close to my ear. She looked so male now that I wondered if she had somehow changed gender. A passer-by came by and she spun around to beg from him in a deeper male voice, the disguise immersive. *I found Salgueiro for you!* -she hissed, turning back to me. She indicated a sinister bag she had under her arm, stained with dirt or blood it was hard to tell. Something about the package, the vague smell from it, disturbed and threatened me. *I need to show you..* she whispered. *Let me take you some place, my eyrie.*

Your what? I laughed, breaking into a cough.

Never mind, follow me and find out. You won't be sorry. She winked, as voluptuously as she could manage, given the disguise, and the years gone by, the toll on both of us.

Incredibly, Lucia Volo or whoever she really was or always had been, had eked out a secret den for herself on the rooftop of an ageing 1970's towerblock, by using a disused fire escape stair that everyone had forgotten about. Up there she had some sort of tent made of tarpaulin, and a brazier stolen from a building site, on which I saw she had been cooking small animals, rodent smorgasbord, as if they were the finest delicacies, roadkill kebabs.

She handed me a bottle of Tequila and we perched together on the edge of the parapet to admire the spectacular view. Lucia withdrew the mystery object from her rucksack at last. Even after all these years, I somehow half expected it to be Salgueiro's severed head, but in fact it was only a falcon. But wait. *Only* a falcon; what am I saying? She slipped its leather hood off and rested it on a thick towel around her arm, preparing to loose its rope and set it free, presumably to go pick up smaller birds for her to cook over her open fire.

Did you ever see Salgueiro yourself, face to face, Hunter? Lucia asked. She seemed to be laughing at me now. *What makes you think he was a man? Why not a woman? A bird, even?*

BANG!

The name means willow, who bends in the wind.

Before the falcon took off, it climbed onto my lap and began tearing gently at my clothes and skin. Numb, bemused, I somehow didn't mind. It reminded me a bit of something Lucia had done to me ten years ago, or was that ten days, ten minutes? Know thy self, as the ancient Greeks said, every day a school day. Beneath the tanned and sullied brown of my skin, the bird progressively exposed scraps of reptilian green, scaled flesh, revealing what? I was salamander, gecko, lizard, phoenix bird. Beneath that, digging deeper still, it exposed black pinstripe fabric again. A man within a man within a man. Until seemingly satisfied that I was immortal and eternal as it was, the falcon spread its wings and leapt into the air to sail down again towards the hot, raging city below. Even if I followed it now, I knew that nothing would ever be over.

Savor Life

Jamey Gallagher

The sidewalk was still stained where the insured had landed, reddish-brown Rorschach blots against gray concrete. Resisting interpretation, Reyersen slid black and white photos out of a manilla folder and held them away from his face, telescoping his arm because he was nearsighted. One of the stains on the sidewalk was from the crik of blood that had leaked out of the man's mouth, another from the brains that had escaped the cage of his skull when it cracked open against concrete. The poor sap. Or the fortunate fellow. If what he'd intended was to end his life, he had ended it, definitively, in one violent stroke. In the photo the man wore a tan raincoat over a black suit. His tie hung loose around his neck, exposing the hairy notch below his Adam's apple. He'd landed on his back. Reyersen imagined him waving his arms and legs as he fell, as if he could catch on to something in the air and hold himself back.

The man had worn glasses. The wire frame had come loose from around one of his ears. The close-up photos of the man's head had an artistic look, like they'd been shot by Man Ray. Disquieting, but also aesthetically appealing. Reyersen wondered how drastically the features had been jarred out of shape, how different the man would have looked before his head impacted the pavement. The face in the photo looked lopsided, but also dependable, the kind of guy you could trust. There were dozens of men like that at Savor Life, the insurance company Reyersen worked for. The logo of the company was a white bird against a blue circle, a positive spin on the insurance business. Everything public-facing about the company exuded positivity. Reyersen worked the dirty jobs. Jobs like this, where he had to determine whether someone had killed himself, been killed, or whether the fall had been, as reported, an "accident".

He compared the photos to the sidewalk again before sliding them back into the folder and crouching. He touched the rough concrete, then lay in the position Ed Wholley had been in when he landed. The sidewalk was on a sidestreet, an alley, really, so there wasn't a lot of foot traffic, but a young couple walked past arm in arm, cutting through to get to the next street, glancing down at him curiously. Not that Reyersen cared. He had a job to do, and he was damn-well going to do it.

It was a cool early March day. Birds had returned to the city. A few crows hunched on the molding of the building across the alley, a brownstone that'd been there forever. The building from which Wholley had fallen, on the other hand, was modern, built within the last ten years — new but far from nice, a brutalist structure that already looked in need of repair, if not demolition. A cheap hotel with small balconies attached to the sides of all the rooms. It didn't jibe with the older buildings in the area, with their cornices and brick faces. It looked temporary. Glancing up at the top of the building gave Reyersen vertigo.

He placed his cheek against the stained concrete, which smelled like ozone and iron, then looked up at the sky between the buildings. The "accident" had occurred eight days earlier, on one of those gray February days that feel both interminable and too short, days that shut down like guillotine blades, days everyone was happy to see end. Reysersen raised his arms and legs in the air, shook them a little. A man wearing a raincoat identical to the one Wholley had worn passed on the sidewalk, his face hidden.

Reyersen clambered up from the pavement, brushing grit off his jacket. It was a little after lunch – he'd downed a crab cake at a local bar with two colleagues – and he felt full and, thanks to the martinis, loagy, yet the case intrigued him. Not because there was any great mystery to it but because he recognized something of himself in Ed Wholley, the part he wanted to kill off.

He entered the hotel from the side door in the alley, a simple red door with no windows or markings of any kind, unlocked. The maroon carpeting inside was thin, the walls dark, half the lightbulbs in their cages on the wall dead. The ammoniac stench of urine rose from one corner. A large man, as hairy and stout as a wrestler, emerged from a room down the hall, clad in an undershirt and loose gray pants. A towel, even from this distance visibly dotted with blood and snot, was draped over his shoulder, and he held a shaving mug and razor. He passed Reyersen with a grunt, possibly of warning. A little down the hallway, Reyersen heard the sounds of what might have been sex or might have been a physical altercation behind one of the doors. He had his money on sex but wasn't going to hang around to collect.

He eschewed the elevator and climbed the stairs to the tenth floor, the floor Wholley had "fallen" from. The stairwell was dark, his footsteps echoing against concrete. A lightbulb flickered on one of the landings. He had the feeling only prostitutes and drunks ever used this stairwell. He expected to see a body slumped against the wall at every turn, not dead but not in any appreciable way alive, but there was only interminable darkness, the concrete stairs, his echoing footsteps.

The tenth floor hallway was identical to the one downstairs but bookended by two small windows. Weak light stroking through the windows made the walls look darker, more desolate than those on the bottom floor. Reyersen walked to the end of one hallway, looked out the window. Half the buildings were taller than the hotel. He looked down on the old basilica a few blocks away, its stone walls breaking up all the brick. He could almost see the harbor, in the process of being built up into some kind of tourist destination. As if that was ever going to work. He could see small local businesses and tall old buildings. The Masonic Temple. It was a city overlaid on a dark history. Enslaved people had once been driven through the center of the city, and, before that, the land had been ripped away from Native tribes.

Room 1021 had been discretely blocked off. Instead of ostentatious yellow caution tape, a simple seal covered the doorknob. Reyersen slid the blade of the putty knife he kept in his coat pocket into the slot of the door, jimmied the latch, slipped into the room, and closed the door behind him. He could have gone to the hotel management and explained who he was and what he needed to do, and they might have let him into the room anyway, but he'd been in too many situations where he couldn't get what he wanted by following official protocol. He did what he had to do to find out what he needed to know. He was a professional. Besides, he liked the risk of being caught, the frisson of potential danger. Part of him *wanted* to get caught. He'd been like that all his life.

An empty fifth of whiskey stood on the bedside table beside an ashtray full of five or six cigarette butts, smoked to the quick. None of them had lipstick on their filters. Beside the bottle and ashtray was a ragged paperback copy of a dimestore novel, *The Last Days of Lucky Lamore*. Reyersen pocketed the book.

The furnishings in the small room already looked dated. The accommodations would have been acceptable ten years ago, but now they belonged to an earlier era – the world had changed since the forties. Gone ultramodern. Supposedly. There was a fuzzy carpet under the chintzy bed. There was wall art featuring landscapes that were supposed to look grand and high class but only managed to look sad – some kind of country scene from three hundred years ago, back when there were natives and the land looked dramatic. The lighting in the painting was all golden and verdant green.

Reyersen settled onto the bed. Wholley had been wearing his raincoat, so he must not have been in the room long before "falling". He imagined Wholley, with his dependable head and features that didn't project any emotion, entering the room, sliding the whiskey bottle out of his pocket. Maybe it had been empty already. Maybe he'd spent the night before drinking in one of the seedy bars around Fells Point. It had been 2pm when he fell/jumped off the balcony. Maybe a good greasy lunch would have saved him. Or a nap.

Reyersen paced the room. He walked to the sliding doors letting out onto the balcony. To call it a balcony was a kindness. It was a cheap structure, walking onto it at all an enactment of suicidal desire. The balcony was not even large enough for a folding chair. The only thing one could do was stand on it, smoking a cigarette, looking out over the city. On the day Wholley jumped, the city would have looked monochromatic. Dull browns, dull reds, dull grays. An ugly soup. The balcony looked like it had been designed for suicides. Reyersen imagined dozens of people jumping from their balconies at the same time, a ballet of human desperation. He imagined all of them landing with dull thuds, barely audible from ten stories up. The railing around the balcony was four feet tall, and Wholley would have had to climb it. There would be no accidentally tripping over it.

Suicide was the only reasonable option, besides murder, and there was no sign that anyone had broken into the room or that there had been a struggle.

Reyersen went back inside, settled onto the bed, his back against the wall. He crossed his legs and removed photos and files from the manilla folder. He had copies of the police report and all available public records about the man. Married for fifteen years. Two children, a son and a daughter. He'd lived in a suburb of Boston called Newton. Had been working for his company, which manufactured calculators, for twelve years. Aside from his wife and children, Reyersen didn't see how his absence from the earth made any difference at all. To anyone.

*

Reyersen returned to the office, a few blocks from the hotel, in the dead zone between City Hall and the construction around the harbor, to fill out the necessary paperwork. It was a blocky building built in 1912, and the rooms were small, his desk in an office crowded with three other desks. "Suicide," he wrote, in neat black letters, in the space marked "cause of death". He slid the report into his boss's inbox then made small talk with his coworkers, who were all waiting for the day to end. Janson and Hedges and Gray. None of them had any idea that Reyersen was recently married. He kept things like that to himself – not that there were many things like that. They talked about the start of the baseball season, the Orioles' chances, which were about nil, as usual, and the turn in the weather.

Then it was quitting time, and, as Reyersen walked down the hallway toward the elevators, all he could think about was Jayne, back at the apartment, waiting for him. At least he hoped so. Jayne would be wearing those pants that ended just below the knee and a shirt that tied around her stomach, an outfit meant for younger women, though Jayne could pull it off. In her early thirties, she was still in college, an undergrad, pursuing an anthropology degree. There was an about-equal chance that she wouldn't be at the apartment, that she'd be out drinking at the local bars with friends, or at the library alone, finishing a paper or studying for a test. He was working on his jealousy issues, acting as if things like that didn't matter.

Reyersen had "met" Jayne while investigating another mysterious death, though that one had been cut and dried, in terms of the insurance pay-off. Her fiancee's head had been found propped on a log beside a trail in the Patapsco State Park. It was too bad they hadn't been married at the time, because Jayne would have received the poor sap's not inconsiderable death benefits. Instead, the money went to the victim's parents, who didn't need it. Reyersen wasn't sure what it was about the police reports that made him zero in on Jayne, but he'd read and reread transcripts of the interviews the cops had conducted with her. Something about the way she responded to their questions had piqued his curiosity. She'd been in shock, so nothing definitive could be said about her based on her responses, but there was a quiet stoicism to her reaction, a glacial calm he found alluring. He'd read all the news stories about the incident. Gristly murders were just starting to make their way into the newspapers. Unspeakable murders had always occurred, but at one time they'd been buried under a blanket of propriety. Now they were becoming fodder for the public. There had been a few photographs of the grieving fiancee in the newspapers, photos Reyersen had cut out in his apartment at night, a few stories meant to scare the squares, before interest in the story had waned. No one had ever been caught, and no motives were discovered for the murder and decapitation of Ted Graber, which was not as rare as people wanted to think. People got away with murder all the time.

Reyersen had found her address in the police reports. Easy as pie. At the time, Jayne had been living alone in the county, in an apartment complex that catered to single younger women, teachers and nuns. He'd sat in his car watching the apartment for a few days before catching sight of her emerging from a back door. He couldn't say what it was about her – the pants that ended just past her knee?, the way she walked? There was something about her, something both laden with the tragedy she'd experienced yet somehow lighter than air. He'd felt a keen urge to meet her.

He wasn't proud of the fact that he'd spent so long tracking her, and he was still surprised that his pursuit had produced results, that he had netted his quarry. It was not something he'd ever done before. For weeks he followed her, and when he wasn't following her he thought about her. She spent most of her time on the University of Baltimore campus, walking from building to building between classes, carrying books close to her chest. She was a regular at a coffeehouse Reyersen started frequenting – dark walls and hand-drawn advertisements for rooms to let and musical instruments for sale. There was often music and loud laughter, but sometimes, in the afternoon, there were lulls when the wannabe beatniks kicked back, sipping their coffees and writing pretentious verse in little notebooks. It was during one of those lulls that Reyersen approached Jayne as she sat by the window, gazing at the rainy street. He knew he looked like a square, with his button-up shirt, loose linen pants, and fedora, but when he leaned forward, looking at her out of a face that still bore the ravages of severe adolescent acne, he exuded a wolfish charm. He could feel it working on her. Sometimes it did.

They'd talked about Miles Davis, who was playing quietly over the soundsystem and had just released *The Birth of the Cool*, a new direction for the musician. They had differing opinions on the album – he would realize later that she was right, that it was a step forward not a step back. Then they talked about artists, mostly older artists out of an earlier era, Man Ray, Mondrian, the Italian Futurists. Reyersen dabbled in drawing, had since he was an idealistic kid, though he no longer had serious aspirations. A doodle here, a doodle there. They talked about Jack Kerouac's *On the Road*, of course. Jayne wanted to be the next Margeret Mead, traveling, mucking through the world of ideas and the world of man. When she got excited about ideas, something inside her would glow out through her eyes.

Strangely, even when Reyersen was with Jayne he couldn't manage to see her clearly. He would forget what she looked like the instant he looked away from her. Her hair was on the edge of auburn. Her nose was not large, not small, straightish, her lips full-ish. Were her eyes green or gray? Sometimes one, sometimes the other. The light slid off her face rather than reflecting from it. He had never been so attracted to someone he couldn't see in his life.

They'd been married for exactly one week, following a simple ceremony at City Hall, his buddy Proster a witness. He never told her, and never would tell her, that their meeting at the coffeehouse had been more than accidental. Despite the fact that she was nearly ten years younger and more in tune with what was happening in the world of art and music, more *current*, and at least two times as smart, they were meant for each other.

*

The days were getting longer, so light still clung to the edges of the sky when Reyersen walked to the bus stop outside City

Hall. A dozen sad men huddled around the benches near the bus stop, all wearing dark suits under light raincoats. It was like stepping into a crowd of Ed Wholleys. They were all returning to their kids and row houses or suburban manses, the noise and clamor of family life. Reyersen thanked god he was free, had never taken that route. Propagation. Breeding. He and Jayne were in accord on that. No children. Some of the squares lived in the county, others in the middle class housing developments that ringed the city proper, housing developments with covenants to keep undesirables out. Some of them were probably Poles or Irishmen or Jews, but really they were all just gray men who commuted to work every day, carrying briefcases and wearing raincoats. Why did Reyersen think he was any better? Maybe because he had a mind of his own, had not given up and thrown his lot in with the raging stream of sewage that was modern civilization.

Maybe.

He thought of the way Jayne had looked when he had left the apartment that morning. Under the covers, she smelled like mushrooms and sunlight. Her hair over her face. Reyersen was no poet, but he found himself tempted to write poems about her. Which was a kind of sickness all its own. If someone had told him a year or two earlier that he would fall victim to love, he would have laughed in their face. But here he was, feeling the lack of something he was about to have again. Looking around him, he suspected the majority of men at the bus stop had never felt what he was feeling.

He wondered if Wholley had ever felt this way about his wife. He suspected that someone who decided to jump off a ten story balcony must have experienced happiness at one point in his life. If there was no happiness, how could there be the kind of dejection that drove a man over a balcony? Reyersen pictured the big man falling, arms and legs streaming out behind him. The fall wouldn't have taken long. He wondered how many seconds it would take a two hundred pound man to fall ten stories. A mathematical equation. That's all it was, really. A question of numbers. A calculation. He felt sorry for the wife, who would now, thanks to a single word he'd written on a form, not be receiving death benefits, but that wasn't his concern. The jump not the word was the prime mover in that decision.

The bus driver, a gray and hunched old syphilitic he must have seen hundreds of times before, nodded at Reyersen as he climbed aboard, and he stood there, loophanging, watching the city pass, appreciating the way the light went lambent out the window. It was an ugly city, but the ugliness carried a kind of beauty along with it. It was a mostly brick city, but there were some already-green patches of grass. Trees just starting to bud. By the time he got off the bus, across the city, it was dusk and then it was night and then he was walking through the night and he could taste her already. He imagined her spread out on the bed for him like a buffet. She had never done that before, presented herself to him like a gift, but maybe someday... A man could dream.

He lived in, now *they* lived in, what had once been an old clocktower, converted into apartments. He'd been living here for seven years, but returning to it now, when it held his new wife, it took on a different aspect. He liked the clocktower because it was tall and odd, and the apartments inside were large and open. Half were studios where artists either did or didn't work. There were often parties. The blare of hard driving jazz. This was what passed for the arts district in this small city. Weirdos and transvestites, beatniks and druggies, along with people who didn't fit and wanted to get away from the world – Reyersen, despite his square appearance and his square job, counted himself one of them.

He and Jayne lived in an apartment on the second-from-the-top floor. There were two apartments on their floor, but the other one had been unoccupied for four years. The door to their apartment was ajar, which was not terribly troubling. Since the second apartment was empty, no one ever walked onto their floor unless they were visiting, or lost. What *was* troubling was that none of the lights in the apartment were on. It surprised him that Jayne would leave the apartment without closing the door behind her, but apparently she had. Or else someone had broken in. When he walked in and saw the state of the apartment, Reyersen was not entirely sure someone hadn't.

Along with leaving the door ajar, Jayne had left the apartment in a state of disarray. A tan milk-crusted bowl sat on the coffee table. A coffee mug half-full of brown sludge. A bunch of books splayed out around the foot of the couch, textbooks and monographs. He closed the door behind him, trying not to feel annoyed or upset or jealous. Living together was so new, he had no idea what to expect from Jayne. If he had to come home to a mess and an open door every day, what was the big deal? It was a fair trade, considering what he got in return.

The apartment's decor was eclectic. Reyersen had to admit to some wannabe beatnik proclivities in himself. Most of the art on the walls was original, paintings he'd bought or bartered for from his clocktower neighbors. Sometimes artists had open houses in their studios and sold their work for cheap. His favorite piece was a garish abstract behind the couch, a painting that looked like a gash of red blood against spatters of intestinal yellow. It made him think of life and death at the same time. He cleaned up Jayne's dishes and piled the books neatly, glancing at the titles. They were mostly anthropology books about Quaquitals and Inuits.

In the bathroom, a pair of Jayne's nylons were hanging from the showerrod. Reyersen could imagine her gorgeous legs, substantial and shapely, ghosting inside. He crumpled the nylons in his fist and shoved his nose into the bunched material. He knew it wasn't right, the way he felt about her. The feeling of sexual mystery, of overwhelming erotic desire, was not the way a husband was supposed to feel about a wife. It was the way a middle aged man felt about his young mistress, or the way a teenager felt about an older lover. He was bowled over by her presence, even the presence of her presence, the hint of her left over after she'd left. He felt raging desire. But there was nothing he could do with that desire until she got home. He had to bank it so he could stoke it later on.

He poured himself a bourbon, put the needle on the record that had been left on the turntable. Billie Holiday's

"Strange Fruit" came bristling out of the speakers, the horns slow and dragging, the rhythm section plunking along. It was a haunting song, the music and lyrics and vocals creating a dark mist. The deep darkness of U.S. history. The shallow shadows that infected all of them. "Southern trees bear strange fruit," Billie sang in her broken voice. It hit him and held on to his heart as he walked to the window to look out at the city. He was higher than Ed Wholley had been when he'd jumped off the balcony to his death. He could probably squeeze himself out the window if he wanted to, but, at least at the moment, he didn't have the faintest desire to do away with himself.

He awaited Jayne's return, awaited taking her up like a bad habit.

Billie stopped singing about the tragedy of U.S. history and started singing about love. "Love is like a faucet," she sang, coy and knowing. "It turns off and on."

*

Three hours later Reyersen was sprawled on the couch, a glass of bourbon on the floor, his head heavy, a bit deranged. He'd read the first third of *The Death of Lucky Lamore*. The book was standard fare, about a gangster in a turf war with another gangster. There were pretty dames, rumrunners, and violence in spurts. He appreciated the aesthetics of the book, paid little attention to its plot. The characters were flat, but the atmosphere was rich. He knew Lucky Lamore was going to die, yet he invested emotional energy into the character anyway. Through the floor came the rumble of a party in process. The beating of percussion, maybe a blaring saxophone. Hard to tell. A comforting sound that would only get annoying when he tried to sleep.

In the bathroom, he put the nylons over his mouth and nose, breathing in, detecting the faintest trace of Jayne, while sitting on the john. There were atoms of her, her legs, her crotch, her ass, embedded in the nylons. No matter how hard she scrubbed them, she could never erase her scent. Now

Reyersen couldn't hold back the emotions he'd been fighting all night. They flooded him, breaching the dam of his reserve, pressing against his eyeballs. Where the hell was she? What the hell was she doing, and who the hell was she doing it with? It was well past the time when she should have returned.

Even after being with her for almost a year, there remained things Reyersen didn't know about Jayne. There were great gaps in the history of her. Shadows and elisions. He had thought that was preferable to knowing everything about her. It gave him something to look forward to. He pictured her like a closed clam shell. He would pry her open eventually, sliding the edge of a putty blade between her lips, and reach in under the pink tongue that was her body. There were raw spots that made her recoil whenever he put his finger near them – maybe just the death of her fiancee (she never mentioned Graber), though he suspected something more fundamental. She never talked about her family, her childhood, where she'd grown up. She shared none of that with him. It was hard to tell if she had an accent or not. Maybe.

He poured himself another slug of bourbon, settling his ragged breathing, then grabbed his coat and walked back out into the night. The halls of the clocktower were dark and mostly quiet, but in the apartment one flight down the clatter of laughter and music sounded from behind a door. He knew a jazz musician lived there; he'd heard him practicing at all hours of the night, phrases bleating through a tenor sax.

It was colder outside now. This late at night, the buses were intermittent, at best, so he hailed a cab and headed to Fells Point. He and Jayne didn't make a habit of drinking in the bars out here, it wasn't their scene, but he knew some of her college friends did. The streets were cobblestone. Dozens of people staggered from bar to bar. It was cold, but, compared to how cold it had been a few weeks before, the weather made them forget it was still winter. Pretend to forget, anyway. There were dockworkers and fishermen tying one on, and groups of college kids making a nuisance of themselves. A volatile mix. Reyersen paid the cabdriver then walked the streets, hunched inside his raincoat and fedora. They probably mistook him for a fed.

He went into a hole in the wall and ordered a bourbon from a bartender with a red face and long blond hair. As he sat half-listening to the conversations around him, he realized how stupid he was. What if Jayne returned while he was out searching for her? He should have left a note. He had half a mind to return home and get back to waiting for her; instead he ordered another bourbon and looked around.

No way was Jayne going to be in a place like this, so he walked down toward the docks, where the more popular bars were located, and waded into the crowds. Here the ratio of college kids to working men evened out. They were insufferable. Most of them came from money and had no idea how fortunate they were. Beef-fed football players and effete intellectuals. In every group, Reyersen looked for Jayne's amber hair. A few times he thought he saw her, then he'd realize it was a younger woman, actually college-aged. He imagined the interest the college boys must have shown in Jayne, an experienced woman. They were probably all after her. And Jayne too innocent to realize it. Maybe she'd been led into some dangerous situation, getting into a car with a half dozen young men with ill intentions. Rage spread through Reyersen's body, his ribcage, his arms, his fists. If he caught one of them he'd pound him to a red pulp. Then again, he knew Jayne was too smart for that.

The night got away from him. His eyesight blurred. He got a drink only in half the bars he walked into, but even that was too many. He blurred and bleered and banged into beef-fed bodies that pushed back at him. He looked at the face of every woman in every bar, which he knew was putting him in danger. Someone was going to take it the wrong way. The women were shrinking violets and open white pages and sluts and saints, and not one of them was Jayne. He narrowly avoided a few fistfights. He didn't ask anyone if they'd seen her because he didn't have a picture and wasn't sure he could describe her. Average height. Brownish hair. Green or gray eyes. The description fit a million women. Yet somehow Jayne was singular.

When he felt something rising inside him, he scurried around the side of the docks to vomit up gray bourbon mash, and he breathed through his nose for a few minutes. The bay was before him, stars sliding off dark water riffled by wind. Across the bay, cranes outlined against the sky.

When he turned back around, he saw her, Jayne, scampering away, holding the hand of a college boy. It was just her back, the back of her amber hair, but Reyersen was sure it was her. Had to be. Though he didn't think she had a red dress like that. By the time he came to the mouth of the alley they'd disappeared down, he saw nothing. He was too drunk to be angry, too drunk to be sad. Still, he felt as if his entire life was spilling out from his insides.

*

He had no memory of making it back to the clocktower, his shirt and slacks miraculously free of vomit flecks. He still wore his shoes, not so miraculously clean. His hat sat on the bed like a bad omen. He groaned out a deep red bourbon-soaked bog, turned onto his back. Sometime during the night he'd gone through all Jayne's things, ripping her clothes out of the closet and strewing them around the room. It had been quite a bender. There were a lot of collegiate clothes, pants that ended past the knee, bobby sox, cardigans, but there were also professional-looking clothes, a pencil skirt he'd never seen her wear, a suit dress. There were a dozen shoes. Reyersen staggered to his feet before settling back down onto the bed, head pounding, mouth a wad of cotton. When he coughed, his heart squeezed inside his chest, like he had three fists.

On the floor was a shoebox he'd obviously rifled through the night before. There were a dozen photographs inside. An old black and white photograph of a family in the mountains. A father with a large forehead and a big grin wearing a suit. A dark haired mother wearing a fur stole. A child that didn't look like a child but like a miniature version of the mother. He assumed the child was Jayne. Then there were photographs of, he assumed, Ted Graber. In one of the photos the young man was shirtless, smiling at the camera, cocky. Reyersen felt an instant dislike for the man he recognized as jealousy. He pictured the young man's head by the side of a trail in the woods, flies buzzing around his open mouth. There were a few photos of Ted and Jayne together. A series of three from a photobooth, mugging for the camera, their heads touching. They were so obviously in love it made Reyersen want to puke or cry, maybe both at the same time. There were letters Graber had written to her, but Reyersen was in no state to read them. He tucked them back into the shoebox for later. Then he tucked the shoebox back into the closet. If she returned, he'd never have to look at them again.

Already late for work, Reyersen made himself a hangover special. Scrambled eggs with cheese, bacon, toast, the works. He put *The Birth of the Cool* on the turntable and let the geometric jazz spread throughout the apartment. For years he'd been alone. He had never minded being alone. He could do whatever he wanted, whenever he wanted. He'd been a loner all his life. So why was being alone so hard all of a sudden? He had been with Jayne for less than a year, had lived with her for less than a week, yet somehow he felt like insects were clawing inside his skin trying to get out. Was it possible to change so completely, so quickly?

He was angry. Of course he was. She'd been gone all night without leaving a note. He hadn't heard one word from her. There had been no phone call. Nothing. He was angry, yes, but now he was also worried. He knew the kinds of unexpected, nefarious things that could happen to people out of the blue. Disappearances, murders, accidents. One second everything was fine, the next…. Men and women faked their deaths more often than anyone realized. There was an underworld of dark doings that, thanks to his job, Reyersen was privy to. What if Jayne had run across the wrong crowd? What if she wound up washed up in the harbor, her pale body bloated, crabs nibbling her entrails? What if she'd jumped from a balcony like Wholley, her hair streaming out behind her? There were all kinds of things he didn't want to imagine.

Most likely, she had simply wound up drinking too much at a girlfriend's apartment and had spent the night somewhere. The time had got away from her. They didn't have protocols yet. Maybe this was how she was going to treat him – like an afterthought. He took a long hot shower, trying to push the dregs of his soul out through his feet, trying to stop the pounding of his head, then dressed in a clean white shirt and linen pants too thin for the March weather. He took a cab downtown, walking into the office two hours late. By the grace of a God he didn't believe in, no one noticed his tardiness. They probably assumed he was out investigating another suspicious death. It made him wish he'd slept later.

Two new files had been slapped on his desk. Nothing unusual. Nothing he had to investigate. Two simple, uncomplicated deaths. Most of his job was just this: routine paperwork, checking things over, searching for false notes that usually weren't there. Most deaths were perfectly explicable. Maybe once or twice a month he had to go out and do fieldwork, investigate shady dealings. He lived for those times, wished there were more of them.

*

The black phone on his desk rattled Reyersen out of his reverie. An angry jangling, the insides of the squat black box battering away. He lifted the receiver.

"Reyersen. Savor Life."

There was a pause over the line. He almost hung up. Then a voice started in on him. It was the voice not of a woman but of a harpy. It tunneled into his ear and sliced through his brain. Ed Wholley's wife. God, if this woman were his wife he would have jumped from a balcony, too. She told him she couldn't believe that the insurance company had had the *audacity* to claim that her husband, who loved her and cared for her, who loved and cared for his two children, who were now without their father, would ever do such a thing as kill himself. Is that really what they were saying?

"I'm sorry, ma'am. The investigation is over."

BANG!

He hung up on her. When she called back, he took the receiver off the cradle, laid it on his desk, stared at it. It was a strange object, black and oblong. He could hear her voice coming through like a nattering insect. He pictured her in a tenement house, crowded onto a street with a bunch of other tenement houses somewhere outside Boston. He pictured a swarm of immigrant kids, some kind of Dickensian nightmare. When the nattering wore itself out, he replaced the receiver on the cradle. He looked around. Janson, Hedges, and Gray had their heads down, working away at their own paperwork, or pretending to. It struck him that they were all extraneous, that if all four of them went out and did away with themselves – a gunshot to the head, death by train, jumping off a balcony or into the harbor – it would not make a whit of difference to the world. Not the faintest ripple would be felt.

*

In the afternoon he pretended he had a case to investigate, grabbing his hat from the hatrack, leaving the raincoat where it was. It was beautiful outside, buds unfurling, birds returned to the city in flocks. It must have been sixty or sixty five degrees. He walked without knowing where he was going, until he realized where he was going. There was only one place he could be going.

The campus was mostly brick buildings, with greenswards here and there. They were all out in the warm weather, men and women barely men and barely women. Reyersen had not gone to college himself. Instead, he'd gone to war, an education in its own right. The Pacific Theater. Which was something he refused to think about, an unexplored region in his deep memories. Coming back, jaded, he'd found a job, then another. He'd worked his way up, until now he was a company man. Before the war, he'd been a reader, a budding artist, interested in culture. He'd gone to museums. He'd been soft, but the war had blasted that softness out of him. The people walking around him on the campus were still soft. Like marshmallow people. He could step on them and smooth them into the pavement. Many of the women, the girls, were attractive, but none of them held a candle to Jayne, and he barely looked at them. Their legs, their arms bared to the weather, their cupid bow mouths. He was too busy looking for Jayne to pay them any mind.

He remembered how he'd seen her everywhere he looked the night before, how every woman in every group had looked a little like her. Today, by contrast, none of the women looked like Jayne. They all looked younger, in every sense. They lacked her sophistication, the knowing way she moved her hips. He wished suddenly that he knew more about her, about the family in the pictures he'd found, about her time with Ted Graber. He felt like he had when he'd been following her, more than a year earlier. He had the same hopeless sense of hunt, the same endless hunger.

He walked into a few buildings, wandered down the hallways. He stood at the head of a lecture hall and looked inside at the tiers of seats. They were all lined up, listening to a professor with a beard and a tweed coat, a man who looked like a representation of what he was supposed to be. How could anyone live like that, Reyersen wondered? A shadow of the thing he was supposed to be? Then again, what was he? Anyone looking at him would spot him for an insurance man. And all the students were just shadows of students. The professor stood behind a podium rattling on about the initiating events of the Sino-Russian War. The man didn't know the first thing about war, had never been in one, had never *smelled* one. He was a brain in a case. He was nothing, really.

Reyersen walked down hallways that smelled like stone, then he walked back outside again. It was all pointless. There were hundreds of classrooms, and without knowing Jayne's schedule he'd never find her.

She was not in the coffeehouse, which was the same as ever, either.

*

BANG!

It was shocking, how quickly Reyersen reacclimated to solitude. Already it felt natural to be alone again. When he returned from the office, early, the apartment still smelled like Jayne, but that smell would fade. He unwrapped the sandwich he'd bought on his way home from the office, opened the bourbon, sat at the table eating and drinking. His time with Jayne already seemed like a dream, half-remembered. Had they really been so hungry for each other? Had he really been able to bring her to completion, time and time again? Had they had happy times? Had it been that word they all feared, love? Maybe it was better that she was gone, because now they would never have to watch what they had fade. It would remain pristine and untouchable.

He listened to *The Birth of the Cool*, again. Intricate lines moved inside the music. The instruments seemed to be saying something to each other he could barely decipher, talking in a language just beyond comprehension.

It was when side A of the record was over, the needle returning to its arm, that Reyersen noticed the bit of red cloth on a nail by the window sill, and noticed the open window. It had been open since last night, he realized. Had it really been open since last night? The apartment was always comfortable, even in winter, heat rising from the other apartments, and he could often open the window even in the middle of winter. Now, in the lambent light of evening, he saw the bit of red cloth and felt something stick in his throat. Knew, already, even before he had moved to the window and looked down. Knew without any doubt.

Time To Say Goodbye

Roxanne Dent

New York City, 1950

Nick Santos walked out of *Solly's Bar* on Avenue B in the East Village stone, cold sober. It was almost midnight. The driving rain struck him like a blow from the Grim Reaper, Enforcer for the Italian mob. Nick pulled up the collar of his beige raincoat.

On the way to his dented, grey Chevy, he ignored a drug deal on the corner and a homeless man shrieking about Jesus' blood. His life was in the crapper.

Nick's Investigative Services hadn't had a decent case in months. He was behind in his rent. This morning, his bank informed him he was overdrawn.

He stepped on a soaked, candy wrapper and nearly fell into a filthy puddle full of cigarette butts and dog shit before he managed to regain his balance.

His key stuck and he cursed as he yanked open the rusty front door and slid onto the vinyl seat. His black hair, worn too long from missing a few haircuts, dripped down his neck. The car stunk. He checked his shoes. Wet but clean. He leaned over the back seat to grab a box of tissues to wipe his face. A body lay on the floor. Nick pulled out his forty-five.

"Get out, buddy."

The mook didn't move. Nick grabbed the flashlight from the glove compartment and shined it in the back.

Asher Gilford's lifeless, blue eyes stared back at him. He was wearing his lucky, Hawaiian Aloha shirt with flowers and birds. It didn't bring him luck. His face was a pulpy mess; his body riddled with bullet holes.

BANG!

A police siren sounded a few blocks away. Nick hated cops. The feeling was mutual. When Detective Ryan saw him across a street, he spit on the sidewalk. He'd be arrested for his ex-partner's murder. At the station, they'd take turns giving him knuckle sandwiches until he confessed. He'd wind up fried like a chitlin in the hot seat at Sing Sing.

Partners for three years Nick and Asher parted ways six months ago. As usual, it was over a dame. A redhead with green eyes the color of absinthe and gams that wouldn't quit. Nick was in love with her. Asher married her.

When he went to their home to deliver some papers, Myra came to the door. Nick took one look at her bruised face. His temper got the best of him. He and Asher had words. And went a few rounds. Their neighbors called the cops. They hadn't spoken until yesterday morning.

Asher phoned him out of the blue.

"Meet me at *Solly's* tomorrow night at ten sharp."

Nick was about to tell him to drop dead, when Asher added, "I got a case that could use your special skills. It's right up your alley and the pay is sweet."

"How sweet?"

"Five grand."

Asher wasn't above lying but never about money.

Before he hung up, he added, "Make sure you aren't tailed."

Nick arrived the next evening at *Solly's* at ten on the dot and stayed until just before midnight. No Asher. Nick nursed a beer all night. Solly wasn't happy and Nick got a bad feeling which grew as the hours passed. Asher was never late. That remark about not being tailed was like a flashing light in his brain.

He checked the body again. Six bullet holes. No blood. Asher was murdered elsewhere.

Three police cars whizzed by, reminding him it was time to scram.

A whore with frizzled blonde hair in black leather who hadn't made her money yet, stepped out of the shadows of a shuttered, Gold for Cash shop under a yellow umbrella and headed his way in thigh-high boots.

Nick gunned the motor. The skinny blonde gave him the finger as he sped past. He could dump Asher's body in an alley. But with his luck, someone would be looking out a window. If he weighed it down and dropped it in the Hudson, Asher might never be found. Nick thought of Myra waiting at home and drove to Big Mike's junkyard in Corona, Queens. Once clear of *Solly's*, he drove like a nun. He couldn't afford to be stopped.

*

Big Mike's had piles of everything from refrigerators and sinks to old furniture, rusty cars, toilets, and broken toys. Every night, he locked up on the dot of eleven and went home. When Nick was low on funds and needed parts for his car, he used his skills to open the padlock and raided the place. He always left at least a fin under the door. This time Nick planned to deposit Asher's body minus the lettuce where Big Mike would find it when he opened up.

The amount of bullet holes in Asher's body indicated a mob hit. But he knew Asher made it a cardinal rule never to get in bed with mobsters.

Whoever fiddled with the lock on his car, and deposited Asher's body knew about their meeting. If they wanted Nick to take the fall, why hadn't they called the cops with a tip while he was inside *Solly's*? It didn't make sense.

Returning to Corona brought back a flood of memories. His stepfather's fists. His mother's murder. Buying ices at The Lemon Ice King of Corona with Rocko, Joey and little Jimmy, after winning a baseball game. They were all eager to sign up for war. No one thought they'd die.

Nick's friends were ghosts who haunted his dreams, blown up at Dunkirk and in the Pacific. He lucked out with a leg wound that took it's time to heal and left him with a slight limp.

Big Mike's was deserted. The torrential rain had turned into a fine drizzle. The few remaining wooden houses were boarded up. The land was cheap, but no one wanted to live next to a big pile of junk.

Nick opened the glove compartment, removed a pair of leather gloves, and put them on. He stood still for a second. Silence and the occasional rodent or squirrel scrounging for food or scurrying for cover were the only sounds in the night. He opened the trunk. Inside was a crumpled blanket he took to the beach for a picnic last summer, a set of skeleton keys and a rake pick. He grabbed the rake pick, walked over to the gate, gave the padlock a few twists and it popped open. He swung the gate back with a minimum of squeaks and made a return trip to his car. He pulled Asher out of the seat onto the blanket. Rigor Mortis was just beginning to pass away. He lifted the wrapped body over his right shoulder, trying not to breathe in the sickening aroma of decomposition.

Nick carried him up the hill and inside the yard. He laid his ex-partner on top of the crushed bones of what was left of an old, silver Packard near the front entrance.

Nick stepped back. If he wore his fedora he would have taken it off.

"You were never one for religion, Ash. Me either. Rest in peace."

Nick returned to his Chevy, cleaned out the back with an old plaid, work shirt and what was left of a bottle of Lestoil he kept in the trunk, grateful there was no blood.

On the way back to the city, he held his breath until two cop cars in back of him zipped past sirens on.

*

Asher Investigations was located on the sixth floor of a dirty, beige, office building on 39th Street. As soon as Nick entered the city, it started to pour again. The area was deserted. Even the prostitutes and drug dealers were gone. He needed to know who hired Asher. The set of keys to the office were still attached to his own keys. He'd never returned them, and Asher never asked for them back.

Nick parked two blocks away. He entered the building and walked up. The elevator attendants were long gone, the elevator locked. There was something creepy about a deserted office building at night. A squeak on the stairs behind him made him pause. He decided it was mice.

When he arrived on the sixth floor, he didn't need to use his keys. The door was open. He removed his forty-five, turned on the light and stepped inside.

Files were scattered over the floor. Asher's desk was upended. The wall safe stood open. This was no robbery. Papers were ripped up and stomped on by a wet boot as if the thief had a tantrum at not finding what he wanted.

Nick knew something the intruder didn't. He went to a closet where Asher kept a change of clothes. The tux, white shirt, dress shoes and an old pair of boots were on the floor. Nick bent down and punched the lower back wall. A section popped open.

He removed a grey, metal box. Inside were two photographs.

In one was a tall man in a tux in his fifties, with an aquiline nose, a jutting chin, light eyes, and fair hair. The arrogant coldness in his eyes reminded Nick of SS commanders in charge of the death camps. The photograph was taken from afar on a terrace at night. Across from him was George Dorsey, Chief of Police in civilian clothes. Each had a drink in their hands. The civilian handed Dorsey a fat packet.

The second was a naked, slender, slip of a girl with small breasts, long, slinky, blonde hair past her tiny waist and hips, unbuckling the arrogant guy's belt. Her face was that of a twelve-or-thirteen-year-old.

He heard a squeak behind him.

A thug with a nose like Jimmy Durante and fists like Joe Lewis landed a punch on Nick's jaw that knocked him out cold.

The first thing he noticed when he opened his eyes was the thug's dead body. Somebody shot him in the back of the head with Nick's forty-five. The pictures were missing.

The sound of police sirens told him this time the murderer called the cops with a tip. He groaned and grabbed his gun.

BANG!

He forced himself to stagger to a window in the hall that overlooked a back alley, opened it and managed to speed climb down the fire escape without falling. He made it a block away before cop cars descended on the building like ants.

As he drove past, Nick spotted a short, overly muscular bald man step out of the shadows. A Continental Mark II picked him up and took off.

*

Nick drove to the only man he trusted. Max was a mutt like him. Jewish on his mother's side and colored on his father's. His dad died when he was a kid. When war broke out, Nick joined the army and was placed in the US 12th Armored Division, one of only ten US integrated divisions during World War II. That's where he met Nick.

Max was a reader of books, a lover of archaic words, and a man who could make you laugh. Despite the violence, slurs, and racist remarks, he believed in the American dream. One day America would be for all Americans, no matter their race or religion.

When Nick walked into a house in Germany that was supposed to be empty, a German sniper shot him. Max rushed right in and dragged him out, only to get shot by a second sniper. The bullet crushed his spine. Unlike Nick he wound up in a wheelchair. Max wasn't bitter. It didn't keep him down.

After Max came home, he went to live with his mother in the rent controlled, first floor apartment on Bleecker Street in Greenwich Village. She made sure her son's name was on the lease when she moved in. Once she passed away, the landlord suggested Max would be happier elsewhere. Max declined. Since his name was on the lease, he was a wounded Vet, and the building was filled with bohemian, community activists, made up of actors, writers, and artists who loudly threatened to go on a rent strike in support of Max, the landlord changed his tune.

It was late and most folks would be annoyed if someone rang their bell around 2am.

Max drew the curtain aside. When he saw Nick's face, he grinned and buzzed him in.

"Welcome to my humble abode, Shamus. It's been a while since we had a chinwag. Sit yourself down on my new, second hand couch. Beer? All out of the hard stuff."

"Sounds great."

Max's building was built in the 1880s. It had an ancient, working fireplace and bare, wood floors, little furniture, and a massive collection of books, magazines, and newspapers. He was a bit of a hoarder about the printed word. Max hardly ever threw out any newspapers for fear he'd miss an editorial he needed when he wrote the articles he sent to the various members of the black press. They were stacked by date along the walls of his apartment and reached halfway up to the ceiling.

"So what demons have driven you to me in the middle of the night?" Max said as he handed Nick an ice cold, Rheingold. And by the way, is that blood on your collar?"

"I need a safe place to crash and to pick your bookish brain."

"Tell Max all about it," he said as he handed Nick an ice bag for his jaw.

"Thanks!" Nick started at the beginning and didn't leave out a word. When he finished, Max's dark eyes were worried.

"Holus-Bolus, Nick. Looks like whoever murdered Asher picked you to take the rap. Who was Asher's client?"

"The numbskull didn't live long enough to tell me."

"Look on the bright side. You didn't end up like the goon with the lead fists. You always were a lucky bastard."

"Lucky's not the word I'd use."

"Sounds like the brewstered dude was being blackmailed and went to Old Roley, Poley Dorsey for help."

"If brewstered means rich, yeah."

"Any idea who he is?"

"He looked powerful. Probably been in the news at some charity event or other."

"And since I have an extensive collection of newspapers, you wanted to peruse my property. You have my blessing.

I'm going back to bed. Keep the papers in order by date. You know how picky I am. There's two beers in my brand new refrigerator. Keeps things colder than the ice box and less messy. Besides beer I got coffee. The pot is on the stove. Coffee in the fridge. See you at breakfast."

Nick smiled as he watched Max speed wheel down the hall into the bedroom humming "Good Golly, Miss Molly", and began with the most recent newspapers.

As the darkness outside gradually turned lighter, Nick found what he was looking for. The *Daily Mail* ran a photograph in the society pages about the Director of a leading chemical company, the elegant Carson Schmidt.

He stood beside his stunning, twenty-three year-old daughter, Eden and her equally wealthy, good looking fiancé, Chad Barrington attending a fund raiser for the Police Union. There was a rumor Barrington might go into politics.

As the sun came up, Nick made a second pot of coffee and drank it black.

A great schmoozer, Asher knew a lot of people from different walks of life. His words, "It's right up your alley," got Nick to thinking.

While Asher's pet peeve was gangsters, Nick's was dirty politicians. The war had taught him if your family had money and influence, you could stay safe at home in a cushy job and let the slob in the street bleed out overseas. Dirty politicians meant shoddy equipment at the front, poisoned water near a school, inferior housing, and back room deals that benefited them. Screw the little guy. Politics was a dirty game. It pissed him off.

The more he thought about it, Asher's remark described the person who hired him. The client had a grudge against dirty politicians. The trouble was lots did.

Max wheeled out of the bathroom while Nick listened to the weather. "I see the cops found the bodies and you made a fresh pot of coffee, put out the cream cheese, and dropped a single bagel in the toaster. Does this mean you won't be joining me for bacon and eggs?"

"Another time. Thanks for the hospitality. If anyone asks, I was here all night."

Max wheeled over to block the front door. "Where do you think you're going, gumshoe? The goon's body was pumped with bullets from your forty-five. Hand it over."

"No."

"Say your gun was stolen. They can't prove otherwise."

"This is my mess."

"Listen, Sherlock. Unlike you who walks alone, I know people who know people who know people. I'll see it disappears faster than a rabbit in a hat."

After a couple of seconds, Nick dropped the gun into his lap. "I owe you."

"You bet you do. Be smart. Don't antagonize the fuzz. Handle your mess with the utmost mansuetude."

Nick laughed as he left.

*

Weary by the time he found a parking space, Nick walked to his one-bedroom apartment on the top floor of Cornelia Street. Nick's office was a large, bright room on the second floor next to the only bathroom. For the addition of the tiny bedroom, living room, and kitchen upstairs, he paid sixty dollars a month, more than he could afford at the moment.

He'd just inserted the key into the front door when Sergeant Becker appeared on his left loudly snapping a wad of blackjack gum. On his right he heard the scratchy, smoker's voice of Detective Bill Ryan.

"Been looking for you, black bean."

Nick stiffened. "My father was Puerto Rican, not Mexican."

"Who cares. You all look alike. Where've you been all night?" Ryan demanded.

"None of your busines."

Becker gave Nick a kidney punch. "Show some respect."

Nick grunted, "Try that again jughead and you'll wish you hadn't."

Ryan shoved Becker back and got into Nick's face. The stench of a cheap cigar lingered on his breath. "We need to talk. Your place or the station."

Nick opened the front door. They went inside.

His nosy, first floor neighbor, Mrs Mungo-Park stuck her head out the door.

"Everything all right dear?"

"Right as rain," Nick muttered as he continued up the stairs.

When Nick reached his second-floor office, he shut the door. Detective Ryan sat in the chair behind the desk as Becker rammed Nick into one of the wooden chairs.

Ryan's face had a sour look as he glanced at the framed pictures on the walls, the area rug, fireplace and three large windows letting in a weak sun. "Your ex-partner was found on top of a junk heap in Queens early this morning. Tenderized and shot six times. Know anything about it?" he growled.

"Ash and I parted ways a while back."

"Yeah. I remember," Ryan said. "You two came to blows."

"We had a disagreement. I'm sorry he's dead."

"He's lying, boss."

"I'm not dumb ass," Nick said.

Becker started toward Nick, fists raised.

"Sit down, Becker."

"He's got a smart mouth, boss. Let me soften him up."

"Another time. So hot shot, where were you last night?" Ryan said.

"Shooting the breeze with an old army buddy. Max Williams. A crippled vet."

"Yeah? Got your alibi all dusted off and ready. We'll see. Asher was shot twelve hours earlier. Not in his office by the way. That was another guy. Maybe you knew him. Eddy the Tank. One of Joey Gallo's wannabees."

"Never heard of him."

"The office was trashed," Ryan added.

"Sad how the criminal element has taken over the city," Nick drawled.

"Any idea what case your ex-partner was on?"

"Not a clue."

Detective Ryan sat forward. "The other night, we got a call about a dead body in a Chevy in Alphabet City next to *Solly's Bar*. I believe you frequent *Solly's*."

"Me and a dozen other guys."

"A black and white was on its way but got called away to a liquor store robbery. When he got around to checking out the tip, no car.

"You question Solly?"

"He said he's only interested in people who buy his liquor, not their cars. Don't you have a Chevy, Santos?"

"1949 four door."

"Mind if we look it over?"

"Sure. If you got a warrant."

Ryan smiled. "Don't worry. We'll get one. From what I hear, Asher's pretty wife gets the house, car and fifty grand in life insurance. The rumor is you could use an infusion of cash and I recall the fight you had with Asher was over his wife. Maybe you hired the Tank to off her husband to make it look like a mob hit, then got rid of the joker who killed him."

"Not me. Murder for profit and a dame is dumb. I'm not dumb."

"You own a registered forty-five."

"Lost it a month ago."

"Is that right!"

"Yeah. I was upset."

"I bet. Convenient since the bone crusher in Asher's office was shot with a forty-five. How'd you lose it?"

"A brawl upstate with two guys who, like you, took an instant dislike to my mug. When I got home the gun was gone. One of them must have lifted it."

"You report it?"

"What for? Never saw them before or since. You're saying Asher was shot with a forty-five?"

"I didn't say. What case was your ex-partner working on?"

"Again, don't know."

Detective Ryan stood. "I know a liar when I hear one. We'll be back when we can prove it. Come on, Becker. Let's go."

As soon as they left, Nick took a shower, shaved, and changed clothes.

When he came downstairs, he skipped over the squeaky fourth stair and managed to slip outside without Mrs Mungo-Park opening her door.

If Asher was shot with a forty-five too, Ryan would have said. And now he knew why his car hadn't been searched while he was in *Solly's*. Maybe Max was right. He was a lucky bastard.

Strapped under his arm was the Luger he brought back from Germany as a war trophy. He had the paperwork but never registered it. With two people dead and him up for an award as patsy of the year, Nick felt it was too dangerous to go out unarmed.

*

Nick parked his car near Washington Square Park. The folk singer, Rambling Jack Elliot, was tuning his guitar, drawing a crowd. Nick checked the trunk to be sure there were no dead bodies before he got in and drove to Woodside, Queens. Asher put a down payment on a small, red brick house for him and Myra shortly after they were married.

Since his chat with Detective Ryan, a grain of suspicion had slithered into Nick's mind.

He rang the bell. Myra pushed the curtain aside.

The door opened.

She wore a red satin blouse and black slacks. Channel No. 5 wafted over.

Tears filled her eyes. "Oh God, Nick. Ash is dead. Murdered."

"I know. May I come in?"

She hesitated for a second before she pulled him in and indicated the big chair in the living room. Asher's chair. Along the wall were two suitcases.

"Taking a trip, Myra?"

"I have to get away. I'm a wreck."

The side table next to the flowered couch held an ashtray in the shape of a pistol, with a lit Pall Mall and a glass of smoky, golden liquid next to it.

"Murder does that," Nick said.

"Want a scotch?"

It was too early for him, but he nodded. "Sure."

When she returned and handed him the glass, her fingers felt like ice.

She sat on the edge of the couch across from Nick. Strands of wavy, golden hair brushed her cheek as she sipped her drink. When she looked up, those gorgeous eyes drew him in. He thought they were filled with terror more than grief.

Her voice shook. "I'm scared, Nick. Really scared."

Nick believed her. He could almost hear her teeth chattering. He just wasn't sure why.

"Ash and me. We loved each other something fierce."

Nick was a gentleman and didn't remind her of the bruises. "No one else?"

"Never. All I ever wanted was a normal life. It's my fault Ash is dead."

His voice hardened. "Why is it your fault, Myra?"

"When Sergeant Quinn first contacted Ash about surveillance work, he was leery. Chief Dorsey had contacts in the mob. I told him we needed the money. It wasn't true."

"Patrick Quinn?"

She nodded.

Quinn, an honest cop, was fired from the police force. A year later, he won a packet on the horses and began paying out large sums to anyone who had damaging information on cops which he then mailed to the press.

Nick watched Myra take a drag on the Pall Mall. "The name Carson Schmidt ring a bell?"

He thought it was only in books people slowly drained of color. She shook her head, too scared to speak and looked at her watch.

"What about Eden?"

The glass slipped out of Myra's hand and fell. Heavy duty, it didn't break. She watched the liquid seep onto the powder-blue carpet, ground out her cigarette and stood.

"You should go," she said. Her face despite the makeup was chalk white, full lips red as blood.

Nick went to her. "Who is Schmidt and Eden to you?"

When she didn't answer, he grabbed her shoulders and shook her. "Damn it, Myra, talk to me. I want to help."

She burst into sobs. He held her until the sobs let up and brought her a refresher. "Drink up."

She did.

"I saw the pictures Asher hid in his office. It looked like this Schmidt guy was being blackmailed for sex with a minor. Was that what Quinn wanted Asher to do? Dig up dirt on Schmidt and his relationship to Chief Dorsey?"

"Shut up," she screamed. "You don't know anything." She threw the empty glass at the wall, and it shattered.

The loud crash seemed to settle her nerves more than the liquor.

"Myra," Nick pleaded.

She walked over to one of the suitcases, removed a manilla envelope and brought it to Nick. "Besides the pictures there's two thousand dollars in cash. Take it."

Nick glanced inside at the photographs. He whistled.

"Ash missed you, Nick. He used to say once you got your teeth into something, you never let go."

"What do you want, Myra?"

"Justice. She sat and removed a fresh cigarette from the pack with shaking hands. Nick flicked his lighter. She took a deep drag. "Schmidt bought two sisters once. Twelve and thirteen. Eden was the pretty one. She had blue eyes. His favorite. She did what he wanted." Myra stubbed out her cigarette. "I cried and cried."

Nick stared. "You and Eden are sisters!?"

"He said I was a pale imitation. Eden sparkled. I fizzled. He called me stupid. He adopted Eden and gave me back to the agency."

"You report him?"

She stood and laughed, a note away from hysteria. "The agency was run by one of his friends. The cops told me they would prosecute me unless I stopped telling lies."

"Jesus, Myra! I'm sorry."

"Ash was furious when I told him. He wanted to destroy

Schmidt. He took the photos for Quinn but kept a few back. They're inside."

The sound of gunshots shattered the windows. Nick tackled Myra. They fell to the floor.

He went for his gun.

"Myra, get up. We have to get out of here." She didn't move. A red trail snaked along the blue rug. Her eyes were wide open. Nick felt for a pulse. There was none. Someone kicked in the front door. There was no time to split. Nick stuffed the envelope inside his jacket and stood with the Luger in his right hand.

Detective Ryan entered carrying a Smith and Wesson revolver.

"Myra's dead," Nick said.

"Did you do it?"

"Hell no. You?"

"I was her ride to the airport."

"You?"

"I knew Myra when she was Shivon Murphy. She got a raw deal. After Asher was killed, I heard a rumor she was next."

"Was it you who tried to frame me for murder?"

"No. Don't get the wrong idea, Santos. I'm not your amigo."

"I got that."

"But the scum who think they can get away with anything because they're richer than God, I like even less."

"Who killed the Tank?"

"Someone who didn't trust loose lips. Be smart. Leave the city and don't come back. Ever!"

"You tell Quinn that?"

The sound of sirens was close.

Ryan's red face turned a deeper red. "Patrick Quinn's dead. A hit and run this morning. He was a good cop. Now get the hell out before I change my fucking mind."

Nick ducked out the back. The sky was a steely grey and overcast.

Three dead bodies. None was his. His luck held. He'd drop the incriminating photographs off to leading newspapers and smut magazines. There's nothing like a major scandal to boost sales. Pictures are hard to deny. Schmidt and Dorsey were screwed. A cynic, Nick doubted Eden and Chad's engagement would be long-lived.

It was time to say goodbye. Nick would go to Florida. Get a tan. He'd be back in a couple of months. New York City was in his blood like a shot of adrenalin, or the memory of a dame with eyes the color of absinthe.

Avocado Noir

Charles West

Nate Valencia was sitting at his worn desk, trying to position himself in front of an old circular fan in a mostly futile effort to combat the heat of another Los Angeles summer day. He had the sleeves of his white shirt rolled up as he spoke into the landline phone. "Yeah, it's a hundred and forty freakin' degrees in here. When can you come and fix the air conditioner?" He grimaced as he listened. "November? What would it take for me to move up on that list?" He re-grimaced. "Three hundred dollars. Plus what it takes to actually fix the unit, huh. I'll have to get back to you." He hung up. "After I get three hundred dollars," he said to himself.

There was a knock at the door. "Come in."

A woman entered the office. The room seemed to get warmer just by her presence. She was dressed all in white, a somewhat translucent dress, which contrasted with her thick dark hair which just brushed her shoulders. She was wearing high heels and carrying a large handbag which probably cost more than his car. "Are you Nate Valencia?"

"Could be. Who's asking?"

"My name is Eden Giordano. My husband is missing. I would like for you to find him. You recently helped an acquaintance of mine, Julia Heffelfinger, find her husband."

"I *did* find him, but only after he committed suicide, leaving a note saying, 'I don't want to live in a world that has Julia Heffelfinger in it'."

"Well, you've met Julia. I'm sure you could see his point."

"What about your husband? Does he harbor any similar opinions about you?"

"I don't know and don't care. When I say I want you to find my husband, it is only because he took something that belongs to me and I want it back."

"And what would that be?"

She reached into her handbag and extracted an avocado, which she put on the desk. Valencia picked it up and examined it. "I'm going to need a little more information."

"He took my avocados."

"Just how many avocados are we talking about?"

"Twenty."

"Seems like a lot of trouble for twenty avocados."

"You misunderstand. Twenty tons of avocados. That's two hundred thousand dollars' worth. He took them from my ranch."

"Why not call the police."

"Julia said you were discreet. I would like to avoid any scandal or embarrassment."

"Where could he get rid of twenty tons of avocados?"

"They're good for a few weeks, so pretty much anywhere in North America."

She brushed the hair from her shoulders, and said, "It's very hot in here."

"The air conditioning is on the fritz."

"Why don't you open the window?"

"I don't know if you noticed the restaurant downstairs, but if I open the window, we will both smell like kimchi for a week. Welcome to Koreatown."

"Do you have any water?"

"Sure." Valencia handed her a lukewarm plastic water bottle, not one of the posh brands from France or Fiji, but one of the cut rate kind you get at the corner store on Olympic Boulevard.

She slowly put it to her lips, but then spilled it down the front of her dress. "Oh, I am so clumsy," she said breathlessly, as Valencia watched the white dress go from translucent to almost transparent.

"Do you have any idea where your husband might be?" he said, regaining most of his senses.

"If I knew that, I wouldn't need you, would I? Here is his personal information. He used to live in the valley, Canoga Park."

"I'll give it a shot, but I need an advance."

"How much?"

"How about three hundred dollars."

She didn't react to the price which made Valencia think he should have asked for more. She reached into her purse and put the money on the desk.

Valencia watched her go as he fanned himself with the three bills.

*

It was twenty six miles from Valencia's office on Olympic and Normandie to Canoga Park. It took two and a half hours, spent mostly on the 405 Highway. The air conditioner in his car didn't work any better than the one in his office. Eden's husband was easy to find, Valencia thought, as he knocked on the door. "Are you Michael Giordano?" he asked the man who opened it.

"I am."

"I'm Nate Valencia..."

"Did my wife send you?"

"She wants her avocados back."

"I don't have her stupid avocados."

"Then why did you run off? Why are you hiding out?"

"I didn't run off. I left her, sure, but I didn't run off. I don't have her avocados and I am not in hiding. You found me, didn't you?"

"Yes, but I'm a professional detective."

"So, what did you do, Google me?"

"Maybe," Valencia said hesitantly.

"Listen, I left her because she is a psycho, and she may be getting into something dangerous."

"Like what?"

"You're better off not knowing. Or even getting involved with her. She can be extremely persuasive and manipulative, believe me." Giordano suddenly raised his hands, and said, "Don't shoot."

"I'm not going to shoot you," Valencia said.

"Not you," Giordano said. "Behind you."

*

Valencia woke up with a headache, but considered himself lucky when he noticed the puddle of blood near him on the floor. In his experience a puddle of blood was often a sign of foul play. A man was standing nearby writing in a notebook. "What happened? Who are you?"

"Well, you got knocked on the head, and Michael Giordano got shot in the head. He's dead. And I am Inspector Zepeda."

"LAPD?"

"USDA," he said. Sensing Valencia's confusion he continued, "The United States Department of Agriculture. I am a fruit inspector. It looks like we're both looking for some missing avocados."

"Did you find them? Did Eden, I mean Mrs Giordano, get her avocados back?" Valencia asked.

Zepeda smiled. "How hard did you get hit? Eden Giordano is our main suspect in the avocado theft."

"What?"

"The recently deceased Michael Giordano tipped us off that Eden was dealing with a Mexican drug cartel. They were using her avocado ranch to sell their avocados and launder their dirty money. We followed her to your place. We thought you were in with her and the drug cartel, but it doesn't look like that now."

"Why would a Mexican drug cartel get involved with avocados?"

"They found out how much money they could make. All they had to do was apply the same tactics they perfected in the drug trade to the avocado business – robbery, bribery, corruption, extortion, murder. And avocados are a lot easier to get across the border. Mexican and Californian avocados are a billion dollar industry. The average American eats over seven pounds of avocados a year."

"That's a lot of guacamole."

"Not just guacamole," Zepeda said. "There's avocado soup, avocado oil, Cobb Salad, sandwiches, sushi, avocado toast."

"Did the cartel kill Giordano?"

"Maybe. But it doesn't look like their work. His head is still attached. And then there is the other thing."

"What other thing?"

Zepeda produced a clear plastic evidence bag containing several avocado pits. "These were stuffed down his throat. It suggests a crime of passion to me. Crazy psycho passion."

"What happens now? What happens to Eden?"

"Probably nothing. There's nothing connecting her to her husband's murder. All we have is suspicions. The avocados are gone. She will probably even collect insurance on the missing fruit."

"That's the pits."

"No," Zepeda said, holding up the evidence bag. "These are the pits."

*

The next day, Valencia was back in his office in front of the fan, his skull wrapped up with an ice bandage. A knock at the door reminded him of the headache he had. "Come in."

Eden Giordano entered. She was wearing a different white dress, with different high heels, and with the same handbag. "Oh, you poor thing," she said approaching him. "Is there anything I can do," she added, as she gently touched his bandaged head.

"No, there's nothing left to do," Valencia said. "I didn't find your avocados and your husband is dead. I guess I blew it."

"Oh, don't say that. I'm sure you did your best." There was a brief awkward silence, until she spoke again. "Would you like a cookie?" she asked out of the blue. She reached in her handbag and produced a clear plastic bag containing cookies. She offered them to Valencia who accepted a cookie and took a tentative bite.

"Wow, this is really good," he said both pleased and surprised. "This is chocolate and something else."

"It's avocado."

"A chocolate chip and avocado cookie? That's brilliant. But not as brilliant as you."

"What do you mean?"

"Oh, you are very smart. First you hire me so it looks like you must care about your husband, and want your avocados back, though they most likely came from the Mexican drug cartel you were dealing with. Then you sell the avocados on the black market, then report them stolen and collect on your crop insurance."

"Why are you saying such hateful things?"

"Because they are true."

Her voice softened, "I thought we, you know, you and I, could, you know, get together. You said you like my cookies. You could have my cookies anytime you wanted. If you know what I mean?"

"Oh, I think I know what you mean," Valencia said. "Your cookies are great. The best I ever had. Oh, you are good. You conned your husband, you conned the Mexican drug cartel, you conned your crop insurance company. But I won't play the sap for you. You're good all right, but you made a couple of little mistakes."

"I don't know what you are talking about."

Valencia held up a piece of paper. "Your shipping invoice says you had forty thousand pounds of *Hass* avocados," he said.

"That's right."

"I suppose you know that ninety-five percent of the avocados grown in Mexico and California are of the *Hass* variety."

"So?"

"The avocado you gave me the other day is an example of the *Fuerte* variety, a little smaller, greener, with a smoother skin, and generally harvested a little later in the year, and certainly not as widely grown as the more popular *Hass* avocado. Did you know *fuerte* means *strong* in Spanish?"

"What's your point?" Her voice hardened slightly.

"I checked up on you. You *are* an avocado grower all right, but your trees are *Fuerte* avocados, not *Hass*. So how can you sell forty thousand pounds of a product you don't even grow? Your avocados are still on your trees in Ventura."

"How do you know all this?"

"Because I went and saw them. I'm sure you've heard of the Ventura Freeway."

"You can't prove anything," she snarled, completely abandoning the seductive voice.

"I don't have to prove anything. I'm not the police or the District Attorney. But they might be able to prove something if they can match the *Fuerte* avocado pit taken from your dead husband's throat with the *Fuerte* avocados on your trees in Ventura. And your crop insurance company will just have to glance at this invoice," he said, holding it up, "and figure out they don't have to pay for a crop you don't even grow. And as for the Mexican cartel, I'm sure their standards of proof are probably somewhat lower than those of U.S. law enforcement. You, my dear, are toast. Avocado toast."

"You think you are so smart, don't you?" Eden said, angrily.

"Not really," Valencia replied. "I got my head cracked open, probably by you. I've solved a case for the benefit of the police, an insurance company and a Mexican drug cartel, and the United States Department of Agriculture, all for three hundred dollars and a chocolate chip and avocado cookie," he said, as he took another bite. "Seriously, this is a great cookie. Is there any chance I could get the recipe before you get arrested?"

"You can't arrest me."

"No, I can't arrest you, but Inspector Zepeda here can," Valencia said as Zepeda came in from where he was listening to their conversation.

"Actually, I can't arrest her," Zepeda admitted. "But the police outside certainly can."

Eden stormed out of the office. The voices of the police were somewhat muffled, but Eden's mellifluous voice could be heard clearly. "Get your hands off me, copper!"

"I can arrest produce, but not people," Zepeda explained. "Anyway, thanks for the help."

"Sure, but I didn't really do much, did I? In fact, I'm thinking why should I even bother. What's it all for? No matter what we do, how hard we try, things are never going to change are they? You can't change the world. That's just the way things are. It doesn't matter how hard we fight it, there will always be evil, injustice and darkness in the world."

"Forget it, Nate," Zepeda said. "It's Koreatown. You wanna get lunch?"

"I could eat."

The Also-Rans

Benedict J Jones

You'd have to be a proper mug to knock over a bookie's these days. I'm talking clucking crack-head mug here, you get me? You got about a grand, tops, that you can get at with the rest locked away in time-lock safes that the poor bitch in the polyester polo shirt who runs the place can't get at either, no matter how much you make her sweat with a knife to her throat. For that, you may as well try to jack an offie. Granted, the Bangladeshi working there has most of the takings in his sock, but you can grab a decent bit of stock, and it's a bonus that most of them don't have security glass up. Yet.

So yeah, you'd be a mug to try and do over a bookie's. A normal bookie's that is, you know the type: there's at least two on every high street (next to the pound shop and the pawnbrokers). Except the thing is, there was a place that wasn't your normal bookie's and some mug had decided to try and knock it off. And they'd succeeded.

Pony Pete looks proper pissed off. They call him Pony on account of the watches he wears that he tries to convince people really are Rolexes and Tags, except I've never seen a watch with Tag Hour written on it... No one calls him that to his face but it's what he gets called, he's heard the talk and reckons it's because of him doing the bookie thing with the horses. He runs a bookie operation above a pub between the drive-thru McDonalds at Deptford and Surrey Quays Overground (I won't tell you the name of the place because, trust me, you don't want to go in there). You walk into the place and it looks like a lot of other pubs – tired decor that hasn't been updated since the late eighties, a barmaid who's seen better days (they were probably in the late eighties too), and a pool table that doesn't work. A dying boozer somehow staying on its feet, except that the real action is upstairs. You get a lot of people who get banned from your regular betting shops; dickheads on the whole who like to shout the odds, smash the machines and spit at the staff. Even after they're banned from all the local joints, they still want to bet. You'd think, what with this being the twenty first century, they'd just go on-line but, and again you'll have to trust me, these idiots think dial-up is what you do when you want to buy some cheap coke and get it delivered. Pete pays a couple of heavies who keep the clientele in line, and the big boys play cards in the back room so the pond life mind their Ps and Qs.

"They fucking done me over, Charlie, me! Who the fuck do they think they are?"

"Not sure what you think I can do about it, Pete."

He looks at me, eyes all big and sad like he might start bawling any second.

"Look into it, like."

"Ain't you got backers who can help you out?" He looks uncomfortable.

"Tell the truth, it's them I'm worried about. They don't like things like this, they'd worry I was in on it."

I can feel his pain.

"Alright. Tell me about it. How much they take you for?"

"Fifteen large."

I whistle.

"They must've come over the back wall into the beer garden. No cunt out there to see them and then they were into the pub. Margie didn't even see them till she got whacked over the head."

"How many?"

"Four."

"Carrying?"

"We'd have hardly given up the money if they weren't, would we?"

I concede the point and gesture for him to continue, scribbling in my notebook as he does so.

"Two of them had 'atchets, one a big old revolver, like something out a war film, and the last one was carrying a sawn-off shotgun but cut right down so it had no stock and a short arse barrel – you could almost see the cartridge poking out at us."

"Masks?"

"Well, obviously. Jesus, not much of a fucking detective are you...?"

"Oi."

"What?"

"I'm trying to help you out here, Pete – get me?"

"Sorry, Charlie. These cunts got me ulcers playing up." He takes a bright pink bottle of Pepto from his pocket and necks a load.

"So they had masks on, then?"

Pony Pete nods. "Silly cunts were wearing rubber horse masks."

"Horse masks?"

He nods and shakes his head. "Like getting stuck up by four Mister Eds."

I hold back a chuckle.

"Alright, I'll have a look into it and see what I can find out."

"Thanks, Charles."

He makes no move towards his wallet, and I sigh.

"My name Oxfam?"

"You what?"

"Save the Children, maybe?"

"Course it ain't."

The penny drops and he gives me a wink. "Here you go, mate. More when you got something, like." He passes me a fifty. I hold it up to the light to make sure it isn't snide. He sticks his lip out like a naughty schoolboy.

"I'll get back to you if I find anything – and there'd better more than that in it for me."

*

BANG!

I remember the days when I wouldn't have even got out of bed for a fifty but times have changed. I start off doing the rounds; *Wheelan's*, *The China Hall*, *The Moby Dick*, *The Ship and Whale*, *The Aardvark*. What strikes me most are the pubs that are long gone; *The Ship York*, *The Prince of Orange*, *The Three Compasses*, *The Jolly Caulkers*, *The Prince of Wales*, *The Quebec Curve* and all the rest. My trip down Rotherhithe Street turns into a thirsty walk up memory lane until I stop for another beer in *The Blacksmith's Arms*.

I squeeze the lime inside the neck of my Corona and take a pew at the end of the bar. My mum used to like me bringing her here for a Sunday roast but it's been years since we've been in. The manager is still the same: a big South African guy with a bald head and a bushy beard, rugby top, and a gut that shows he likes to sample his ales.

"Put another one in there for you, Cole?" I say.

"Decent of you, Charlie," he nods to the barmaid, and she reloads his glass. I pay, and then turn back to him.

"Anyone been in dropping a bit of change? People who wouldn't otherwise?"

He looks at his pint and takes a mouthful before answering.

"Now I'm not one to talk about my customers, my regulars, but them idiots, well..."

"Which idiots are we talking about?"

"You know Derrick, with the gimpy leg? Looks like he stinks - and he does. Banned from most of the pubs around here – including this one. Course, Carly," he gestures at the barmaid, "she's new and didn't know. I'd had to run over to the cash-and-carry for some more prawn crackers. Anyway, they were all in here – Derrick and his cronies living it up; pints, chasers, food, and for once, all paid for with no trouble."

"Who's this little crew of cronies?"

He laughs.

"Crew? They aren't a fucking crew, man. You got Derrick with his gimpy leg. Aldridge, black feller, got dodgy eyes so he has to wear sunglasses all the time. Who else now... Stevie Q,"

I nod, I know Stevie Q; story goes, his mum was an old goer and when she was eight months gone she went on a bender, drank a lot of Thunderbird before she let a gang of pikeys run a train on her. No wonder he came out the way he did. Not sure of the term you're meant to use now, but the kids used to call him Spacko Stevie.

"Last one's called Colin, I think. Same as the rest, though."

"How's that?"

"Fucking gimp. Got a hunched back and walks funny. Right bunch of charmers."

A coachload of American tourists file through the doors.

"Ah, shit. Fucking yanks, why can't they all just go down to *The Mayflower*," mutters Cole, and he downs his drink. "Have to catch you in a bit, Charlie."

I nod and raise my glass, already lost in my thoughts.

*

If there's two things I know, it's pond life and where to find them. I head back up Redriff Road and past the old bridge down to the *Wetherspoon's* opposite the kebab shop I used to work in. *The Surrey Dock's Tavern* – used to be called *The Warrior* until it got shut down in bad circumstances – isn't too bad as far as chain pubs go, better than some. The staff in here tend to be students but I know one of the managers a bit from back in the day; he was in the year above me at St. Michael's and I served coke and draw to him for a few years after school. He's gone straight-arrow now; missus and two kids and a two-bed in Lewisham.

"Hello, Matt."

"Alright, Charlie – what's happening?"

"Not much, man. Looking for a little bit of information."

"That right?"

"Yeah, 'bout a few people you might know?"

"Me? Don't think we know any of the same people anymore."

"Customers – yours."

"Mine?"

"Or maybe people you barred."

He takes a sip of his Diet Coke and nods for me to continue so I lay out a description of the people that Cole told me about, his face sours.

"The Also-Rans, that's what I call them – none of them are ever going to be coming first at anything. A right bunch. What d'you want with them?"

I tap my nose and slide a tenner across the bar.

"You don't happen to know where any of these geniuses might live, do you?"

*

I'm standing outside a block of flats in Layard Square, just behind Jamaica Road, trying to work out the best way of resolving this that doesn't involve anyone getting their legs broken, when the door opens. The door I'm watching.

A man steps out. He hobbles along the landing and then down the stairs. The man walks with a pronounced limp, rolling gait, and I know that this is Derrick. To be fair, he doesn't look like he smells; his hair is freshly cut and slicked back, and he wears a decent blazer over a pink-and-white gingham shirt, with chinos and boat shoes. Just a well-dressed chap about town. I wonder how much of that bank roll is left... He limps out of the estate and onto Jamaica Road. I follow him down to the bus stop on the little piazza and spark a Benson while we wait.

He boards a 381 bus and I'm three people behind him. I tap my Visa and stay standing while he gets offered a sit down on the priority seats, which he takes. Where are you going, Del? He looks happy, smiling and whistling to himself. We stay on till Dockhead, and he gets off near the closed down *Nine Bar*. We cross at the lights and head down past the Circle into Shad Thames. When we get near the La Pont de la Tour restaurant, he starts checking his watch and looking about. I check the time on my phone – three minutes to seven. I walk past him, catch a smell of Lynx, and keep going before stopping and pretending to check the laces on my Timberlands.

A woman is walking down towards him; looks Malaysian or maybe Thai, tall – pushing six-foot in her heels, a gym-toned body shown off by the tightest of tube dresses, this is a fine-looking woman but the way she's dressed screams pro. He waves at her and his grin gets so wide I think his face will split. I watch as they air kiss and he hands her an envelope. She slips it into her bag and then links her arm through his. They turn into a small alley and I reach the corner as they step into The Chop House. I watch through the window as they get taken to their table. I carry on through the alley until I'm standing on the river looking out on Tower Bridge and get to thinking about what I'm planning to do.

I smoke a Benson down and then head inside. Tell them I only want a drink and sit at the bar with a gin and tonic: double Bombay Sapphire and Fever Tree tonic. I look over into the restaurant proper and see Derrick smiling and laughing, the woman with him doing the same. I watch their starters get delivered and take that as my cue. I throw back the last of my drink and walk towards them. Derrick looks up at me and his smile falters. I give a smile.

"Might be best if your friend goes and powders her nose."

She looks up at me and I reach into the watch-pocket of my jeans and palm her a half wrap of chang. The woman gets up quick and vanishes off to find the toilets.

"Hello, Derrick."

"Hello," he replies, studying the spoon he had just dipped into his lobster bisque.

"How is it?"

"The food?"

"Mm-hmm."

"Pretty decent. Better than what I'm used to – I'm more of a beans on toast man."

He picks up his champagne flute and downs the contents. I don't wait for the server. I take the bottle from the cooler and top his glass up. I turn the bottle over in my hands.

"Laurent-Perrier, the good stuff. I have a friend who likes the rosé of this."

"Can't say I've had it."

I shrug and raise my hand to the waiter.

"Another glass, please." I look at Derrick. "I think you know why I'm here, no?"

"I reckon so. Knew someone would come knocking eventually. You were quicker than I gave that prick Pete credit for, though."

I stay quiet while the waiter fills my glass.

"Why did you do it?"

Derrick looks me dead in the eye.

"Tired of it. Tired of the shit: the budget lagers, people laughing, not enough money to keep the electric on, benefits, sanctions and shit. I said to the lads, fuck this – every dog has his day and when's ours? Got bored of waiting for something to come along, so we did it." He shrugs at me.

"The tools?"

"Oh, them. The Webley was a display piece, a replica."

"The shotgun?"

"Aldridge's nephew had stashed it in his flat so we borrowed it."

"The horse heads?"

"We just wanted to fuck Pony Pete off – he'd banned Stevie the week before because he pissed himself in the upstairs bookie."

"Sounds fair enough to me. You do realise that nothing can be the same after this?"

"Always knew that. Didn't care. A couple of days of living how I should've been living is all I wanted."

"Much of it left?"

Derrick gives me a half-smile and reaches into his blazer pocket. He tosses a thin wedge on the table. I pick it up and thumb the notes: about a grand left.

"You all doing things like this?"

Derrick nods.

"Like our bucket lists. We knew they'd find us eventually. Aldridge said he'd be going back to Saint Vincent but he'll only have got as far as the nearest bookies that'll let him in, Stevie wanted to treat a girl who works with him in Poundland, and Colin, well, same as me – except he'll be with a young fella, I imagine."

I almost want to laugh but instead I raise my glass to him. I check the notes and peel off two hundred.

"That should cover dinner and a cab home. You paid the brass already?"

He nods. I look up and see she has come back from the toilets. I pocket the rest of the money and down the last of the champagne.

"Then enjoy it. You ain't got anything to worry about till the morning."

"Thank you," he says, but I wave it away and head off out of the place.

*

I meet Pony Pete at *The Old Salt Quay, Spice Island* as was, early doors. We both have lattes, no stomach for booze this early – although he looks like he'd hit it hard last night.

"Please tell me you've got something for me, Charles?"

"Might just have names of them what done you over and some addresses."

"Really? Oh, lovely, lovely. Go on then, run 'em past me."

"In a minute. First off, what are you going to do to this lot?"

"What you worried about that for?"

"I always worry."

"Not what I heard – weren't you there when that kid, the one who turned Queen's evidence, got his hands broke into chalk?"

Shit, that takes me back. And, yes, I was there – did a stretch for it as well. Fucking prick for mentioning it, though, Pete.

"Long time ago. Don't take me for a mug - what are you gonna do to them?"

"Me? Nothing. My backers, well…"

He smiles and puffs out his chest, a little man with big backers.

"We talking leg breaking, or burying them somewhere?"

"Legs, I'd imagine, but I can't promise."

"Fair enough. And second, my fee..."

"Your fee?"

"You think I run my arse off buying drinks and paying people out the goodness of my heart?"

"Course not, course not." Pete takes out a roll and peels off a couple of hundred. He lays it on the table next to me. "There you go, Charlie-boy."

Boy? I smile at him and regard the meagre pickings.

"Cheers." The piece of paper with full names and addresses stays in my pocket along with most of the bundle I'd recovered from Derrick. "The guy leading it is called Derrick Finlan, hop-a-long leg, he lives over near Southwark Park, not exactly sure where. Geezers with him were Aldridge Brown, Steve Quinn, and Colin Warde. They aren't exactly hard to find. All locals, you might know the names."

Looking up, I see that Pete's jaw has dropped.

"Them cunts?"

"Yep, them cunts. Did you over, mate. Came in your place and took fifteen large off you – made you look like a right mug, didn't they?"

"That bunch of crips and spazzos?"

"The very same. Walked in your shop bold as brass and took the money."

I take a long drink out of my coffee and then pocket the money from the table. I'm enjoying this.

"It can't have been."

"I'm sure it'll go down well with your backers, finding out who did it."

The look on Pete's face says it won't. I imagine the bookies might be getting run by someone else from now on. I finish my coffee and get up.

"See you later, Pete."

He raises a hand. The colour has drained from his face knowing who it was who'd done him over. I guess the also-rans finally did come in; for themselves and only for a day - but they came in.

A Stretch of Ground

Grant Tracey

1

He was a thin scarf bending with the lines of snow.

The call came twenty minutes ago, north, twelve miles from Winsome, on one of them numbered county roads, 215. His red windbreaker had a stuck zipper so he held it closed with a gloveless hand. Why he didn't wait in the small house on the hill, I don't know.

He crumpled into my hack, words clouded with liquor. He pointed at his car, a Ford Falcon pressed into a large oak tree. The headlights and grill were now a lopsided grin. Take me to the Daws Motel, he said, words crashing hiccups.

He was on the run from Mike Dietrichson, owner of Winsome Pontiac Buick on Franklin. I bowled against his team now and then, Wednesdays, Mohawk Lanes. Mike hated to lose. He had big hunching shoulders, a hard stomach, and heavy hands. He always talked trash, badgering us to pick up 7-10 splits.

My fare rubbed at the cold spots on his face with shaky fingers. A white beaded wristband puffed against the fleshy part of his hand. The band was full of letters—some I could make out: ANA.

"How much have you been drinking, cowboy?"

"Drinking?" His eyes darkened. "I don't drink—" He introduced himself.

Jimmy Feddersen? A week or so ago, his face was under the yellow glare of WKLL's news cameras. He had found $2300 in a black doctor's bag near a storm drain on Water Street.

Word had it the money was dividends from a high-stakes poker game Dietrichson ran above the Armory. Nelson Griggs of Young and Beggert Realty was there. Winsome's Chief of Police was there too.

The black bag should have carried $12,300, he admitted. That meant ten large was unaccounted for —

Two hours ago Dietrichson grew tired of Jimmy's good Samaritan bit. Two of his boys rousted Feddersen from Regehr's and brought him to the dealership. In a back room, they worked him over with sawed-off baseball bats. "Where's the rest of the money, thief?"

"Did you take it?" I asked.

He looked away. Two bandits in Mardi-Gras masks had broken in on the poker game and hijacked the winnings. Jimmy — narrow shoulders, small hands — fit the bill. The other bandit was a woman.

His hiccups returned. "I don't know how I got away —" He coughed. "I needed the money," he mumbled, something about a stretch of ground.

He had a family two hours east of here that he wanted to give back to. He was working at the Sizemore pulp and paper mill but the returns were slim, slow. He needed a bigger stake. He missed his girls, six and ten. Maybe I could drive him there?

We never made it.

Jimmy's hiccuping slid into wobbly laughter and then burbles of blood.

He crumpled against the dash — dead.

There was no money in his pockets.

2

Some fucker was tap-tapping my face like a drummer riding his hi-hat too damn long —

They sat at the couch's edge, guns on their thighs. The room was full of cigarettes and coffee. "Wake up, soldier." The older fella's face barely moved, lower lip loose. He must have had some form of palsy.

A STRETCH OF GROUND

Thin sands of light filtered through my trailer's musty windows.

I'd seen these guys before, Mohawk Lanes, Wednesday Night Bowling, Dietrichson's posse. The one with the drooping lip was Kyle Kangas. His eyebrows were a heavy zipper and his pock-marked face looked like a dry lung. Terry Jack Kotter was in his early twenties, with gray eyes the color of rain and the fragile skin of a Hummel. He sported a bolo tie, cowboy hat with an Aztec band. Several razor nicks dotted his chin. A spot of Kleenex was stuck to one of them. "Where's the money, soldier?"

The tap became a stinging slap. "Ten G's—"

Under my pillow was my Army-issued .45. I had slept with it since the Ice House incident several months back. Keep talking assholes.

"Jimmy didn't leave it with you before he, uh, checked out, did he?"

"He barely said anything—you guys gave him a real working over—"

"So, he did talk?"

"Nothing about money—"

Another short lash—my head exploded with scorpions.

They had searched Jimmy's apartment—nothing. Talked to the girl in the farmhouse—Ellana. Another fat nothing.

One of the poker night robbers was a woman, Kangas reminded me. And Jimmy's car crashed into a tree by Ellana's pad. "Coincidence?" He shrugged with sulky languor.

She said she'd never seen him before, Terry Jack added, the gun raised like a semaphore flag. "But we didn't believe her. Worked her over a little—" There were some shadows in his smile.

The beaded wristband. ANA. Ellana. "You give her the Louisville Slugger treatment too?"

"My technique is varied." Kyle rubbed his chin. "Relax, soldier. She's still alive—"

"The soldier bit. You overuse it," I said.

Bronze star, Korea. Greased a few Red Chinese, huh? He smirked. You were a real bad-ass.

"I was a radio operator—"

Truth be told, I had killed more since coming back. Three in an ice house rescue a few months ago on the Ojibwe reservation. That "operation" put me in the hospital for four weeks—flashbacks, nervous breakdown. "What did you do to Ellana?"

"Relax—" Terry Jack straightened the shoestrings on his bolo so that the aiguillettes lined up. He gently tapped them together.

Kangas's lips barely parted. "Maybe it's all like she says. Just a coincidence."

"Right." Terry Jack laughed, air slipping slowly from a slashed tire. The sand in the room grew thicker. "Dietrichson wants the money."

"I'm telling you, I know nothing about the money, Jimmy said dick about the money," I lied.

The gun under my pillow was too far away. *Keep talking—*

"Our boss hates to lose," Kangas said. "You hear anything, you see anything, money-wise, you let us know? Dig?"

"The guy was a real loser," Kotter said. "And the boss hates losing to losers."

"I only met Jimmy yesterday—"

"That's enough time to learn a dying loser's secrets—you don't want to be a loser too, do you?"

My mouth was full of bile. "If I find the money, you'll leave the girl alone—?"

They looked at each other. "Maybe—"

"Yeah—maybe," Kangas winked. "Life's full of uncertainties, motherfucker."

They laughed

Then Terry Jack handed me a wad of Kleenex. "Now, clean up your face—"

3

"They cut off two of my fingers," Ellana said.

Her left hand was wrapped in a bandage the size of a

cave man's club. Spots of blood showed through the mummified gauze.

We were in back at Regehr's, red-lined booth, yellow Formica table. We were drinking orange egg creams from glasses with more curved rings than the Michelin Man.

She sipped and swallowed two painkillers. "I think I've passed my limit on these but it hurts like fuck—" She grimaced. "What the hell do you want? The goddamn money—?"

"I want to help you—"

"You work for them—?"

"Fuck no."

She smiled, suddenly recognizing me. You're the fella who punched-out that school teacher for sleeping with his daughter. And you rescued Irene Sizemore from her sadistic husband and his ice house of horrors. Killed three, she said.

"Yeah." I rubbed at the edges of my mouth. *Funny how it works: after bringing Irene and her son safely back home the alleged charges against me for supertuning fellas who supertuned women suddenly disappeared.* Cabbie turned hero. My war record helped. And the four-week stay in the hospital generated quite a bit of sympathy. "Tell me about Feddersen—"

She flicked curled ends of blonde hair away from her black eyes. Look, she said, me and Jimmy did the robbery—but you already knew that. I wasn't going to tell those bastards—she looked at her club for a hand. "He needed the money for a stake for his family. A stretch of ground, he called it. A farm or some damn dream. Me, I just wanted money. Nothing noble." She shrugged effortlessly and sipped more egg cream.

Ellana was a waitress at *Gus's Diner* and was tired of a life clearing tables and plates dotted with cigarettes buried in mashed potatoes. And there she heard talk of a poker game, Thursdays above the Armory. "So we got a couple of Mardi Gras masks—"

"Was Jimmy in love with you?" I told her about the wristband—

"Yes." They had a thing. "Like you and Irene had."

"Yeah—" *Killing her husband who had been plotting to kill her kind of ended our thing.*

Jimmy's wife and kids live above a grocery store, two hours from here, Bingston, she said. Jimmy came here to make more money to buy his own place—"He wrote letters home every day." She reached into her bag. "I haven't had a chance to get a stamp for this but—it's to his wife—"

It lay on the table between us as her voice sank down a well. I noted the address.

"Why the whole black bag ruse—"

She popped a third painkiller. The bottle now had a very thin rattle. She shrugged at it vaguely. If Jimmy "found" some money it might divert suspicion from us, from me. "That was the thinking—Jimmy was worried for me—"

"But $2300 ain't going to placate Mike. He wants it all—all back—"

She nodded and played with the charm of a dolphin on her necklace. "Yes. The cheap S.O.B. I'd wait on him at *Gus's*. Seven per cent tip he left, like paying a goddamn sales tax. Seven per cent."

I shook out my pack of Luckies, offered her one, lit it for her.

"I'm not giving that bastard back my share of the money—" They each pocketed five.

"Jimmy send his share to the wife?"

She puffed quickly. "Yeah—I think so—" Another puff. Her words were muddy—

"You should slow down on those things—"

"Who asked you?—"

I leaned back, took a long slow pull, my eyes narrowing. "I'm offering you the same protection I offered Irene—"

It had been just over a year since the ice house incident, and three months since the Salinger Files, a caper involving a manuscript written by that *Catcher in the Rye* fella that was stolen from Polis College on the hill. A librarian, a college prof, and a student from the rich exurbs, Colin K. Hoops, were involved in the shenanigans that devolved into sexual assault, kidnapping, and killing. The librarian was dead, the prof dismissed by the Board of Regents and sent to prison, and the student, the rapist? Well, he walked free of all charges because his family could afford the best lawyers. That is, he walked, until he met up with me in a ski mask late one night under the shadows of the campanile and I broke his legs.

"I won't let Dietrichson or his boys hurt you anymore—"

She smiled dimly, and then popped the last painkiller in the bottle.

4

I don't know why it hadn't occurred to me before, but when it did, I called in sick and drove east to Bingston and the address on the letter Ellana had yet to post.

It was a small town of about 3500 with a motel, a bar, hardware store, and four-corner gas station. The mom and pop grocery was right next to Rexall. I drove down Main Street and on over to an excluded spot on Taft and Third. Lit a Lucky. The sun was high and bright and the street was empty.

If I had a horse I'd be looking for a goddamn hitching post.

I tugged at the back of my leather jacket, covering up the .45 in the waistband of my khakis.

Jimmy's wife was behind the grocery counter. She had a plain face, chestnut hair, and tortoise-shell glass with wide frames that showed off her blue eyes.

I grabbed a box of popcorn with an elephant on it and a bottle of Pepsi.

"Rebekah?" She nodded. The smell of bubblegum and detergent filled the spaces between us.

I was the cabbie who was with your husband when he died, I said, and regardless of the bogus police story that it was a mix of alcohol and the crackup that led to the brain trauma that killed him, I told her that was all bullshit. He had been beaten to death by Dietrichson's boys, only he didn't know he was dead yet until he was in my hack. I lied a little and said his last words were about her, and the girls.

She smiled awkwardly. "You don't have to say that for me." Her teeth were narrow and her chin dipped as she spoke. "Jimmy was drifting away from me, from us —"

The tops of several cans along the shelves were flecked with fly matter. Beyond her swayed a frayed curtain. Behind it, cinder block walls, a cot, and a hot plate.

I took a short drag of what was left of my cigarette and offered her one. She didn't smoke. She used to, but Jimmy quit so she did too.

"He was sending you money, right?"

"Yes —"

"To buy a stretch of ground —"

"Yes —"

"Did he ever send a large lump sum, like 5K? I'm not with Diestrichson or the cops. But, a couple of beefy guys are going to come this way — if I figured it out, they will — and — they cut off some fingers of a friend of mine —"

She shuddered and glanced down at the cash register and rang up no sale. From under the drawer she pulled out a short letter. "This arrived last week —"

It was a long goodbye from Jimmy:

"Dearest Becca. I don't know how to begin and this isn't what I want to tell you but I must. I'm in love with someone else. I love you too, and I think maybe a person can love two people, at the same time, but I'm afraid I love Ellana more, and I, I, want you to have this money, $3,000, to have a new start for you and the two girls. I remember so many great things about life with you, and I'll always remember those great things, but — things change, I don't know why. Maybe it's part of God's plan. I don't know. I still love you, but, like I said, I love Ellana more. Money has no conscience. I took it for you. Please put it toward something good. Sorry I lost my way. Sorry I lost you. Hug the girls for me. Love, Jimmy."

The letter shook in my hands. The money was severance pay. *Three K? That meant he held back 2 large ones for himself, his own nest egg.*

With Jimmy dead, Rebekah was re-thinking the dream of a farm, and instead wanted to move west to Winsome or

North to Watertown. The suburbs. But she couldn't just up and leave, she said, the kids liked it here. They had friends.

Sure. You got friends, family in the Midwest? Those guys will be coming, they're killers, I muttered. Let me stay in the back room. I'll camp out there. Soup, sandwiches, I'll get by —

She showed me to the room.

I smoked a half a pack of cigarettes, the .45 on my thigh. The Pepsi had turned warm.

5

On the third day, they arrived in Sloan Wilson grays, flipping over the open sign on the door to "Sorry, We're Closed". They wore gloves. Terry Jack still sported the black cowboy hat with the Aztec band. It was parked in a jaunty manner on the squared-off shelf of his head.

All the light in the room dimmed, disappearing behind the heavy shadows of their thick shoulders.

"Cold day, huh? Much business?" Kyle smiled faintly, his eyes elsewhere, hands in the pockets of his camel hair coat.

They spoke barbed-wire fences of menace, commenting on what nice girls Rebekah had, and wasn't that them, playing in the backyard, making a snowman? "It's getting kind of dark." Terry Jack glanced over his shoulder into the thin night.

Kyle picked at a tooth with the corner of a matchbook he'd grabbed off the counter. "Shouldn't they be inside? Safe — ?"

Rebekah gasped.

Hate to see something happen to them, one of the two said.

"Guess, you can't keep an eye on them girls, because your man's gone, huh?" Kyle closed the matchbook, his face an even dryer lung than it was a few days back. "Give us the money — "

"The money he sent home — " Terry Jack said.

"To you."

"Five large — "

"It wasn't five, it was three, assholes—" I mumbled loudly.

Terry Jack reached inside his pockets and pulled out a .45, but before he could do anything with it, my gun was barking as I stepped through the part in the curtains. I put two in his chest. His hands folded in front of him and he fell to his knees, vague half-words tumbling from crimped lips.

"Sands—!" Kyle's coat was buttoned too tightly and he never did get his gun free. I took off half his head and he tumbled back, thudding hard on the store's gray-green linoleum, brains and bone, a scraped streak stretching like long fingers—

Terry Jack swayed, and then a big blood bubble burst between his lips and he fell forward. Rebekah shook against my shoulders, and then asked for a cigarette.

The staties held me for close to three hours. But Rebekah vouched for me, saying I was a friend of the family, had come to visit, had come to give my condolences over Jimmy's tragic death. These two men, whom she had never seen before, came into the grocery store and held her up. "Pulled guns and everything. Threatened my girls." Thank god, Mr. Sands was here, she said. Did you know he was a hero? Bronze Star in Korea? Why these other men would want to rob such a place, she had no idea. "I guess some people think there's a lot of money in groceries. Maybe there used to be, but there ain't no more."

Once I got home I called Mike Dietrichson, told him he'd have to get some new boys, his two had said their long goodbyes. Becca has the money. Consider it payment for the murder of her husband. You do anything to her, or Ellana, I'll kill you.

Sinatra played in the background and Mike didn't say much. "You're a real red-ass, aren't ya?"

"You could say that."

"I understand, you left my name out of it—"

"I did."

"Okay. Okay. Case closed." I could feel him smiling through the phone. "You ever grow tired driving a hack, give me a call —"

The next night was bowling night. Dietrichson had a couple of newbies on his team and they couldn't bowl worth a damn. He gave them as hard a time as he gave us, but he was a good sport about it all. Between bawling them out and talking smack to my team, Mike bought us all several rounds of beer. He even tipped the waitress twenty bucks.

Bang!
Bang!

PAYDAY

Saira Viola

Mark Schneider. Law school dropout. Part-time drunk. Serial masturbator. High- functioning meth addict. Sex bot devotee. Ex-husband, and one of LAPD's finest.

Early morning: Parked outside Baby Blues in an unmarked grey Chrysler 300, still code 3 equipped. His white shirt unbuttoned, revealing a full pecan tinted rug. Cuff sleeves turned back. His black pants were unzipped, and his cock poked out of striped jockeys. Schneider had a sock missing and a solitary long frizzy white hair dangled from his left nostril. Checking his face in the rear-view mirror, he yanked the hair out. "Son of a bitch. You still got it." He ran the tips of his fingers down the right side of his face. A face, chequered with mistakes, money fights, and unreported murder.

Schneider smoothed his shirt down, zipped up, and rummaged around in the back seat. Sifting through paper coffee cups, potato chip packets, a half-drunk bottle of Jameson, and a dozen grease spotted Five Guys burger bags, he grabbed his anti-perspirant stick. Twist. Click. He slicked both armpits. Then he spied a little mouthful of sunlight. A sparkly faced cutie Marla Cortez skipped right in front of him. She had just finished her shift at the Golden Banana and was on her way home. Marla had to take care of her mom who had a heart condition and her little brother Oscar.

She flung off her denim jacket revealing a sea green tube top and hiked up her skirt allowing the youthful rush of summer heat, to embrace her as she wheeled her hips around. Her pink-string tanga on show. High High High. Smiling honkers on display. She was all taste as she hop-scotched towards the patrol car, caterwauling, tuneless karaoke style rhymes, with a Kool Aid cup in her hand. Her apple-shaped ass winking. Jiggle. Jiggle Jiggle. Like the soft round sound of a Tenor trombone.

Schneider's smutty eye preyed on Marla's intoxicating euphoria. "Fresh."

He leant back in his seat, slid his hand down to his leg, and winced as he lifted the hem of his pants. A dime-sized hole in the middle of his right calf dripped blood. He blotted it dry with a stained paper towel and tossed it in the back seat. "Small fish are easy prey," he muttered. "Pat and frisk. Every curve. Inside thigh and sugar walls." He opened the car door using the Dutch Reach technique, so he could easily spot any oncoming distractions, or potential witnesses. "Excuse me Miss."

Marla was in her own kookookechoo bubble. A boho suede purse hung from her neck. "Yeeeeeh."

"Could you please step this way?"

"Er…What for?"

"Coz I asked you to."

Marla sniffed.

"You got no right to ask me anything Officer. I'm not doing anything wrong. Lemme pass please."

Schneider looked at her like a captive animal. "You ain't shit baby. You ain't nuthin and you ain't going nowhere."

"But I've done nuthing wrong."

Schneider's power was sewn up tight in the furrows of his face.

Marla tried to side step away, but Schneider blocked her path with his leg and showed off his gun tucked in his waistband.

"Sir. Please. Just let me through."

"No. Fucking. Way."

Marla spat on the ground. "What the fuck is going on." Under her breath she hissed "Bbbbbbastard!"

"Whooooa. Eassseee tiger." Without blinking, Schneider pinned her arms behind her back and used his left hand to control her. Within seconds, she was cuffed. He forced her to stand, against the car legs apart, and placed his big meaty fingers around her waist. After patting her down, he groped her left butt cheek. "You got your ID?"

Marla flinched.

Then he groped her right butt cheek.

Her eyelashes instinctively quivered "D...Don't touch me!"

"Cool it honey. You're slurring your words, and there's that crazy eye twitch. You reek of weed and pcp. And you're in a lot of trouble. It doesn't look good for you. Not at all. No mam. Thing is liddle lady, I'm entitled to touch. Anywhere I want. Cos, I got a feelin' you're concealin'. And your freaky-deaky necked shit makes me think you're under the influence of a drug or controlled substance. But I'm a nice guy. I'm thinkin' you and me can work somethin' out." He caught the warmth of her body as he stood behind her with his cock pressed hard against her ass and slipped his fingers into the back of her panties. "You know what I want."

Marla opened her mouth as wide as she could, her tonsils trying to spread the injustice. "Arrrrrrrrrrrrrggghhh!"

Schneider lunged deeper and squeezed her snatch. "One more word and I'll fuck the shit right out of you."

Marla tossed her head back and mule-kicked him in the shin.

He stumbled, picked himself up and untied the purse from her neck. "Now what we got here? Some kind o' prairie hippie shit?"

Inside her purse, Marla had her driver's license, cell phone, a tiny tube of cherry lip balm, an EBT card, and some foil wraps. Schneider held the purse under his right arm, walked her to the other side of the car then placed her headfirst into the front passenger seat. He sat on the driver's side and pretended to run her intel through his police laptop. "We got a real messy situation. Clearly, you're under the influence of some kinda drug, probably some alkhi–hol too. Completely outta control in a public place. So, you're a danger to yourself and everyone around you."

BANG!

He held up the foil wraps. "And what we got here? Some leftovers? A little angel dust. Krissst."

Schneider's face grew uglier. "Girl you're fucked! Well, what's it gonna be, Big Jim and the twins or a trip to the precinct and county lock up? Get down girl. C'mon. Get down."

A string of tears beaded Marla's eyes "You wa...want mmme t' suck yoooo off th... then y yyou let ...me go?"

"That's right."

"Bbbbbbbbastard!"

"I saw the EBT card. Dunno why they bother with that shit. You can't buy jack. No vitamins, no beer, and no cigarettes. So, what the fuck's it good for? If you accept my offer, at least you'll be getting a dose of good ol' American protein. Just you and me. It's a very generous offer."

Marla clawed her own hands. A form of self-protest. "Wh..what kind of fucked up po-po are you anyway?"

"The real kind. Dirty. Reliable. Now we got a deal or what?"

Schneider unzipped his pants.

"Now give it a long, slow suck, lollipop style..."

Schneider forced her head down. One hand gripped the back of her neck. Pastel ribbons of vomit began to build in her glottis.

Schneider's 45 calibre Kimber Classic was aimed at her the whole time.

Marla felt as if her tongue was buried in white America, as if she had no control of her own body. Terror. She wanted to run. Run from his blistered thumbs and his sickly cologne. But one look at his malign little eyes and she hung on, like a trapped bird feeding her wounds into a deadly snake. When it was over, she remained perfectly still for a while, staring out of the window at a singing wave of blue sky.

Schneider dropped her off at a vacant parking lot near Family Dollar minimart. She sat on the curb and threw up. A five minute technicolour barfing opera. All her dreams, missed opportunities, and nightmares splattered to the ground.

Schneider adjusted his pants and drove away, spanking the tarmac at speed. Pounding on the steering wheel, he screeched the lyrics to AC/DC's *Highway to Hell*: "No stop signs... no one's gonna slow me down." In the cavities of his mind, Schneider believed he was a renegade, reacting against a system he'd stopped believing in long ago. To everyone else he was a lyin' dealin' snortin' stealin' crooked cop. The god of the unflushed crapper feasting on fresh blood.

*

Three weeks later in Brodies Food Mart Marla watched as Schneider punched open the cash register and jammed his pockets with a stack of bills. The owner simply shrugged and turned away. Marla had been marking time: At the Rape Crisis center in West Hollywood. At the free clinic for contact dermatitis. At the unemployment office. At Danny G's pawn shop hocking her sick mother's wedding ring so the family could eat. They were being squeezed left right and centre for car payments, credit card bills, and back rent but all she could think of was the greying stink of a dead white fish. She followed Schneider out of the door and hovered in a side street all the while fingering her small silver Milagro she carried around for luck and her newly acquired pocket knife. You look like a big fat calf standing there waiting ...just waiting for the slaughter. Schneider whistled at a petite strawberry-blonde wearing a tight lavender sweater over black jeggings and long black boots. She glanced at him nervously and hurried away. Schnieder was about to say something when suddenly out of the shadows two beef heads covered by ski masks fired three shots into the air:

BAM ! BAM! BAM!

They raced towards a blacked-out Lincoln pushing past a phalanx of party goers waving their hands in the air. The driver in the Lincoln spun around and caught Schnieder reaching for his gun, radioing for help. He jammed the brakes, calmly pulled out a 38 caliber from the glove box and shot him straight through the window. Schneider arched over. His legs splintered and he took the full fall on the rump of his ass. Screams! A swash of blood and a welling crowd.

Schneider screeched, "I'm hit, Jesus I'm hit."

Squad cars and an ambulance arrived a few minutes later.

Marla edged her way through the rabble and stared at a sputtering red neon sign above her. *PAYDAY*.

Slap Happy

Andrew Humphrey

We're sitting around the scarred old coffee table at Eric's, drinking Stella and rating our favourite serial killers when a skinny, bearded guy bursts in. He's waving a gun around. There are three of us in the room. He can't point the gun at all of us at once, but he has a good try. Eric's flat is small and there's a kitchen opposite the front door. There's no way the man could know that Danny is in the kitchen, fixing himself crackers and cheese. It's sad for him that he doesn't, though, as seconds after he breaks in, Danny emerges. He scatters the plastic ribbons covering the doorway, then shoots the guy twice in the head who then slides over and down, like a clothes horse being folded away.

No one else has moved. A smell seeps through the fug of pot and body odour and cordite. Eric looks at me with desperate eyes.

"I think I shit myself."

Fuck's sake.

I'm better than this, I think. But I'm really not.

Happy sits on the floor, motionless, joint at port arms, Stella bottle cradled in his lap.

"Shipman?" he says, looking at me. "He's your favourite? That's so lame."

"It's all about the numbers, man," Danny says, tucking the gun into his jeans pocket.

Happy nods slowly at him as though considering the point. Then he sees the dead guy cooling in a scruffy puddle across the doorway. "Who the fuck is that?"

"Seriously, Happy, you only just noticed?" Eric's voice is shrill. Even shriller than usual. He stands gingerly.

"To be fair," Danny says, "Happy's barely been sober this millennium."

"True that," Happy says. He points his bottle at the dead man. Lager sloshes over a filthy bare foot. "So. Who is he, then?"

"That," I say, "Is a good question."

Happy nods, satisfied, then tries to lick a dribble of beer from his big toe.

After Eric's cleaned himself up we stand in a loose circle, looking down at the body. Danny's been through his pockets; a Samsung phone, newish model, locked, of course. No wallet, but there's a bundle of greasy notes; about three hundred quid, maybe, in tens and twenties. Danny hands us a couple of twenties each and keeps the rest for himself. No one argues.

He holds the guy's gun in the palm of his hand. It's small and black; snub nosed and ugly. "Piece of shit," Danny says. "He could have picked this up anywhere." He checks the chamber. "It's not even loaded."

"Huh," I say. To Danny, "You okay?"

"Sure. He dealt the cards. You break into a man's crib waving a gun around, you take the consequences."

"Preach," Happy says.

"How about the shots, man?" Eric says. His eyes are bright and anxious. "Someone must have heard. If the feds turn up, we're screwed."

"The feds?" I say.

"Fuck you," Eric says.

"I think we're golden," Danny says. "No one around hear gives a shit."

"That is one of this neighbourhood's better points," Happy says.

"Perhaps the only one."

Eric starts to protest, but he can't be bothered. He nudges the body with his right foot. "What are we going to do with him?"

"I'll take care of it," Danny says, as we knew he would.

Danny ushers us all out of the flat, Eric too. It's a little after two in the morning and the streets are stark and empty in the moonlight.

"Stick together," Danny says. "Don't come back here until..." He thinks for a moment, eyes averted, breath pluming in the chilled air. "Midnight."

"That's ages," Eric says. "All my stuff is stashed in there. What are we going to do ..."

"You're big boys," Danny says. "You'll figure it out."

He closes the door, locks it from the inside.

"Jesus," Eric is as jittery as ever. "Fuck's sake, man." He's talking to himself mostly. His arms and hands are moving constantly. His head turns this way and that but his eyes don't settle and he won't look at me or Happy.

Happy seems oblivious. He is entirely relaxed, leant back against the front door. He has a thick beard that's so bushy it looks as though it has something living in it. Knowing Happy, it probably does. He runs a hand through it slowly. His face becomes animated and then slackens again. Danny's right. I can't remember the last time Happy wasn't drunk or high. It suits him, though. He wasn't really made to be sober.

"You hungry, Happy?"

"What?" He looks at me and I see him come back into the present. "Yeah. I could eat."

"Food?" Eric says. "How can you think about food at a time ..."

"We'll go to Jan's," I say. "Have a cuppa and some cheese on toast. Talk this out."

"Talk what out?" Happy says.

"Jesus Christ," Eric says.

Jan's is on the seafront, about a ten minute walk away. It's late October. Summer was brutally hot, but it left suddenly, as though it owed money. Now the season is dying slowly and inelegantly, bit by bit as the weekends crumble away and vendor after vendor packs up for the last time. They'll be back next spring: probably, most of them. This is a small coastal resort in the East of England. It's tired and broken and shabby at the best of times. And this isn't the best of times. As the summer trade recedes it leaves its traces in the chilling air. Ghost scents; used chip fat, candy floss, sweat, a sense of quiet desperation. Still, this is home, for the four of us. It's where we wash up, men of our kind.

Jan's is a greasy spoon tucked between a mobile phone shop and a bookies. Jan himself is a large, slab-like man of uncertain age and ethnicity. He's behind the counter when we enter, a copy of the *Daily Express* propped in front of him. We are his only customers. He folds the paper in half and looks at us with flat eyes.

"We close soon."

"Two hours, Jan, give or take." I try a smile. I shouldn't have bothered.

"Soon," he grunts. Jan's closes at four every morning and opens again at six. I asked him once why he bothered closing at all. "Man has to sleep," he said.

I order toasted cheese and tea for three. Jan waits for a moment, then says, "No cheese."

"What?"

"You hear. No cheese."

"This is bullshit," Eric says under his breath.

"No worries," I say, cutting Eric off. "Just toast then."

"Just toast," Jan says. His eyes shift downwards and his voice becomes even gruffer. "Tomorrow, no toast."

"No toast?" Eric says.

"Tomorrow, nothing." He points the newspaper at each of us in turn. "You three, banned."

"Banned? What the fuck are you talking about?"

"Too dangerous. Too much bang, bang."

Eric's mouth hangs open. "Too much ... how do you know ..."

"Not Danny. You tell Danny, he welcome."

"What's happened, Jan? What do you know?" I say.

"Jan know nothing." He stares at the counter, his expression surly and closed. "Tea and toast. On the house. Then you fuck off, yes? Give it week, maybe two. If you still around, come back then."

"If we're still around?" Eric says, incredulous. But Jan is making himself busy, boiling water, toasting bread.

"On the house," Happy says. "Sweet."

We huddle around a chipped, Formica-topped table, sipping tea and chewing pieces of flaccid toast. Jan is wiping the floor behind the counter. The tang of bleach cuts through the smell of old food.

"Are we safe here?" Eric says.

I shrug. "Who knows?"

"What does safe even mean these days?" Happy says. He stares at us in turn, his expression suddenly intensely serious. "What does it mean?" His head tilts towards the cold half-round of toast languishing on Eric's plate. "You done with that, man?" Eric nods and Happy folds the toast into his mouth and chews quickly.

While Happy eats and drinks I look at Eric and say, "What have you done?"

"What?" It's impossible to read Eric as his expression is constantly cycling through various stages of fear and guilt and anxiety. He looks guilty now and close to tears. "Nothing. That guy earlier? Just some rando, some smackhead looking for a fix."

"That's what I thought, but with three hundred quid? And that phone? Pretty high end for a junkie."

"Could have nicked it."

"Maybe. But that stuff with Jan ... something's wrong."

"And it's my fault, is it? Of course it is. It's always Eric."

"To be fair, mate, it usually is." I try to soften the words with a smile, but Eric clings onto his indignation as though that's all he has left. Perhaps it is.

*

We'd met in a foster home, twenty years back. They weren't bad people, the Bacon's; they were not unkind, at least and that made them an improvement on what Eric and I had previously known, although that was not saying much. Our stories were similar and familiar and depressing; absent fathers, exhausted mums. A revolving carousel of male role models; all neglectful, some violent. We exchanged war stories occasionally, but not often. Eric's usually trumped mine which was why I tried to cut him some slack as he fucked up over and over again. He was feckless and lazy and untrustworthy, but how could he be otherwise, given his upbringing?

We'd washed up here because of him. After we left the foster home we lived on the streets for a while; Brighton, Worthing, Southend eventually. We begged and stole and now and then Eric would disappear for a few days and then turn up again with some cash in his pocket. He didn't say where it had come from and I only asked once. He would share though, more or less. I tried not to forget that.

Then, out of nowhere, on a mild evening, with dusk circling and the air soft and forgiving, a lean ascetic man with small, mean eyes and a mouth set in a permanent sneer approached us as we sat propped against a breakwater. We were drunk or high or both. The ocean whispered at our back. Life was as good as it was going to get, probably ever.

He walked straight up to Eric and passed him some keys and a small bundle of notes. "I need you to look after my flat. I'm not sure for how long. You know which one." He put a hand on Eric's shoulder and I saw the fingers digging in. "I *will* be back. Don't fuck it up." Then he turned on his heel and walked away. His footprints were barely visible in the pale sand.

"Who the fuck was that?"

"No idea," Eric said.

I stared at him. He wouldn't meet my gaze. "Come on, man. He literally just …"

"Like I said, no idea." He counted the notes out and handed half to me. "Thing is, we've got somewhere to crash."

I asked where the flat was and he told me. I held the notes up. "We could catch the train."

"We'll hitch," he said.

"Sure," I said. We fetched some more White Lightning and got absolutely wasted.

*

The door to Jan's creaks open and a small, thin girl creeps in. She's wearing a sparkly gold top with spaghetti straps and a pair of oversized fleecy pyjama trousers. This is Candy. She's a stripper and a prostitute. She's not as young as she looks, which is just as well as she looks about fourteen. She sees us and freezes like a deer caught in a clearing. "Fuck," she says, "You three."

"What?" Eric says. "What now?"

"Bad news, that's what you are," Candy says, pointing at us. "Bad fucking news. Sorry boys."

"What have you heard?" I say. Her eyes fix on mine. She quivers, on the verge of bolting. She holds the door open and looks out at the dark street. "You're safer in here," I say, although I'm not sure I mean it.

"The stupid man is right," Jan says. He comes out from behind the counter and hands Candy an oversized coat that she slips gratefully across her bare shoulders. "You come in the kitchen. Is warmer. These three just leaving. I get you something to eat."

Eric's face becomes indignant again. "I didn't think you…"

"I get you something to eat," he says again, ushering the faun-like girl towards the counter and the kitchen beyond.

She glances back, almost hidden by Jan's bulk. "I'm sorry," she says. "Tell Danny …"

"Tell Danny what?" I say.

"Nothing," she says eventually and then she disappears from view.

Jan's voice booms back, "You three go now." He does not sound unkind. But all things are relative, I suppose.

*

The flat was compact and bare. It had been stripped of all personal belongings. There was no trace at all of the man who had approached Eric on the beach. There was a smell, though, in the living room and the small bedroom. One I couldn't trace. It was poorly lit. The rooms were small and seemed to consist of mostly shadow. It gave me the creeps although I wasn't sure why. It was warm enough, though. It had a roof. There was some tinned food in the kitchen cupboards and a few bottles of Stella in the fridge.

"Sweet," Eric said, opening one and passing it to me. "We're on easy street, mate."

"Yeah," I said. "Something like that."

It didn't take long for Eric's paranoia to resurface and he woke me in the early hours, his face too close to mine, his breath rancid. "It's too good to be true. It's got to be."

I pushed him away from me. "What do you want me to say? Maybe it isn't, Eric. Maybe everything is fine. Go back to sleep."

But it wasn't fine. Of course it wasn't. Two days later we found out why.

*

We stand on the street, the three of us. It's cold and bleak in the dead hours. A chill breeze picks up and nips at our edges. An empty crisp packet eddies briefly and drops at my feet.

"Do you think she'll be okay?" Eric says. "Candy? With Jan?"

I shrug. "Probably." Jan is protective of the street girls. They seem easy enough around him and we've never heard anything untoward. "Perhaps he sees himself as a father figure."

"The state of our fathers I'm not sure that's saying much."

"Sweet like candy," Happy says. He's staring at his feet, jacket open, seemingly impervious to the cold.

She is sweet, in her way. It's common knowledge that Eric has a crush on her. Predictably it is not reciprocated. Still, he cares, which is something. Perhaps we all do, fellow travellers that we are.

"We should keep moving," I say.

"Why?" Eric says.

"To keep warm as much as anything else."

"We could go to yours."

"No," I say quickly. Too quickly perhaps and much more sharply than I intended. Even Happy reacts, his eyes widening in surprise as he looks into my face. "I mean, it might not be safe." I don't mean that at all. I just don't want them coming to mine. I don't have to tell them that though.

Happy looks at his feet again. Eric grunts. "Okay. I don't get Danny, though. He shouldn't be leaving us like this."

"He's cleaning up, man," Happy says. "Did you want to do it?"

Neither Eric or I have anything to say to that so we huddle into our coats and walk towards the beach.

*

It was late morning. The day was already hot. The flat was stifling and unpleasant, which was unsurprising as Eric insisted on keeping the curtains drawn and the windows closed. He was sniffing the armpits of a t-shirt, seeing if he could squeeze another day's wear out of it, when the front door opened and two men walked in.

"Didn't you lock it?" Eric's eyes were wide. He pulled his top on hurriedly.

I started to say that of course I had when the lead guy said, "No point locking doors round here, lad."

He was in his thirties, I supposed, with a thick Liverpudlian accent. He was lean and hard looking with blonde cropped hair and a complexion pocked with old acne scars. He wore a suit jacket and a formal shirt. His lower half was clad in dirty red tracksuit bottoms and a pair of white trainers.

He saw Eric staring at him. "What's up, lad?"

"Nothing."

"Good. It's rude to stare. Didn't you know that?" Eric's eyes dropped. He shook his head. "Well, you do now." He rubbed his hands together. "Anyway, business."

He moved to one side and his companion – tall and broad, dressed all in black – stepped forward wordlessly and dropped a zip up canvas bag embossed with the Liverpool FC logo onto the floor in the middle of the room.

"Look after this for a few days, alright, lads?" the first guy said. Eric started to speak but I nudged his shoulder and he shut up. "Stick it somewhere safe. Then don't touch it. Don't open it. If you open it Rob here will break something." Rob nodded. "Doesn't matter to Rob. I think he might enjoy it. It's hard to tell. He doesn't talk much. Do you, Rob?" Rob shook his head. "So be good lads and leave it the fuck alone, yeah?"

"Okay," Eric said.

The lead guy looked at me. I tried not to blink. "What are you, the strong silent type?"

"Well, silent, anyway."

He laughed, short and ugly. "Nice one. Funny. Sense of humour. We like a sense of humour, don't we, Rob?" Rob's expression remained blank. "Anyway. We'll be back in a week or so. Pick up our property. You'll get a little something for your troubles."

They left, closing the door gently behind themselves.

We both stared at the bag.

"I wonder what's in it?" Eric said.

"What do you think?" Eric said nothing. "Don't open it."

"I won't," Eric said.

And he didn't. Not this time.

*

It's dark by the beach. The stars have given up. We can hear the sea flexing behind us.

"What's the point of this?" Eric says. "I'm fucking freezing."

"We've got the sea to our back. No one can creep up on us."

"Aquaman," Happy says.

"What?"

"Aquaman could come up behind us. Easy."

"Yeah. About that ..."

"I'm just saying."

"I know, Happy. And you're right. He could. But ..."

"The thing is," Eric says, "we can't see anything anyway. Could be anyone out there."

He's right, although I don't want to admit it. I haven't really thought this through. "It'll be light soon. Everything will seem better then."

"Yeah," Eric says. "If there's one thing that improves this shithole of a town, it's daylight."

*

They came back a week later. Eric fetched the bag and handed it to the blonde guy. He made a show of examining it and looked at us both in turn. "Good. I'd have known if you'd opened it."

"I said we wouldn't."

"And you seem very trustworthy, mate." His voice took on an odd, lilting quality. "Salt of the earth. Butter wouldn't melt." He stepped up to Eric and put a hand on his cheek. "But I find it hard to trust. Do you know what I mean? Been hurt too many times. Too soft, that's my problem." His fingers dug into Eric's cheek. Eric's glance shot sideways at me, wide-eyed, frightened. "Don't look at him. Look at me. Good lad." His hand dropped suddenly and he shouldered past Eric into the kitchen. We heard the fridge door open and he was back a moment later with a slice of cold pizza and a bottle of Stella. "Fucking starving. It's been a long night." It was six o'clock in the morning.

He ate the pizza slowly, deliberately, his eyes fixed on Eric. When he'd finished he drained the bottle and tossed it onto the sofa. "See you soon, lads," he said as he turned towards the door.

"I thought you said we'd get paid," I said.

Rob had the door half open. He paused. The blonde guy said. "I did. I did, lad. I did say that." He pulled a hand across his acned-scarred face. "Thing is, it's been a tough week. Times are … hard. As Rob will attest." He said the word attest oddly, extending it, lingering, as though it was new to him and he was trying it out. Rob didn't move, didn't speak. "Thing is, we haven't broken anything. We haven't cut anybody. I'd call it a win, lad and leave it at that."

They left then, quickly and quietly. Eric exhaled. "Jesus Christ. Did you see his eyes?"

"What about them."

"There's nothing there, man. Nothing at all."

*

We skirt the edge of the beach, huddle in a bus shelter briefly then walk along the promenade and past a row of amusement arcades. They are padlocked, desolate. Gaudy in daylight, now they seem to consist only of silence and shadow. We barely speak. Light comes in dribbles from a reluctant sky. We head back towards the town.

*

The summer wore down. We had three more visits from our Liverpudlian friend. The first couple of times he was accompanied by Rob, but for the third he was on his own.

It was mid-September, chilly, indifferent, Autumn coming on. Eric was back after a couple of unexplained days away. He had no cash, at least none that he told me about, but he was pale and exhausted.

It was mid-evening when our visitor called and deposited the same old Liverpool bag. He dropped it from a height onto the sofa and stared at us both in turn as though willing us to say something. We remained silent and waited for him to leave.

"The more observant among you will have noticed that Rob is not with me today." He sniffed deeply and rubbed his nostrils hard. His eyes were sunken and red-rimmed. "It turns out that Rob was not quite the reliable employee that he was thought to be. Following a most unsatisfactory quarterly review it was decided that we had to let him go. With regret, obviously. Rob was given severance. Rob was severed." His voice had taken on that odd, lilting quality again. He wasn't looking at us. He wasn't looking anywhere in particular. "I cannot lie, boys, I've taken this hard. I liked Rob. Rob and me were close." He jabbed a finger at Eric suddenly and his eyes and voice became animated again. "I told you, didn't I? I'm too soft. I feel too much. That's my trouble." For an awful moment I thought he was going to cry. Thankfully, he didn't. He straightened, gave another lengthy snort, then pointed at the bag. "Don't open it, lads. I'll know if you do and I'll fucking hurt you."

He backed slowly out of the door, leaving it open. I followed him and watched from the doorway as he shambled towards the seafront.

"What was that all about? He's off his tits."

I looked back into the room. Eric had opened the bag.

*

There's movement ahead of us and we pause at the mouth of an alley. "What the fuck," Eric says, shuffling behind me and Happy. A tiny figure becomes clear in the darkness as we approach.

"Candy?" I say.

She stands in front of us, arms folded, her head bobbing from side to side. "Are you okay?" Eric says, stepping forward, reaching for her. She eases backwards and Eric is left grasping awkwardly at empty air.

"I'm fine."

"Is it Jan? Has he ..." Eric falters.

"No. Jan is ... Jan. He gave me this." She pulls the coat tight around her shoulders. It's too big for her, black and shapeless and ugly. She seems pleased with it, though. It's keeping her warm, I suppose. That's something. She looks at the three of us, eyes lingering on each in turn. "Men," she says, giving a sigh that's almost bigger than she is. Then to Eric, "You should go. Now."

"What?"

"I'm sorry," she says, more gently. Turning to Happy she says, "Gant. That's the name you want. The name that Danny wants. He's also called the Grey Man."

Happy's head tilts towards her. "For fuck's sake, Candy," Eric says. "I was good to you." Happy steps off to the side. I see the glow of his phone. "You've done for me. You might as well kill me yourself."

"You know, it would have been easier if you had just fucked me."

"What?"

"I'm not a counsellor, Eric. Or a priest." She chews on a thumbnail briefly and spits it out. "All that stuff you unloaded onto me. All that ... poison. Should have just fucked me, mate. Like Happy. Like Danny."

"Danny?" I say. I'm totally ignored, which is probably just as well.

"Just go," she says softly. "Now."

"Go where?" he says. He glances towards Happy but he's yards away now and talking quietly on his phone. His gaze skitters between me and Candy. "Cunting bollocks," he says and runs headlong towards the beach.

I grab Candy's arm. "What was that all about?"

She jerks away from me. "As though you don't know."

"I don't. Honestly."

"Okay. If you say so. Not that it matters. Right under your nose, mate. Some friend, huh?"

She disappears into the alley. Happy has gone too. I spin around stupidly in the reluctant dawn.

*

It was drugs. Of course it was drugs.

"Coke," Eric said, sifting through the contents. He stood, a small plastic bag of white powder in each hand. "I'm having this."

"What?" I looked nervously at the door.

"I'm selling it, mate. You can help if you like."

"No. Eric. No."

"What are you so worried about?"

"You know what. He'll be back. He's fucking mental."

"Lost his muscle though, hasn't he? And you said it yourself. He was off his skull. There's two of us and only one of him. You need to grow a pair."

It felt odd, being talked down to by Eric. I also thought he had a point. "You'll be stepping on toes. And what do you know about selling drugs?"

"You have no idea, mate." He threw a bag at me and I caught it instinctively. "You don't know what I know. What I've done." I looked at the floor. I felt ashamed suddenly and I wasn't sure why. "It doesn't matter. I don't need you. I'll do it."

"I've got my job to think about."

"Job? Cleaning at McDonalds? Yeah, it'd be terrible if that went wrong."

"It's cash. It's something." Actually, I liked it. The routine. And some of my colleagues. I didn't want to admit that to Eric, though. I didn't really want to admit it to myself. "I'm drinking less. I'm not getting high as often. I haven't nicked anything for a month."

"Well, that is awesome and I am so fucking proud of you it's bringing tears to my eyes, it really is, but back here in the real world we need some serious money and I am sick to death of selling my arse so I'm getting out there and moving this shit and I don't care what you or that pock-faced cunt have to say about it."

"Selling your arse?"

"I'll start with Candy and the girls. Christ knows they need a pick me up. And Jan. Jan has contacts. He does frighten me though, Jan." He saw me looking at him. "What?"

"Eric."

"Well, what did you think I was doing?"

"I don't know. You wouldn't say. I did ask."

"Once. You asked once. Otherwise you're too wrapped in your precious job or got your head stuck in some book. And it wasn't just … *that*. It was … other stuff. Contacts, man. Real fucking scum, but … contacts. With money." He threw two more bags of cocaine at me and I let them bounce off my chest. "They'd love this shit. Lap it right up."

"Cool. You do you, Eric. You do you."

"Same as it ever was," Eric said. He stuffed a handful of the bags into his jacket pockets and walked out of the door. I next saw him three days later.

I'd just finished my shift. Debbie was opening up. I liked Debbie. She was older than me. She tried to seem stern but there was softness underneath that she couldn't hide. She made me a coffee before I left.

"Come back in a bit and get some breakfast. On the house, obvs. Got to milk those perks."

"Thanks, Debs."

"Then maybe get some sleep? You look like shit." She was smiling though and she patted my hand as she passed me my drink.

I walked along the front and found a bench with a view across the estuary. The light was blue-grey, flat against the water. I drank my coffee and read. Ross McDonald, *Find a Victim*. I was lost in Lew Archer's world and didn't notice when someone sat beside me.

"I think I may have something that belongs to you."

I jolted back into the present and turned towards the source of the voice. Compact, clean-shaven, sat upright, his head canted in my direction. "What? Who are you?"

"I'm Danny." He extended a hand and I took it. He had a firm grip, but he wasn't a dick about it. He smiled, wrinkling the flesh at the edge of his eyes. "I know who you are."

"Eric." Danny nodded. I folded the corner of my paperback and stuffed it in my pocket. "He doesn't belong to me."

"I know. Just banter, mate. Keeping it light."

"Where is he?"

"He's at home. He's not very cosy, though." He stood. "Follow me."

It was a ten minute walk. We didn't speak. Danny

seemed comfortable in the silence. We entered the flat and I saw Eric, bound and gagged, lying across the sofa. His eyes, wide and frantic, flicked towards me then away again.

Danny released him, quickly, efficiently, and removed the tape from his mouth. "Be a good boy, Eric. No shouting, no running. We need to talk." Eric nodded, cowed. Danny sat next to him on the sofa. "Actually, I'll talk. You two listen. I'll take questions at the end." That smile again; crinkly, almost warm. I sat opposite and didn't speak.

"The first thing you need to know is that I work for Slater."

"Fuck," Eric said. I thought the same but kept my mouth shut. John Slater ran everything around here. Everyone paid their dues; Candy and the girls, Jan, all the other low lives, us included. Even the money that Eric earned, however he'd earned it, a cut would have made its way back to Slater.

Danny put a finger to his lips. "An understandable reaction, but still … shut up." Eric's head dropped. "I get it. You don't know me. I'm new. Mr Slater needed some new blood. There's been some trouble, some lads from up North trying to muscle in. I understand you met a couple of them. We've affected a takeover. A hostile takeover. Very hostile, as it turns out. They underestimated us quite badly. So you won't be seeing them again." He looked at us both in turn. "You don't have to thank me." Eric started to speak. "Shut up," Danny said, his voice flat. "The thing is, Eric here has been naughty. Naughty and stupid. I think we can all agree that's a worrying combination."

He leant forward. It was as though he was speaking to me now and me alone. "You know what he did. What he tried to do. It's actually quite hard not to make money selling coke. Especially when you haven't actually paid for it in the first place. But Eric here …" He shook his head sadly and patted Eric's arm. Eric shrank away from him. "So. You can speak now, Eric. What do think your first mistake was?" Eric, wretched, broken, mumbled something. "Clearly now. So the whole class can hear."

"Candy," I said.

Danny's gaze fixed lazily onto me. "Candy? Is that her name? Yes. Well done. And can you guess what the second mistake was?"

"I should imagine that he didn't take payment in cash."

"You imagine correctly. And so, children, how did Eric take payment from Candy, do we think?" He gripped Eric's arm. Hard. "No need to answer. We all know, don't we? And when you think about it, looking at the state of this thing next to me, it's poor Candy, isn't it? I mean … Jesus. But she's a game one as it turns out and she takes her hard earned goods and she sells some on to her colleagues. And she takes cash, because she isn't a moron. And to prove that point she passes some of that cash onto Mr Slater. And Mr Slater has a word with me. So here we are."

"I didn't fuck her," Eric said.

"What?" Danny let go of his arm.

"I didn't fuck her. We just talked."

"Oh, Eric," I said.

"Okay. Okay. I suppose that is adorable in its way and I am every bit as much of a romantic as the next man, but what the *fuck* difference does that make, in the scheme of things, from a business point of view?"

"Not much, I suppose. It matters to me, though."

Danny stood. "Brilliant." He took a breath. "We are where are then, aren't we, as someone no doubt once gouged into the side of a plague pit. The question should be," he nodded at Eric, "do I strangle you or cut your throat, but I'd like to think that there's a bit more room for nuance in this volatile, post-Brexit world."

"What?" Eric said.

"Shut up."

"Listen to your friend," Danny said.

*

There are skeins of light now and I can make out the edge of the beach as a jolt of adrenalin drives me forward. I hear Eric before I see him. His breath is short and laboured and he is whimpering something although the words are indistinct.

I reach him and he relaxes a fraction when he realises that it's me. "What are you doing? If you need to run this is a strange way to go about it. What are you going to do, swim to France?"

The sea flexes behind us. The beach becomes scrubby and pebble ridden. I hear the scrunch of my footsteps as I move towards him. "I trusted her. I mean, I paid her, but I trusted her."

"What have you done, Eric?"

He appears insubstantial in the watery light. "Nothing, man. I was just a go between. These things ... these things would have happened, with or without me."

"What things? Who is Gant?"

His body twists. He appears exasperated now, almost angry. "Seriously? You read, yeah? You've got a brain? Maybe even an imagination? What do you think this is? Really?"

"But ... you're not ... that's not you, Eric."

"Of course it isn't. I was a middle man." He searches for a word. "... a *procurer*. That's all."

"Jesus, Eric."

"You remember the Bacon's?"

"Of course I do."

"Good people, right? She used to bake on Sunday, you remember that? Those apple pies, hot from the oven. Quite a treat for kids like us."

"So what?"

"They still foster. We've kept in touch. All those children. Damaged, vulnerable. To a man like Gant ..."

"What are you saying?"

"They took their cut. The Bacon's. We all did. That's what this is about really. Money. Well, not for Gant, maybe. But still, the stubborn old bastard didn't think he should have to pay Slater anything. So here we are. It was a matter of principle, he said. Principle. Fucking hell."

I'm close enough now to feel his breath on my cheek. "So this is all because Slater didn't get paid?"

"Yeah," he says, but his eyes slide away from mine as he speaks.

I feel the adrenalin seep away. I am spent and I suspect that Eric is too. "Let's head for the station. Get you on an early train."

"It's too late," he says. I hear footsteps behind me and I know that for once he is right.

*

Danny went through the small hallway into the bedroom and came back with the Liverpool bag and what was left of the drugs. "Stinks in there. Do you two share?"

He was looking at me. "I sleep on the sofa."

He nodded. He held the bag up above his head. "Right. This is yours. Consider it a gift."

"What?" Eric said.

"You sell it. Where you like, for how much you like. I'll be back every week or so for our cut."

"How much?" Danny just looked at him. "How much is your cut?"

"That's up to you, Eric. It can be as much or as little as you like."

"I don't understand."

Danny threw the bag to Eric who caught it with difficulty. "This is a freebie. It cost us nothing, it cost you nothing. It's a starter pack. A free hit. Just do your best with it. You pay me something every week. How much is up to you."

Eric didn't attempt to keep the scepticism out of his voice. "Right. So how about if I give you a quid?"

"If you give me a pound, I'll take a pound."

"Right," Eric said again. "Fuck's sake."

Danny sat and crossed his legs, adjusting the crease in his chinos as he settled. "IBM, back in the day, sold more computers than anyone else worldwide. Do you know how they did that?" Eric shook his head. "They set their sales people piss easy targets. They thought it was a joke. Their competitors thought it was a joke. But it took the pressure off, see? They sold and sold, well beyond expectations. I like that.

Taking the pressure off. I'm aware that I've come in here and been a bit of a dick. It goes with the territory in my line of work. I don't enjoy it." He frowned and held a finger up. "That's not true. Sometimes I *do* enjoy it. *Really* enjoy it. But not often. Not now." He held his arms wide open. "I'd rather be a nice guy. Take the pressure off. What do you say, Eric?"

"I don't know."

"Give it go. Give it your best shot. Let's see where we end up. It's fair to say that Mr Slater was a little sceptical, just like you. But then if he'd had his way you'd already be floating face down in the North Sea. So … there's that. Isn't there?"

"What about me?" I said.

Danny looked puzzled. "What about you?"

"Where do I fit in?"

"None of this is directed at you. You're not a drug dealer. You've got a job." Eric snorted. Danny moved quickly, striking the side of Eric's face hard. There was a crack like a gunshot. "Don't take the piss. So he's a cleaner. I don't care if he scrapes shit out of u-bends, he goes to work and earns a wage. That puts him several rungs up from you. Got it?"

"Got it," Eric said. His cheek was scarlet. A single tear ran down it.

He was back a week later. He knocked on the door and I let him in. He wore a fleece jacket over a white t-shirt that was tight against his chest. "Is laughing boy in?"

I opened the door wider so he could enter. "Kitchen. I'm off to work, I'll leave you it."

"This won't take a minute. Hold on and I'll walk with you."

I waited outside. Autumn light. A tiny breeze that could barely be bothered. Danny appeared a couple of minutes later, whistling. "He paid up, then?"

"More than a quid."

"Good for him."

"How's it going?"

"I wouldn't know. I've barely seen him. We don't really speak. Not since …"

"Not since I turned up."

"Something like that."

"It's for the best. I'd keep my distance, if I was you."

"You've seen the flat? It's not easy. Anyway, why should I? We go back a long way, Eric and me."

"I know."

"How do you know?"

He sniffed. He walked quickly, his hands stuffed deep in his jacket pockets. "Don't insult me, lad. I know enough. Not everything, not yet. Not about Eric, at least. But enough. Guys like Eric ... it doesn't tend to end well."

"So I should steer clear?"

"If you've got any sense."

"Why do you care?"

"Who said I cared? It's just a bit of friendly advice. Take it or leave it."

We crossed the road, slowing as we approached the McDonald's. "So what's your story, then? You seem to know all about us. It's hardly fair."

"Fair?" He laughed. "Nice one." He pointed at the paperback jutting out of my coat pocket. "What's that?" I pulled it free and showed it to him. *The High Window* by Raymond Chandler. "Fiction. Huh. I don't get the point of made up stuff."

"Does there have to be a point? It's just an escape. Sometimes, it's good to be in someone else's head."

"Depends whose head it is, doesn't it?"

"Not really. I don't often care. So, what do you read, then? Apart from the *Guardian*?"

"The *Guardian*?"

"That line about something being gouged in the side of a plague pit; that's from Marina Hyde in the *Guardian*. I read it online and it kind of stuck."

"Could be coincidence."

"Could be."

"Anyway, so what? I read loads of stuff; financial pages mostly, but all sorts, I pick up bits from here, bits from there. I'm a proper magpie, me. Is that okay with you?"

"I wasn't accusing you of anything."

"Weren't you?"

"No."

His eyes which had become flat and hard softened a little. "You'd best get to work. Keep an eye on Eric for me."

"I thought you said to keep my distance?"

"You're a clever guy, I'm sure you can do both."

He was there later, at the end of my shift. I was surprised and wary. "What?" I said. It was colder now and I pulled my coat around me. Danny's jacket was zipped to the throat and his hands were buried deep in the pockets.

"I was in the army," he said. "I thought you'd have guessed, what with my military bearing." I hadn't but I could see it then, I supposed. "I saw action; Iraq, Afghanistan."

"For Queen and country."

"For a while … but …" He made a face. "I had a disagreement, with an officer. The army and I parted ways."

"What happened to the officer?"

"Bits of him are scattered over Basra. My fault, apparently. They couldn't prove anything though. So … bye bye, Danny. Keep your mouth shut, lad."

"Was it your fault?"

"Oh, I killed the fucker. He. Was. A. Cunt. Of the first order. He would have done for all of us; all my lovely boys. Can't be having that."

"Okay."

"I still served though. In a private capacity."

"You were a mercenary?"

His eyes went flat. "We don't like that word. Private contractors, that's what we were. Back to the old haunts; Iraq, Afghanistan. And Chechnya, Georgia. And some other stuff; off the books, dark web shit."

"Am I meant to be impressed?"

He shrugged. "You asked. There it is."

"How did you end up here?"

His grin was dark and off centre. "The last op, ten of us went in, only two came back. No one knows. Just me and

Happy. No one cares. A boy's got to eat. Mr Slater saw my CV and here we are."

"Happy?"

"Friend of mine. You'll meet him soon."

"Can't wait."

His hand snaked towards my face and stopped inches from my cheek. "Don't take the piss out of Happy. He's good people. I mean … he's utterly fucked. Broken. But who wouldn't be, what he's done, what he's seen?" His hand moved gently to my shoulder. "When you meet Happy, you be nice to him, you hear me?"

"I hear you. Jesus."

"Good. Good. I've got to go. But just so you know, Eric's using."

"Of course he is. Eric's always using."

"Too much, though. It might be that he can make some money for us. But … there's a limit."

"No pressure, I thought you said?"

His hand touched my cheek briefly. It was dry and warm. "You didn't believe all that bullshit, did you? Have a word with Eric. Get him to rein it in a bit. There's a good lad."

He straightened and turned and made his way inland. I looked back towards McDonalds and saw Julie through the window, watching from the counter.

*

There are three of them and they stand in a line. Eric and I are side by side. The sea fizzes and laps behind us. "Aquaman," Happy says and I almost laugh.

He stands on the right of the trio; Danny is on the left, at ease, hands linked behind his back. In the middle is a stout, avuncular looking man in his fifties. He has neat hair and a greying beard and wears a smart coat that is a little too big for him. "Morning, boys," Slater says. His voice is pleasant and even. He points at Eric, "You are quite the nuisance."

*

"I only gave him a ton, can you believe that?" Eric paced the living room in uneven strides. "Do you know how much I've made?" His eyes bulged as he leant towards me.

"I don't care."

"Come on …"

"Seriously, Eric. I don't fucking care."

"Jesus. You're always pissing on my chips. You're just jealous because I've found something I'm good at."

The bloody Liverpool bag was sat in the corner of the room. Of course it was. It was almost empty now. I pointed at it. "You heard Danny. This is a freebie. If they keep using you after this then shit gets real. You've got to get your act together, Eric."

"Danny this, Danny that."

"What's that supposed to mean?"

"You figure it out."

"You'd already be dead, if it wasn't for him."

"So he says. We don't know that he even works for Slater."

"Eric. Fuck. I don't think I can take much more of this."

He sat, stood again, running a hand quickly through his greasy fringe. "Is that right? I'm so sorry, princess. For all the trouble."

"What?"

"You heard. You snotty cunt. What makes you so special?"

"I'm not special."

"You think you are."

"I really don't." He glanced around as though searching for something, then looked at me again, his eyes glassy. "And lay off the gear."

"You. Are. Not. My. *Mother*."

"You're going to get yourself killed."

"What do you care?"

"Of course I care, Eric. I'll always care."

I think it was something in my voice, rather than the words, that brought him up short. The regret, perhaps. After a moment's stillness he nodded slowly. "You need to get your own place, man."

"I know." I had to get out of there. I looked at my watch. "I've got to get to work," I lied.

"Of course you have."

At the door I hesitated. "Who is he, Eric?"

"Who is who?"

"The man on the beach? The guy who owns this flat?"

"I don't know."

"Come on. Seriously?"

"It doesn't matter." He found half a joint in an ashtray and lit it. "It is, as they say, of no consequence."

"I think it matters," I said.

It did.

A couple of weeks later Danny came into McDonald's just I was finishing my early shift and ordered breakfast. I waited for him outside. He brandished the polystyrene box containing his food as he joined me. "I saw this guy on TV, a chef, Michelin stars and everything and they asked him what his favourite breakfast was. This is it; Sausage and Egg McMuffin." He extracted the food from the box and took a bite. "Fucking hell. Remind me never to eat in that guy's gaff."

"I could have got you a discount."

He dropped the remainder of his breakfast onto the ground and rubbed his hands together briskly. It was dry, cool. The sky was steel-blue, becoming lighter. "I think I can take the hit."

"I'd have thought you'd have eaten McDonald's before."

"Nah. I'm very particular. Always have been, even in the army. Got no end of stick about it."

"That's interesting. What do you want, Danny?"

"Straight to business. Like it. How's Eric?"

"How would I know? He's out all hours selling your shit. You probably see him more than I do."

"Yeah. He's keeping his nose clean so far. Paying his dues."

"Perhaps you underestimated him."

He shrugged. "Doubtful. I expect I'll still end up killing the fucker."

"Jesus. So, why ask me how he is?"

"Has he said anything?"

"About what?"

I walked towards the town centre. I thought I'd sit outside the tiny library and wait for it to open. Danny kept pace beside me. "That flat of yours. How did that come about? Last I heard you two were drifting, on the streets. Then you wash up here, with your own place."

"It's not my place."

"I know. But it's not really Eric's either, is it?"

I felt wary. I knew this mattered but I didn't know why. "I dunno. It belongs to a friend of a friend, I think."

"You think?"

"Yeah."

He moved ahead of me as we approached a corner, cutting me off. "Find out, will you? It'll be easier coming from you."

"Why?"

"People are asking. That's all you need to know." He stuffed his hands into his pockets and watched a white delivery van negotiate the shallow bend ahead of us. "By the way, there's a flat. Just around the corner. If you want it. Nothing flash, but it would be your own place."

"What? Why?"

"I'm just a lovely bloke, aren't I? Anyway, it suits me. I'd rather Eric was on his own."

"How did you …"

"Pulled some strings with Slater. He's got a contact at the council, this place came up, easy–peasy."

"Thanks."

"No skin off my nose."

"Still …"

"It'll do you good. Get a bit of distance from that smack head."

"He's not a smack head."

"Oh, mate, well if he isn't, he will be soon."

"He's still my friend."

"Good. So have a drink. Have a burger together. Ask that question." He leant forward and patted my cheek. "And make it snappy."

*

"I've made you money, Mr Slater." I'm surprised by the firmness of Eric's voice.

"This is true," Slater says, equably. "You have."

It is lighter now but I cannot see the town. There is only beach and sea and these three men. Danny looks at me for the first time. He has a fresh white t-shirt on beneath his black jacket. "You've changed," I say.

Danny shrugs. "We all change. As Sartre said ..."

"Your clothes. You've changed your clothes."

"Messy job cleaning up."

"Who was he?"

Danny looks at Slater who rolls his eyes and raises his arms in the air. "I've already apologised. I thought you were taking too long, Danny. I am not a patient man. It was a mistake. He was ... under qualified."

"You get what you pay for," Danny says.

"You do indeed."

Danny produces something small from his pocket and holds it up. I squint towards it. Eric is very quiet and still beside me. "It's a memory stick. Eric was looking after it for Gant."

"Thank you, Danny," Slater says. "I'll take that."

Danny doesn't move. "I had a look at the contents."

"I told you not to. I'll ignore that for now, but just hand me the ..."

"Just some pictures you said. You and a women doing what men and women do. No big deal, not really, but embarrassing, for a man of your ... stature."

"Gant is ... was ... a business associate. He owes me money. I didn't know that he filmed ..."

"And yet you never mentioned him? Gant? We had to wait for Eric's little girlfriend to cough him up." Eric shifted beside me but said nothing.

"So?"

"You know his reputation. You must know that I'd know it too."

"Business is business. I just wanted you to get *that*." He jabs a finger at the plastic stick in Danny's hand. "And you have. Eventually. Well done. Now ..."

"It's not a women, though, is it, Mr Slater? On the film. It's not a man either, not that it would have mattered, if it was."

"They can fake things, these days. You know that." Slater was not so equable now. "Anyway, you work for me, Danny. Give me that fucking thing."

"It's too late. Everybody knows."

*

Julie helped me move in, which was good of her. She had a daughter who was about my age, maybe a little younger, who lived away. She gave me some furniture from her old room. "She won't be needing this stuff anymore," she said, eyes averted. "Not after all these years."

She brought me small, homely things as well; candles, a mirror, prints for the walls. Most Sunday's she'd come round and cook me a roast. "You're wasting away," she'd say if I refused a second helping of pudding. If she had a second glass of wine with lunch she'd talk about her daughter perhaps, but not that often and not for long. She fussed over me, which should have been annoying, but it wasn't. It was nice. I liked it.

Danny dropped in occasionally. Eric never did.

But things got easier between Eric and me once we weren't living together. We'd hang out from time to time, at his mostly, or on the beach or in the dark, shabby pub just around the corner from his. I asked Danny's question, as casually as possible, whenever an opening arose, but Eric would always shrug and change the subject.

Then he brought it up himself, obliquely, unbidden, one January dusk as we stood on the beach surveying the burnt out shell of a Mini Cooper that had been dumped there the previous day.

"I need to move out, man. Get out of that shit hole. I need somewhere better. I can do it. I'm earning now." He rubbed his fingers together. "Serious money. First time in my life."

Well, maybe. But he was gambling too and using and Candy, one of his best customers, still wasn't paying cash. But Danny got paid on time and he hadn't threatened Eric for ages so maybe he was exceeding expectations. Especially his own.

"Do it then. What's stopping you?"

He was quiet for a while. He picked up a pebble and threw it at the ruined car. It clanged off the bonnet and skittered into the darkness. "That dude. You know?"

"I know." I waited.

"He'll be back. I need to hold on until then." He brought his hands together, his fingers clenching and unclenching.

"Why?"

"I have something of his. He gave it to me. For safe keeping." He found it hard to get the words out. His head twisted away from me.

"Eric?"

"Look … if anything happens to me, if you hear anything … I'm not a bad guy, you know that, right?"

"Of course I do." Did I? Not really, but what else could I say? "What's going on? I don't understand."

He wiped his eyes. "You don't need to. It'll be fine. But if it isn't, there's some cash, hidden in a box under a floor board beneath the bed. Half is for you, half for Candy. If … well, I'm trusting you, man."

"If you trust me, tell me. Everything."

I heard a siren in the distance and Eric turned his head towards the sound. He hunched into his jacket. "It's freezing," he said. "We'd better get back."

*

"Jesus." Slater moves towards Danny. His coat falls open. Happy eases to Slater's side and places a hand, almost tenderly, on his left shoulder.

"It turns out that you are just a tedious old paedophile, Mr Slater." Happy's right hand moves smoothly from his pocket to Slater's chest. Slater squeals as Happy seems to punch him three, four, five times. He falls backwards. His legs thrash weakly from side to side. Happy drops to his knees and presses a hand over his mouth so that he makes no sound. "I really fucking hate paedophiles," Danny says. "Always have."

After a moment Happy walks to the shoreline and runs his knife through the inky water. An oil-dark stain spreads around Slater's body. He joins Danny again and stands calmly next to him.

"That's that, then," Eric says.

"Is it, Eric?" Danny says. He holds the memory stick high in the air. "It's not really about this, is it?"

"What do you mean?"

"Gant will have copies. He could've hidden this anywhere. It's about the flat."

"The flat?" I think of it, the smell and the shadows. The flesh on the back of my neck contracts.

Danny looks at me. "It's a crime scene, mate. The stuff on here. The … things … I watched. All filmed in that flat. So much DNA. All those bodily fluids, all that blood."

"Blood?" I say. I can feel Eric cringing, diminishing next to me.

"Yeah. Blood. Think about it." I don't want to, but I do. He turns to Eric. "Gant just needed you to mind the place. That's all."

"Yeah," Eric says. "That's all. No big deal."

"No big deal. How old was the boy, Eric?"

*

I dropped in at Eric's on a warm day in early Summer and found Candy sitting next to him on the sofa. Eric stood suddenly. He looked awkward, embarrassed almost, although I wasn't sure why. Candy wore a short silver dress but she sat demurely, skinny knees pressed together, feet splayed. She looked up at me with her doe eyes. She was pretty, I supposed, in a haunted kind of way.

"You could have knocked, man," Eric says.

"Sorry. I didn't mean to interrupt."

"I was just leaving," Candy said, although she didn't move.

The front door opened again and Danny came in, followed by a squat man with a thick, unruly beard. "Cosy, cosy," Danny said, taking in the scene. Candy stood and, without speaking or making eye contact with anyone, slid past Danny and out of the door. "I have that effect on all the girls," he said as he ushered the man into the room. "Bye, sweetheart," he called theatrically to Candy's departing back and then, turning to us, "This is Happy." Happy nodded and Eric and I nodded back. "I know, he dresses as though he's been kicked through a charity shop and he smells a bit funny … no offence, Happy."

"None taken."

"But we've been through some shit together, haven't we, mate?"

"We have?"

"You remember that time in Khandahar?"

"Khandahar?"

"Black ops, with those two guys from Bradford. They went one way, we went the other. They got caught, ended up having their fucking heads cut off. We didn't. Do you remember that, Happy?"

"Not really."

"Christ," I said.

Eric said, "Well, this is lovely …"

"Happy will be staying here for a while."

"What now?"

"You heard. You find it hard to settle, don't you, Happy?" Happy nodded. "He'll be coming to yours as well, at some point," Danny said, looking at me.

"Okay," I said.

"Cheer up, boys. Happy's lovely. No trouble at all. Just keep him topped up with booze and pills."

"Especially booze," Happy said, pointing a grubby forefinger in our direction. "And especially pills."

Actually, Happy was fine; he was usually vacant, occasionally gnomic, invariably good-natured. We grew used to him. Eric found him rooting through the drawers in his bedroom once but he said he was looking for drugs, which seemed to make sense.

Julie started seeing an older man who she met through a dating site. I was seeing less and less of her. How much this had to do with Happy's occasional presence, or with Danny's for that matter, I didn't know. I never asked. She probably wouldn't have admitted as much anyway. It was sad. I missed her. I started drinking more and using pot again, from time to time, just to take the edge off.

We hung out together most weekends, the four of us, smoking and drinking and talking rubbish. Danny seemed to have become almost a friend. But he listened more than he talked, I noticed. And he didn't miss much.

*

There is a small, charged silence. It's almost full light now but I still can't see beyond the edge of the beach. Happy's head tilts gently to one side. "What boy?" Eric says.

"Eight? Ten?"

Eric skitters backwards and foam laps at his feet. He turns and for a moment I think he is considering simply walking into the sea. "He made me do it. Gant. He wanted insurance. So I'd do what he said."

"It's never your fault, is it, Eric?"

"I'm not a pedo."

"There's a lad somewhere who might dispute that. At least I hope there is."

"Eric?" I say, but he won't look at me.

"You need me," he says to Danny. A single tear trickles down his cheek.

"I need you? Interesting."

"To find Gant."

"Why would I want to find Gant?"

"He is a pedo. And worse. You hate them, you said so yourself. I can help you. Help you get him."

"I've recently inherited a business, Eric. I'm going to be a very busy man."

"Here comes the new boss," Happy says suddenly. "Same as the old boss."

"I sincerely hope not, Happy," Danny says mildly. He doesn't move. Neither does Happy. Eric's breathing is ragged, uncertain. I imagine him slumping sideways, bleeding into the sea.

Danny's eyes meet mine again and I try not to look away. "The first thing a good boss learns is to delegate. So, I'll leave the decision to you."

"What decision? What are you talking about?"

"Eric. He's your friend. He's scum, on that I think we can all agree, but he's your friend. Over to you."

Eric's neck twists from side to side as his gaze darts from Happy and back to me. His eyes are wide open. Then his face settles, becomes flat and calm. I wait for him to cry and beg but he doesn't.

The Last Best Thing

Mia Dalia

For Chelsea

The woman floated in the middle of the pool on an inflatable raft of pure white. It looked like she was reclined on a cloud; comfortable, serene. Her hair was blonde, luxurious; her body - a flawless sunscreen-ad hue of gold. Eyes hidden behind an overlarge pair of sunglasses and a body barely covered by a bikini provocative enough to start a riot, she was a perfect embodiment of a California dream: young, beautiful, relaxed, happy. Bathed in the warmth of the sun, swayed gently by the postcard-blue water.

The pool was large enough so that the other guests had plenty of space to swim without disturbing her. Plus, she looked too picturesque in her repose to disturb. Perhaps that is why it took everyone so long to realize that the woman was dead.

Sunday Morning. Those few precious hours when the sinners are still sleeping off the excesses of the night before and the saints are in the church praying for their souls. I love this time – the quiet.

Not a cloud in the sky, the blue above is mirrored in the blue below; the hotel pool is a thing of legend and many legends had swum in it. Well, once upon a time anyway. Nowadays, The Lux is something of a thing of the past. A faded beauty of yesteryear. A beauty still, certainly, you can see it in its proud tall bearing, the decadence of its Art Deco lines, but time and age had come for The Lux, and no one can defy that tenacious duo for long.

BANG!

The Lux puts me in mind of an old Hollywood starlet; it has those same airs, the same stubborn desire to hold on to the past. I'd seen those actresses around The Lux over the years, wearing too much makeup, their hair garishly dyed and fooling no one, and yet still, beneath the wrinkles and wear and tear, recognizably the same faces that had beguiled cinema goers for decades.

They make me sad. Their stooped shoulders, their perfect diction. I don't know why. I guess at heart I'm a perfectionist, and who wants to see the afterlife of perfect?

None of them are around today, but the place isn't empty either. I recognize some of the faces, discreetly study those I don't.

It's my job, you see. No, I'm not a pool boy, though some days the way some of the guests treat me I'm sure they can't tell the difference. I'm a hotel detective. That is, I suppose, the most respectable version of my title. I do not respond to colloquialisms.

It's questionable whether The Lux has a need of a detective, but it certainly has a want of one. The management likes the optics, says it's good for business. Makes the establishment seem trustworthy.

For me, it's easy money. There's never much to do but reassure the old-money clientele that their precious possessions are safe during their stay.

I haven't done any real detecting in years. Most days I can't tell if I miss it. I ask myself but all I get is a warped whiskey bottle reflection of a frown.

Once upon a time, I was somebody. I went from one uniform to another, from the Army to the Police Force. Guess the latter just didn't take. The official version is that I was 'retired' for excessive violence. I still don't think it was excessive. The punk got what he deserved. He beat a young woman half to death for daring to say "No" to his advances. I made sure he'd never be able to do that again. He survived. My career didn't.

To tell you the truth, I don't remember the entire episode. I can vividly recall hitting him the first time, the way the bones of his face felt on my knuckles, but afterwards is a blur.

THE LAST BEST THING

Maybe it's good they let me go. It's easier here, at The Lux. I get a comped room; one too small for guests, with an alley view, but still. I get to have my routines, co-workers I can almost call friends. The pay's crap, but I don't need much. I had a dream, or at least an idea of a dream when I came here. A story I wanted to tell, something that happened to me during the war, and I had been trying to make sense of since. Bought a typewriter and everything.

Night after night, I'd sit down in front of it, a glass of whiskey in hand, but most days words wouldn't come. And whiskey flowed. Guess after a while I learned to go with the flow.

The story remains untold; the typewriter left alone to gather dust - my very own heavy-duty dreamcatcher.

Maybe I wasn't meant to be a writer. These days I'm not sure what I was meant to be. Just getting from dusk to dawn can be a chore. At least, the dawn to dusk goes easily enough.

I watch the woman in the pool. The fresh-driven-snow whiteness of her float. When did she come in? How'd I miss her? I must have closed my eyes.

I think about what it must be like to go through life beautiful. To have the world welcome you with wide open arms and an approving smile.

Maybe I'm tired. Maybe I'd drank too much the night before, which often brings with it a certain sort of contemplative melancholy.

Sometimes it takes me to dark places. Places I brought home from the war and my mind had framed as nightmares since, redecorating my mind palace in tenebrous and macabre. I fight the good fight, I will as long as I can. And if the time comes when I'm too tired to, well, I have something for that. Something that'll take me away kindly, quietly.

Clear liquid in small glass vial held onto like a life preserver, like a last resort, like a way out.

I'd never been beautiful. Not before the war, and certainly not after. I learned to wear my scars proudly. I earned them. But mine will never be a face a woman will look upon with love.

Pity. Sure. I'd had some of those dalliances. I took it too, all that pity. But it never lasts. It isn't a self-perpetuating emotion like love. It's more like lust, it wears itself out after a while.

Maybe I've been in LA for too long. This place lives and dies on beauty, prides itself on attracting it, flaunts it. Beauty is the only currency a town like this can understand and appreciate.

I don't belong here, but the woman in the pool does.

I close my eyes, again, just for a moment, against the relentless morning sun. The screaming rouses me. A rude awakening if there was ever one; I hadn't even realized I dozed off. Sleeping on the job, sheesh, how the mighty have fallen.

There's a body in the pool, that's all I see. It's enough to jump start me into action. I kick off my shoes and dive in. It's the beautiful blonde. She must have just fallen in, must have rolled off her float and gone under, but her body is too wooden, too unresisting, too...

Dead. She's dead. She'd been dead prior to falling in. I'd been watching a dead woman in the pool. Some detective.

I bring her up, lay her out on the pool deck. Everyone has left the pool. There's panic, agitation.

"Call for help," I tell the closest reasonable-looking person. "Call for help, now." The man rushes off, presumably to do so.

The woman has no pulse, no heartbeat. She's beyond resuscitation efforts. Without her sunglasses, which had stayed somewhere in the pool, she looks...if not older then certainly less innocent. This town has a way of stripping innocence away.

There are ghost lines where wrinkles would have one day creased the corners of her eyes and now never will. Whatever age she was, she'll now be forever. A certain, least desirable, brand of immortality.

One of the other pool goers is mumbling something about tipping the float unintentionally. Their voice is choked up with tears and guilt.

"She was already dead when she went in," I reassure the guest.

It seems to have the opposite effect on the rest of them. These well-heeled individuals who'd never spent too much time around the dead, the thought upsets them. I say nothing more until help arrives. Just kneel there on the wet stone, next to a beautiful dead woman, and wonder why none of it feels quite real.

Frank Callow and Tim O'Rourke, LAPD's finest, are leading the circus. They recognize me and, like most officers who do, never waste a chance to showcase what passes for a sense of humor.

"Still the hotel dick, eh? How's the business? Been dicking ya 'round or what?" O'Rourke gets fatter every time I see him. His gut is straining his uniform shirt and I'm expecting to be hit by a popped-off button any moment. His round face is surprisingly jolly for the job, ruddy and smooth, like someone who never has to shave. Which is likely a good thing, because a wispy ginger beard to match his wispy ginger hair would have been a most unbecoming look.

If O'Rourke hasn't been skipping any meals, Callow looks like some of those meals might have been his. He is a bone-thin, sharp-featured, shark-slick sort of man. Smart, but the man's got an unreadable sort of face I'd never been able to trust.

I take a deep breath, steady myself, and relay the pertinent facts to the officers. I try to leave out the part about me sitting there cluelessly observing the dead woman in the pool. When I realize I can't quite do that, because the timing of the thing is very much pertinent facts, I at least leave out the part about me dozing off.

The pool area is cordoned off. Names are being taken; people are being interviewed. This is exactly the sort of thing the hotel desires to avoid: the scandals, the sordid publicity. This is exactly the sort of thing I was hired to prevent. It doesn't bode well for my future employment prospects.

There were only five others in the pool that morning.

BANG!

Sadie Strickland – a once pretty, once young wife of an important man. They come into town regularly on business. He deposits her in the hotel and goes on to do whatever it is an important businessman does in LA. Presumably, making deals and spending time with pretty young things his wife once was. Mrs Strickland reads romances by the pool while sucking down an endless procession of mimosas. She's a harmless petite brunette with too-wide eyes that make her look permanently semi-startled.

This morning's events have sobered her right up and I wonder if deep down she is imagining some tragic romance-gone-wrong scenario for the dead woman.

Bernard "Bear" Stone. Once a legendary movie producer, now retired. A corpulent bald man with a permanent self-satisfied grin and an ever-present cigar. Rumor has it, Bernard Stone has more money than he knows what to do with and doesn't own a home, preferring extended stays at a series of hotels. The Lux has long been his August choice.

Mindy and Mandy Rutherford. The twin heiresses to the Rutherford textile empire fortune. The forever bickering and yet Siamese-twins-inseparable duo whose mutual resentment is only eclipsed by mutual devotion. Much to the exclusion of the world around them.

I'd always found the Rutherfords to be strange birds, the way they seemed to exist on the world of their own, a private bubble set amid the rest of us. They could have been anywhere from 30s to 50s, unmarried, childless, and never in need of doing a day's work in their life, they had a certain timeless quality to them. And something else too. Something almost childlike or, at least, untouched by adulthood, untouched by the ugliness of life.

They loved LA. Loved the movies, which must have seemed to them as real as their own not-quite-real lives. Giving money to productions they liked over the years had earned them a reputation. Patrons of the art. Mercurial and favoring only a certain particularly dreamy, none-too-realistic kind of motion picture, but wealthy enough to be forgiven any eccentricities.

THE LAST BEST THING

This town is like that. Dollar signs are everywhere. All is forgiven for the right amount.

Last but not least Emory Penn. An almost perfect named author of the bunch. The articles written about him were always full of Penn/pen puns. Well, the cheaper fodder, anyway. The more serious journalists would talk about Penn's lyrical sophistication, the unflinching depiction of the post-war generation, the haunting quality of his fiction.

I'd read Penn. To be honest, I'd read everything the man had ever written. It was as good as everyone said – a rare thing in a hyperbolic mendacious publicity world.

Penn was the only guest I had ever wanted to talk with, ever went as far as imagined befriending.

This is, of course, frowned upon in business. A good hotel staff member is a near-invisible presence, easily summoned, easily dismissed, helpful yet unobtrusive.

I always did try to toe the line.

The few times I entertained the dreams of a writer's life for myself, I think I always, subconsciously or not, pictured Penn's life.

The man was Hemingway-handsome, the same sort of effortless masculinity, with an easy manner and intelligent eyes. People enjoyed talking to him and he seemed to enjoy talking to them. Despite, as he claimed in his interviews, spending most of his time in front of a typewriter or doing research in a library, he had the tanned skin and social skills of a beach-side bartender. I could just picture him in a cabana-style tiki bar somewhere, mixing up amusingly named cocktails. Sandy toes and surfing jokes. Eyes squinted against the sun.

Penn had to be in his early 50s by now but could pass for younger. No grey in his blonde hair and only some in his neatly trimmed beard and mustache combo. A permanent twinkle in his blue eyes that no female reporter had ever failed to comment upon.

A perfect Hollywood author and a rarity: someone as good-looking as he was talented. Someone who could, it seems, make a living out of his looks, and chose to use his brains instead.

A few of Penn's books had been adapted for the silver screen. A few were said to be unadaptable, meaning it was only a matter of time.

The books sold. The man sold. His romances with actresses were gossiped over and photographed. And yet he was too good, too charming to resent. Only admired.

It was, it seemed to me, a perfect life. A life as close to perfect as one could get.

And of course, none of these people had anything to do with the dead woman in the pool. Or so they said.

They didn't know her. Had never seen her before.

O'Rourke and Callow might not have me on their Christmas card list, but they don't seem to mind my offer of assistance. They think the guests might open up to me more easily because I'm a familiar face; little do they know the people who stay at The Lux do not consider staff to be familiar faces, do not even consider them to have individual faces, just all one indistinct help engine.

Nevertheless, I do my best to interview every witness. O'Rourke and Callow don't let me forget that I am a witness myself.

How is it that I can't recall the exact details of the victim's movements that morning?

"Sleeping on the job, dick?" O'Rourke spits at me.

I don't answer. Sometimes my mind just drifts. I used to think it was trying to free itself from real life's constraints to help me write a story, but now I'm no longer so sure.

The examiner suspects the cause of death to be poison but won't know for sure until the proper tests are carried out. That makes it a murder.

A murder on my turf.

I had one job. An easy job. Only to keep the guests alive. Keep them from murdering each other. Was that too much to ask?

O'Rourke's insults are broad and crude like the man himself, but Callow's are sharp, daggers that slice straight through.

THE LAST BEST THING

In Callow's eyes, I'm scum, the lowest of the low, a failed city cop, a failed private cop. I can see myself through his eyes and I shudder.

Mrs Strickland is a shivering mess. She wants her husband, she wants her lawyer, she saw nothing. Yes, she eventually admits, she saw the woman enter, saw her speak to Penn. Yes, she swam next to the woman's float, but only briefly. Yes, she screamed when the woman tipped over. Who wouldn't? And might she have another drink while she waited?

The Rutherford sisters don't talk in unison. Their speech is overlaid one on top of the other so that none of the sentences ever have a proper ending.

"Yes, we saw, the woman, so pretty, so very pretty, thought she was an actress, couldn't place her, tried to think what we might have seen her in, couldn't, she talked to that man, that charming man, that author, everyone talks to him, we talked to him once, he was very nice, such a gentleman, such a gentleman, and then she had a drink, some drink, we don't know, she drank it, and took the float to the pool, such a nice float, we thought of using it too, but of course, we'd need two, side by side, and that would take up too much space, and then we didn't think about it, we were talking, until we heard a scream, that woman, that small woman with all the mimosas, she was screaming and we saw, the woman, she was underwater, and then pulled out, and then everything happened and we just…"

Bear Stone is a man made magnanimous by his good fortune. He has an easy, well-fed manner of someone who is done fighting his battles and is happy to sit back reaping the rewards. He is a large ungainly man on land, but the moment he hits the water he turns into an aquatic animal, slick and graceful. Naturally, he enjoys swimming and is one of the few guests who actually comes to the pool to swim. It was him who inadvertently tipped over the dead woman's float.

Yes, he had noticed her before. "You don't miss a broad who looks like that," he grinned. Then remembered the circumstances and put on a serious face.

He remembered the woman talking to Emory Penn, wishing she'd come over and talk to him instead. "Back in the day, a girl who looks like that, with stars in her eyes and movies on her mind, she came to talk to me first. Always." Stone brags.

"Is that all you remember?" I ask him.

"Yeah. What? Is that not enough? Where were you? Aren't you the one they pay to pay attention?"

I smile politely. He's right, of course. Each one of them is a better witness than I am because at least they were alert and awake.

I'm the one who let a beautiful woman walk into a pool on my watch and die. I'm the scum here.

O'Rourke's and Callow's abuse feels right, deserved; I revel in it, flagellate myself with it.

The hotel's owner has been summoned and is on the way. I can only imagine what my conversation with him is going to go like.

I dread having to look for another job, another place to live. I hate change, been through too much of it already.

"Speak to Penn," Callow says. "See what he says."

Did he pick up on me avoiding the writer? I can't help it; Penn intimidates me.

But it seems I can't put it off any longer.

Up close, the man does have a twinkle in his eye. He looks at me and I feel the scars on my face set aflame.

"You look familiar?" he says. "What was your name again?"

"Treacher."

"That a first or last name?"

I shrug. I don't think he remembers me, but he continues to search his memory.

"Ah, yes, didn't you come talk to me last time I stayed here? Something about a book you were writing?"

"I think you're confusing me with someone else," I say evenly.

He gives me a look that translates into 'a face like that is tough to forget' but doesn't push it.

Our interview continues.

Yes, he remembers the young woman coming up to talk to him. She flirted. Of course, she did, I think.

"Did the most peculiar thing, too. Leaned over and drank my martini. Then ate the olive. And winked. I was going to come join her in the pool but had some editorial notes to go over first. To think if only I had…"

Penn's handsome face turns pensive, remorseful. He couldn't have saved her, probably, but he thinks there might have been a possibility. His writer's brain is already whirring, creating a world where things had gone differently, where he came out a hero, with a rescued damsel in his arms beaming at him with gratitude-fed admiration. I can already imagine him spinning this into interview fodder, perhaps even a new book. Midas-ing this tragedy into storytelling gold.

I've been around long enough to know how these things go. Police will look into it for a while, talk a good game, sure, but if no easy solution appears, it'll be swept under the proverbial rug, one woven with indifference and uncaring. Because the dead woman is just another victim in a city that is admittedly almost proudly rough on its denizens. Her beauty will merit her some attention in death the way it did in life, but time will pass, and she'll be just another dead girl. An utterly forgettable tragedy.

If there isn't someone behind her throwing cash to fuel the investigative fires, if her name had never been on a marque in the lights, she'll fade away like so many before her and, surely, so many to come.

My cynicism doesn't make me inaccurate. My jadedness doesn't make me wrong.

One day, sooner rather than later, this'll all be but a blip in our collective histories.

Sadie Strickland will go on to drink her sorrows away. The Rutherford sisters will continue to perpetuate in the world of their own making, one only tangentially connected to ours. Bear Stone will continue rolling through life as a self-satisfied congratulatory parade of one. And Emory Penn will continue to be a golden idol, a wordsmith of the world, a poet of his time.

And me, I'll land on my feet. Somewhere decidedly lower grade. Shabbier. Doing another meaningless job. Perhaps a bouncer at a club, someplace my scarred countenance can be used, a Cerberus at the gate, growling at strangers. Dreaming about stories I'll never write. Words that'll never come.

I'll be forgotten by everyone from this day, I know. Forgiven by all but one.

Emory Penn will never recollect in any great detail a conversation he had with me two years before, during his stay at The Lux on a promotional tour for his latest novel. The way I approached him with uncharacteristic shyness, the writing advice I asked for. A manuscript I asked him to read, clutched in my hopeful sweaty hands.

He was so gracious, so polite, so charming – it was easy to take his good manners for acceptance, for approval. Later, I saw him throw the manuscript in the trash bin. I still remember seeing it there, amid banana peels and coffee dregs. It looked the way seeing it made me feel – like nothing.

I never said a thing to him about it. Not then, not later. Why would I? He only did what was in line with his nature.

And I did a thing most out of line with mine. I poisoned his drink. Served it to him too, and he never even looked up to notice me. One hotel-white jacketed arm with a tray as good as the other.

I had no idea the martini would never reach his lips. That it would be drunk instead by a beautiful woman who wanted to flirt with a famous man.

It was a slow-acting quiet sort of poison. One meant to offer death as a gentle sleep. She didn't suffer. It's what I tell myself. But still, she'll haunt me, I know. Rob me of my sleep, perhaps eventually my sanity.

In the days and years to come, I might write this story over and over again, never deciding on the ending. Telling the truth seems too confessional, too dangerous; lying – well, then I'd have to think up an ending and I've never been particularly imaginative.

Maybe, I'll wait. Me and my beautiful ghost. See what she wants. It'll be the least I could do, considering. The last best thing I can offer.

Reciprocity

Cate Moyle

The soupy evening foiled Hazel Wallace's plans for a moonlight fishing expedition on the river, so he unhitched the Hydra-Sport, then threw in a line on the small branch running through his property. A thick fog had settled for days across Burnt Springs — the nighttime marsh and all its wandering souls missed the bright autumn moon. The fish were fierce and biting, though, tempted to surface by the vibrations of cool mist precipitant meeting the warm spring's waterline. An incessant series of plops, like the sound of rain, echoed atop the surface, although nothing fell on Hazel except a dissatisfied mood.

This election he had gotten himself into was complicating his schedule in ways he disliked. Beside campaign events, he had to spend more time playing the dutiful family man than was his custom. He found the stepping-stones into office slick with pretense. Even this local run for the sheriff's office seemed rife in expectations. *Not certain how dad remained sane all those years.* As Alabama's Attorney General, Hazel's father left a legacy to be endured, in addition to admired.

Tonight, it felt good to be out of the spotlight. Back in his hunting grounds. The Burnt offered his rustic side a murky space to hide and his fish camp was one of the few places where his wife Georgina would not follow.

Bullfrogs wheezed their last seasonal song and plunged into the wet to warm. Hazel envied the simplicity of life and death out here. He cast his line rhythmically and remained unspooked by the sounds, including a few larger noises signaling large reptilian movements, until his hound dog acted alert to something behind them.

Little Red placed his paws on the boat's bow and growled into the vaporous evening. Hazel patted the dog's head in reassurance. They listened together. *The noise of crushing rocks under car tires?* Hazel saw a halo of brightened mist followed with a slight movement that stirred the lit fog and presupposed it was a car door. This was confirmed by the reverb of slamming. In the dense fog, shapes were muted, but with a darkened roof and the way its vehicle body disappeared into whiteness, he'd guess a patrol car.

"You down for the weekend, Hazel?" Sheriff Boone's voice cut through the mist.

"Reckon so." He started up the small outboard.

When Hazel landed his jon boat on the muddy bank, he saw the silhouette of two figures standing in the headlights of the vehicle. The diminutive shape was Boone and by the large-rim-hatted fellow next to him, he had brought a deputy with him as if he expected trouble.

"Evening officers," Hazel said in the politest tone he could muster.

They returned a mere nod. "You remember the disappearance of that Fowler girl? Ethel Fowler." The sheriff began abruptly.

"Yeah, of course, Eldred's younger sister. About five years ago. Wait a minute, you're out here questioning me about an old crime? Committed over in Baton Rouge?"

"You're not a suspect. Or the topic of my conversation."

"Then do share, Sheriff Boone." Hazel coughed to keep his sarcasm in check.

"We have some new evidence. Concerning a local."

"Who?"

The sheriff held up his palm in denial of further questions. "Hell, I can't say, you know that." He scowled. "Will say, this evidence isn't exactly new, only recently brought to my attention. Seems my assistant sheriff was sitting on a key element to the case all these years. Didn't bother to keep me informed." Sheriff Boone kicked at a nearby rock as if to underline the severity of this breach.

"Are you telling me Smith is inept? Or complicit?"

RECIPROCITY

"If I were speaking plainly, I might say a sheriff needs his second in command to oversee investigations with the book in mind. And more importantly, mishandling orders is unacceptable, even if the public is none the wiser."

"Christ. Well, won't have that sort of incompetence around long when I become sheriff. Nor will I drag my feet on getting rid of dead weight."

"Hmm. Let's just say I'm working on rectifying that situation before the election ends." The sheriff studied the camp, what little he saw through the murk. The pause in conversation seemed purposeful. Little Red began a nervous low-throated growl. Boone shushed the dog and moved closer to the boat where Hazel sat.

"Fishing looks good, Hazel, but you up for a little hunting later?"

"Buck?"

"Better. Two-legged game. Wants to take flight." The sheriff turned to his deputy and they grinned.

There was some operative distinction they were hiding. "A murderer?" Hazel's interest was piqued.

"Tastier," the sheriff laughed. The officer joined him.

Hazel rubbed the back of his neck thinking of a way to resist.

"I'll make it worth your while, trust me, boy." Sheriff Boone gestured at the deputy and they disappeared in the fog enveloping their patrol car.

"We'll be back by at four o'clock then," the sheriff said from behind the swamp smog. Hazel remained quiet in the sounds of their departure.

Sure as November burn piles, a truck honked outside Hazel's cabin at the appointed hour in the morning. Boone gave Hazel a brief wave from the driver's seat and thumbed him toward the rear. Even in the dark before twilight, Hazel could make out it wasn't a personal vehicle, or the deputy's car, but a large black and white Escalade SUV with the county logo on the side and "Sheriff" painted atop the hood.

Obviously, doesn't do undercover work. Hazel slipped into the seat. The sheriff drove off. *Two grown men sitting in the rear like teenagers.* Hazel turned to the other man. "Deputy?" He offered his hand.

"Chapelle." The officer shook with a firm grip.

Hazel remembered a number of Chapelles from his schooldays in Burnt Springs. The family had an endless supply of redheaded kids to grace the muddy roads. But he declined from mentioning this familiarity. As the SUV tore through a still darkened landscape, the sheriff spoke not a word, concentrating on the road. Chapelle occupied himself within the dim back seat by cleaning a gun. Hazel looked out the window for familiar sights and wondered why he hadn't called Georgina to tell her about this outing. Or at least, his buddy Eldred.

When they arrived at their destination, morning light glowed at the horizon. Hazel recognized the dimly lit blind and surrounding fields as part of Judge Tanner's plantation. It was a great spot for pass shooting waterfowl — built up on a ridge between a very large pond and the Burnt Springs slough. A natural funnel for birds flying between the two bodies of water. Tanner's property backed up to the Fannahoochee Wildlife Refuge and the judge often bragged about the quail that convalesced on his lands. Hazel had been invited here once before to game for wild turkey years ago.

"What are we shooting for today?" Hazel noticed that there weren't any dogs with them.

"Sandhill Crane."

In a climate where the seasons are defined by the type of hunting allowed, this was unrecognizable; Hazel never heard of Sandhill Crane open season. The turn made him uneasy, but he knew better than to inquire about the crane's protected status.

"Sandhill..." He whispered eyeing the dawn.

"Crane. Hazel my boy, you ain't never had meat this tender before — fourteen pounds of the finest flying steak." The sheriff adjusted the lens on a set of field glasses.

"Like ribeye in the sky." His deputy grinned.

Boone chuckled. "They fly through here on their way to Florida this time each year." He returned to the glasses. "Those retirees won't miss a few."

"I suppose they can always buy a fancy statue of one to stand by their condo pond." Hazel tried to appear light in the moment as he stroked his goatee in concern.

"Alongside their damn plastic flamingos," Chapelle snickered.

"That's a good one, Chap." The sheriff slapped his deputy's shoulder.

"Is the judge gonna be joining us?"

"Nope." The sheriff appeared satisfied with that reply until he met Hazel's eye. "Tanner knows we're here though, don't worry your pretty boy head over that." He reached into the ammo bag and drew out a dozen twelve-gauge shotgun shells. "Always knows when I'm here," he said, "and smart enough not to ask questions."

Taking this as a warning, Hazel threw his camo pack, supplied with a day's hunt of provision, on his back and strapped a Remington 870 over his shoulder, then followed them across the judge's half-cut field to the pit blind where they loaded their guns, listened for the Sandhill Cranes.

They had been lying in wait for about twenty minutes when the sheriff decided to talk. "So, the judge tells me you ain't able to pass the bar exam."

Hazel felt an angry heat rise from his collar. His finger flinched slightly against the gun trigger. "I'll take it again and pass. Not that it's needed to qualify for sheriff, as I'm sure you know," he countered, hoping he didn't sound peevish.

"Hmm." The sheriff ran his thumb along the design on the side plate of his shotgun. Boone's pork-rind finger stroked the delicate etching of a war eagle.

Hazel scanned the skies behind them.

"I've got a cousin over in Birmingham," Boone stated a few minutes later.

"You don't say." It was apparent the sheriff planned to make his point lengthy and as painful as possible.

"Yup. Works for the Alabama State Bar."

Hazel decided to play along, "A good job?"

"Good as they come. Supervises the admissions office and the bar examinations."

Hazel waited to discover where this was going. His pulse beating so loud he was afraid they could hear.

"She tells me someone can be admitted without state exam through, um, res-sip- pra-city."

"Reciprocity, yes—meaning someone has practiced law in another state—meaning someone has passed the bar exam somewhere else."

"Meaning the supervisor of admissions attests to having received paperwork to support such reciprocity. Funny word. I looked it up—exchanging things for mutual benefit." The sheriff became quiet again, letting the conversation soak into the morning air. In a full emptiness, he asked, "You graduated from Stetson Law School, right?"

"Yes."

"I got a cousin in Tallahassee."

Hazel had to smile. "Damn, Boone. You have one hell of a family."

"Boy, ain't that the truth." The sheriff smiled with him.

"I give, what's the exchange?"

"Well, it took me a while to figure out what you really wanted, but me—this'll be right quick. I'm a simple guy. I want you to drop out of the race."

"No," Hazel replied with an angry laugh. "In fact, hell no."

"Let's stand down for a minute," the sheriff said. They rested their shotguns in the holders on the blind wall and moved back from the camouflage. "Chap!" He called to his deputy who was ten yards away, "We left decoys in the truck. Go on and get them, will ya? We're gonna have to draw the cranes nearer, they're not passing close enough to shoot."

Chapelle secured his gun and scampered off.

"You can't want this job that bad, Hazel. I know you have your sights on the state attorney's office like your daddy. And his daddy."

"True. But maybe I feel the county could be better served."

"And how the hell am I supposed to take that?" Boone barked.

Hazel, stroking his goatee, lifted a couple of fingers in a vague gesture.

"Look, this ain't some stump speech where you get to talk sweet and mighty, or impress with your hundred-watt smile. This is where you've got to make a decision—grab the life you want by its balls or waste time floundering on some supposed high road."

"As with most situations, sheriff, it's a bit more complicated."

The sheriff tugged on the rim of his John Deere cap. "Here's what is not complicated, boy, you are running out of money and I have the traditional supporters deep in my pocket."

"Then why not wait for me to fail?"

"I want the fight gone out of you. You're a worthy opponent but I can't have you around raking up muck on me. Let's have it done. This is an easy trade."

Hazel absent-mindedly slapped his gloves against the side of his thigh.

"I swan, you ain't gonna decide, are you?"

"I've made promises to my own *cousins*."

"Then set them straight."

"Yeah, well, this one particular person wants to have an *in* with the sheriff's office. Real bad." Hazel scratched his goatee. "Also, after all the time we've spent on the campaign, Fletcher, Eldred, even Georgina, I don't think they'll believe I would just quit."

"Look, I wasn't going to mention this unless you went hardball, but I'm working to have an opening for an assistant sheriff in a week or two. You could take the job and still get some law and order experience. Make good with your people. Get yourself admitted to the Alabama Bar."

"Maybe." Hazel walked to the pit's edge. "Putting my campaign manager off the scent will be an ordeal, though."

"Boy, my advice is if they can't see it your way, cut them loose. They're between you and the prize."

Hazel nodded and swallowed, loud and dry. The weight of his family's legacy pressed at his throat like a chokehold.

"You have to the end of next week. Once I get wind of your withdrawal, I'll make some calls. Otherwise," the sheriff drew a line in the dirt with his boot heel, then picked up his shotgun, "It's every man for himself."

"Okay," Deputy Chapelle called from a position where he'd been hanging back studiously avoiding the conversation after he had placed a dozen or so windsock decoys, "Ready boss?"

Sheriff Boone gave him the thumbs up, lifted his weapon, and he, Chapelle, and Hazel took aim past the decoys standing four feet tall in the wide valley field below them.

The trio made pass shoots at cranes but not a single flight came close to their spread for a clean kill in the early morning hours. After mostly quiet air, a large swoop of Sandhill finally flew across the field low over the trees heading back to the refuge, right in line with their windsock decoys. The men fired and saw the heavy dive of a crane fall to the ground.

"Well, lookey here, it's an early holiday package compliments of F-L-A. They must miss you down there, Hazel."

"Did you see that? It dropped like a feed sack off a barn roof," the deputy said.

The three men walked with the purpose of recovering the fallen bird, all wings and legs, bobbing on the marsh.

"Stay away from that neck. The crane might try to peck your eyes out," the sheriff warned. As if on cue, the Sandhill flopped itself and aimed its long beak at them along with a tremendous honk. Boone drew a pistol out of his holster and dispatched the bird through its neck.

"Watch the claws, watch the claws," the sheriff said as the crane's legs flayed. Eventually, it went still.

"What sauce you planning, Chap?"

"Thinking bourbon and five-spice powder this time, boss."

"Sounds great. Can't wait to grill this up boys." Boone walked toward the truck.

"Ribeye, I tell you," Chapelle said and play punched Hazel on the bicep. He bent down over the crane and grabbed a wing then indicated Hazel to take the other.

*

For three days, Hazel tried to get his campaign manager, Fletcher Norris, alone to have a conversation about ending the campaign. Every phone call was interrupted. His email requesting a meeting remained unanswered, though Fletcher fired off a series of messages that committed more politicking at a host of PR events. In his usual style, each email concluded with a quote from scripture that echoed the message content.

Obviously, there was time to craft custom messages, yet days passed with no reply to Hazel's request. *Was he elusive by intent or happenstance?* Hazel couldn't figure, because even after all these months living with Fletcher's line of thought, he found the man's mind moved as errantly as his exotropic eye.

Sitting in his Jeep hidden outside Fletcher's yard, Hazel watched him pull up on a motorcycle and enter the mobile home. It occurred to him that their minivan had remained in the same spot for days. *Money problems?* Hazel ran through the current state of his campaign finances, which was a losing proposition, regrettably. Money would make it easier to fend off the Norrises.

Through the lit family room window, Hazel observed Norris pantomime a domestic scene with his wife. It seemed heated. After the wife shook her arms in rage, the couple disappeared from view. *Now was not the time for a personal appeal.* Hazel backed away.

It would be nice to simply send out a concession email, but ineffective since he found his manager fanatical. A personality trait no doubt ingrained; a background check on Norris had revealed he was voted 'Most Likely to Start a Religious Cult' in high school.

Later that evening, Hazel received a "YES" to his offer of a guy's weekend at the fish camp. Although his typical reply ended with "Fletch", this email was signed "F. Norris". No bible verse decorated the signature line.

*

Hazel placed the fishing gear creek side, his own Shimano combo in the rod holder next to his Stetson U chair, and a lesser model Zebco for his guest by the other folding chair. The deep hole at this bend provided a resting area for largemouth bass and was the primary reason he'd bought this particular property — reeling them in was easy from this spot. He didn't want to be stuck in a boat if the upcoming conversation agitated Norris. Hazel had an ugly feeling about telling him the campaign was over. No matter the outcome, he admitted confronting his manager would be a damn sight easier than if he had to tell his deceased father. *God rest his soul. And his terrible temper.*

Double-checking the lid on the bait bucket, he whistled for Little Red and caught sight of a lank hare in the swamp grass near the chairs. Hazel rubbed at his goatee. *Seeing a rabbit while fishing was plain bad luck.* "Dammit."

After two failed attempts, Fletcher cast his fishing line a foot further than Hazel's. "How's this crane? Taste-wise?"

"Somewhere between duck breast and steak. Dark red meat. Chapelle cooked it rare as a filet. Seriously, when he called it ribeye from the sky, he knew what he was talking about."

"For once," Fletcher snorted. "I'd rather stick to smaller fowl, one that can't look you in the eye. Heard there's a bunch of quail out there."

Hazel whistled for his dog that had disappeared into the dark woodlands. "It's far away easier with smaller birds. You want quail? I can get us hunting time there."

"Are you garnering invitations from Judge Tanner himself these days?"

"Possibly, but not necessarily; I have an inside connection where any day can hold an invite."

RECIPROCITY

Little Red came back into the illumination from the cabin's floodlight, tail wagging.

"No. Hazel, that's the corruption we're running against, can't you see? This is the sort of favor the sheriff passes off as nothing." Fletcher removed his eyeglasses to check for spots. "As if influence ain't consequential."

"Merely an offer. I didn't mean to be controversial, just thought we'd add a bit of hunting to the weekend." Hazel patted the dog; it turned circles before lying down next to Fletcher.

"Sure, but let's stick to genuine invitations." Fletcher reached down to pet the dog. "Remember the high road. We are running a different style of crusade; you said it yourself when you hired me."

Hired being a loose term. Hazel recalled how Fletcher weaseled his way on the campaign. "And I think you called me a choir boy for that," Hazel snapped.

"Maybe this world needs a few more choir boys. Like my daddy always used to say, salvation got from the devil ain't gonna take you where you think." Fletcher reeled in a fish after sensing a tug on his line. "Illicit hunting would not be the way I'd go."

Hazel's face reddened with the truth of the conversation. He opened the awaiting ice chest and Little Red jumped with excitement.

"Besides, Jesus made miracles with fish," Fletcher concluded. "I'll be happy to make do with them for dinner." The blue of the creek surface rested serene in moonlight, untroubled by the current underneath. Fletcher threw another line in the water and they watched the ripple.

"There doesn't seem to be much of a high road in politics, Fletch. It's a path filled with mud slinging. And confrontations that force a man to reveal the worst part of himself."

"True. I believe you're right about that," Fletcher nodded, "but once you've won, you can set a better tone for the county."

Hazel shooed the dog away from the bait. "I can't see a way of winning this thing without compromising myself... or my family," he paused and stroked his goatee as if deliberating. "My campaign has failed to raise the money. At this point Boone has powerful contributors, and he's warned me he will spend whatever it takes to dismantle me." After what constituted a meaningful lapse of time to Hazel, he opened his palm in a helpless gesture, "What if I stopped?"

"And hand the election over to an amoral man? No. What are you thinking Hazel?"

"I'm realizing it's best for Georgina and the kids to end this mire of a campaign. Probably better for the county, too." Hazel reeled his line in closer and replaced the rod in its holder. "And the sheriff, amoral? That's a little strong now."

"Well, other people have their opinions, but tell me," Fletcher leaned forward. "Would you trust your daughter with him? Alone? In his squad car, being driven off into the dark of night? If yes, then there's a good man and vote for him. If you wouldn't…"

Fletcher let his words hang between them. "And I don't blame you. Look here," he pointed to his eyes indicating Hazel should not be afraid of direct contact. "I'd never leave my little Meagan unaccompanied with Sheriff Boone. Or my wife. Ever."

Hazel busied himself with the bait, realizing this question bothered him. His response irritated him, too.

"Boone might be on his best behavior up in Chiggersville but down here on the Burnt our way of life's blighted with his corruption. Just so you're schooled correctly—there's a troupe of topless dancers that move through small towns putting on striptease shows. They'll use an abandoned barn or any back room offered. The group bails a couple nights later after the sheriff's office is called." Fletcher adjusted his eyewear again. "Folks think the sheriff enforces our laws and upholds our values." He snorted. "What they don't realize is that Boone is the when and the where of goings-on in this county. And he profits from it, crime and all. That's the sort of person you're handing the election."

"How do you know the sheriff is involved?" Hazel skewered a minnow.

RECIPROCITY

"Same reason I know your answer to my question about your daughter. A good man senses these things." Fletcher placed his rod in the holder and wiped his hands down his face, "Plus, I have a reliable source in the sheriff's department."

Hazel stood, cast his line, set the rod in a holder and walked behind their chairs. He motioned the dog to stay put. Hazel admitted Fletcher had extraordinary instincts and an ingenious mind.

"That means others are aware about this. So, we go at Boone from another direction, from the inside. With the truth on our side." Hazel talked while he paced in the floodlight between the lawn chairs and his cabin. "If this activity were brought to light, he'd be forced to resign."

"Have you not watched our sheriff at work? He tells lies Arkansas style." Fletcher waved his arm, "Nothing ever sticks!"

Hazel moved closer and stared out across the water.

Fletcher studied the stars overhead and then Hazel's agitated expression. The Senator's son appeared upset— reddened all the way from his two hundred dollar haircut to his neck as smooth as his St. Croix shirt. Fletcher couldn't help the incessant calculations of Hazel's spending habits. The guy's fishing gear cost more money than Fletcher's monthly bills, including grocery and medical.

"Quit messing with me, Hazel, gimme it. Straight up." Fletcher tried looking Hazel in the eye, willing his own to remain forward facing. "I can see it swelling inside you."

"Monday, I'm announcing that I'm out of the election."

Fletcher shook his head. "You seem to have forgotten there's a moral imperative here," he said in a disgusted tone. "I've been wrong about you, haven't I?"

Little Red hopped up at the raising of his voice, knocking into the bucket. Fletcher steadied the container and stroked the dog's head. "I thought we were kin-minded. Thought we were friends."

Arms folded, Hazel remained still. He sighed and thought about his next move. Fletcher did the same, moving forward on his seat.

"I know about Georgina's troubles. The shoplifting. I don't just have it on reliable sources either—made copies of the arrest records."

The men measured the resolve in one another.

"Yup. I was worried you might succumb to pressure, so I placed the documentation in a firebox. I have stuff on Boone in there, too. For security."

Hazel thought Norris was rubbing the dog's throat a little aggressively; he lunged forward and pushed Fletcher out of the chair. Hazel clenched his fist in an urge to throw a punch.

Fletcher stepped away and cowered creek side. "Hoped not to use any of it, but in these types of situation one can't be too careful." He blanched like a man gone vicious with regret, but his words loomed, threat inherent and personal.

Hazel hated being made the fool. Flush with emotion, blood pounded in his neck. "Don't even..."

"Listen, you can't trust Boone further than a hog's breath. I've got a nose for trouble, Hazel, and I smell a double-cross." Fletcher pointed at Hazel, who retreated, putting distance between the two.

Hazel tried not to glare at Fletcher's egg-shaped head. He paced again.

Fletcher stared the other direction, watching Hazel's thin shadow on the water as the man tread agitated, into and out of the camp floodlight.

Little Red ducked under a chair and began to shake.

"What you are smelling, Fletch, is reality. It's not that I choose to surrender—it's that Boone is too powerful and popular."

"Damn it Hazel, where is your compass pointing these days? Popular? Is that what this is about? Like when you used to decide who was the 'in' crowd? The rest be damned." He tapped his chest with a forefinger. "Like that kid who dated Georgina freshman year? The one that never recovered from the hazing you and Eldred put him through. Everyone else gets sacrificed so you can be popular. Again." He rambled on, the curl of his lip lopsided as his eye. "Maybe it's time someone stopped you from your own ambition."

"That's enough, Norris." It was Hazel's time to point.

"Sounds like you've already decided: cut Norris loose." Fletcher gazed at the gathering heavens. "You're in deep if you do this..."

The dog whimpered in the direction of the cabin and Fletcher wrenched his haunted eyes from the sky above to find himself peering into the barrel of Hazel's gun.

An evening that had started clear and calm now blew in a damp and bitter edge. Hazel waited on the arrival of his high school buddy Eldred Hagan, who he'd instinctually called when at a loss for the next move. Old habits hold in times of trouble — especially after thinking through who would be awake near midnight and would come hither with few questions. And the oddity of the situation increased the probability of Eldred showing.

Fog fingered through the trees and in the mist Hazel relived those last moments: the involuntary raising of Fletch's arm, his errant eye straightening at imminent death to stare defiantly at his killer. *Mortifying*. How Fletcher seemed to get the last word, even silently. Mostly, he knew Norris didn't deserve this and he wished for a different end.

Hazel folded the chairs and tidied up the fish camp until he heard a vehicle pull off the road, then sauntered over to the headlights heading up his driveway. A blare of rockabilly music moved along with the approaching van.

You're in deep, deep, deep. Rolling down the vortex of love...

He caught wind of Eldred singing before lowering the volume, "Deep, deep, deep."

Typical, thought Hazel. Listening to old fifties songs like that Val Dunford tune. Lovesick and wronged: these were his friend's favorite moods.

Eldred cleared his throat. "This gonna get you in trouble with the missus?"

Hazel nodded, then grimaced like there was more.

"With the law?"

Hazel rubbed his neck. Silently, he walked Eldred over to

the spot of the shooting. He gazed around the camp behind them as his friend took in the scene.

"Ah jeez, is that Fletcher Norris?"

"Yeah." Hazel didn't meet his buddy's eye. "Like I said, it was an accident."

"I don't need to know about it. None of it." Eldred held his head low and wandered a bit; he knew it would be one of those conversations to not make eye contact. "So, you want the body disposed?"

"A guy mysteriously vanishes while getting ready for a hunting trip with his buddy, uh, hell no. It has to be an accident. I'm prepared to call the authorities."

Eldred took a moment to look back over Norris' body, pacing a slow circle.

"An accident? I'm not judging your story, Hazel, but that," he pointed, "is not an unfortunate flesh wound."

"They will believe the story if I have an eyewitness, Eldred."

They studied each other, hunting for an answer the night winds wouldn't take up in whisper. A cold fog rolled around them, nuanced and weft.

"Given the shot, he'd have to have been coming straight for us. But at that close a range?" Eldred sounded as if he was talking to himself, "Maybe he went deranged? So, it was self-defense?"

"Maybe. No, I don't want his good name harmed. It'll be an accident, pure and simple."

"Okay, whatever you want. Not sure that will hold under forensic testing, though."

"I'm not worried about that," Hazel said. At Eldred's curious expression he added, "Yet."

"Well, I'll get my hunting gear, then you give me a story before the sheriff squad gets here." Eldred walked back to his van to gather the necessary props.

Hazel noticed duct tape around his boot tops and at his wrists—a strange outfit, even for hunting. Though, in truth, he forgot to ask what Eldred was doing when he called him. Hoped it wasn't important.

*

Deputy Chapelle finished his questioning and joined a number of his officers to survey the campsite. Hazel turned to thank his buddy but found Eldred already absent from the bleary scene.

Looking across camp, Hazel could only make out the briefest red glow of taillights. *Amazing, how quickly a white van disappears into fog.* Sometimes a man wants to be that inconspicuous, he mused. *Like fog sliding past forest limbs. A soft falling on the swampland.* A presence barely noted.

He sensed breathing behind him.

"Guess this means an end to your campaign — good to have you on the team." The deputy offered his hand. "Got to admit, I'll miss that TV ad with the family." Chappelle leaned in adding, "And that pretty missus of yours."

Hazel stared, feeling the energy of a fist course through his arm but compromised by gripping the man's hand tighter. He held it until he saw Chappelle wince.

Shall We Not Revenge

Gary Fry

I was sitting in a café using my phone to surf the net when I learnt what had happened to Indeedy since our school days.

Life hadn't gone well for me. I lived in a small flat in a grubby district of Manchester and hadn't held down a job since my early twenties. I was smart enough not to establish a direct link between Indeedy's schoolground bullying and my current state of mind, but even so this news about him hit me hard. My fists clenched, a little of that anger – which my therapist had done good things to control – stealing in. It was only after several seconds that I was able to glance again at the screen.

Facebook was showing Matthew Deed's page. With characteristic recklessness, he'd revealed that several years earlier he'd won the National Lottery jackpot, over eight million pounds. He'd posted pictures of a big house in Wetherby, a red sports car, a trophy wife (she really was beautiful), and also two boys who'd be well into their schooling by now.

My fury came again in a wave. An elderly lady in one corner of the café stared my way, but I somehow forced a smile. What was a more rational way of dealing with this development, I wondered? It was Dr Kelly's voice in my mind, suggesting a sensible solution, a triumph of reason over the savage heart. In the event, I simply left the building and got back inside my brother's vehicle.

Jake, a self-employed electrician, had lent me the ride for a fortnight. I hadn't been able to afford a car since running up debts while taking drugs in the late 'nineties, something else my elder brother had helped me through. He was currently holidaying in Spain with his family and relied on me to feed his two cats.

Feeling more depressed than I had in months, I drove home and let myself into my tenement flat. I tried to keep my mind off certain sensations which seemed to form in my body, beneath conscious awareness. I switched on the television and watched the news. Somebody famous had reached an out-of-court settlement after committing a misdemeanor, and his victim seemed pleased. Was retribution these days always a bloodless arrangement? Could hurt be alleviated by money? I switched channels, settling on a documentary about the social behaviour of fish. Whenever others threatened their progeny, they retaliated viciously. There was no additional layer of mediation.

Pacing back and forth in my disorganised room, I reflected on what felt like pertinent matters. My late parents (both dead in a car accident half-a-decade ago) had been decent but hadn't appreciated the importance of education. I'd been bright, particularly in the humanity subjects, but also the shyest person at my school. No wonder I was such an easy target for the likes of Indeedy. Every day he'd played some new trick on me, almost always a cruel one. I dreaded daily attendance, and once my brother had left at sixteen to start work, I was at Indeedy's mercy in the playground.

Dr Kelly has instructed me to focus on the boy's social deprivation, the council estate on which he'd lived, and his shitty parents. But that only helped to some degree. Certain acts leave scars, simple as that. After trying so hard to come to terms with such a dark period in my life, I'd learned that many similar experiences resist convenient dismissal.

So was it revenge I now sought?

I'd once attempted to achieve that in the past. On a school day, pushed to the limits of endurance, I'd turned and punched the boy after he'd jumped on me during a games lesson. The teacher had spotted the altercation and marched us both to the headmaster's office, where I'd shed humiliated tears. This situation typified my identity: I was always afraid of which aspects of my character troubling events might reveal. That was largely why I held myself aloof from the world at large, feeling isolated from it, a profoundly empty sensation. But it wasn't my fault.

Finishing off yet another bottle of strong white cider, I turned in for bed, imagining all kinds of grisly events which soon burdened my dreams.

*

The following day I had a hangover, acute pain behind reddened eyes. Nobody ever looked twice at me in the street, and I dealt with that unhappy truth by drinking more, which compromised my appearance further still, a vicious circle. And so I drifted through life, moving from one disappointment to another, with neither direction nor motivation.

But suddenly I had a point of focus: Matthew Deed. He'd originated much of my suffering, and now I'd decided that he needed to be reminded of that. His luck was just about to change. And so perhaps was mine.

By lunchtime I was in the car, playing something moribund on the stereo. My mood fluctuated as I steered along countless roads headed sixty miles north. Despite the summer heat, I kept the windows up to ensure my violent exclamations couldn't be overheard by other motorists. After reaching the small town of Wetherby and parking in the high street, I pushed aside many intrusive deliberations and addressed my ad hoc plan.

After devouring a plate of paella in a café, I visited the tourist information centre to consult its reference books. Here in the local telephone directory I found MR. M. DEED & MRS. J. DEED, followed by an address inscribed in the same self-important bold print, all of which made everyone else in the list appear negligible. He hadn't changed, then … or had he? I was intrigued to find out. Recording the details in my phone, I returned to my vehicle and moved swiftly on.

I'd put the postcode into Google Maps and used the app to help me navigate. It wasn't long before I sat in the car idling outside the Deeds' family home. It was a considerable property, a large detached with a double garage and sprawling garden. There was a Porsche on the shale drive but no sign of activity in the grounds ... until a figure eventually emerged from the building's entrance and then climbed inside that blood-coloured vehicle. It was the wife I'd noticed on social media, even more attractive in the flesh.

As she drove away, I followed, deciding that this would serve as a reconnaissance stage. In the woman's absence, I might have taken the opportunity to knock at the house door and confront the husband, but right now confidence had left me. Still, I had time on my side. I'd unfold my impromptu plan cautiously.

My beautiful quarry led me all the way to a plush-looking school, where she was soon joined by her children. I bet bullying rarely occurred at this institution. As soon as the two boys – as elegant as their mother and a little older than in the photographs online, maybe ten or eleven – climbed in the rear, they buckled up to maximise their safety. The Porsche performed a swift U-turn and then steered off. Blending in with other parents waiting with transport, I didn't pursue them. I'd avoided being spotted on the route here; it would be unwise to take additional risks at such an early stage.

As I headed back for the town, I wondered why I'd never managed to retain a lover. My body suddenly ached with regret. I was thirty-seven; I'd probably never be a father, either. After parking in the high street, I took out my phone and accessed Facebook again. Then I wrote a private message to Matthew Deed:

Dear Indeedy,

Remember me? I'm Luke Cashman, the poor sod you taunted for years at school. Anyway, I recently read of your windfall and I'd just like to express a sense of injustice. I've received treatment for depression for most of my adulthood. I live alone and find life difficult. I feel that my experience at your hands did much to contribute to all this unhappiness. So what do you think we ought to do about that?

Keenly anticipating a reply,
LC
PS I'm presently in town ...

I'd noticed that he hadn't updated his account for a long while, making me think the message I sent would sit in his inbox forevermore, pitifully unread. Suddenly apprehensive, I tried to justify my actions. Perhaps I was offering him a chance to redeem himself. Rather than some pitiable vigilante, I might be an agent of nature, prompting decency at the heart of everyone I chanced upon. That evening, after securing a room in a budget hostel in the town, I took a walk along the riverside, considering all these matters.

I paused at a bend in the river, examining its waters. Here was a sliver of irrepressible nature trapped in an urban mire. Fish – trout, salmon, carp; I knew my stuff – snapped at one another, conducting their own forms of justice to resolve dispute. When I glanced up, I saw a young couple bickering on a bench beneath a tree. He'd bought flowers, perhaps to apologise for some dishonest act. Would she accept them? Was that the way such breaches were patched up in the modern day? I wondered how Indeedy might propose to make up for all his disgraceful actions.

On one occasion years ago, he and a bunch of toadying adherents had caught me alone on my bike in woodland. They'd stolen my tyre pump, which had prompted a sudden flash of inspiration from the boy. After a brief whispered consultation, three of them had held me down, blocked up my nose and prised apart my jaws. Then Indeedy had inserted the pump's nozzle between my lips to wank air into my mouth. Sensing my head about to explode, the act had felt like some sexual violation – the press of his flesh, a hard object thrust between my teeth. I'd had nightmares for weeks.

How was anyone ever supposed to come to terms with something like that? What must the offender do to make amends?

I pondered such questions while trying to sleep that night in my room, and the following morning I felt alive with determination.

*

BANG!

Amid infuriating spam in my social media account, I found a reply from Matthew Deed:

Dear Luke,

Thank you for your email, yes I do remember you. As you know, everything changes, and I have too. Why not meet me, since your in town, in the car park at Kippers Wood tomorrow (or today if your reading on Tuesday) at noon. We can have a chat.

Best wishes,
Matt

The man hadn't improved at all. His punctuation and spelling were dreadful. But his proposal troubled me most. He'd asked to talk in what sounded like a deserted location – was he planning to pull another violent trick on me? It was possible, but all the same, I thought I could handle myself. A few years ago I'd chased a burglar out of my flat, wielding a hammer. And I certainly couldn't deny being curious about what Indeedy intended to say.

Jake carried a tool in the boot, a large wrench he might sometimes use for purposes other than his work. After driving and then parking near the woodland's entrance, I took the wrench and slipped it in an inside jacket pocket, ensuring immediate access if the necessity arose. But now I was frightened. Such physical activities weren't really my preference. To minimise mounting anxiety, I entered Kipper's Wood and observed that it was far from secluded. Although no housing could be seen hereabouts, there were several people letting dogs off leashes, encaged domesticity giving way to the brief madness of freedom. As midday approached, heat thrummed from a bright sky.

Soon I heard another vehicle arrive.

My heart drumming, I turned and spotted a grey Mercedes pulling up alongside my brother's Ford. My discomfort was heightened, surely because I was about to reopen part of my mind cordoned off many years ago. As a man climbed out from behind the steering wheel, the thumping in my chest was transferred to my head. I'd begun to shake all over.

He *had* changed, if only in appearance. He didn't look as bullish as he'd been as a teenager. He was scrubbed up, fashionable, even elegant – fuck, he also wore glasses. The teenager I vividly recalled would have strutted around with a squint before succumbing to such effete apparel. Having just spotted me emerging from the woodland, Matthew Deed slowed a little, looking nervous. His hands brushed back a swatch of curly brown hair. I supposed he had it styled, possibly at his wife's behest.

My attitude flitted between anger and relief, relief and anger. The metal weapon felt cold against my heaving chest.

There was nobody else in the area. We now stood in a clearing of sand and shale, eyeing up each other like vengeful enemies in some old film, about to engage in a showdown with words, those modern weapons of debate. Only five paces soon separated us. I drew first.

"You came."

"Any reason I wouldn't, mate?"

He sounded defensive, as if he was trying to figure out what would happen next. All the same, his voice had possessed an apologetic tone, the kind I'd often detected when people felt ashamed. That pleased me. My fingers fell away from my jacket's parting.

I decided to address the matter at hand. "I guess you're wondering what I'm after?"

"It had crossed my mind."

"Short journey," I replied without conscious intention, the juvenile joke invoking our childhoods, the last time we'd met.

The man sniggered but offered little more than that. Perhaps he didn't live in the past the same way I did. With so much money, a family and a future, he wouldn't need to, of course. I watched him squint in the sunlight I'd craftily arranged to point his way.

"So what do you want?"

I was about to reply when he continued.

"Look, I'm different these days. A husband ... a father. I do a bit of business, but it's all honest stuff. In fact, I'm well known around this area for my charitable work. So if you're looking for the person who … well, who did such stupid childish things, you're out of luck."

It's you who's out of that, pal, I considered saying as one hand felt again for the bulge inside my jacket. But somehow I resisted that temptation.

"It's easy to better yourself when you're cushioned in life."

"How do you mean?"

"I'm on about your Lottery win," I said, observing him without blinking.

"Ah. I see." He looked briefly around, as if searching for someone who might witness this scene. But nobody was here right now. Then he glanced at me again and said, "I suppose that's what this is all about. You … want some of it, right?"

Did I? It certainly seemed so. Unsettlingly, my plan appeared to have its own agenda.

"Why the hell not?" I told him, still holding his stare.

His gaze grew fierce. But his body never moved.

"How much?" he asked.

"Twenty thousand," I told him, as if plucking the figure from midair.

He suddenly looked incredulous, a familiar bullish attitude in that large frame. "You've got to be fucking joking!"

"It's only a fraction of what you won."

When had I calculated this? In my sleep?

"It doesn't work like that," he said, anger rippling across his expression. "I have the business to run, a house to upkeep, my kids' school fees to pay …"

He paused, perhaps realising that his excuses had just strayed into risky territory. I seized the opportunity at once.

"Oh, please tell me how your children enjoy their privileged education. It must be fantastic to be free from all the shit involved in our – sorry, I mean *my* – days back in the classroom."

He now appeared torn between guilt and rage. Maybe he couldn't decide whether to come at me with his fists or rather negotiate an amicable solution to this problem. Whatever the truth was, I was prepared to retaliate.

Moments later, his voice flinty, he said, "Just leave my family out of this."

Was it they who'd had transformed him for the better? In that case, what hope was there for me, a single, childless man? But I remained silent, simply watching as my companion suffered any number of corrosive emotions. Finally, still glaring my way, he went on.

"I'm prepared to offer you a grand. As a goodwill gesture, or whatever they're called. I *am* sorry, you know. All … all *that* was wrong of me. But I just want to move on. So … what do you say?"

My reflections became audible. "It's not enough, nowhere near."

Before he could respond, I added more.

"Have you any idea how much basic living costs? In your position, maybe not. A grand wouldn't allow me more than a few months of relief. Money offers security, if not even an opportunity to change. That certainly seems to have happened to you. And now I want some of the same. I've had a shit life, pal. Perhaps you did, too, as a kid, but mine goes on and on – "

"Okay."

" – and on and on and – "

"I said, *okay.*"

I'd planted a truth right at the heart of him. I could observe him relenting. In the peripheries of my vision, I spotted a man out with his dog, trying to get it to fetch a stick, another triumph of social forces over biological ones. Perhaps I believed that I was in the process of achieving the same.

Just then the man continued.

"Let me go away and think about this. I need to consider my options. And obviously I don't carry large amounts of cash around with me."

If he did, might I be freer with the weapon in my pocket? But who was I kidding? I was no fighter; I had a sharp intellect, that was all, and one which currently came to my aid. I realised that he might depart and never contact me again, though I doubted it. He could phone the police, but where was evidence of any sharp practice? It was he who'd proposed making a settlement payment and not me. Indeed, it would be my word against his. Oh, I'd been smart. The same was true of having first learned where his boys schooled and then casually mentioning this to the father. He surely wouldn't want his wife to learn anything so negative about his past. She was classy; he'd probably attracted her with his newfound refinements. And for the sake of a relatively negligible payment, it surely wasn't worth having so much potentially damaging material revealed.

The whole planet seemed to hold its breath until I reached a conclusion. Then, calmly eyeing Indeedy, I spoke plainly. "Okay. But I'll need a decision *today*."

"I'll message you. Check your account at four o'clock prompt. I'll be at my computer for five minutes after that, and if I don't receive a reply by then, any deal is off."

"I'll be waiting," I said, as the man strode away and got back inside his vehicle. He fired up the throaty engine and edged away. "Bring it on, old pal."

*

Ideas bedevilled me all that afternoon. I have a recollection of marching up and down the town's high street, my forehead furrowed with concentration. God knows what other pedestrians thought as I barrelled on past them. For a short spell I thought I might have grown slightly unhinged.

I wasn't a criminal, but hadn't I just committed an illegal act? In whatever way I tried to story away my behaviour, this surely amounted to blackmail. However, the most disturbing aspect was that I liked the taste of it, like copper in my mouth. It was the sense of transgressing social rules that thrilled me. I wasn't the puppet or pawn I'd believed myself to be. Under the surface, like some fish in a riverbed, I'd begun to rise for bait, but with no intention of getting caught. I was striving for a form of justice that obeyed natural laws. And I'd soon be rich – or at any rate, better off that I'd ever been.

When four o'clock approached, I stared and stared at my

social media account. Three-fifty-six, three-fifty-seven … My heart hammered maniacally. I recalled that I'd left the wrench inside my jacket. At three-fifty-eight, I began to look furtively around my hostel room, expecting police to burst in at any moment, Indeedy in the background using so much cash to keep this whole sordid situation away from his new existence, like a fish occupying unpolluted waters. Three-fifty-nine …

The message arrived with the turn of the hour. My palms greasy with sweat, I unfurled the communication.

Dear Luke,

Your right, I do owe you something. I hope this will be enough. I'm prepared to pay you ten thousand pounds in cash, same place, tonight at 8pm. Then I want you out of my life for good. I'm sorry to sound so harsh. These are sad circumstances and I have to protect them I love. Take it or leave it. Respond at once, please.

Matthew

He'd clearly given the issue some thought, despite expressing it with more bad spelling and sloppy punctuation. I felt almost bad about what I was doing. But then I reread his sign-off. The day before he'd written "Matt", and today it was the formal full version of his Christian name. He had no compassion for me, though he was anticipating that *from* me. He hadn't even apologised. I felt my fists clench anew. The digital screen clipped away the seconds like a stay of execution.

Thinking more charitably, I realized that he was offering half of what I'd asked for spontaneously. In hindsight I'd regretted the reckless size of my demand, but it had obviously promoted him to settle on a realistic compromise, increasing his original proposal by a thousand percent. It would be unreasonable to refuse. Dragging my mind back to the everyday, I clicked to reply and typed:

Fine. See you there.
Cashman

BANG!

*

I murdered the intervening hours by sitting on my bed in the hostel, watching a small television on one wall. Soon I lost myself in a documentary about evolution. It was claimed by some Open University type that human beings had started out in the sea, a single-celled entity which, upon emergence and adaptation, had interacted with other creatures to ultimately forge a communal world. Human society was a product of such embodied exchanges. The scholar went on to assert that money was a method of mediation between interacting agents. Where animals tore chunks out of each other to settle disputes, people negotiated fiscal compromises. This was apparently a triumph of the rational, civilized mind.

I wasn't convinced by this conclusion. What about victims of senseless violence? Could the rage of the unjust really be supplanted by cold cash? To suppress such speculations, I rose at once and hurried downstairs to exit the building. I got into my brother's car and drove for Kipper's Wood, that tool wedged against my thumping ribs like some outrageous talisman. Once I stood again in the clearing and awaited my adversary's arrival, I felt my hands clench tight, tighter, tightest.

He eventually arrived ... and he wasn't alone. *His wife*? I was thrown into sudden confusion by that possibility. If he was trying to keep this situation private, why had he now involved her? But then, as I looked on unblinking, both figures stepped outside, one certainly Matthew Deed, and the other burly, skin-headed, tattooed. And so the bully had brought in reinforcements again, just as he'd done in the past. He hadn't changed, after all.

While the driver and his brutal-looking passenger met in front of Jake's car and then began strolling my way, I noticed a briefcase in my old enemy's weaker left hand. Did he carry a gun in one pocket, leaving his strong arm free to pull it on me if required? But in that case, why had he also drafted in the support of another? Something didn't add up here ... When the two men crunched into my proximity, I readied myself for action – fight or flight, as it's known in the animal kingdom.

"You came," said Indeedy, his expression disarmingly neutral.

"*Every* reason why I should," I replied, eyeing first him and then his companion. Next, I glanced at the case. Both men shuffled on shale. There were no other people out here; maybe that was why Indeedy had selected this relatively late hour. The world released a breath, the chill evening breeze pushing against our tender flesh, as the man spoke again.

"Here's the payment." Hoisting the case, he hesitated, tilting his head to indicate the huge man at his side. "I expect you'd also like to be introduced to my security."

I didn't speak, simply glared somewhere between the two men. Indeedy jostled his luggage again.

"I'm offering you this because I'm genuinely sorry about the past, Luke. We all change, and I hope with this help, you can, too. But I'm also very cautious. As I said in my message, I have a family to protect, and if there are any – what's the term? – any comebacks from this deal, then my friend here – a good friend involved in my business ventures, selling horses abroad; some foreigners can be, shall we say, rather unscrupulous – yes, my friend here will be forced to do what he does to some of them. It usually ends in – again I'm searching for the right phrase – an *incapacity*. Do you understand?"

"Yeah, I get it," I said, realizing that something of the boy I'd once known still remained inside the man. But then, looking away from the skinhead and tattoos to my right, I simply reached out to take the money from my left.

Would this finally repair the damage? Moving up close to Indeedy, I'd suddenly wanted to produce my weapon and strike him. But that would have been impetuous and irrational; people, Dr Kelly has regularly instructed me, can be better than this. Indeed, wasn't my old enemy proving this point by offering me so much compensation? I recalled him mentioning that he now did charity work. Perhaps there was good and bad in everyone, an ever-shifting inner conflict.

When I stepped back, the two men immediately turned and strolled away. I watched as they drove off. It was over.

BANG!

Cautious to the end, I carried the case behind a nearby wall and located a long, uncoupled tree branch. There were no locks on the lid, just a basic flip and lift mechanism. Next, I used a brittle end of wood to click the latches on each side, which both snapped up. But nothing else happened. When I stooped to open the case, I saw stacks of notes placed neatly inside. This wasn't a trick; there was no nasty trap awaiting me here. I resealed the stash, returned to my brother's car, and left.

*

It took me a few more weeks, but I finally figured it all out.

Having money changes nothing.

It was Matthew's lads who convinced me. I'd learned that their parents had won the lottery about five years ago and yet both children were at least twice that old. That meant that Mr and Mrs Deed had met *before* the family became rich. Whichever way he'd managed to attract a beautiful wife, Indeedy had done so *without* affluence. He must rather have willed himself to become a better person, a process perhaps enabled by his cocky attitude.

Me, I'd never been anything other than timid and anonymous. I was alone, damaged, and *still* angry.

I hadn't spent any of the bribe, and so I could afford to take a risk. I spoke to my brother who passed on some useful information from his dark world. Then, after scouring the internet using a tor-encrypted account, I found an advert for a mail-order company specialising in different species of fish. A typographical error on the homepage set my hungry heart racing:

Please enquire for trout, salmon, kill, carp ...

All but the most informed would assume that this was a misspelling of *krill*, but I knew better. Krill is a sea shrimp while the others occupy rivers; the creature was out of context in this passage.

I made the call. A woman answered, her voice disarmingly pleasant, the kind of person you'd never suspect of anything but an honest life. Could she have been hurt in the past, too?

I said, "I know what you do."

"Oh yes, sir?"

"The error on your homepage. I'm interested."

"I'm putting you on hold."

Before long, a man came on the line, his tone curt and efficient. "The product in question will be nine thousand pounds. Please indicate where you would like it delivered, along with the name of the recipient. Use a single piece of paper which, along with the cash payment, should be passed on to us in a single padded envelope. Once we are convinced of your dedication to this matter, we will exchange. We aim to satisfy the transaction within a calendar month. Thank you for your custom. Goodbye."

It was done. I hung up. A few days later I got a call back to request my attendance at a public site near Manchester, where I was interviewed by an implacable young woman who rigorously assessed my circumstances. When she appeared satisfied, I handed over the cash along with my victim's details. Then I left.

A week later I went on holiday to Spain for a month, drawing on the grand left over from the deal. I enjoyed every moment of the trip, my mood sweetened by anticipation. Indeed, a fortnight before returning to Manchester, I read about the incident in a national newspaper.

Lottery winner murdered in his home; despite suspicious social media activities, detectives admit to having no obvious suspects; possibly botched burglary; the victim leaves behind a loving wife and two heartbroken children.

I felt guilty about the last fact, but this failed to overwhelm me. I was getting stronger, sensing my past recede like an aging scar. I'd recently come to terms with my experience the only way a person could. And those two boys – well, they had a fortune to comfort them, didn't they? When this proved insufficient, as it certainly would, they'd perhaps come looking for whoever had taken their father away. But they'd never identify me. Just as my handling of police interrogations lately has proved – yes, I did receive a payment from the late victim but was demonstrably out of the country when he died – I'm far too clever for that.

The young men will get over it somehow.

After all, I have.

Blow Jobs and the Meaning of Noir

Maxim Jakubowski

It was Paris and we were young.

We'd meet in an old bar by the Place Saint Michel, owned by a widow from the Auvergne, who had adopted our motley Left Bank gang and allowed us to spend hours on end sipping on coffees and the occasional beer and probably deterring better-paying customers from venturing into the joint. She didn't seem to mind. Maybe she thought of us as her adopted family. I found out a few years later, that shortly after we had all departed Paris for our real lives, she had promptly sold the bar to return to her terroir and it had become yet another of the kebab joints that now blight the Latin Quarter.

We never talked much about the things we were studying or learning. No, we conversed about movies, books and women. Or, more specifically, girls. Those we had known, those we had not known in the Biblical sense, those we yearned for, those we had lost.

Two or three times a week we would meet up near the rue d'Ulm and go and see films at the cinématheque. They were the cheapest seats in Paris and, on most evenings, we had no clue as to what we were about to watch. Often, it would be an obscure Mongolian film with Swahili subtitles or worse, but Henri Langlois or one of his minions (many of which would go on to become famous critics, writers or directors) would formally introduce the film and swear it was an undiscovered masterpiece and this was the only remaining print left in the world, one of the thousands of rarities the mad curator had squirrelled away in his vaults, many such illegally, during his notorious career; when we were luckier it was a series of Buster Keaton shorts. To this day, I still kneel at the altar of Keaton's genius. Charlie Chaplin can't compete!

Not all of us in fact were even students. Max was working for a British bank in Paris, Michel supplemented his income from painting and illustrations by working in the music archives of French radio, the ORTF, Marcel was an accountant for a multinational. They were the core of the group. There was also Roland, Philippe, Pascal and his brother. Others drifted in and out on the whim of exams, budgets and a lack of steady relationships. But we had somehow congregated together through a set of common acquaintances and accidental friendships and now formed a distinct group of drinkers, complainants and dilettantes. There were others on the periphery of our group, who would join us from time to time, then disappear, including a fat pretentious twat who shadowed us like a lapdog, until we managed to insult him away, and to our great surprise actually became famous manning the barricades in May 1968 and even got himself elected as a French MP. He was probably still a twat, but he became a famous twat!

It was then that Maryanne Armshaw crossed our paths.

Max had been walking down the Boulevard Saint Germain on his own, when he had noticed her strolling in the opposite direction with a girlfriend. He'd heard them speaking English together, though with an American accent, and had turned round and begun following them on a whim. They led him a merry dance, but he only had eyes for her legs. She made him think of Julie Christie in BILLY LIAR, a film that had made an indelible impression on him, or rather the actress had. Eventually the two girls, after walking miles in circles, from Les Deux Magots down Boulevard Montparnasse, Avenue Raspail and then back north toward the Luxembourg Gardens, decided they needed a rest and sat themselves down at a trendy and expensive café on the corner of St Michel and St Germain. Certainly one he could not afford. But he was smitten. He found himself a table close to theirs and ordered himself an espresso; the cheapest choice. From overhearing their conversation, he found out they had only arrived in Paris from somewhere in the Midwest a few days previously, but the blonde one was staying on for several months on some course while her companion was only in Paris for another week. Eventually, he summoned up the courage to speak to them, using the fact that he was English ("wow, we're all strangers in a strange land" was his feeble opening gambit; he'd been reading the Heinlein novel just a few weeks ago) as a perfect pretext and offered himself as a free guide to Paris for the rest of their joint stay in the city. The red-haired American girl politely declined, arguing she had already made plans, but the blonde agreed. Her name was Maryanne and she was from Cedar Rapids.

Maryanne was a mixture of prudishness and sensation-seeker. She openly admitted she had not come to Paris to study properly, but wanted to live her life. Not that, coming from her native Midwest, she had even seen the Godard film. She was happy to be kissed, felt up in strategic places but couldn't stand the thought of someone, let alone a man, touching her breasts. They were slight; a bit like Jane Birkin's. Max courted her for weeks and never succeeded in getting much further than first base, introduced her to his friends and she became a regular hanger on, after which to everyone's surprise, a week later, Marcel confessed to the others that he had managed to bed her. Marcel was a sly one. No one even knew he had been seeing Maryanne behind their backs. He confirmed, with a wry smile, that the young American blonde would allow him to do absolutely everything to her between the sheets, but shrieked to high heaven if his fingers, mouth or tongue ventured within an inch of her nipples. It was frustrating, he admitted, but beggars can't be choosers, and it was his first American girl after all and there were other pleasures to assuredly enjoy with her. She gave great blowjobs, he informed them, grinning.

The problem with Maryanne was that she knew nothing about books, movies, philosophy or politics and remained mostly silent and blank looking when they all met up to draw out their coffees in the bar, which made her something of an uninvolved hanger on. By then, her college friend had returned to America and she was staying in a small rented room by Ménilmontant, to which Max often escorted her back to late at night after all the others had dispersed. Marcel never stayed up late because of his day job and only saw Maryanne proper at the week-ends.

They had all been to see 'Gun Crazy' at the cinémathèque. Maryanne, who had never watched a black and white movie before, had unlike them all not been impressed. Why was it a noir movie when it wasn't in colour; why not noir et blanc? Why did the characters get up to such stupid things knowing it would do no good, and accepted their fate so easily. They all tried to painstakingly explain to her what the essence of noir was, but she refused to take them seriously. "You're pretentious old farts," she complained.

Max, on the other hand, pictured her at night while he was jerking off with her face and slight body to the forefront of his mind, like an image projected onto a silver screen, as the epitome of the femme fatale. American, blonde, slim, unattainable (to him). He was happy to forgive her intellectual failings which he blamed on her youth and sometimes dreamed they improbably became lovers and were fleeing along mythical American highways on some mad mission to get away with the loot, dodging crooked cops and malevolent villains and staying in sordid motel rooms to the loud sound of rock'n roll music.

She had become the siren of his dreams of noir.

Eventually, Marcel tired of her. No doubt fed up with her bothersome and often noisy protests every time his hand strayed in the direction of her breasts when they were in bed. He was assuredly a tit man and the frustration got to him, even though all her other sexual parts were readily available.

Max was encouraged and began courting her again. He convinced himself he would become the first man to be allowed to kiss her nipples and make her writhe with pleasure. It would be his mission. After all, she had come to Paris to escape the clumsy embraces of American jocks and surely his carefully constructed air of sophistication would win the day.

BLOW JOBS AND THE MEANING OF NOIR

He drifted away from the group and spent more time with Maryanne. Taking her to movies, reading to her from books he admired. Somehow he felt she was moving in his direction, step by step, fascinated by his knowledge of popular culture, his passions. He liked teaching her things.

They watched 'Double Indemnity', 'Rififi', 'The Lady in the Lake'. He even took her to see his favourite film, Louis Malle's 'Le Feu Follet'. A movie about the last 24 hours in the life of a man who would commit suicide and wanted to say goodbye to all the women he had known and loved. Max found it profound and romantic. Maryanne found it boring, but after they argued came back to his flat and went down on him for the first time. Oh yes, she was good! Was this the sort of thing girls learned best in American high schools? he asked her, spent, on cloud nine, his trousers still around his ankles. No English or French woman – not that there had been many he hadn't paid for – had been so skillful.

Odd then that she had such a phobia about her breasts!

But he would remember the first time she had taken him inside her mouth forever. A feeling, a warmth he would find unforgettable. He would live on that memory for years. It would return in his dreams, in his imagination whenever he least expected it. To the extent that thirty years later, adrift and between love affairs, the disturbing thought occurred to him of how it might have felt for Maryanne (and all the other women who eventually followed in her path) to take a penis between their lips. Was it pleasurable? erotic? unnatural? tactile? It became a subject of fascination and one day, when his mood balanced between loneliness and grief, he resolved to find out and looked up ads in the personal section of Craigslist and met another man and agreed to suck him off. He didn't find it unpleasant, nor did it trigger him sexually though he would begin to do so on a fairly regular basis, but that's another story.

"Of course," Maryanne replied, with a mischievous smile. "We have special classes about it; it's on the curriculum..." You couldn't say she didn't have a sense of irony. "In America we take that part of a girl's education very seriously. A bit like all you Europeans study the essence of noir..."

She was adamant Max and his friends took certain things much too seriously. Which they did.

He ground her down and she consented to sleep with him.

It lasted a couple of months during which time they lived in a world of their own, no longer seeing his friends – she had none in Paris – and gravitating between bed and movie theatres around the Rue des Ecoles, where a trio of arthouses screened the classics on a regular basis and afternoon tickets were half-price. She enjoyed musicals, Busby Berkeley, Fred Astaire and Ginger Rogers, Gene Kelly, Cyd Charisse, but still couldn't fathom his passion for film noir and its doom laden stories.

A distant cousin of hers from Iowa was coming to Paris with a group of college friends and Maryanne had planned to spend time with them over the week-end. Max declined joining them as he wanted to see 'Pierrot Le Fou' again and it was only playing at the Dragon on Sunday afternoon. It would be their first week-end apart in ages. He had a bad feeling about it.

They were on the phone. He was at work. She was supposedly in her room going through her study papers, not that she had done much in the way of studying since she had arrived in Paris.

"How did it go with your cousin?"

"It was OK."

"Just OK?"

"Yes."

"What did you do?"

"You know... the Eiffel Tower, Notre-Dame, a bateau-mouche on the river... Not the sort of things we do together."

"Good..."

There was a lengthy silence on the line.

"So how was he, your cousin, his friends?"

"Hmm... He's OK, a bit of a jerk. But he came with Justin."

"Who's Justin?"

"Someone I knew in high school."

Max felt guilty that the very moment she said that he pictured her practicing her blowjobs on Justin, deducing the fact that this was how she had perfected her oral skills.

"Oh..."

Another silence.

"What is it?"

"Well... on Sunday night, Pete stayed in and I went out to have a couscous with Justin and..."

"And?"

"We slept together..."

"What?" It felt like a knife digging deep into his guts.

"And it was good, Max. He was my first boyfriend, you know... I like you, but it's not the same. We're so different. You're so... European, I'm simpler, you know."

"I see..."

"It felt like... coming home... I even..." she was hesitant.

"What?"

"It felt just, how can I put it... right... when he touched my boobs..."

They agreed not to see each other that week, and meet up when her cousin and Justin had returned to Iowa.

By then, Maryanne had decided she no longer wanted to be in a relationship with him any longer. Didn't think it was fair on either of them. She was sorry and all that. It's not you, it's me. We think differently. You're a nice guy. All the habitual clichés.

Max was gutted. His mind in a tizzy.

He knew Maryanne Armshaw wasn't special and that deep down they were not particularly suited for each other. Came from different worlds. But there was anger inside of him that rose to the surface. He rang her. Begged for one final meet. A chat. Not even a mercy fuck. She reluctantly agreed.

On the day, an hour or so before Maryanne was expected at his flat, he carefully prepared the scene, tidying things up, looking at the place through her eyes.

He took a razor blade and meticulously cut into his wrist. The blood began to run. He'd left a towel on the floor by the couch to absorb it. He hadn't done his homework though, and cut the wrong way. He would carry that small white scar for the rest of his life. He'd prepared an A4 sheet of paper and pinned it to his chest.

On it he had written with a black felt pen: 'This is essence of noir.'

Spite? Wit? Madness? He wasn't even sure himself.

When Maryanne punctually arrived, he was woozy and half-conscious.

She screamed when she saw him sprawled out on the couch, with his arms hanging over the side and the crimson stain on the towel below it.

She ran out onto the landing.

An ambulance came quickly and he was rushed to the nearest hospital. He was only kept there two days while the doctor explained how he had botched the job by cutting in the wrong direction. Next time, the disapproving medic said, you'll at least know how to do it properly.

He found out from her landlord that Maryanne returned to America within 48 hours. Max lived on and began the next chapter in the book of his life, in which he would enjoy some blowjobs (as well as give them). He still has a passion for film noir.

Going Clean

Gabriel Heller

In memory of Steven Murray

We were on our way out of town. Two days before, Galen had surprised us in the bedroom and come at me with a knife. Holding his arm at bay, I wrestled him onto the floor, and pried the knife from his hand. The next thing I knew I was standing in the middle of the room, completely naked, unable to move, feeling all my strength running out of my body, while he gurgled and whispered for help, and Eve, also naked, was crouched in the corner, sobbing behind her hands.

The truth was that for a couple months we had been entertaining the idea of robbing him and going down to Florida and starting fresh, but the killing was not part of the plan. That's how it happened though, and we took as much cash as we could find, scattered in hiding places all around the apartment. There were drugs, too – plenty of them – different sized vials of cocaine and heroin, neatly packaged in tin lunch boxes, but without much difficulty we stayed away from those. For some time, we had been talking about going clean, and now we had enough money to disappear for a little while, and then in two or three years time, our thinking was, we could re-surface on the West Coast, in California or Oregon or even Washington State.

*

BANG!

We packed in a hurry, and in the cab on the way to the airport, I watched her where she sat across from me. I put my hand over her hand and let it rest on the seat between us. The bright autumn street passed behind her and the sunlight and shade passed over her lap. She took her hand from under mine and lit a cigarette and rolled down the window, and the traffic sounds grew suddenly louder – horns and trucks rattling – and over everything I heard a baby crying, and then our driver changed lanes and raced to make a light, and the crying became the machine gun pounding of a jack hammer destroying the sidewalk.

*

By the time we landed and checked into our hotel, it was dark. Out the window you could see the decrepit towers of a church, all gray, with stone saints and angels engraved in them.

Eve put her head on my belly. The church bells went off a few different times.

After a while, we went downstairs to the bar. There was a man playing a guitar and others clapping and singing. We ordered a bottle of rum and a bottle of mineral water.

I felt happy. I believed we could live above the codes and conventions that bound other people, that our love would carry us.

"To what?" she asked, as we clinked our glasses.

"To going clean," I said.

She leaned across the table and kissed me hard.

"To starting over," she said. "A blank slate."

*

The next day we went over to the park near the hotel. We lay on the grass and smoked. The good feeling from the night before was long gone. My mind raced, and every time I closed my eyes, I saw the look of panic on Galen's face, as I pressed the knife down into his neck.

GOING CLEAN

Walking back to our hotel in the evening, we found ourselves amid a ragged carnival. I threw some darts, popped a few balloons, won a stuffed unicorn that I gave to a little girl, who looked frightened when I handed it to her but took it anyway.

In the room, Eve wanted to make love, but I couldn't. My whole body felt tight and constricted. My heart pounded. It was difficult to breath.

"It's going to be ok," she said, pressing her face into my neck and hugging me. "Let's go downstairs and get a drink."

At the hotel bar, we met a pharmacist who wore a cheap brown suit, a brown tie, and thick black-framed glasses, who gave us some morphine and took us to a dance club nearby. Eve was a good dancer, and I watched them together. The morphine released me from the bad feeling that had clamped down on me, and I could just enjoy the music and watch my girl enjoy herself on the dance floor, and later we injected some more to get to sleep.

*

In the morning, Eve felt bad about it.

"I thought we were going clean," she said.

"We are," I said.

"This is very important," she said.

"I know it is," I said.

We were drinking coffee in the hotel bar. Through the window, we watched a boy with no shirt or shoes, dirty face smeared with scabs, run out into the street when the light turned red and kneel down and unroll a red handkerchief full of broken glass. He lay down on it, first on his stomach then on his back, then he gathered it up and went from car to car collecting his tips all before the light went green.

"We know what to do if we run out of money," I said, trying to lighten things between us.

But she didn't laugh.

She couldn't stop watching the boy, and after a while she got up and went out and gave him some money. That was the thing about Eve. I knew she could never be good, not really, but she could be tender, especially towards the damaged or the mistreated or the crushed.

*

That night we got a bus going south. She fell asleep soon after we pulled out of the station, her head resting on my shoulder, her cold hand on my leg. We wound up into the mountains, where I had the feeling that we were traveling along sheer cliffs, and then down through groves of palm trees where the air was thicker and warmer, and the houses on the side of the road stood exposed and broken down on small plots of dirt.

When I woke up it was still dark, but the bus had stopped, and people were standing in the aisles gathering their bags down from the rack above us. I kissed Eve on the ear and squeezed her thigh, and she stirred and stretched her arms, her eyes still closed.

"I dreamed I was walking on broken glass," she said. "You died."

"How nice," I said.

Outside I could smell the trees and the ocean. A taxi driver with a thick mustache jogged over to us and took our suitcases. He drove fast through the darkness dodging potholes and bumps in the road. When the road became sand, he stopped the car.

We took our suitcases and walked down a path to the beach. There were palm trees all around us. The ocean was loud, but we could not see it. We took off our shoes and sat with our feet in the warm sand, listening to the invisible waves crashing very near, one on top of the other, full of shifting, unstable melodies. Gradually, the sky began to lighten and the silver crests of the waves began to show. Then a man in blue shorts appeared behind the gate of the hotel, rubbing his eyes, and Eve told him that we wanted a room, and he led us up the stairs to the second floor.

*

We slept for a little while and then went down to the beach. Here and there workmen were building cabanas on the sand. You could hear the sound of their hammers over the waves.

The ocean was blue-gray and rough, and you could hardly look at it because the way it reflected the sun.

Eve wanted to go to a beach on the other side of some rocks, which she thought would be more secluded, so we had to do some climbing to get there. But there were more people there than on the main beach. Then she wanted to go along a path that took us into the jungle.

We walked for a little while among the tall trees and the dark green flowering plants with their huge cupped leaves. In a clearing, we came to a thatched bungalow. Beneath the roof were hundreds of bats, cooing like pigeons. They were gray and furry. We watched them for a little while. These small, winged creatures. They were climbing all over each other, trying to get as far away as they could from the light.

"I like bats," Eve said. "It wouldn't have been so bad to be a bat."

"It wouldn't be bad at all," I said.

*

We found a nice spot in the sand on the edge of the jungle.

I watched her as she walked down the empty beach, waded into the bright, blank ocean, stood knee deep in the swirling foam. She bent down and tossed water above her head. Then she disappeared and came up sparkling, blinking the salt out of her eyes and reaching up behind her head to squeeze the water out of her hair.

As I walked toward her, the tiny, sand-colored crabs ran out of the way of my feet just in time. The ocean was warm. The undertow pulled steadily at my legs as I waded out to her. She kissed me and pressed against me. She pressed me so tight. She hugged me with all her strength, then let me go.

She took my hand and we walked out to where the waves were breaking. We watched a swell come in from the distance. She squeezed my hand. Slowly the water rose into a wall

185

before our eyes. She screamed and I took her by the waist and lifted her up, and she screamed louder as I heaved her into the smooth curling belly of the wave, and then it swallowed up her scream, and I closed my eyes and it swallowed me up too. I went flipping backwards underwater and skidding along the sand. When I came up, Eve was laughing. I was laughing too.

Again and again, we dove into the waves. They flipped us around and crashed down on us. I followed her further out, and we rose up with the swell, but this time the wave didn't break until it passed, and my feet didn't touch the sand anymore, and she was about twenty or thirty feet ahead of me and still swimming. I swam after her. I swam with all my strength to reach her.

By the time I did, the beach was maybe two hundred feet away.

She was too exhausted to go any further, and she was crying. "Just let me go," she said. "Please."

And then she went under. I dove after her and got hold of her underwater with both my hands, and she struggled against me, but I held onto her. I could see the washed-out sunlight on the surface of the ocean. I felt my air running out, as she flailed against me. Finally, she went limp, and I kicked madly, and we broke through the surface into the sunlight, gasping for air.

Then she was screaming. Not any words, just screaming. The ocean was making a furious sucking noise.

I begged her to stop, to calm down.

I took hold of her thighs and tried to pull her legs up, to get her on her back. For a second, she went under again and came up coughing.

Then I slapped her hard in the face. It seemed to wake her up. She went quiet and blinked her eyes a few times.

We got on our backs and started to swim parallel to the shore. Finally, we were out of the current. We swam back towards the beach, slowly, and we caught a wave that took us into the shallow water.

*

That night I dreamed about a drowned child. I could see him floating way beyond the waves. A man with tattoos up and down his arms and neck came ashore carrying the limp, pale blue body of the child. He still had his pants on and one shoe.

The man with tattoos laid the kid down in the sand.

Galen was there.

"A kid is dead," he said to me.

"At least you're still alive," I said.

He looked at me sadly.

A circle of people closed around the boy. I figured someone was trying to bring his life back.

After a while I saw Galen carrying the body away. The dead boy's long hair hung down, like a black curtain. It's just a thing now, I thought, its soul gone. A woman followed close behind. She kept falling and getting up and falling again.

"I should be the one crying for you," I said.

But there was no answer.

The waves kept coming in, just the same as always. They rose and fell, rose and fell, without remorse.

*

We woke up late, and started drinking almost right away, blacking out at night. Days passed. We smoked and looked out at the ocean. But we didn't go back into it.

In a bar, in the dusty little hub of town, we met a man who gave us some oxycodone. He spoke English and had big, bulging eyes like a fish.

"You have a lovely wife," he said.

"Thank you," I said.

"What is her sign?"

I cleared my throat.

Eve laughed nervously. "Gemini," she said.

He chuckled and bought our drinks, and we took some pills, and then we walked with him down to the beach.

There was a bonfire, and we sat around it for a little while. There were people drumming and juggling fire. We drank and watched the fire and listened to the ocean.

BANG!

The first thing that happened was the fire turned black, but I could still see it. And then I tried to move, but I couldn't. I felt two hands on my shoulders pushing me back. I lay down in the sand. I heard Eve laughing. Then I started to spin and spin, and when I stopped spinning, it was like I was looking out of the wrong end of a telescope. Everything was very small and faraway. I heard a lot of noise around me and laughter and the drums got loud and then stopped, and I couldn't hear anything at all. Everything was black around the edges of my vision. Eve and the man who'd given us the pills were dancing very close, and he had his hands under her dress. Then her dress was down in front, and he pointed at the sand and made circles with his finger and she turned and turned next to the smoldering remains of the fire.

*

When I opened my eyes, it was light out. The seagulls were walking around and flying above the beach and making a lot of noise. I got to my feet and vomited in the sand. I sat down and vomited again. Eventually, I staggered back toward the hotel.

I went up to our room and lay down on the bathroom floor. I don't know how long I lay there, my mind full of disconnected images.

I saw the drowned boy from my dream. He was alive and laughing. I didn't know how I knew him, but I did.

I saw Galen at the stove frying eggs, shirtless, wearing tan cargo shorts, while Eve was sitting at the table, painting her toenails pink.

He turned and smiled at me.

The pan was sizzling.

"You hungry, Joe?" Galen said.

"Yeah," I said.

He clapped his hands and rubbed them together.

"Then let's eat, my friend."

Then I saw the panic in his eyes, and I knew I'd never be able to get away from them, and I saw him dead on the bedroom floor, the knife sticking sideways in his neck and the blood pooling on the hardwood all around him.

"No, no, no...," someone kept whimpering, and after a while I realized it was me.

*

When I came downstairs, the sun was high in the sky. I ordered a beer from the kid behind the bar and took it and went out to the beach and sat down in the sand.

A little while later, I watched Eve come towards me down the beach. Her dress was all torn along the front and barely covered her breasts. She sat down next to me in the sand. She had dark circles under her eyes, and her lips had no color in them.

I went up to the bar and got us both a margarita.

"I don't want it," she said when I came back.

I set it down next to her in the sand.

I watched the light tilt back and forth on the ocean, moving in the swells.

"What happened?" I asked.

She took a sip of her margarita.

"This drink sucks."

"It's just a fucking drink," I said.

"Oh, fuck you," she said. "Like this was my idea."

I was quiet. I just looked out at the seagulls and the ocean.

"You passed out," she said. "I tried to wake you up, but you were out cold, so I just let you sleep. You were breathing fine."

"He poisoned me."

"Nobody poisoned you."

"I saw you two together."

"You had a bad dream."

"Where were you just now?" I asked.

She smiled at me, a terrible smile, showed me the thin glass pipe.

"I hate smoking crack," she said. "The high goes too quick."

She lit a cigarette. Her hands were shaking.

We sat there watching the ocean, huge beyond imagining, the waves rising and falling. I knew that all the light on the surface of this ocean was almost nothing compared to the darkness inside it.

"My mouth hurts. I think something's wrong with me," Eve said. "Will you look into my mouth?"

She lifted her upper lip. I could see how the top row of her teeth all fit into the bone. I could imagine her with no skin at all, just a skull with teeth.

"You've got a blister on your gum," I said.

She let her lip drop.

"It hurts."

"I bet."

"I feel like I'm having a nightmare," she said. "Like I don't know where I am. I don't understand what's happening."

"Galen's dead. He was your husband. I killed him. We stole his money."

She turned and stared at me. There were tears in her eyes. She opened her mouth like she was trying to say something else, but no more words came out.

Bang!
Bang!
Bang!

Film Noir

Yvette Viets Flaten

I

You don't believe it
when you finally surface at Jake's
and climb the two grimy flights
to hear Vivian purr "You got a customer,"
arching brows over those big lavender
eyes of hers

and you go through the glass and mahogany door
into the office, drop your hat on the blotter,
turn to face the customer, sure it'll be some
dame with a grudge against her old man

but it ain't a dame; it's a lady
sitting in your chair, ankles trim
as any Santa Clara filly, shin bones
straight as arrows, the hem of her
black wool skirt just kissing that spot
below the knee cap that says: Look But Don't Touch.

And you're lucky you got Irish blood
on both sides so you can make easy talk
while your eyes do the rest of the number: slim
waist, salmon silk blouse, jacket lapel sporting
a Van Pelt brooch, and the brim of her hat just
shading her eyes enough so that half your brain's
recalling that Marine's story of Morocco, the Kasbah

BANG!

and white slavers while the other half's picturing
the Pump Room and some quail dish with a fancy French name.

And she waits for you to light her cigarette, places
her hand on yours to steady the flame, draws the taste
down deep into her chest and holds it there, while you turn
away and light one too quick, snapping the Zippo hatch shut,
before your fantasies escape.

She says her husband's been acting strange.
Receiving odd phone calls, going out late...
She's worried he's in trouble...
She wants to know...

You lean back against your desk.
Money comes up. Your fee.
You feel cheap. Bought.
It's never bothered you before.

*

At first glance
the black maid
knows you a dick,
knows you a liar,
knows you ain't but no count...
But she puts on the right face
takes you out to the pool
and says: "Ma'am, dhey'ze a Mr Gordon
here to seez ya..."

And she looks like a movie star
in a black suit and a yellow wrap
and all you can think about is the master
bedroom and those long legs up around your hips

while she orders Singapore Slings, invites
you to sit down, asks if you've discovered

FILM NOIR

who drives the DeSoto she's seen cruising
the boulevard outside the gates?

You'll find out, you promise.
You mean it, too, sipping the cocktail
but wishing it was a double shot of whiskey,
wishing it was Jake's house brand, potent
but uncomplicated; not the stuff she's feeding you.

She waits for you to light another cigarette.
She waits, knowing you're hooked; you wish it
weren't so, but you flip back the top, roll the wheel...
the light blazes... "Come again," she says. "Soon..."

II

The phone jangles in the outer office
and you listen to Vivian's throaty give and take.
She laughs; her office chair squeaks, rolling backwards;
she raps her Woolworth paste on the beveled glass:
"It's McIlhenney, 5th Precinct..."

McIlhenny takes her out for ravioli once
or twice a month, sends a box of chocolates
around on her birthday, spends the night
whenever his wife hauls their kids
up to his mother's in Sacramento.

He's usually good for an address
an alias, a tag;
but today he don't know nuttin'
about the lady
about the husband
about any DeSoto making the rounds
in that part of town.

"Yeah, yeah, thanks," you say,
dropping the receiver in its cradle,

BANG!

"Thanks for nothing..." and you know
you're gonna have to do this the hard way.

*

So you dip into Jake's, down the steps
into the confessional dark of his afternoon
and buy a pint, ease it into your inside
pocket, while Doris slides down a couple
of stools to see if anything's going
and in the corner Joey the Gimp runs his hand
over his mouth, judging if you're ripe for a touch

but you're not. You pay and hike for the Herald,
slipping in through the loading dock, down the iron
snail shell stairs, your heels ringing all the way down,
round and round, down to Sub basement B, down
to the Tombs where Ma Schuester squints up under
her green shade as a snake of smoke coils up past
her beady eyes, and she greets you: "Well, look what
the cat-"

And you start giving her the business, telling
her you've got a real tough nut this time
and she'll never crack it, and she snarls:
"Get to the point, you s.o.b"

and when you drop the name Fisher she rasps
out a laugh, disappears into the maze of green
metal stacks, comes back with a clipping file
and a '36 yearbook...

...Fisher, John Abernathy Malcombe, III
Money; philanthropist, supports a half-dozen
libraries, endows an Ivy League chair
in Mathematics; married to one...

she flips the yearbook open, turns it around
to you like a nasty hotel clerk with a point

to make, taps a nicotined nail on your lady's
forehead and says: "Madeline LeRoi, New York City."

And there she is, posing on the steps
of the Marble Collegiate Church, dazzling
you with that smile, in a bridal gown covered
with a million seed pearls, any one of which
you would trade places with in a flash

but you tear your eyes away and focus
on the husband, little horn-rimmed egghead
with a pencil moustache, and you wonder why
every looker finishes up with a mouse...

and Ma rasps out another laugh and says
"Pay up, sonny" and you slip her fee across
the counter, into her claw greasy with ink,
watch her crack the seal and swig down
the first belt

and turning, you tell her: "Ma, too bad you
ain't a man; you'd be Editor by now" and as
you clang back up the spiral, she lifts
the pint to the disappearing flash of your
heels and cuffs, murmuring: "Don't I know it,
sonny...don't I know it..."

III

The brass bell jingles as you enter DeMarco's Dray
and Freight and you tell the old biddy at the desk
you want to speak to Freddie but she keeps you sitting
tight in the waiting room drinking tasteless water
out of a paper cone for what seems hours 'til Freddie
gets off the blower and she nods you in without a word.

And there's two other guys in with Freddie
but they don't say nothing; they don't even

BANG!

so much as blink their eyes up at you from their
Sporting News, and Freddie asks what you need
and you tell him: a plain, fast car that no one
will eyeball

And Freddie sends one of his boys
outta the room and half an hour later
you're driving down Wiltshire in a old
souped-up Buick, blue-black as midnight

but now you got all of two bucks left
so you go eat Chinese, sitting in a back booth
killing time, trying to concentrate on the paper
but all the while thinking of her and that mousy
husband, trying to figure what business he's got into.

And when you leave it's not quite dark
so you run the Roadster up along the coast highway
to see what she'll do and she purrs like a big kitty
under your touch, and when the sun's finally down
you turn her around, ease back to town like a regular
Sunday driver

and you drift over to her neighborhood, turn down her street,
pull up slow, switch off, roll to a stop in the dark so you can
watch the drive yet still make out most of the house through
the palms, and there you sit, waiting, waiting.

*

And you wait more, watching; 'til the lights of the house start
clicking off one by one, till there's just one left upstairs and
you guess it's the master bedroom and you figure him for a
reader and her sitting at a vanity
with a silver brush, in white —

And you stop it there, light a cigarette, drag the smoke down
into your lungs like you're trying to drown it, the way you'd

like to drown this desire that surfaces every time you think of
her, your heart hammering under your ribs.

So you wait more, smoking, thinking, 'til the last light snaps
off and the house glows in the moonlight like a big white
tomb. And you lean your head back against
the leather seat and light another
cigarette, watching the smoke weave
its way out your window...

...and you keep checking the house over
for some sign of life but the windows
are dead blank and you know you're
getting tired...

...so you light up again...
and this time the curl of smoke
is the color of Vivian's eyes
and you can't help picturing her
outline whenever she's bending
over the file drawer...

and you remember the first night she worked late...
that sweater...that laugh...the phone, spindle,
goose-neck lamp hitting the floor, the wild shadows
on the ceiling; and the next morning her changing
your desk blotter, winking at you, so that now
you're wondering if McIlhenney ever-

The wind picks up; fans the business end
of your butt bright orange; lifts the palm
branches across the street, shivering them
like the feathers of some carnival hochie-koch-

Headlights!-flash in the rear view-
You tense, squash the smoke,
sit tight, watching...

BANG!

...watching as the lights near...

the car coming up behind you, slowly...

...passing...

It keeps going...

DeSoto.

Just like the lady said.

IV

So now you gotta decide
whether to follow it
or stay put...

but before you turn the key,
it comes drifting back up the street
and you dip down in the seat so they don't
make you out, and you're sure it's 'they';
sure there were two guys in front...

You wait more...
then sit up...
but there's nothing on the street now

So you wait longer...
till first light...
but still nothing...

and you decide to pull out, before
the milkman shows, before the maid's
up sweeping off the back steps, long before
the lady ever gets her breakfast tray...

FILM NOIR

*

You go back to your rooms,
strip down, just start climbing
into bed when Mrs Mihjac hammers
on your door asking for that something
on the rent you promised, and something
for all the clean shirts she's pressed...

So you hand your last dollar out
through the door, and she's peering
in, eyeing the half of you she can
see with those black gypsy eyes
of hers that are like hot rivets
going into your flesh...

and it's useless to lie to her
so you confess you're broke
and she grumbles but you know
she'll carry you – for a while,
anyway – because you always square
up when you finally come flush...

And she flaps her slippers downstairs
and you pull the shades, drop on the bed,
stare up at the fixture, trying to figure
the angles, listening to the chip, chip, chip
of #3's typewriter, smelling paprika and onions
drifting up from below...

V

You wake with a jolt of white hot
fear flooding your veins, from falling
off a cliff, or the roof of some downtown
bank building; coming to when you're half-way
to the ground, when you know there's no hope...

BANG!

And your heart's going sixty miles to the minute
and you sit on the mattress edge, trying
to shake off the feeling...

And after a while you dress, back
the Buick out of the garage, drop
by Jake's for a quick one before
you drift over to the clean streets
of her neighborhood where the palms
are still waving and the gardener's
cutting back the azaleas...

and you park in the same spot and sit
and watch the sun go down...watch the house
go dark one light at a time, just like last night...

...waiting for the DeSoto...

*

The first thing you see
is a coupe turning out
of her driveway and you start up
and drift along but hanging back
so the driver won't tumble to being
followed too soon...

And you check your watch
and it's quarter to one
and you figure this'll be
the husband going out for
his rendezvous and you're
still trying to guess
if it'll be a dame
he's hooking up with...
or some pretty boy...
or poker...
or a floating crap game – though
it don't square up with his look –

FILM NOIR

– so you consider blackmail...
or fraud...
...or maybe, he's dipped into the wrong account...
And you think of her that first day
sitting in your office with those trim
ankles and the word 'trouble' hanging
on those carmine lips...

And now you realize you're downtown
and the coupe stops in front
of the Pacific Mercantile Bldg.
and from where you sit it looks
like a guy in a hat goes scuttling
through the front doors and before long
another light goes on up on the 6th floor
and you're just about to pull up closer
when the hat comes out and drives off fast...

and you tail him,
follow him all over town,
until he turns in the drive-way at home...

So you park and wait, but no light
comes on in the house, anywhere;
no light at all, and you wonder why...
why?

And while you're sitting there
figuring, the DeSoto cruises up
the street like a tiger shark
on a blood hunt.

VI

From instinct
you reach for the ignition,
turn the key, but the DeSoto
veers to the curb, cutting you off,
and while you're stabbing for reverse

BANG!

the driver's out, grabbing your wrists
through the open window, and the passenger's
on your running board, shoving his Police Special
up your nose...

And they haul you outta the car
and, straight off, the bigger cop lands
one on your face and then a couple more
in your gut; and you guess from his steady,
measured way that he's a bull who likes his
work, and you're thankful you got Polack
blood on both sides so you can stand this
kind of public service and still see straight...

And they heave you against the hood,
frisking you, but you're savvy to their
ways so you don't say nothing, not when
they find your piece, not when they lift
your wallet, not till the Driver's studied
your license and hauls you around by the lapels
asking: "What's a cheap gumshoe like you doing
in a swell neighborhood like this?"

And you know you gotta answer straight
but it comes real hard, so you jerk your
jacket back onto your shoulders and dust
the cuffs, buying time till your wind's
back, till you can stand up full under
the nose of Fists and say: "I'm on a case..."

And Driver wants to know who and why,
and you say, forget it, that's private;
and he wants to know about the car and how come
you're on this street and you repeat, forget it;
and he threatens arrest and you scoff; he says
'suspicious person', you say, free country;
he snaps your empty wallet inside out to your
face and says 'vagrancy', smirking

and then Fists mutters how about 'resisting arrest'
and smashes your jaw and you feel the black
coming down over you like a heavy velvet curtain
and you know your knees are crumbling the way
Jimmy Samposa's did, losing the welterweight,
but that your head ain't gonna bounce on this
pavement the way his did on canvas...

*

They leave you alone
in interrogation till
your brains unscramble
and then two new cops
bring you a mug of coffee,
and the younger one asks
if you want a doughnut
but you can't even groan
without it hurting
and eating is out
of the question.

And the other cop asks
how a bright dick like
you trips on the curb
so bad?

And how come you happen
to be on the same street
as O'Donnell and Richter
at 2:30am, in a black car,
the same as which –
(flipping open a notebook)
 – one Mrs John Fisher,
of number 3730, claims
to have seen in her vicinity
on several occasions
and subsequently reported
as suspicious...?

BANG!

And how is it
that said roadster,
which you was driving,
has a tag registered
to DeMarco's Dray and Freight
operated by one Freddie 'the Meathook'
DeMarco, known to have connections
to Chicago and Newark?

"So what?" you say. "So I hire a car...
So I pick a bum name outta the phone book-
So, go tell it to the G-men."

"So, what were you doing there?"

"Like I said before, I'm on a case..."

"Alright, wiseguy, let's start
over from the beginning..."

And it goes on like this for a couple
more hours till a fat sergeant sticks
his cue-ball head around the door
and says to the dicks: "Forget this gumshoe;
I got a stiff waiting for you guys over on Hamilton-"
and from the other side of the glass, you hear him
add: "6th floor, Pacific Mercantile..."

VII

At the booking desk, they pour your property
out of a manila envelope, eye you as you strap
on your watch and count your change, make you
ask for your piece, handing it over as grudgingly
as a miser doling out money to a nephew...

FILM NOIR

And you double-check your P-I license,
making sure it's still in your wallet
before you pocket your .38 and head
for the door...

And Vivian's done exactly what you told her
over the phone: she's waiting at the corner
in a cab and she's got you ten bucks
and a flask of whisky; and you take a couple
of long pulls, shaking her off your arm
when she starts doing the nursey number,
dabbing at your eyebrow with her hankie
and cooing about your purple eye...

And you get out of the cab where the Buick's
parked and tell Vivian to go back to the office
and sit tight by the phone till you need her...

And you fire up the Buick
roar through the gates of 3730
pull right up to the front door
and lean on the bell...

*

At first glance
the black maid
knows yo' is trouble
and says: "Miz Fisher ain't home"
trying to shut the door

but you push past, asking:
"What about Mr Fisher...?"
And the maid says: "Mr John's
gone to 'Frisco dis morning..."

And you march through the hall, straight
into the drawing room, right to the fancy

BANG!

fireplace already laid with logs, trying
not to gulp like a beached carp because
you didn't dream it this plush,
and turning, you say: "I'll wait"

but the maid's bulldogging your heels, growling
'bout calling the Po-lice and you needing a bigger
thrashing than the one you already got...

and then you hear the swish of satin and her
voice saying: "That's enough, Marvel" as she
enters from the library, sheathed in a bottle green
wasp-waist number with a string of pearls, clutching
a matching purse and trailing a cloud of French perfume
that you know is real just by the way it floats up
your nose, straight into your brain...

And before you can begin, she orders an ice bag
for your head, and the brandy decanter, offers you
a seat on a leather chesterfield that welcomes you
like a grandmother's lap...

and you sink, lean back against the soft leather,
watch her light a cigarette for you from a silver
table lighter, feel the brush of her fingers as she
passes it into your hand...

And Marvel wheels in a trolley, and the ice feels
good over your eye, and the brandy slides down
into your gut like a ribbon of warmth and when
the maid's gone, she asks, "What happened to your
face, Mr Gordon?"

But you're not gonna be derailed, so you ignore
the question and ask instead if Mr Fisher owns
a gun and she says...yes – he keeps it in his study
– in the desk...

FILM NOIR

And you ask if he has business downtown
in the Pacific Mercantile Bldg.? A stockbroker
maybe...an accountant...a lawyer...?

And she thinks for a moment, pursing those perfect
Bing cherry lips, then shakes her head no-no, she
doesn't recall her husband ever saying so...

And you ask what time Mr Fisher left for 'Frisco
this morning? and she says, why, she has no idea...
So you ask what time he got up? and she says, really,
she has no idea...

And you ask why not, and she pauses a moment,
looking you straight in the eye, replying: Mr Fisher prefers a
separate bedroom... Always has...

And it's just like someone threw a switch
on you because now all you can picture
is her alone, tossing in a big wide bed,
while he's next door buried in some
butterfly book...

And before you can salvage your thoughts, she's up,
pressing a buzzer, pulling on her gloves, excusing
herself to some hoity-toity cocktail party, instructing Marvel
to draw you a bath in one of the guest rooms
and for Cook to fix whatever you'd like...

And she's gone – before you can ask about
the husband's car, before you can ask about
his business in 'Frisco, long before you can
pry that picture of her out of your mind.

VIII

The guest room is bigger than the flat
you and six others were raised in, not to

209

BANG!

mention the tub and hot water; and when you
finish, your suit's laying on the bed
waiting for you, brushed down; shoes shined,
and in the kitchen the little Filipino cook
scrambles two pair without asking and cuts
the crusts off honey-colored toast.

And between the brandy and the soak,
the ice and eggs, you feel better,
eye less swollen, teeth less loose,
but when Marvel carries in your hat
you know this fairy tale's over.

But even so, on the way to the door
you ask if Mr Fisher drove his coupe to 'Frisco?
And Marvel says: No, he rung a taxi to catch
da Limited...and then she adds: Dat coupe
belongs to Miz Fisher, anyway...

And you stop dead, and on the wall beside you
there's a portrait of the lady standing
with a horse and Marvel sees you looking
and says: Miz Fisher rides most every day...
either dat horse, or else her new one...

And she hands you a framed photo from a sideboard
full of framed photos; and there she is, holding
the bridle of some big-headed nag, dressed in a man's
suitcoat and tie, smiling out at you with those
perfect teeth, her eyes just shaded by the brim
of a man's hat...

And Marvel's saying dat horse is a Tennessee Walker
and how Miz Fisher is aiming to win some prize
with it – but all you can think of is the shape
of someone scuttling into the building wearing
a hat just like that...

FILM NOIR

And you ask: does Mr Fisher have a bum leg...
a limp, maybe... a queer walk...?

And Marvel puffs up like an ugly sculpin
and snaps: Course not! Who put dat thought
in yo' head...?

But you don't reply;
you already know the answer
as you go down the front steps to the Buick...

*

You stop at the first drug store
and drop a nickel and Vivian answers
on the 2nd ring, and you tell her
to shut up, shut up and listen, you
tell her to get hold of McIlhenney
and find out who the stiff was
on the 6th floor of the Pacific Mercantile.

And you tell her to hurry it up,
that you'll call in a couple of hours
and you hang up and get back in the car

and before you know it you're heading out
to the coast again, and the sun's setting
just like last time, and you pull off, watching
it sink into the satin pillow sea, wondering if
she's back from the party yet, picturing her
after a bath, in some red silk wrapper...

And you figure Vivian's had enough time,
so you call, but there's no answer...
so you wait ten minutes and call again
but still no answer... and the third time,
someone picks up but doesn't speak...

BANG!

IX

So you head downtown and when you turn
the corner you see police cruisers
and a meat wagon...

And you take the grimy stairs
to your office three at a time
and there are cops all over
the landing, and detectives,
and you recognize a couple
from the 5th...

And two of them way-lay you
in the hall, and ask where
you've been all day, and who
gave you the shiner, and they
make you to turn over your piece,
which they sniff like finicky pups
and pass along to some guy with glasses.

And you ask what the hell's going on,
push your way through the front office
into your own, crunching broken glass –
and they're both dead; McIlhenney through
the heart and Vivian in the back of the head...

And from what Vivian's not wearing there's no
doubt what was up; and one of the smart dicks
is saying: Shot from the other side of the glass,
and another asks: How could someone see through the bevels?
And the smart dick toes your desk lamp laying on the floor
with its neck wrung and says: Maybe this was lit...?

But to you, there's no maybe about it;
that's how Vivian liked it: afterhours,
with shadows on the wall-

FILM NOIR

And then McIlhenney's partner
shows up, along with the Precinct
captain and some brass from downtown
and a couple bowties from the DA's office,
and one of them asks you: "What have you got
to say about this?"

And you look at McIlhenney dead in your chair
with his fly buttons undone and Vivian
at his feet and you tell him the truth;
you say: "Looks like he went happy..."

And McIlhenney's partner lunges,
growling 'you bastard', swinging
at your head, but the others haul
him back and the Captain says:
"Put some cuffs on that mouthpiece..."

*

In interrogation
they start working on
theories why you'd murder
McIlhenney and for starters
they say: Revenge-
and you say, for what?
Then they say: Jealousy-
and you say, again, for what?
and then they suggest
Lovers' Triangle –
and you say, why would
I wait three years...?

And they look at you
like chimps at the zoo,
and you say: Yeah, that's right,
three years – he wasn't no saint...

BANG!

And they gotta admit your gun's
clean; and no one in your building's
seen you around for days, nor at
the corner diner, nor over at Jakes...

And you say: you got nothing...
and they want to know where you were
all day, so you tell them you drove
up to Topanga Beach to see the sights
and you were just stopping to pick up
the mail when you saw the melee...

And they want some witnesses and you shrug,
and they ask about your eye again, and you
tell them you tripped on a curb real bad...

Then they put you in a cell
with a couple of bums who mumble
you to sleep and the next thing you know
they're clanging back the door and telling you
it's check-out time...

X

After a night on that bunk
you drive straight to your rooms,
wash, shave, change clothes, promise
Mrs Mihjac through the door that you'll
be squaring up tomorrow.

And they've snagged your piece as evidence
so you lift a floorboard, pull out a .32
Smith and Wesson, a hammerless little honey
that slips into your pocket without a bulge

and in a different diner, where you're just
another joe, you order the meatloaf and when

a newsy comes in pushing the late morning edition
you see McIlhenney's made the headlines but what
you really want is on pg. 2:

PACIFIC MERCANTILE BODY IDENTIFIED:
Well-known Attorney found shot dead
City Desk: Police have identified
the man found shot to death in his
6th floor office as Warren J.
Orloff, 58, a man known to the public more for his philanthropy and
good-works than for his professional
career.
 Orloff was apparently working late
at his desk when he was shot in the
back of the head at close range by
one or more unknown assailants.
 Police are unable to state a clear
motive for the crime, although robbery has been discounted because numerous valuable works of art displayed
in the office remained untouched.
 Orloff, originally of New York City,
had a distinguished career at
the New York Bar before moving west,
where he became far better known for
great generosity to many civic parks
and libraries, as well as endowing
other institutions of higher culture.

And you push your plate aside,
lean back in the booth
considering...

considering...

while the waitress refills

BANG!

your mug, recites a trilogy
of pies, tucks your slip
under your plate after you
shake your head no...

and you leave a dime tip,
go out to the car, drive
across town to her place,
making the turns without
thinking, realizing how
this trip's become a habit...

*

You pull through the gates of 3730
and ring the bell, but no one answers
so you ring it again, and no one answers,
so you open the door and step inside...
walk across the foyer...

And you stop there

stand still...

listening...

but the house is quiet...

...eerie quiet,

and you stand longer...

And your gut goes over in a knot
and the skin on the back of your head
tightens because you know she's here somewhere
and if you're right, she's already killed three people
and she thinks you're one of them...

FILM NOIR

The french windows to the terrace are open
and you step out, start down the steps toward
the pool when her voice stops you–
"Why, Mr Gordon, what a surprise…"

And she comes down behind you, wrapped
in the same red silk you dreamed about,
in a cloud of that perfume, her hair
brushed back different somehow, her eyes bright…

and she comes straight to you, close,
asking: "Care for a swim…?"

And as she walks toward the pool, she slips
the silk from her shoulders, trailing it behind
like a broken wing, trailing it like a stain
of blood on the jungle path…

and you watch her measured walk, the sway
of her hips as she slides into the green shade
under the shifting palms, and every word you
rehearsed is gone, and you know better but you
follow anyway, watch her drop the silk, stand
for a moment on the pool's lip before she
dives in and swims the length and back.

And there's a towel on the chaise
and you're holding it when she climbs out,
walks toward you, turns, lets you drape it
around her shoulders…

and your hands linger…

…and she's so close that every thought
you had of blackmailing her, every thought
of squealing on her vanishes, and all you
can feel is her body pressing into yours
and your heart jackhammering your ribs…

BANG!

...and she turns in your arms, smiling,
offering up those ruby lips like some
exotic fruit...

and you bend forward...taste her kiss...taste it
just the way you tasted your first communion wine
at St. Ignatius...closing your eyes...holding your breath...
knowing Father Schwartz, Christ, and the Holy Mother
– all three – were watching you, watching you just
the way she is now...

Just the way she is now.

The sound of the shot is muffled
between your bodies and you don't
even recognize it at first, just feel
the kick as your own bullet tears up
through your gut, into your lungs...

And then you're staggering backward
to the edge of the pool, trying to catch
your breath, mouthing the word 'why?'
because you've got a hundred questions
and time's running...

And her eyes have gone dark and she's
whispering how sorry she is for making
you a decoy but she had to kill Orloff,
...recognized her from New York, remembered
a hat-check girl he'd once prosecuted
for picking pockets...blackmail...
going to tell Fisher...

...everything would be gone...
the clothes...horses...ruined...
she couldn't let it happen...

couldn't go back to that life...

FILM NOIR

watching the swells...
angling for their tips...
trying to make ends...

And while you're still staggering
she laughs...
says now she won't have to...
says she's fixed it...
framed her husband... used his gun on Orloff
...they'd just quarreled over some
rare book, anyway-

Some stupid rare book-
Books – her husband's only passion...
only thing he loves...
only thing he takes to bed...

And as your knees buckle
she steps closer, fires again...

and the lead catches you high in the chest,
spinning you backward, and as you fall
into the pool that old white hot fear
flashes through your veins and you realize
it'll be a crapshoot whether you drown first
or bleed to death...

And as you start to sink, you picture her
that first day, in that black suit, with those
red lips; and you can see yourself coming up
the stairs to your office, and Vivian giving
you the look, and how you waltzed in, dropping
your hat on the blotter, figuring your customer
would be some dame with a grudge against her old man...

And now, as things dim, you realize
that you had it figured right, all along.

Neon Graveyard

Melissa Pleckham

Until I laid eyes on him, I never knew how quiet death could be — how it could sneak up on you before you ever heard it coming and lay you out cold on the slab. I guess I thought it would announce itself somehow, like there'd be some fanfare. But when it finally happened, the only sound was the wire pulled taught as a guitar string around my neck, and the rhythmic hum of the neon pulsing on and off.

You had to laugh, you know? At how ridiculous it all was. How silly death turned out to be.

When my eyes closed for the last time those glowing shapes exploded on the backs of my lids like fireworks in Vegas. They were gauche — tacky. I thought everything would be so much darker.

I never knew death could be so bright.

*

He walked into my office in a tailored suit and hat, like he should be flickering on a big screen in black and white and not there in the flesh in a tiny little strip mall in an ugly corner of North Hollywood between a dingy Thai restaurant with great lunch specials and a disreputable massage parlor that was always getting raided by the cops. His face was angular but his lips looked soft. His cheeks and chin were darkened with stubble. And he smelled good — real good. Like stale cigarettes, whiskey, and incense. My one weakness has always been a good-smelling man.

"You open?" he asked, taking off his hat and closing the

door behind him. His hair was slicked back, save for one errant lock that kept escaping like a secret he couldn't quite keep.

I chewed on my tea tree oil toothpick and smirked up at him. "I try not to make it a habit, but you caught me off guard." I gestured to the sagging green sofa oozing stuffing on the other side of my desk, but he ignored me and walked toward the window.

"I've never met a female P.I. before." He said it low, like a come on. I bristled, annoyed and aroused in equal measure.

"Don't get out much? It's not 1942 anymore. Us 'broads' have jobs nowadays."

"Don't get hot," he said, slipping two fingers between the horizontal blinds and parting them to peer outside. "I like it. I'd prefer a woman." The Thai place had a huge neon lotus right outside my window that lit up the office day and night if I didn't keep the blinds closed, and it made his handsome face glow pink, then red, then pink, then red as he stared out at the cracked pavement of the dusty parking lot, the power lines that sizzled across the sky, the cars driving by on Sherman Way. The afternoon was becoming evening fast. The sun would drop into the Pacific any minute now, somewhere on the other side of that hill that separates the city of angels from this little valley of devils.

"You know what the lotus symbolizes, don't you?" he asked, his eyes staring straight ahead. "Purity. And resurrection." His lips pulled back in a dangerous grin and I felt my stomach drop, felt an ache in my knees that burned all the way up my thighs.

I was tired of being at his mercy. Time to cut to the chase.

"What do you need me for?"

He pulled his fingers out of the blinds slowly and turned towards me, smiling. "There's going to be a murder."

I narrowed my eyes at him. "Tell me what I need to know."

Taking his time, he came over and perched on the edge of my desk, so close I could hear the ticking of his wristwatch. He had a way of moving slowly in small spaces that made them feel bigger than they were — suddenly my tiny office was Union Station. Then he reached out toward me, and my hand shot out to grab his wrist just as he fished a toothpick out of the antique silver holder I kept near the blotter on my desk. The toothpicks clattered to the floor but I held his gaze until he started to laugh. His eyeeteeth gleamed vampire-sharp.

"Ms. P.I.," he breathed. "What's your name anyhow? It's not on the door."

He pulled his arm up and I rose with it and he yanked me toward him and put his soft lips on mine. He tasted like trouble. My favorite flavor.

I whispered my name into his mouth, then covered it with mine again. Funny — I never thought to ask for his before we fell onto the sofa that all too often had a nasty habit of becoming a bed.

Outside, the neon lotus pulsed pink and red all night, the blinds slicing through the colors like knives.

*

He had a story, of course. Everyone who walked through my door had a story. Something about a shady deal to turn a profit by selling a floundering business, and his associate-turned-adversary who was going to frame him for murder so he'd be out of the way with no claim on the dough. He'd sussed out the plan though, and he wanted me to help him nail the guy before the murder could happen.

It was a flimsy story, but I was a flimsy woman and I took him on — in every way I could. We spent a week driving all over the Valley in his burgundy 1970 Porsche 911S, a gorgeous car the color of dried blood. I wish I could say the engine was the only thing that purred every time he stroked his gear shift, but I was smitten as a school kid.

We cased joints together, following the fat man with the mustache so thin it looked like it was ashamed to be on his lip who he said was his would-be killer through the shoulder-high stacks at the used bookstore in Burbank, the one with the mural of writers and movie stars on the back wall. I had him at Hemingway, but I'd lost him by Greta Garbo, foiled by one of the bookstore's resident cats, who wound her way between my ankles and sent me spinning into a stack of sci-fi. Outside, in the parking lot, he kissed me. He kissed me that day like he really cared about me.

We tailed the redhead in the green velvet turban who he said was the fat man's wife, sending the Porsche soaring down narrow alleys and wide residential streets with leafy trees standing sentinel until we finally hit Cahuenga and rode it halfway to the Hollywood Bowl, taking the turn up to Mulholland where the lights of the city glittered on the dark hillsides like diamonds tossed into dirt. Later, in the Porsche, with the city stretched all sluggish before us like a starlet with a benzo problem, he kissed me. He kissed me that night like he really wanted me.

At the end of each day, we'd show up, starving, to a local restaurant for dinner, realizing we hadn't had anything but black coffee for hours. We had pizza and red wine at the Italian place painted to look like a vineyard, green plastic vines snaking along the peeling stucco walls. We had tamales and margaritas, blended ice cold with so much tequila we could hardly see straight, at the Mexican place with the crimson vinyl booths and Christmas lights on Ventura. One night we even ended up on the other side of the hill, and for our troubles he treated us both to steaks so rare our plates looked like crime scenes and martinis so strong they came with a second glass to hold all the booze, at the oldest restaurant in Hollywood. Later, when his lips touched mine, I let myself believe in love.

He wasn't the first client I'd slept with. But he was the only client who ever kissed me like that. He was the only man who ever kissed me like he meant it.

I forgot myself. I forgot my work.

I forgot that men can be a lot of things, but no matter who they are or how they kiss, they can always, always be cruel.

*

So that night in my office as I stared out the window at the cerulean twilight lapping up the last of the Valley dusk, I never heard Death sneaking up behind me, never felt the whisper of his lips on my ear as he stood up close against me and slipped the wire around my neck, pulled it taut, stole the breath from my lungs and the light from my eyes. The lotus outside burned neon pink, red, pink, red. I struggled, but not much. Why bother?

"I hope you take him for all he's worth, baby." I tried to say it, but it was already too late. I didn't have a breath left in me to push out even one single word. I could feel his smirk against my cheek though; I think he knew what I was trying to say.

Satisfied with his handiwork, he kissed my lips, already cooling, one last time and then slipped out quietly, the deed complete. He had a friend to frame, or maybe just a quick getaway to make. As for me, my eyes were empty, save for the tiny neon lotus pulsing in each dark pupil. I did not blink.

I only wondered why he'd waited so long. Why did he need the week? Why didn't he do it that first day?

Why does any predator play with its prey? It'd be easier just to end it quick. But I guess the game is part of the hunt. Maybe the best part.

That's not for the prey to know. But take it from me: If you end up being hunted, you're one of the lucky ones if you enjoy the feeling of those jaws around your throat.

Fortunately for me, I did.

*

I'm still not sure about the particulars of his plan. I'm still not sure who they were — the fat man with the thin mustache, the redhead in the green velvet turban. They didn't like the looks of us, that's for sure, but I'll never know if they actually were who he said they were. I'll never know who they were to him, or if they meant anything to him at all. Of course, you could say the same for me.

If I'd stopped to think — if I'd been able to think at all — I probably would have seen the warning signs: The way he drove too fast, kissed too hard, laughed too loud, stared too long. The way his eyes looked when he watched me. Like a wild animal on a fraying leash, like he didn't quite belong in those suits, in that car. Who knows where they'd come from. They could've been ripped off from a dead man just as easily as they could've been his from day one.

I am sure of one thing though: Wherever he is now, whatever steering wheel he's behind, whatever name some woman is breathing in his ear, he's doing alright. This world is a shipwreck and men like him are survivors. Women like me? We're just the leaking life rafts they ride back to shore.

*

As for death? I never heard it coming. And I thought it would be darker, I'll admit that. But that neon burned my eyes and seared my brain until it was all I could see, until it was all that I was. Until there was nothing else left. Darkness? I'd have prayed for it, maybe. If I'd been the praying type.

The lotus blinked on and off, spilling cheap red light through the window and into the spreading pool of blood beneath my garroted throat, shining even cheaper than the neon there on the dirty floor. Purity. Resurrection. There would be none for me. Not that I'd ever expected it.

I did think it'd be darker though.

You had to laugh, you know?

Fifty Shades of Maigret

Rhys Hughes

When Detective Chief Inspector Maigret returned to his office on Quai des Orfèvres he found Lucas pacing the room in agitation. Maigret puffed placidly on his pipe and waited for Lucas to speak. "A man came to see you when you were out."

"Where is he?" asked Maigret.

"He refused to wait here. Said that he felt more nervous inside the building. He went to the Brasserie Dauphin and is waiting there."

"Anyone with him?"

"No, and he insisted that you come alone."

"What is he like?"

Lucas seemed strangely embarrassed. "Expensively dressed in an elegant manner. He is a highly trained manservant who works for an old aristocrat. That's all he was willing to state about himself. He was very reticent."

"And he said nothing about why he wishes to see me?"

Lucas blushed. "Not much."

"But something at least? What was it?"

Lucas swallowed and averted his eyes. "He has information about a crime of perverted desires. He mentioned chains and whips."

Maigret raised his eyebrows slightly then shrugged. Nothing could truly surprise him at his age, after all his experience, but Lucas was still young, callow, not yet jaded by relentless exposure to the darker side of life. "I see."

"What are you thinking?"

"Nothing!" boomed Maigret. He tapped out his pipe against his heel, turned and strode out of the office and along

227

the corridors to the main doors that led onto the street. "When will they learn that I don't think?" he muttered.

It was a dull afternoon in October and a fine rain was falling.

He reached the Brasserie Dauphin and ordered a beer before looking around. While he was lifting the glass to his mouth he felt a respectful tap on his shoulder. He took a gulp first and then glanced at the owner of the hand that had tried to attract his attention. A tall man in archaic clothes, his bearing ramrod straight but his facial muscles slack. The retainer of some eccentric comte or duc, his soul stuck in a previous century. He beckoned to a tiny table with two vacant chairs and Maigret shrugged.

He followed the tall man to the table and they sat down. The tall man tried to shake his hand over the vase in the centre of the table but Maigret ignored the gesture and gulped more beer. The tall man withdrew his hand and smiled.

"It is an honour to meet you. I am Ferdinand Freluquet."

Maigret merely grunted.

Ferdinand was flustered but did his best to retain his self-control. "I have followed, of course, many of your cases in the newspapers. I know what an incisive mind you have. The crimes you have solved are numberless!"

"My mind is irrelevant," snapped Maigret, wiping his mouth with a cloth. "You told my inspector that you want to report a crime?"

"Ah, straight to the point, I see. I don't exactly want to report a crime. I mean, if it goes through official channels then considerable difficulties might arise for my master. My loyalty to him is total. I was hoping for secrecy."

"Who is your master? What is his name?"

"I am not at liberty to say."

Maigret stood and began to walk out. Alarmed, Ferdinand shot out of his chair, caught up with him and whispered sharply, "Piqueur!"

"What do you mean?"

"The Marquis de Piqueur is my master."

Maigret hesitated for a moment, then turned and sat back down, signalling the waiter to bring him another beer.

Ferdinand heaved a sigh of relief and ordered a glass of troussepinette from one of the obscure dusty bottles on the shelves behind the bar, a bottle that surely hadn't been opened for half a century or more.

Maigret feigned indifference but was carefully watching Ferdinand's reactions when he sipped the strange liqueur. Then he said:

"I don't know him."

Ferdinand winced, recovered himself quickly, smiled. "Very few do. He prefers to keep himself to himself. He values his privacy."

"How long have you been working for your employer?"

"The Marquis de Piqueur took me on when I was eighteen years old. I rose through the ranks of servants until I achieved my present position. He is a secretive man but he confides fully in me. I know all his business."

"Can you be absolutely certain of that?"

Ferdinand spilled a little of his drink and coughed. Maigret drained his beer, fixed the servant with a penetrating stare and waited for him to recover his wits. His expression was stern as he added, "Tell me about the chains."

Ferdinand seemed to shrink into himself and Maigret almost wanted to laugh. Not that he enjoyed making the servant uncomfortable but it must be admitted that these oleaginous people, lackeys of the anachronistic nobility, had nobody to blame but themselves when the modern world declined to offer them the privilege of discretion. Maigret decided to press his advantage just a little further. "And the whips."

Ferdinand licked his lips and said, "That inspector of yours wouldn't promise to pass on my message to you unless I told him something about what I wanted to discuss. It is essential that I secure your help. So I told him."

"But you didn't tell him very much, I gather."

Ferdinand pushed aside his glass of troussepinette and his sagging face drooped lower, as if the flesh were about to slide off the bones, before he replied, in a steady enough voice with words that had obviously been rehearsed:

"My master is a man of honour but he is also a man of desires. That's the truest sort of man, isn't it? To be pulled in different directions at the same time by duty and needs. He has always been wealthy and able to pay for the fulfilment of his passions, no matter how strange those passions might be. But he has ethics!"

"I don't follow you," said Maigret, filling his pipe.

"He has a conscience!"

"In my experience even the lowest criminal has a conscience or at least the remnants of one. That information is of limited use. You are trying to tell me that the Marquis de Piqueur is a pervert of some kind. Lately he has been growing anxious about something. And now he wants to soothe his agitation but escape the consequences of his actions, whatever they might be, at the same time. This isn't unusual."

"You don't understand. He didn't ask me to speak to you."

"Ah, that was your idea, was it?"

"Yes. My idea. I see the torment in my master's soul. I know he is a good man at heart. I want to help save him from an unfair fate."

Maigret inserted his pipe between his teeth, bit down to hold it in place, struck a match and lit the tobacco. Then he took the pipe out and forgot about it until it went out. He used the bowl to aid his gestures while Ferdinand pouted.

"French aristocrats are renowned for perversity and warped eroticism. The question that really ought to concern us is whether a criminal offence has been committed or not. You must be perfectly candid with me, hold nothing back."

"I am finding it difficult."

"Of course! If it was easy would you have even bothered?"

Ferdinand frowned at this question.

He said, "My master likes to be dominant in amorous activities. He therefore requires a woman to be submissive. Whether she enjoys being submissive in a physical sense is besides the point. He cares only that submission elevates her soul. Sometimes, how shall I put it? She is not fully aware that her soul is rejoicing."

"Is there coercion involved? Answer me directly."

"No. Yes. It's tricky."

Maigret indicated to the waiter for another beer. Feeling mischievous he also ordered a second troussepinette for Ferdinand, who shuddered when it arrived. Maigret was staring at him but the set of his features was placid.

"There is a rather large Château just outside Paris."

"There are many of them."

"To the northeast, in Roissy, in a quiet spot. The grounds are extensive. The walls are solid. If something should happen inside the house it would be quite impossible for anyone outside to hear anything. Do you understand?"

Maigret said nothing but nodded and lit his extinguished pipe.

Ferdinand continued, "This Château is the location of a sort of unique club, a society of men who are emotionally similar to my master."

"Perverts?" ventured Maigret.

"Dominants," said Ferdinand haughtily.

"Husbands beat wives all too frequently and then they apologise. The apology doesn't really compensate for the bruises. But when a pervert ties up his mistress and whips her until her backside resembles a musical stave or – " and at this point Maigret smiled, " – the bars of a prison cell, then all he is required to do is hug her and stroke her hair and provide emotional comfort and everything is considered in balance once again. What is the difference between a domestic wife beater and a 'dominant'?"

"Consent! And love! The intensity of passion! You can hardly compare them! The first is brutal and primitive. The latter is…" Ferdinand frowned and was unable to find words to explain what he regarded as simple truth.

Maigret wiped the foam of beer from his lips.

"Do you believe that too, or are you speaking merely for the benefit of your master? A woman who allows herself to be beaten, no matter the reason, is failing to do her social duty. This doesn't mean we can't have sympathy, but nothing works in isolation. Violence degrades all existence. It is never simply contained."

Ferdinand gave a little start, an involuntary jerk, and it was clear he was having some difficulty reconciling the Maigret who sat before him with the image of the Detective Chief Inspector he had carried in his mind. There had never been any indication from anything he had read or heard that this august policeman was interested in the philosophy of judgement. On the contrary, he had been expressly informed that Maigret had almost infinite reserves of understanding when it came to the complexities of life. Shrugging his shoulders to express a nonchalance he did not feel, Ferdinand said:

"There is my own social duty, of course, and it might conflict with the personal desires of individuals I generally consider superb."

"A loyal servant but one with a powerful conscience?"

"That's correct. Why not?"

Maigret smiled a little. He was enjoying himself more than he supposed he ought to. It had been one of those dull summers full of petty crimes and unimaginative transgressions. If Ferdinand was reliable and truthful and something vicious had taken place in the Château in Roissy then the run of nothing but petty thievery and drunken prostitution might be over. All of them at Quai des Orfèvres were in need of something more exciting and exacting, all felt the same way. Lucas was listless, Lapointe restless, Torrence had practically gone to seed. A sadistic aristocrat might reinvigorate his men.

But most of all, Maigret himself needed a change.

"This master of yours is the sort of man one finds in the novels of De Sade. But how far does he really go? In criminal terms?"

"Not too far, yet. That's why I am here. Because I suspect he is on the verge of crossing the line from, let us say, unusual activity to dangerous practices, and I mean dangerous for the women he deals with and also for himself."

"Why," asked Maigret, finishing his beer, "do I get the impression that you are far more concerned with the 'danger' to the Marquis de Piqueur?" He shut his eyes for a moment, and the muscles of his face seemed to turn to stone. Then he opened his lids and his face softened but he remained somewhat aloof, distant.

Ferdinand inclined his head. "You are right, of course."

"Give me the names of the women."

Ferdinand jerked back in his chair, the legs scraping the floor with a squeal. "But that is information I don't possess. They are anonymous to me. There are many of them, I'm unsure how many in total. At least two dozen."

"Prostitutes, I gather?"

"Never. My master would never pay for flesh. He prefers volunteers and– Women who are not quite volunteers but– They aren't abductees, that would be going too far. They tend to become reconciled to their situation."

The foam dissolved at the bottom of Maigret's glass and he felt his own feelings vanish in a similar manner. He had no opinions whatsoever on anything that Ferdinand had told him but the law was the law and there were very definite steps to be taken. He sighed as he asked the servant for the address of the Château.

"It's in Roissy."

"I know that!" thundered Maigret.

The glasses on the table sang in response to his bellow. Ferdinand turned the colour of the troussepinette he had drunk. Then he blushed furiously but his lips opened and he spoke a precise address in a rasping voice.

The Detective Chief Inspector wrote it down in a notebook.

He stood and turned to leave.

"Don't hurt him," croaked Ferdinand.

Maigret didn't look back.

The Château in Roissy was set in extensive grounds and these grounds were surrounded by a high wall and there was only one gate to facilitate entry. Torrence grumbled as he climbed the ladder that had been found by Maigret in one of the dustiest and most obscure storerooms at the Quai des

Orfèvres. The rungs were rotten and threatened to break under his considerable weight. He hissed down, "Hold it steady!"

Lapointe lifted a finger to his lips. There was ironic laughter in his expression but the shadows were dense around him and Torrence saw nothing of his face. To make matters even worse, the rain, which had stopped, began again, and Torrence's hands, already slick with his sweat, found gripping the wood difficult.

Maigret had given this job to them because he had seen how bored they were. They had accepted with enthusiasm, but approaching the Château at midnight they had seen that getting access wasn't going to be so easy. The wall was higher than anticipated and the ladder unsafe and it didn't even reach to the top of the wall. Torrence would have to stretch up as high as he could to grip the coping. He was a tall man, dwarfing Lapointe, but very heavy and there was a question about his ability to haul himself up. At the moment, he was halfway to the top and the ladder was bending under the strain.

"Keep going," urged Lapointe, and Torrence growled.

"What do you think I'm doing?"

He reached the topmost rung and raised his long arms vertically above him. His hands closed on the rough stone of the coping. He said, "I can't pull myself up without help. Give me a push from below. Hurry up."

Lapointe climbed the ladder until he was directly beneath Torrence. Then he cupped his hands in order to push his colleague's shoes when he jumped off the ladder. Torrence counted to three in a low voice and said, "Heave!"

At the same time he jumped and did his best to pull himself onto the top of the wall. As Lapointe pushed, the ladder finally gave way. It was already bent severely out of shape, like a rattan cane after years of being swished against posteriors. Now it snapped with a report like a pistol shot and Lapointe tumbled down.

But Torrance was straddling the wall. He had successfully propelled his vast bulk onto the coping. Slowly he began to stand, his knees audibly creaking with the strain. His strength was enormous but his agility left something to be desired. Finally he achieved his objective, sweat streaming from his broad forehead.

Standing on the top of the wall, he began to wobble and flung out his arms to keep his balance. With his bulging stomach his silhouette resembled the new moon seen through an old telescope, the shimmering air distorting the image. Lapointe was picking himself up and dusting himself down. He said, "Careful."

No sooner had he spoken the word than part of the coping gave way and Torrence fell on the other side of the wall. Always professional, he uttered nothing more than a very faint groan as he collided with the lawn. Lapointe wondered if he had made a crater but kept this question to himself. He waited and listened.

"I'm fine," said Torrence.

"Follow the plan and do it quietly."

"Of course I will."

Lapointe heard the burly man lurch across the lawn. It was incredible that nobody in the house had heard them. Maybe they were too occupied with their own affairs to notice strange noises in the garden. Lapointe settled himself for a long wait. He sat down next to a shattered length of ladder and squinted at his wristwatch.

He had been instructed to give Torrence one hour and if he hadn't heard from him after that time, he would report back to the Quai des Orfèvres and Maigret would attempt to secure a search warrant from a magistrate. Then the police would arrive in numbers at the gate and a formal investigation would commence. Until then, they had to proceed with their unorthodox methods. It was thrilling and also farcical.

Back in his office at the Quai des Orfèvres, Maigret was working on a new case, that of a gang of bank robbers, and in his mind he had almost completely dismissed the relevance of Ferdinand Freluquet, the Marquis de Piqueur and the Château at Roissy. All that was properly a case for the Vice

Squad anyway, and he regretted giving the bombastic servant his word of honour that he would handle it himself.

But he was sure his men were coping admirably.

He was expecting Lapointe to be the one to climb the ladder and Torrence to remain on the ground to hold it steady, and when he received a telephone call later explaining what had happened, he was close to being astonished for the first time in years. What really motivated him to take events at Roissy more seriously, however, was a minor incident with his pipe. The world often turns on the most trivial signs.

But that is for later...

Torrence hugged the shadows of trees and bushes as he made his way closer to the imposing Château and when he reached the wall he leaned against it and caught his breath. There were lights in all the windows but no sounds reached him. He cautiously peered through one pane of glass and found himself staring into an empty room, sumptuously decorated. He tried the window but it was bolted. He began to make a circuit of the house, testing every window he passed. All the rooms seemed to be empty.

The Château was asymmetrical in shape and it took him a long time to reach the rear of the building. Here at last he found an unlighted window, a small round porthole, and nothing of the room beyond revealed itself to his eye. He tested it and found that it swung open on a hinge. The problem was squeezing his bulk through it. He sucked in his stomach and pushed himself through, and to his surprise he found himself in a smooth chute that sloped down at an increasingly steep angle. He felt panic but it was too late, he was already sliding along and accelerating. He prayed that the chute would remain wide enough to permit him to reach the end. He hated the idea of being stuck for hours or even days in a confined space. With an odd slurping sound, the chute disgorged him into a dimly lit chamber underground. He staggered to his feet, blinked at the damp darkness.

He was in a cellar of some kind, probably the place where wines had once been stored, but now it was devoted to another purpose. What exactly that purpose was, he was unable to discern, but he had a sudden uneasy feeling. The illumination came from patches of faintly glowing slime mould on the damp walls.

He floundered around in the room, hands groping for support. There had to be an exit that would take him up into the main part of the house. He supposed the chute had originally been designed for casks of wine and he found himself wishing he would stumble over some vintage that had been forgotten among the cobwebs by the occupants. He desperately needed a drink. He stumbled and fell to his knees. There was something solid ahead of him and he pushed at it with his fingers. It swung open. Another porthole on a hinge? He supposed it might lead somewhere more salubrious than this curious subterranean grotto. Again he sucked in his stomach, propelled himself as best he could forward, but then there was a click and a twang, as if a hidden spring had been activated, and he was gripped around the waist.

Some mechanism had come into play. He was trapped.

Shouting was out of the question.

He would have to wait for the designated hour to pass. Then Lapointe would summon reinforcements from the Quai des Orfèvres.

It was an uncomfortable situation to be in, but not a disaster. He sighed and vowed that in future he would be satisfied to be bored in the office. Then he heard a door open and gruff voices filled the room. "Bring the women!"

He listened to the shuffling of feet and the scrape on stone of what might be chains. He breathed as quietly as he could manage.

"Fix them in the stocks quickly. We are late."

The creak of wood and the twang of more springs, suppressed moans and gasps. Much to his alarm a hand began prodding his rump.

"This one is already occupied. Who is responsible?"

Nobody answered the query.

"No matter. Get her undressed. She appears to be wearing trousers. A new girl, I guess. But make haste! Piqueur is coming."

Torrance felt a sudden breeze as the cloth of his trousers was cut from him with a knife and whoever held the blade made no attempt to be gentle. He bit his lip to stop himself from whimpering. Now there was disgust in one of the voices. "What huge hips on this one! And such hairy buttocks! It is wrong."

"Maybe an error was made in the procurement?"

"We will check later."

"Proceed anyway," said a more tolerant voice.

The door opened again.

"Messieurs, Piqueur has arrived!"

The new arrival spoke in deep rich tones. He was authoritative and confident, clearly a man highly respected amongst this fraternity. There was humour in his inflection too, but also cruelty under the humour. Torrence, unable to see him, feared him. He nearly blew his cover by shouting out that he was a policeman.

But he understood how dangerous that course of action might be. What if they decided to kill him and dispose of his body? Even if the officers of the Quai des Orfèvres turned up and raided the Château, it would be too late for him. He had been shot before while working on cases and had survived. But luck is rationed in this world, he knew. He had little desire to take any more unnecessary risks. And so–

He would put up with any indignity that came his way.

Piqueur said, "Bring the brazier."

The illumination in the chamber increased slightly.

It was an unsteady glow produced by the flickering flames of live coals. Torrence felt the heat and perspiration slicked his bare buttocks until they gleamed despite their hairiness. What horrors did these unseen men intend to inflict on him? And there were women next to him, all arranged in a line, all secured in stocks.

They remained silent, probably on pain of a greater punishment. Maybe they liked what was happening. Some people are very strange. Torrence was a conventional man. To be taken for a woman was bad enough, to be shackled and tormented was beyond his understanding. It was a hazard of the job, true enough, but one he had never anticipated. To be held hostage by gangsters, yes, but not this. No, not this.

"Bring me a selection of canes," ordered Piqueur.

There was a murmur of delight.

"For those of you new to the club," he added, "allow me to welcome you to our regular music night. I invented this pastime a few years ago and it has proved to be very popular. My hope is that you will enjoy it as much as I do. I have a preference for the old songs and today we will be experiencing a very beautiful piece of music composed by Bertran de Born nearly eight hundred years ago. Thank you."

Even his politeness was menacing, Torrence realised.

"Let us begin," said Piqueur.

There was a loud swishing sound, a sharp crack and a muffled sob. One of the women was being beaten with a cane. Probably the first woman in line. More strokes of the cane now followed, four of them, making five in total. "She's done," said Piqueur. "Move onto the next and be a little firmer, if you please."

The swishing was louder, the sobs too.

"That's better. The stave really has to stand out on their skin. How can we have music if the stave can't be seen clearly? We won't know where the notes are. Hit harder. The second is done. Now proceed with the third."

Torrence judged that he was in the middle of the line. It would be his turn soon enough. To be whacked five times with a cane was bad but he believed he could endure it without too much trouble. It was a test of stamina.

"The welts are coming up bright and scarlet..."

Men were taking it in turns to perform the caning and so far they seemed relentless and muscular. Torrence hoped that a kinder or weaker man, if any were present, would administer his punishment, but he was to be disappointed in this regard. When his turn came, the contact of the rattan on his buttocks was agonising.

He was shocked. The force of the blow was unbelievable.

"Look at that. It hasn't even left a mark!"

"Hit her harder then."

"Such a vast expanse of rump! I think that the force of the impact is being reduced over the larger area. Ripples of fat are distributing the energy and preventing welts. She's too large to be caned effectively in this game."

"What nonsense is that?" shouted Piqueur. "Give the cane to me! I will not tolerate any discrimination in this chamber. See!"

Torrence felt pain even more excruciating than before. Piqueur hit him again and again without mercy. He trembled all over.

"Still no welts," said a voice.

Piqueur muttered an oath, then said, "She's a tough one."

"I already told you that."

"Silence! We will soften her up with a paddle."

The pad of feet as someone rushed off to fetch the implement in question. He was soon back and Piqueur was thanking him. Torrence wasn't sure what a paddle was, but he was able to work it out by sensation alone. A circular board on a short handle, punctured with holes in order to minimise air resistance.

It was like a diabolical table tennis bat.

And now it connected with his flesh. The noise was a fantastic concerto of thunderbolts in distant narrow valleys. Torrence felt sure it must be audible all over Roissy. It slapped him again and again, harder and harder.

Piqueur was losing patience with the world.

He spanked in a frenzy.

Torrence gritted his teeth. The pain was abominable, but beneath the pain a new feeling was rising, some sort of peculiar ecstasy, still in embryonic form but expanding, flooding him through every cell of his tormented body.

The sight of the spanking had clearly excited one of the other men in the chamber, who asked Piqueur to desist for a moment while he relieved himself in Torrence's buttock crack, a procedure that was greeted with approving murmurs. Then Piqueur returned to the fray, froth pouring from his frenzied mouth and spattering on his victim's posterior, while he attempted to tenderise the meat of the inspector's behind.

"Hurler comme un cochon!"

But his efforts were mostly in vain. Only after he paused for a rest and resumed work, a battering even more savage than before, was he rewarded with the sight of dark blue bruising developing on the expanse of rump.

"Her haunches are almost mythological," he gasped.

But success was his. He said:

"Now we can try caning her again. Ready?"

He swapped the bruising paddle for the cutting length of rattan.

It swished and bit deep.

Torrence wanted to howl, but he wasn't sure whether with horror or joy, perhaps both, yet at the same time he vowed vengeance beneath his breath. There were dark pleasures but there was also the law. He knew, ultimately, which side he was on. After the five blows, the caning proceeded down the line.

All the women in the stocks now had five bars of burning red embossed on their rears and these bars resembled a musical stave.

Piqueur's voice came again, "Now to add the notes."

A bellows was pumped.

The illumination in the chamber turned from red to orange.

The heat of flames scorched his legs.

Torrence suddenly realised what was about to happen.

It was worse than criminal.

It was outrageous!

Piqueur, in honour of his music night, intended to brand the women with a hot poker, a devilish method of writing sheet music. Then when all the notes of the Bertran de Born song were in place, he would lead the choir of perverts in their rendition, reading the music off the bums as required. Each posterior represented one bar of the song. Torrence had taken piano lessons when he was a boy. He wondered how complex the music of this old song would be. He hoped there weren't too many notes.

The branding began and now it was more difficult for the women to muffle their howls but nonetheless they did their best to keep quiet. Plainly, they had been warned that to scream would result in even worse punishment.

They soon reached Torrence and amid the stench of burning flesh he heard the voice of the monstrous Marquis, "Now we come to the most complicated passage. Lots of chords here and plenty of grace notes. But pass me the paddle again. This girl needs more softening up, I think. She seems incredibly resilient."

Another man requested a pause in the beating so that he could relieve himself between the mighty buttocks. He did so and the sight excited first another man and then another, who followed his example. Torrence was sticky and sore and thoroughly degraded when Piqueur resumed the paddling. He stifled a sob.

The paddling was followed by the branding.

His entire body pulsed like a heart.

Torrence felt light headed.

The real world seemed to be slipping away and he was sure he was entering some new plane of existence. He wanted to giggle.

The singing began. He strained his ears to listen.

There was a ringing in his skull but the beautiful melody still came through to him and he nodded in time to the rhythm.

He was more than half delirious by now.

And enjoying himself.

Maigret picked up the telephone, listened with a frown to Lapointe, then said, "Wait near the gates. I will be there soon enough."

He shook his head as he struggled to make sense of the news. It was Torrence who had climbed the wall and tried to break into the Château. What had the pair been thinking? As he reflected on the poor judgement of his own inspectors in this instance, the pipe stem snapped between his clenched teeth. It made a sound like a whip as it broke and abruptly his attitude to the case changed and hardened.

He reached for a telephone directory on the edge of his desk, consulted it but found no address for the Marquis de Piqueur. He stood and went to his bookshelves and leafed through a book on French aristocrats. There was no mention of the name. He returned to his desk and called his wife. "I won't be home for dinner tonight, I'm afraid, and I might not even be back for breakfast tomorrow morning."

Then he summoned Lucas and Janvier.

They came into the office.

"There's a chance that Torrence is a prisoner."

While they blinked at him, he continued, "We can't go there officially because it would humiliate Torrence if the press learned about it, which they are bound to do unless we act in a clandestine manner. Listen closely."

They leaned towards him and he said, "There aren't enough of us to force entry, so we must resort to deception. We are targeting a man who calls himself the Marquis de Piqueur. He has never seen me, so I can go in my usual clothes. But I want one of you to dress in dark attire and the other to adopt a disguise."

Lucas and Janvier exchanged bemused glances.

"What sort of disguise, Chief?"

"I require one of you to dress yourself as a woman."

"Are you really serious?"

"I never joke!" thundered Maigret. "Haven't you learned that by now? I plan to arrive at the Château in Roissy with a woman on a leash. I will say that I wish to become a member of the fraternity, that I heard about it from an anonymous source, that I am a rich dilettante and have brought a woman as an offering. That woman will be one of you. While we enter through the front door, the inspector in dark clothes will seek to find an alternative entry and gain admittance to the house undetected."

"I don't really mind being a woman for one night."

It was Janvier who spoke.

Maigret nodded. "We had better get you dressed properly. Remain here. Lucas, go and find plain dark clothes for yourself."

BANG!

The Detective Chief Inspector went out of the office and strolled along the corridor to the glass-sided room where the petty criminals were kept prior to interrogation. It was usually filled with prostitutes and drug dealers. Maigret entered, spied a woman he knew well, went closer, bent and whispered in her ear:

"If you don't want charges brought against you tonight, you can do us a favour in return for freedom," he said and she nodded.

He told her what was required and she agreed to the deal. He led her back to his office, pointed at Janvier and said, "Swap clothes with him. Come, don't be shy. Everything, garters and all. It must be utterly convincing."

While they undressed, Maigret went to the cabinet where he kept a bottle of brandy and helped himself to a large glass. He finished it, licked his lips, and turned around. Janvier had become a seductive woman and the prostitute had turned into a policeman. He smiled with an ironic approval and reached for the telephone, summoning one of the officers who regularly stood guard at the entrance to the Quai des Orfèvres. "Escort this person and make sure they leave safely without being challenged."

The prostitute departed his office and Maigret examined Janvier with a critical eye. As he was doing so, Lucas returned, dressed in black. He had borrowed the clothes from Moers, the forensics expert who worked on the top floor of the building. Maigret nodded. "We need a leash and one other item. We will get those on the way. Let's go down and take a car. Lucas, you drive. You know the way to Roissy?"

"Yes, I do, Chief."

Maigret nodded again. Then he dipped into the pocket of his jacket, pulled out a gun, lifted up Janvier's skirt and thrust the revolver into his garter. Janvier blushed as his fishnet stockings were revealed to Lucas's gaze.

"Hurry," said Maigret.

His expression was grim during the drive. He ordered Lucas to stop near two shops, one that sold pet supplies, the other a shop stocked with wines. Sitting on the back seat of the car with Janvier, he attached a collar and leash to his colleague's neck. He tugged on it a few times to test its effectiveness. Janvier audibly gagged.

"Throw yourself body and soul into the act when the time comes," he told him. "I am your master and you are my bitch. Don't forget. You are totally submissive and have only the desire to serve me, no matter my intentions."

Janvier blinked his eyes in the affirmative. He was unable to articulate words. As Lucas steered around corners, he said, "We are entering Roissy now. I'm sure I know the area where the Château is located. We are very close..."

He turned down a road and pulled up in front of the gates.

"What next, Chief?"

They got out and Lapointe hissed at them from the shadows. Maigret said, "Lapointe, help Lucas climb over the wall on the other side of the grounds. I will ring the bell and seek admittance with Janvier. Don't expect mercy if you are caught. Piqueur is a beast. Good luck and keep your wits about you. There are naked women in the Château. Don't be distracted. Remember that we are professionals."

Lucas ran to join Lapointe and they both hugged the wall as they vanished into the cool shadows of the night. Maigret rang the bell and then jerked the leash so roughly that Janvier collapsed to his knees. "Stay there!" Maigret barked. He was fully immersed in his role, one of those masterful perverted men who are the end result of centuries of aristocratic privilege and selected breeding. He waited patiently as a door in the distant Château opened and a man emerged and began to tramp over the lawn towards the gate. Janvier trembled, his shaking communicating itself to Maigret through the taut leash. The Detective Chief Inspector smiled thinly at this. Fear was a useful tool.

In the meantime, Lucas was assisted to the top of the wall by Lapointe, who allowed him to stand on his shoulders. Lucas was far more agile than Torrence and gained the coping with relative ease. He dropped down the other side, ran in a crouch to the wall of the Château and searched for a way of getting inside.

He found the porthole that Torrence had used before him, but something about it made him feel uneasy. He decided to avoid it. He looked up and saw the wide chimneys on the roof and he came to a bold decision. He scaled a drainpipe, pulled himself onto the sloping slates and bounded to the ridge of the roof. Then he crawled on his hands and knees to the nearest chimney. He stood and peered down it. He saw a very faint glimmer of light at the bottom. It was worth taking a chance. Yes, it was.

The Marquis de Piqueur strode out of the subterranean chamber. "Leave the girls in the stocks overnight. We can release them tomorrow. I want to see how the welts and musical notes look after a dozen hours or so. Let's have supper!"

He went up the worn stone steps to the ground floor.

Other members of the fraternity followed him. Although there was no official leader of the club, Piqueur was respected and obeyed by all. He strode briskly through the many empty rooms on his way to the banqueting chamber.

But he stopped suddenly in the large circular library.

And pointed at the fireplace.

"What is that?" he demanded. All eyes turned to look. A pair of legs and buttocks were dangling from the chimney. The legs were kicking but it was clear that their owner was stuck. Piqueur rubbed his chin as he pondered.

"I suppose someone stuffed her up there in order to give her a whipping? Not a bad idea but they seem to have forgotten to go through with it. Was it the work of one of you?" And he turned to gaze at his followers indulgently.

No one spoke. Piqueur continued, "She is wearing trousers, just like that big girl in the basement. Most inconvenient for the administering of a spanking. Tear them off and give her the belated whipping that she deserves. I will have supper brought here so I can watch while eating. Render her most tender, someone."

There was no shortage of men who offered themselves as volunteers. Lucas's trousers were removed and canes and paddles were fetched. Piqueur seated himself at a reading desk and waited for the food he had ordered.

The whipping began. Unlike Torrence, Lucas made no effort to stifle his screams, and Piqueur arched his eyebrows in wonder.

"How curious! The acoustics of the chimney flue have deepened her voice so that she now sounds more like a man than a girl."

He appeared to enjoy this unexpected effect.

"Kindly whip her harder!"

Lucas squirmed but to no avail. Welts appeared on his flesh and both buttocks glowed like setting suns. Piqueur chewed the supper that had been brought for him. When he finished he was about to wipe his hands on a napkin but then he changed his mind, stood and walked to the fireplace and wiped them on Lucas' fiery rump. The grease and crumbs festooned his rear like samba sequins. Piqueur said:

"Let's improve the sport. Light a fire in the hearth!"

Lucas screamed louder.

At this moment, the door burst open and Maigret appeared with Janvier on a leash. He was about to say something in keeping with the guise he had adopted, but the moment that he caught sight of Piqueur he knew it was pointless. He immediately changed back to his former self, freeing Janvier with a flick of his wrist.

Never before had Maigret been so furious or ferocious.

"Ferdinand Freluquet!"

Piqueur retreated, knocking over a chair.

"I understand everything now," said Maigret, "and I should have realised it sooner. You aren't a Marquis at all. There is no Piqueur with a devoted servant. There is only the servant, a vicious little tyrant and abuser."

"You don't understand. I am battling my demons. That is why I came to you. I needed help and I thought you would empathise. I had been told so much about you, how you never judged anyone. 'Understand and judge not' is your motto. I believed that about you. Why are you menacing me? I am a good man."

"A good man who tortures women for pleasure?"

"It's more complex than that. There are riddles of psychology to be solved. The reward of pain can be an intensely spiritual experience. Many of the women here want to be whipped and degraded. They learn to love submission, the giving up of all control, and a strange magic security envelops them, a feeling of comfort despite the blood and bruises. Please be the man I was told you were, the non-judgmental Maigret. I am torn between my urges and my honour and so I came to you for help. I beg you!"

"What sort of help did you expect me to provide?"

"I don't know. That's not my area of expertise. But I trusted you. I didn't assume a false identity with you. It is these gentlemen in the Château who I have deceived. Show mercy and I will give myself up without resistance."

Maigret was almost convinced by his words, but Piqueur was still stepping backwards, edging towards a cabinet set into the wall. His expression was contrite but his eyes gleamed with malevolence. The two natures within him were wrestling and the darker side was on the verge of winning, and Maigret realised that this would always be the case with him, that his moral side was being systematically whipped into submission in the subterranean chamber of his subconscious mind and that it was close to expiring from its wounds. Piqueur was evil, a menace, a tightly packed avatar of chaos.

Chained to the synapses of his diseased brain, the good side of the false Marquis made a last attempt to reach out to Maigret. "Beware, he's a trickster," came in a whisper from the thin lips. And Maigret lunged. But Piqueur was already at the cabinet and turning a handle to open it. Inside was one of those deadly whips known as a scorpion, with eight leather lashes, each one tipped with a sharp steel barb.

Piqueur gripped it and flourished the hideous weapon.

"I'll whip you dead, man bitch!"

He swung and the eight barbs narrowly missed Maigret. Piqueur went on the attack and anything might have happened, but at this very moment, Janvier lifted his skirt, drew the gun from his garter, aimed at Piqueur's legs.

He pulled the trigger and emptied the chamber.

The Marquis scowled at him.

The bullets ricocheted off his knees.

"I had them replaced with steel caps long ago. Do you think that I whip women without experimenting on myself too? I always try things out on myself first. Many parts of me are no longer flesh but metal. I have whipped huge chunks off my own body. All now replaced with artificial substitutes. I am a monster!"

While he was making this speech, Maigret reached into his pocket and pulled out not a pipe but a bottle. He had obtained it from the wine shop. Troussepinette! He stepped forward and rammed the glass neck into Piqueur's face, shattering his teeth. The bottle was lodged in his throat. Maigret stepped forward, extended his index finger and pushed Piqueur over. The false Marquis landed on his back and the liquid in the bottle began to pour into him, making a ludicrous glugging sound as it did so.

"I felt something wasn't right in the Brasserie Dauphin when you winced when the first drop of this liqueur touched your tongue. A real servant of an aristocrat always takes sly sips from the bottles in his master's drinks cabinet, especially from those alcoholic beverages that the aristocrat never touches, and would be familiar with the taste of troussepinette. Clearly, you weren't. This indicated that you weren't the servant of the master but the master himself."

Maigret knelt and used his arms to prevent Piqueur rising. He held the Marquis down as the bottle emptied itself into his gullet. Only when it was completely empty did he stand and gesture to Janvier. "Reload your gun."

The other men in the room had remained motionless.

"Cover them with it," said Maigret.

He smiled bitterly. "You are all under arrest. Exactly what for, I don't yet know. But I'd say that most of you can look forward to spending a considerable amount of time in jail." As Janvier pointed the revolver at the men, Maigret saw that some of them had erections in their trousers. They had been aroused by Janvier lifting his skirt and exposing his garter. Maigret suppressed his disgust and turned to leave.

He planned to fetch Lapointe and order him to search the Château for Torrence. Janvier would shoot anyone who tried to escape.

Lucas was freed with a chisel and a hammer within an hour. But Torrence wasn't found and freed until just before dawn. Both walked out of the Château with a severe limp, but while Lucas was grimacing, Torrence was grinning.

The days passed and Maigret found the official report difficult to write. He was almost tempted to give the task to one of his men. He felt very awkward as he described the strange activities that had taken place at Roissy and he constantly consulted a thesaurus to find words that were less offensively brutal to his eyes.

Finally he summoned Lucas and said, "Do you think one of you might be able to finish this? I seem to be making a mess of it."

"I don't think I can do it, Chief. Sorry, I'm too traumatised. And Janvier and Lapointe both feel the same way. We were discussing the matter earlier. We never want to hear about Roissy ever again. Our minds are damaged."

Maigret nodded sympathetically. "What about Torrence?"

Lucas stared at the floor.

"He has been on the typewriter ever since we got back to the Quai des Orfèvres. When I asked him what he was writing, he said a novel. I told him that he should do stuff like that in his own time, not in work hours. I didn't want to castigate him too much, considering what he went through. I took a look at some of the pages. It's a rather disreputable story. He says he's going to try to get it published under a pseudonym, Pauline Réage or something, a lady's name, at any rate. I am worried about him. He calls his book, *The Story of O*, and I think the title shows that he has mental health issues."

Maigret sighed, then leaned back in his chair and selected a pipe from his desk. "Leave him in peace. Writing a book is probably as good a therapy as anything. I have never thought of Torrence as the literary sort, though."

"He isn't. His style is faux-lyrical and horrid."

Maigret stifled a laugh.

"Understand and judge not," he said.

Angel Wings

Jenean McBrearty

Detective Kinkaid played his suspects like a musician plays a favorite tune and his favorite melody was "Confession". Fred Hudson had a reputation for being a tough nut to crack, but, according to Kinkaid, it was a reputation built on the erroneous belief that all his interrogators would be dumb Feds. They may have been excellent cops, but they were lousy judges of character because, like all killers, Hudson had no character. He did have personality, though, a pretty-boy actor who required an audience for his headliner exploits. It wasn't necessary to penetrate his psychological defenses, Kinkaid believed. He had only to wait outside Hudson's internal fortress, pen in hand, until he came out, bags packed for a long stay as the star of Cinema San Quentin.

"I figured any dame named Angel Wings would be beautiful. I knew she'd been dangerous when I saw her corpse. The way you posed her told me right off she was a temptress. She liked looking provocative even in death," Kinkaid said. His detainee hadn't uttered a word. There was no evidence that Hudson had posed for a photo, let alone with a violated corpse. It might be the case that Angel's sensual posture was a final act of a wanna-be glamour queen, whose last earthly effort was assuming a come-hither rigor mortis. She might have lasted a minute before she bled out from the quarter-sized hole in her heart.

"I wouldn't have minded putting a couple of ounces of lead in her heart, but I'd never mess with her style. She was one vain bitch, and a guy's gotta respect that when he's into fashion himself," Hudson said and straightened his tie.

"I can see that. Nice threads. Pin stripes are a classic haberdashery statement."

"I'm into Art Deco. The thirties' are my era of choice."

"It's an impressive but expensive choice." Kinkaid had a flashback of the thirty-two hundred-dollar quote he got from a New York antique dealer for his grandmother's Erte lamp. He wrote TOO MUCH on the doodle pad. "Did you love her?"

"Who, Angel? Sure, for about six hours. Then she got naggy, you know? Wantin' me to stay passed breakfast. She got in my face for using my glass for an ashtray. I'd finished my Cuba Libre, so what was the big deal? Just throw the melted ice in the sink. Right?"

Kinkaid was nodding in agreement. "Yeah, yeah. Women don't get it. Reason should rule the day, but …"

"Speaking of reasonable, what happens if I confess to actually pulling the trigger?"

"The up-side, you save the taxpayers the expense of hearings, trials, and appeals. There's a pay-off. No death penalty. Unless you didn't plan to kill her. With your track record, though, the jury probably ain't gonna buy a manslaughter plea."

"Downside?"

"No chance for acquittal. No chance of parole. You want some coffee or something? I think I'll get a coke."

"I could use a beer."

"I'll bring a root beer."

Kinkaid wanted to give Hudson time to ruminate on reality. A wow-wee wardrobe couldn't hide his precarious position any more than it excused a heinous crime. Angel might have been a bitch, but she didn't deserve to die. Kinkaid would have to work that into the conversation. Maybe when they talked motive. He sat in the visitor's lounge wondering if it would be okay to light up. *This Is A Non-smoking Facility* signs were plastered on every wall, but they lacked specificity as far as he was concerned. He'd chance it. He inhaled a mentol light and stared at the floor. Some tough guy he was.

A pair of white high heels caught his eye and he raised his eyes slowly, feasting them on an orange-colored sheath with white trim. "Got a light?" A wide-brimmed white hat shaded the face of the sultry-voiced visitor.

"Can't you read?" Kinkaid said as he pulled a Bic lighter out of his pocket.

"About as good as you. I ain't seen a cop nowhere." She bent down and sucked the flame with her cigarette. "Mind if I sit?" He moved over to give her room on the bench. "I hear they got Freddy Hudson in custody," she said.

She spoke with a slight accent, but he couldn't place it. "That's what I hear. You know him?"

"I introduced him to Angel. I figured they'd get along. Have a few laughs."

"Are you here to bail him out?"

"Like he's going to get bail on a murder wrap. Boy, are you green." She knew her Criminal Law 101.

"Is that what he's being charged with, murder?" He exaggerated a shiver for effect. "Wouldn't want to meet him in a dark alley."

"I've been chasing him down one dark alley after another for years," she said. "He never learns, you know? He's old enough to be Angel's great-grandfather, and he just never learns."

Funny, Hudson's rap-sheet said he was thirty-two. "How did you know Angel?" Kinkaid asked.

"She worked for me. Ironic, ain't it? Her being a working girl married to a cop, and winding up getting killed." She held out a white-gloved hand. "I'm Patty Sage. You got a name?"

"Robert Neil," he lied. "Public defender in the press. Talk about ironic. I'm here to see Mr Hudson."

"Really?" She reached in her purse. "The press always gets special privileges. Guess it's because coppers always like seeing their names in print. When you see him, tell him Patty was here. And just between you and me, Freddy didn't mean to kill that girl."

"You know he did it?"

She looked around the empty room. "Yeah, but he didn't

mean to do it. His thing is robbing banks, not killing pretty girls. He loves admiration, not violence. He's no pervert like Jack the Ripper. Will you tell him Patty was here?"

"Sure, honey. Give me your address and phone number, and maybe I'll come see you about being a witness for him." He expected her to fumble around for a pen and paper, but she pulled out a business card and handed it to him: Patty Sage Escort Services.

"Call at least an hour in advance. I'm real busy in the evenings." She winked at him and sauntered away. Did she turn the corner, or just disappear?

*

He was still wondering if he should make an appointment with his optometrist when he handed Hudson Sage's business card. "A babe was here wanting information on you. You know her?"

"Escort services? Do I look like I'm so desperate for female company, I'd have to pay for it?" Hudson let the card drop to the floor.

"No offense meant. I'm just the messenger."

"But you might want to give her a call, copper. Offense meant." Hudson was wearing a between-us-guys grin. "You look like a lonely guy."

"I might just do that. You want to talk some more reason, or do you want to think on it a while longer?"

"I ... I think I'll think. Maybe I'll remember my alibi."

"Sure, maybe you was at the movies." Kinkaid had second thoughts. Maybe he shouldn't have shown Hudson Sage's card. He obviously lied about knowing her. His whole attitude had changed. From reasonable fop to real asshole in three seconds. He picked up the card and stashed it in his pocket.

*

"Ms Sage? This is the protect-the-innocent reporter you met at the jail. If you can make some time for me, I'd like to give your establishment a little free publicity." It'd taken him an hour to come up with a pitch that was neutral but tempting.

Her sultry voice replied with a question. "What did Hudson say?"

"He said I should give you a call. He needed some time to remember his alibi. What a comedian, hunh?"

"Yeah, he's a riot. Okay, how about my place at eight tonight?"

"It's a date. I'll bring my laptop and a bottle of wine."

"Make it uncut whiskey."

That one threw him. He asked the liquor store clerk what she meant, and he just shrugged. "Manufacturer's haven't cut whiskey since prohibition. Hardly anyone alive who remembers the Volstead Act."

Maybe Hudson was right about dumb interrogators. "Give me a bottle of Johnnie Walker."

"Red, black, green, gold or blue?"

"She wore an orange dress and heels," Kinkaid said, and remembered how it hugged her legs.

"Impress her. Buy green at least."

Forty-five dollars poorer, Kinkaid found Sage's Pacific Beach four-plex that was disguised as a two-story home. She'd swapped her orange sheath for a pink silk kimono over a white slip. It told him this wasn't going to be a real date.

"I'm kinda in a hurry, but since you brought the good stuff ..." She got two glasses from the kitchen while he opened the bottle. She poured them each a healthy four fingers and sat at the opposite end of her rose-colored crushed-velvet sofa. "Bet the booze set you back a pretty penny. Now, I suppose, you'll want details. I guarantee you won't believe me, but me and my clientele have kept up with the times. I used to slam down a bottle of this stuff every day. That kinda living takes its toll on a girl, though. Same with dying."

He took a gulp from his glass to wash down his confusion. "You think Hudson's gonna get the hot needle for killing Angel?"

"If he has to die, I'd say it was better than getting shot down on the street. Would you want to die in public?" She tilted her head back, and he noticed the clean line of her throat. Like a sheep offering its neck to the butcher. She looked over at him. "I'm hoping this time around will be different. I love the son-of-a-bitch. Always have. Most men now days ain't got the same intertest for me. Most ain't like Hudson. Or you."

"Wha'dya mean by that, exactly?" She was driving at something, but it still sounded like Farfetchedville to him.

"I'll bet you showered, shaved and shined your shoes before you came over, didn't you?" Almost involuntarily, Kinkaid nodded a guilty-as-charged yeah. "Of course, you did. I could tell right away, the way you looked at me, that you were a man who cared enough about himself to respect a lady no matter what her occupation. Hudson's like that, too. So are all my clients from the old days. Eventually they all pay me a visit. Luciano. Capone. Segal. Barrow. Gotti. ... I know them all. Different names. Different styles. But they're all real men. Like you."

Her small tender hand inched its way towards his thigh. "If you let him go, I promise he won't never kill anybody else. We'll go away together. He always like the idea of Cuba. Or Rio. I could teach him to tango. I could teach you."

Hudson never let on he had a crazy girlfriend. What did he need Angel Wings for when he had a loony-tunes like Patty Sage waiting for him? "I ... I don't know how to make that happen. It ain't my call."

"All you have to do is stay with me a while. A half an hour. I'll know when he's ready to come home. You will too. Promise me you'll stay and drink this bottle with me."

He didn't want to stay, and he didn't want to go. She was crazy, but she was lovely, too. Like a Silver Screen star that's been colorized and is playing her last scene in a movie made for two. "Tell me," he whispered, "about yesterday." She fell into his arms – at least it felt as though they were falling together. Somehow, he knew that even though she loved Hudson, at that moment, she was his, and his alone. That's what escorts are trained to do. They're actresses, he thought for a speeding second, and then lost himself in forgetfulness of touches and lips and slippery-ness.

He heard a gentle knock, and Sage kissed him once more before going to the door. "Who is it?" she asked.

"Dillinger," a voice said, and Sage turned to Kinkaid.

"Go out the back door. There's a staircase," she whispered. "And thank-you!" She was glowing. Kinkaid had never seen such happiness on a woman's face.

*

Just as crazy men like Hudson needed a female audience, crazy women like Sage needed male approval, Kinkaid concluded as he pulled into the police station parking lot. Or, maybe all men and women were like that. Maybe that was the nature of the sexes. He could imagine the scenario playing out in bedrooms all over America. People calling themselves Sage and Dillinger, role playing with others who pretended to be famous tough guys for women who loved tough guys. It made him laugh to himself the way he responded to domestic calls. Playing the role of cynical cop who worries about damsels in distress who could kick his butt to defend their crazy lovers. Most of humanity seemed to struggle to be who they aren't because reality is just too damn boring.

"Is Hudson still in his cell?" he asked a real live Sgt. John Walker.

"Sure, why wouldn't he be?" came the abrupt answer.

"Just checking."

"He wants to see you."

Kinkaid went to Hudson's cell and there he was, still sitting on his cot. "What's the word? Have you given any more thought to confessing your sins?" Kinkaid let himself into the cell, and leaned against the top bunk opposite Hudson's.

"I remembered my alibi. I took a little nap, and it came to me in a dream. I was with Patty Sage the night Angel Wings was killed. Go ahead, ask her. She'll back me up in court too. You'll see."

Kinkaid looked into Hudson's eyes. "You sure about that?"

"Sure, I'm sure. You are too. Why do you think she came to see me? To tell me what I couldn't remember. Me and Sage go way back."

"A guy named Dillinger came to see her, too. Do you know him? 'Cause she sure did look happy when he came knockin'."

To an audience of one, Freddy Hudson played the eeriest killer Kinkaid had ever seen. His whole face seemed to change, as though he wasn't Hudson at all. His smile was sublime, but his eyes were hard and black as lacquered steel.

"Yeah, I know him. I know him as well as I know myself. You gonna call the D.A.?"

Kinkaid never trusted suspects, even ones that had credible alibis. Hudson's alibi didn't pass the smell test. It wasn't close to rational. "What if I tell you I don't believe that bullshit for a minute?"

"Then you'd be lying, Kinkaid. You've been to see her. I can tell. Her perfume is all over you. It's called Beware, by some French company. Gerblaine. I'd know it anywhere. Yeah, it's all coming back to me now." Hudson's grin turned into a sneer. "The pink silk robe with the blue and gold peacocks ..."

"Shut up!" The oracle at Delphi had visions when she inhaled the aroma of incense, maybe Sage's perfume gave Hudson his alibi. Maybe it tattled on him, too.

"Did you take her a present, copper? Whiskey, maybe. She loves her spirits. Calls them her gangsters of love. She'd do anything for them."

Kincaid slowly clapped his hands. Hudson was going to beat the rap. He wouldn't be the first guy to be saved by the love of a good woman. Or a bad one. Maybe this time, Dillinger would do right by Patty Sage. Maybe take her to Cuba where the best rum and cigars were smuggled into Florida. Or up the coast to Atlantic City, where the gambling casinos had high roller bootleggers who just wouldn't stay dead, and made time to see old friends and kill angels who get in their way.

Slimeball

Leif Hanson

"Aye, Mullie, yer not makin' this pimps, awright ya wee
bawbag," Rory Grant yelled at the dark loch, and he saw a
head pop up about twenty meters offshore. The thin-woven
fishing net strained against the weight of the keech ball as
Rory rowed towards the shoreline. A few strands popped
loose as he disembarked and pulled the net onto the beach,
hooking the straps to Caitir's saddle. "C'mon hen," he said, as
he patted her bahoochie, "let's get this howfin' jobby in the
cart. We need to fertilize the barley."

The cuddy dug her hooves into the sand and pulled
against the weight. Rory guided the hardened smelly mess
into the cart as the wood strained under the weight. "Aye,
Caitir, this will spread across all our fields, and make a bonnie
harvest. It'll more than pay for the sacrifice. Maybe triple,
even, especially with the next load," he calculated, as he
latched the gate on the back of the cart. Gathering the burlap
tarp, he tossed it over the mass. "Don't need the Fraser's
pokin' their heads in my business on our way back." Twine
secured the tarp to the cart. He led Caitir to the front and
reattached the modified saddle poles, which had been tied to
a steel hook firmly planted in the ground. The hook
counterbalanced the cart when loading, so that it wouldn't tip
as the giant balls rolled up the ramp.

A breeze picked up, blowing a cold wind through the
valley. Rory pulled his jacket close and took a nip of
Laphroaig. He looked out at the grassy hills and spied Sgùrr
na Lapaich in the distance, as the fog parted ever so briefly.
The green landscape was solemn and wet, as it had been

261

raining all day, and it didn't improve Rory's mood.

The freshly sheared blackface lamb struggled against the rope. Elm stakes secured it against two offset rocks by the shoreline as Rory approached. Gently, Rory tied a blindfold around its eyes, flipped the kerry on its side, and tied its legs together. In one swift move, the animal was in his sinewy arms, and it stopped struggling. Carefully he made his way back onto the rowboat and laid the sheep in the bow, tying it down to a cross plank. Gripping the oars, Rory pushed off and paddled through the water lilies towards the cove where the Allt Taige flowed into Loch Mullardoch.

Rory's great grandfather first discovered Mullie when he was feeding his sheep by the water's edge late one evening. As the sun was setting on an unusually sunny day in mid-spring, a giant head, followed by a long neck attached to a giant dark gray body with flippers, flapped its way onto shore. Old Agan thought he was going to die as he fell back on the soft earth, seeing the head swing down. With a row of sharp teeth, it plucked a fat Linton from the flock, swiveled, and dove back into the water. Agan came to his feet and pulled his heirloom sword from its sheath, but to no avail. The monster was gone, and the antiquated sword he carried dropped from his hand.

Agan waited until the next morning, spending a chilly night by the shoreline, letting his flock graze as he scanned the water for the beast. At dawn, a giant smelly ball washed up on shore, covered in hair. "Aye, that must be Dolly," he lamented. After returning his flock to his pasture, he took his newly built cart to the water's edge to retrieve the Dolly-ball. Dividing and spreading the digested sheep and aquatic plants, his crops out-performed all the neighboring fields, and his yield quadruled the previous-year's harvest. Agan returned the next spring, with only one sheep, and tossed it in the water after rowing out. The lamb struggled and thrashed, and Agan watched in curious horror as a giant head popped out of the water. Looking into its eye, he and the creature came to a silent agreement, and the monster's mouth closed around the meal. A giant slime ball washed ashore the next day.

SLIMEBALL

Agan wasn't quite sure what to call the creature, but when "Nessie" became a sensation down at Loch Ness in 1934, he figured this was one of the offspring, swimming upriver to Loch Mullardoch. Mullie was as good a name as any. The monster, and the fertilizer it provided, was a secret he passed down to his oldest son Robert, and him to Rory. Jack, Rory's oldest, would learn about Mullie in a few years.

The second sheep of the season was about to be tossed when Rory looked over his shoulder to check that he wasn't being watched. "Bloody hell, it's Hamish," he muttered, as he saw a new Ford Ranger drive down the slope to his cart; a Fraser tartan custom-painted on the hood. Hamish stopped next to the cart, exited the vehicle, and lifted the burlap. Rory watched as Hamish recoiled and puked. Making the distraction an opportunity, he untied and shoved the lamb in the water. Mullie's head popped from the loch. "Mullie, you're gonna have to help me," Rory pleaded. Pausing, the beast eyed Rory before dragging the powerless animal to the depths below.

Rory recalled his Da, Robert, telling him how he had to misdirect researchers and sabotage equipment in the 70's. Several science teams conducted searches on Loch Ness, looking for Nessie or her offspring. Robert made several trips to Drumnadrochit, Fort Augustus, and Inverness. Remembering his father being gone for several weeks, Ma explained that he had to settle some business regarding grain shipping, threatening to export out of Ullapool.

When Robert finally passed along his secret, it was more out of necessity than want. Robert had been fighting with a rare form of Non-Hodgkin's lymphoma, Waldenstrom's Macroglobulinemia. He knew his time was short, so he brought Rory, then only twenty-four, with him on his last venture. "Just follow along, laddie," as he strapped a lamb to the bow, "we're gonna paddle out and drop her off."

"Da, it's such a dreich day," Rory replied.

"Gie it laldy. Help me row," as they climbed into the boat. About one hundred meters from shore, Robert cut the binds holding the young sheep. Surprised at its sudden freedom, it struggled to gain its footing and fell off the boat.

"Back her up, laddie," Robert commanded the wide-eyed Rory, too speechless to understand why his father was wasting a perfectly good lamb. Gripping both oars, he paddled away from the struggling animal. About ten meters away Rory almost fell off the boat himself. Giant teeth rose from the water and crushed around the animal, cutting short the bleating. Rory stood up, almost causing the boat to tip.

"Aye, it's a sair ficht for half a loaf." Robert grinned.

"Fuck! Da!" Rory pointed to the head popping out of the water.

"Aye, that's Mullie," Robert waved as the head dropped below the surface, "now sit down before ye fall out." It was a silent row back to shore, but after a few glasses of single malt, the story came out, and the secret entrusted, to be defended for the sake of the family. Rory had only ventured out on Mullie business once, in 2017, when Hayley Johnson published a picture of Nessie. The Loch Ness Monster was a lucrative business, and Nessie brought in millions of tourist dollars every year. The trip to Manchester was simply to let Hayley know to not bring any further unwanted investigations around her photograph, and to keep it under wraps. Or, if asked, say it was probably a sea cow or large eel. However, Rory gave up finding her after a few days, figuring if he threatened her, it would only make matters worse, and might even lead to investigations into nearby bodies of water. Loch Mullerdoch was sacred to him.

Rowing frantically, Rory reached the shore as Hamish recovered his senses and reached underneath the cart to remove a blinking black box. "Yuptae, Rory? GPS Tracker, ya tadger," Hamish yelled out to the craft, holding the device above his head, "I had to ken where ya were getting off to. Last time I had it under your truck, but I lost ya from there."

Rory pulled his boat ashore and tied it off. Hamish, scraping the tracker clean, did not pay attention as Rory circled around the other side of the cart, so that Hamish's back was towards the water. "Aye, Hamish, step away."

"Our barley sales have plummeted due to yer grain. I ken yer secret now, jammy bastard. Is this drookit shiteball how ye fertilize yer fields?"

Silence as Rory's eyes darted between the water and Hamish.

"I thought ye were a clerty necromancer, the way ye makes such a plenty crop."

Walking a few steps backwards, Rory spat, "Haud yer wheesht, Hammy. I dinna meddle with the dead. Ghosts and bones don't make fer good workers."

"Ye need a roadmap to get here." Hamish pointed towards the cart, "What's this? Dinosaur shite? Are ye a time traveler?"

"That's yer clan, Hamish Fraser," Rory retorted, "but aye, dinnae fash yersel, it's a giant slimeball, like ye."

Hamish pulled a Glock-19 from behind his back and leveled it at Rory, who was expecting this move, but took a few more steps backwards. All the Fraser's carried a side arm of some sort, and their clan were never prosecuted due to their family members in key positions within the local government. "I'm gonna have to take this from you, Grant. It's high time our yield outdid yers. But why use an old cart to haul this toalie?"

"It worked for my Granda, it worked for my Da," and looking to the sky above the shoreline, "and it works for me. Goodbye Hamish."

Gnashing teeth muffled a short scream as Mullie extended her long neck and picked Hamish into her mouth. Machinated bones, blood, hair, clothes, and boots became a masticated ball as Mullie tilted her head back and swallowed, like a shore bird swallowing a fish.

Caitir, startled by the sudden appearance of Mullie, raced up the hill, cart in tow. "Shite!" Rory ran after the frightened mare, but she disappeared into the fog, the heavy cart not slowing her down. He found his way back to the road and saw where the cart's wheels dug into the embankment in a sharp right turn. Nodding, he knew exactly where Caitir had gone. After an hour of walking, he came to his own pickup, with a horse trailer attached that had been modified to also fit the wooden cart.

"C'mon girlie, it's all right," and he grabbed some hardened oat biscuits out of his jacket pocket. At first Caitir refused, but with some head stroking and soft words, she ate a few. Rory turned her around, cart still in tow, and they made their way back to the shoreline.

Rory checked the ground where Hamish had been devoured. Three sharp shards of bone, an ear, and several splatters of blood were all that remained. Filling a bucket from his cart, he gathered the Hamish remains, dug a hole amongst taller grass near the bank, and slid them in. A large, flat rock laying nearby served to cover the pieces in the hole, and back-filling with dirt, laid a second stone of equal size on top. The cairn complete, Rory fluffed the grass around it back to a natural state. "Hamish, ye should've stuck to yer own business," and he tried to remember words to a Robert Burns poem. "If there's another world, he lives in bliss; If there is none, he made the best of this." Rory looked out at the water, "God, take this bastard home."

Thankfully, Hamish's truck was unlocked, and the keys were in the center console. Rory breathed a sigh of relief, terrified that they were in Mullie's digestive track. The truck shifted easily into neutral, and after powering down the windows, he was able to guide it down the slope and into the water. It floated away from the shore with the momentum and sank beneath the gently lapping waves.

The next morning two giant balls were floating near the shore. He pulled them in with his net, like his father had taught him. Guiding one into the cart, he noticed a grip sticking out. Rory grabbed the handle and pulled out a crap-covered water-logged Glock. As caber-toss champion of the northern clans, he made the weapon disappear, throwing it as far as he could into the dark water.

The First Suspect

Brian Howell

It was definitely child porn. He needed only to take the briefest of glances. He would not allow himself to look more than in flashes, in any case. Why someone would have gone to the trouble of printing out such horrific acts on glossy photographic paper in this day and age was beyond him. How many were there, anyway? a part of him enquired. Easing them out of the flimsy, half-opened envelope, and trying not to look directly at their troubled content, he fanned them out to count a total of ten, turning over the top one so that it doubly concealed from his immediate perusal the contents underneath, both those of its reversed side and that of the ones it covered.

But why on Earth did he pick them up in the first place? Concern, he hoped.

There was no way he was going to report finding them to the police, not now. Already, his DNA was on them, just as damning as it would have been if he had come across a body, checked it for signs of life, found that it was dead, and dutifully reported that. He would be the first suspect. There was no way around that.

Now, his concern was to shield others from those images. That at least would be one good outcome. If a child came across these, there was no telling what damage could be done. Indeed, he had found them next to the playground of a daycare centre, a small wood that hosted the local shrine. Even worse, if they had been found by a true pervert, or someone, probably a teenager or a young man in his twenties, whose life was ahead of him but whose identity, like a sculpture whose mould has been cracked open too soon and left susceptible to further, deleterious impression, was not hardened sufficiently to be capable of heading off possible corruption.

And yet, if he did not look further at its contents, how could he know this wasn't evidence of a crime that, beyond the initial instance of abuse, however one was able to assess it, was continuing or was the precursor to an even greater crime, or simply the evidence of a cut-and-dried case. If if if...

He decided to keep them, reasoning that if something came to light in the news, he could simply step forward with them. He would have to face the music if he were criticised. It would be all too easy for people to attack him if it came to it, he knew, but he would ask them what they would have done in his shoes.

The only dilemma he now had was whether to show them to someone, in particular to Alicia, as proof of their provenance, and his innocence, as far as that went. Yet even that act might incur criticism and complication in itself. Surely it was better not to involve her at all. Alicia would never find them. She simply never rooted around in his stuff. Never.

As soon as he arrived home, he put the packet in the top drawer of his desk in his study, intending to think of a safer place to transfer it to later. He could hardly lock it because in the extremely unlikely event that Alicia opened it, it would be immediately suspicious.

For the next few months, he went to work by his regular route, which took him past the daycare centre. He had succeeded in putting from his mind the content of the photographs, if not the fact of the photographs themselves, however absent-minded people sometimes said he was, and he had certainly not looked at them again since placing them in the drawer. However, lately, he had found himself paying more attention to the children when he happened to pass by and see them playing outside the centre when he left home or left work. To say he was looking at them was not exactly true; it was more that he looked at the throng of amorphous, anonymous bobbing, jerking, and colourful shapes which, especially at the beginning of the end of his day, meant nothing to him beyond being signifiers of happiness, abandon, and occasional outbursts of wild exuberance.

Or, more precisely, he was looking into them, if not indeed through them, searching for something, which had no immediate substance, as he sometimes might in a forest or wooded area when there was no one about, or, for that matter, anywhere outside. Yet out of this curious, passive searching, something emerged, and it was a face, an oval, blonde child's face, her age around eight or nine. He deducted that the child stood out because she happened to catch his eye a few times by pure chance but then he realised it was something deeper. Terrified, and against his better judgement, he would have to go to the drawer and check.

Although he and Alicia had lived in the area for over thirty years and the daycare centre had been there for most of that time, it was a source of continuing fascination to him that he barely knew any of their neighbours and certainly not any of the children who attended the centre, although one would think they had grown up enough now to acknowledge him. However, these days, men of a certain age were naturally an object of suspicion anywhere near younger people. That's how the world had gone, he thought. And this would have been true as much before the Internet age and mobile phones as now. What conclusions one could draw from this, he had no idea, but perhaps it suited a kind of outsider status he felt he inhabited, regarding himself as an amateur detective of sorts, which Alicia always laughed at, if not exactly mocked. Indeed, he saw himself as a gentle man, if a little bumbling, somewhat eccentric, gentle man, these days, a perception not a little exacerbated by his age, approaching sixty.

Indeed, with no children to worry about, he found himself in recent years observing life around him more closely than he had ever done in the past. 'Looking for trouble,' as Alicia jokingly said from time to time before he went on one of his walks. But it was on one of these walks one evening, as he approached the daycare centre just as it was becoming dark, that he noticed a hooded figure standing by one of the trees. It was possible he was doing some stretches or resting from a run. He could not see exactly, as the negative space that defined the man's shape was a dark grey-green so close to black that he had to question the certainty of his vision, which in this dim light approached something not dissimilar to that perceived in a hypnagogic state, to which he was sometimes susceptible when falling asleep.

These occasions were not disturbing in themselves, but he often felt, after the initial dazzle of coloured shapes and dots had resolved itself that he was looking into another part of reality, one that was happening at that moment, probably in another part of the world, one that often involved people interacting, though not necessarily in a worrying way. He could not ever remember witnessing anyone being hurt in these scenarios, for example.

He stopped for a second to see if he could make out any movement or hear any defining human sound. Nothing.

It was dark, but the children were being picked up by their parents, mostly mothers, transitioning from one form of safety to another, running out of the centre into the alerting illumination of red brake lights.

He looked again, back to the wood, to see if parallax would yield more, but now he couldn't even see the shape he had spied a few seconds ago.

At home, a few minutes later, he spent some time on the web, looking over local news. He wasn't exactly sure what it was he was searching for. Then he turned to the local map online, curious about the topography and their area's history, for once. The wooded area with the shrine had been there forever, as far as he was concerned, and the daycare centre at least twenty-five years. He loved the small wood, especially as the outline of the treetops was visible from some of the rooms in their house. He could not imagine the day those trees might be cut down for development, as invariably happened in the wider locality. Only a few days before, they had finished tearing down a house on his walk to a local bakery, along with the surrounding trees. Murdered, as far as he was concerned.

Some weeks later, on his way for an afternoon stroll, he was perturbed to find that an open space next to the wood at the back of the shrine that was normally used as a car park, and that was between their house and the daycare centre, was cordoned off with temporary barricades. He often took a short cut through this car park, especially at night, climbing over a fence and crossing, so that he didn't have to walk through the wood in the dark, which he had found terrifying even before he had noticed that figure by the tree, or what he thought was a human figure.

Now, he would have to walk through the wood if he didn't want to take the long way round, away from his home. He could not see himself clambering over those fences in the dark, anyway.

As he returned on this particular occasion, there was at least a little light from a few windows opposite the car park along one side of the path that led up to the shrine. From a distance, the short flight of steps to the wood formed the base of a clearing topped by the red tori gate which emphasised the sense of a tunnel penetrating an unending space, even though he knew it took barely a minute to traverse till he was out in the street. For a second, before going up, he stopped, feeling almost as if this space would swallow him up if he walked any further.

He could, once at the top of the steps, still avoid walking right through the main shrine by turning right into an adjacent wood, but the ground was a bit tricky in the dark. He could easily fall over the tentacular tree roots there. But if he just walked straight on, an automatic light would come on for a short time as he approached the small hut next to a sloping path before his successful egress. Unfortunately, that was exactly where he remembered the lurking figure standing, albeit the light at that time was off. In the end, he turned right, slipping down to safety with nothing untoward occurring.

Over the following months, he had managed to time his walks back so that he at least arrived home in the light, which he infinitely preferred. His investigations into the local area had yielded nothing in terms of any significant plans for development, or any historical events of note either. At bottom, this was a quiet, uneventful place, disturbed only by the sound of crows cawing at almost any time of day or night, which tradition had it was a sign of someone having died, which he thought was ridiculous, and by the sound of the children screaming in the playground of the daycare centre, a screaming of an intensity and rawness that almost shredded his nerves sometimes. He could not associate its unusualness with any other school playground he passed.

And then it happened. He found out about the scandal from some neighbours on the way home. They were milling, which was very unusual. A carer in the centre had been arrested for inappropriately touching a child, whereupon a search of his home had revealed thousands of images of child sexual abuse. That was all he could find out.

That same evening at home was momentous in a curiously allied and yet not fully exonerating way.

When he came in, he was not met with the usual cheery greeting.

Alicia was quiet, monosyllabic, in fact. Most of the evening passed without her usual comments. He was reluctant to make anything of her near-silence. He often interpreted others' silences as an accusation that he had done something wrong when it was invariably the case that the person in question, including Alicia, was simply in a bad mood or dealing with some news or event that had nothing to do with him. But on this occasion, it had gone on too long.

"What's wrong?" he asked, finally.

"I heard about that carer, what he did to that child."

"Oh, yes. I heard, on the way. Mrs Sato told me."

"She just stopped you, like that?"

"No, they were in a group, discussing something a bit animatedly. I just had to ask, even though they probably have no liking for me."

"Uh."

"Just that?" he pursued.

"I'm sorry ... I was cleaning in your room..."

He realised that she was holding onto the counter that led into their small kitchen for support. He thought she was almost about to faint, she was holding on so tightly.

"I'm sorry. Forgive me. I just happened to see a drawer open and something made me look. There was an image..."

Oh, no, he thought.

"Oh, I know what you saw."

Her face was pleading, almost retreating within itself.

She wasn't angry, just resigned, it seemed.

"I found them, about six months ago, near the centre. I swear I didn't look at them more than once. I could barely bring myself to check what they were. Please believe me."

"Why didn't you hand them to the police?"

"Why?"

He was trying to control himself, stop himself shaking.

"Why?" he continued. "Because the minute I picked them up, I was a suspect. It was too late. My DNA was already all over them."

"You've been watching too many crime series."

"I thought you were for that."

She let the comment go, even though he was sure it must have come across as mean.

"But you didn't look again?"

"What? For recreational purposes? No! I just told you I didn't look again, anyway."

And yet now he was arguably in a worse position than if he had indeed handed them in. They could be linked to the arrest of the carer, for all he knew, and if so, having kept this evidence to himself all this time, he could be considered as an accessory, albeit unwittingly, after the fact.

"What do you care about most, anyway? If I'm a pervert, or that I could be arrested for aiding a criminal?"

She was silent.

"Both?"

She was still silent.

BANG!

"What would make you after all the years you've known me think the worst of me, anyway?"

He was starting to shake a little now.

She placed a hand on his.

"I'm just worried what they will say."

An image came to him of that girl's face, the one who had looked at him that day in a way he thought might have been some kind of signal. To save her? Was she the victim? Now, he remembered: he had checked the photos in more detail, looking for her face, but it wasn't her he saw. No, they were just limbs, in positions they shouldn't have existed in, especially in their relative sizes. Shocked, he had shoved the photos in the drawer, so disturbed, it was possible, it now seemed, that he had forgotten to close it properly. Perhaps he had a memory of a piece of something sticking out. Alicia, being a very tidy person, might have pulled it open and then just been curious, for once.

Now he wondered again about that lurking figure in the darkness of the wood. Had he seen the older man pick up the photos from the ground near the centre and planned to waylay him to get them back? To threaten him in some way? His mind started spinning. Had the man thought he was the reason for his arrest?

"I'm going out," he said suddenly, seeing no end to this speculation.

He loved her and he knew she loved him and she couldn't really doubt him, but he couldn't take that hesitancy in her look and words any longer. At the last moment, he rushed upstairs and took the photos out of the drawer, not sure exactly what he had in mind.

He was in the wood in a few minutes. He now had a horrible headache. He didn't care any longer about anything. He lay down on a small bench, exhausted. Let some animal eat me in the night, he thought. Maybe some birds will eat out my eyes. Or even some monstrous spirit will put me out of my misery.

A childhood memory stirred.

Waking, he remembered nothing of the night save the sound of some crows. His headache had miraculously dissipated even though his head was half-hanging off the end of the bench. Was he still dreaming or half-asleep?

He was staring at an eye on the floor of the wood, an unblinking eye, embedded in a shallow layer of leaves, staring directly at him. He also saw some globules of light around it in the flatter spaces where there were no leaves. He realised that he was looking at multiple images of the sun thrown onto the ground, an optical even of sorts, made possible by the irising of holes in the leaves on the tree branches by the sun, the very celestial body that had given life to the trees and plants in the first place.

There was a certain malevolence to the eye, he thought. It did not bode well. Or was it pity?

On the ground under the bench, too, were some other images, images of small people, all mixed up, in combinations anathema to his view of the world, and these glossy images, reflecting the nurturing rays of the sun, were shining at different angles into his eyes, some blinding him, not just with light, but with a kind of accusation, and, onto one of these images, which had been threatening to blow away in the small gusts of wind swirling around the wood, stepped a shoe, a strong-looking, official-looking shoe, trapping the image there as the wearer first looked at, then bore down, on him, *him*.

The Liao Women

Song Gao Lei

In the cool damp of the evening, the side of her face red and swelling, Liao Meixiu resolved to kill her husband.

A week previous, she had been cleaning the last of the customers' dishes when from behind her she heard Ma Gang come through the restaurant's main doors after a night of cards. "Meixiu," he called to his wife in an alcohol-slurred voice. "Meixiu, I'm out. Give me more."

Meixiu wiped her hands on her green apron and searched her pockets for the cupboard's key. It was not there and she scared, frightened of the consequences if she had lost it. Another frantic rustle through her pockets turned up nothing before she remembered that the key was in the drawer of her nightstand.

"Wait one minute, Gang," Meixiu said and quickly set forth through the restaurant's serving area and up the stairs to the living quarters she shared with her husband of thirty years. Key in hand, she went back and unlocked the east wall's cupboard above the sink. Meixiu took out a bottle of jingjiu and hurried to where Gang waited in the plywood and glass partition just off the kitchen's opposite wall.

The room was small and accommodated nothing more than a table and two benches. On one bench lay blankets, coats, and boxes of napkins and plastic cups. Gang sat on the other, watching a Second World War prison camp show on the television. Above him hung their family portrait, taken in Meixiu's home village during a Chinese New Year long past. They were a good-looking family then and their child, Ma Huan, was an unscarred boy of three. Now he was a grown man living with his wife and son in Shenzhen.

"Why so slow?" Gang said.

"I had to run get the key," answered his wife as she refilled Gang's plastic cup and his large pink thermos. Gang drank greedily and Meixiu replenished his cup when he set it down empty.

"I don't want these plastic cups," he said. "I told you I want it from a glass cup."

"You break too many of them. Plastic is fine for you."

"You don't know what you're saying woman."

"Last week you broke three glasses, Gang. Drinking has made your memory bad."

It was not merely Gang's memory that was gone. There was little left of the man Meixiu had known and who smiled brightly on the only picture in the room. That man had sharp features. High cheekbones, a strong jaw, and thick black hair. The hair remained, but his sagging jowls obscured his chin and alcohol had turned his face vermillion like the party cups from which he drank.

"Nothing wrong with my memory," Gang muttered and his surly mood, complemented by drunkenness, told Meixiu how her husband's turn at the gambling table had gone.

"How much did you lose?" she said.

"Four," Gang answered, an unlucky number in China due to it sounding the same as the word for death, and Meixiu knew he meant four thousand. "The cards didn't go my way."

"We can't afford this. I have a good mind not to give you your jingjiu whenever you call for it."

Gang grabbed Meixiu's right forearm. Annoyed that this made her spill some of the bottle's amber, syrupy alcohol on the blue tablecloth, he gripped harder.

Meixiu winced. "You're hurting me, Gang. Please stop."

"When I say give me more, you say how much. Understand?"

"Yes. Yes, I understand."

Gang released her. "Fill my cup," he said and his wife did as she was told.

*

The following day the customers came in waves out of the mid-January afternoon. Wearing surgical masks, they flashed the green health barcodes on their phones to gain admittance. In the kitchen it was warm. The woks sizzled and the pots hummed to keep pace. Rice and beef noodles, vegetables and dumplings, cups of tea and bottles of beer.

The restaurant's four women operated in a loose division of labor. Meixiu and her cousin Liao Daiyu prepared and cooked the food. Fatty Zhen, who was not particularly fat, washed dishes and Baby Zhen, who was of no relation to Fatty and at thirty-three was not particularly young, recorded orders and bussed the tables. At any time these roles changed, and more than once Meixiu would go to greet customers or thank them for coming. Covid regulations made this all the easier for her with the mask she wore hiding the physical shame of her smile.

As Meixiu and Daiyu sealed balls of minced beef and leek in dumpling skins, Meixiu looked at Fatty Zhen who was drying plates.

"I need to talk to you," Meixiu said covertly to her cousin. "Not here."

The two women slipped away to the seaside during the afternoon dead period between two and four-thirty. The ocean was a block from their restaurant and on this Tuesday the sand beneath their feet and the sound of the waters lapping the shore was felt and heard only by them.

"What did you want to talk about, elder sister?" said Daiyu, who despite being three years older than her cousin, often referred to Meixiu with this term of affectionate respect.

"We have to let Fatty Zhen go."

"Fatty's been with us two years. She's reliable."

"I know, but a lot of our foreign customers left China once the virus hit and we need to cut some costs. You and I can make up for what she does."

"Fatty shouldn't suffer because Hongbao is losing our money at poker," Daiyu said, using the nickname she coined to mock Ma Gang's alcohol-tinged complexion, hongbao being the red envelopes Chinese people traditionally use to pass along monetary presents. "He's the gift that keeps on taking," she sneered.

Meixiu had no reply, nor could she speak so directly like her cousin, the contrasting pair that they were. Daiyu, short and fiery with a plain face, wore round glasses and her long hair was pulled into a ponytail. Meixiu was the beauty of the family. Tall with wavy, shoulder-length hair and large eyes, at fifty-two she retained the slender figure of her youth. But she was meek, and unlike her cousin, she kept her surgical mask on while they walked on the otherwise deserted beach.

"You should divorce him, elder sister."

"I can't. The certificate of ownership is in his name and we'll lose what we built. You know that."

It was true. In the second year of their marriage, Gang had come back to the village to celebrate the advent of the Year of the Rooster. "I've saved up enough from my construction job for us to start a restaurant in the city," he told his wife. "I know someone who has a spot he can get us next to the ocean. I won't be leaving you for work anymore and we'll be our own bosses."

Afraid of such a sudden change and leaving the land that held her ancestors' graves, Meixiu eventually gave in to Gang's exuberance after requesting that her cousin come and work with them. "Of course," her husband had said, having no conflict with Liao Daiyu in those days.

The arrangement had been a fruitful one. Meixiu and Daiyu's paternal grandmother, their nainai, had raised them while their respective parents were away at factory jobs and part of nainai's education included teaching her granddaughters how to cook. The tutelage paid off in the success of their small restaurant and Daiyu married a traditional Chinese doctor from the city and Meixiu gave birth to a son. She had named him Huan, Chinese for joyous.

And it had been in their early years. Gang had done the maintenance work and heavy lifting and would invite friends and family over on Saturday afternoons. They pushed the tables and chairs to the side and danced to the radio's music, nobody moving as gracefully as Ma Gang. In time, some of these same friends began taking him with them to gamble and drink. The weekend dancing had come to an end and his abusive ways had begun.

"If you can't divorce him," Daiyu said, "then stop giving him money."

"He takes what he wants, cousin."

"That's how you got the welts on your wrist you've been trying to hide from me all day?" Daiyu said in a way that was as much a statement of fact as it was a question.

"I slipped."

"Must be the same place you slipped when you knocked out two of your front teeth."

Daiyu saw the hurt she had caused her cousin and regretted it. This gentle woman who liked wearing a surgical mask because it hid her broken smile didn't deserve such words. "Are we ok for money in the short term, elder sister?" Daiyu said, returning their conversation to its original topic.

"It should be all right for a couple weeks and Gang's been better. Most days he drinks and watches TV which is cheaper than gambling. I also have my savings for Ma Huan. Gang doesn't know about that and we can dip into it if we have to."

"Keep your savings for your son and hold off on telling Fatty. You can take some of my pay for her if you need to and in the meantime I'll come up with something."

"Like what?"

"I don't know," Daiyu said, briefly thinking of their great auntie Liao's husband which made her grin a mischievous grin. "Even if our nainai was a Chen," she said, "remember what she told us?"

"You're Liao women," Meixiu said, the contours of her face lifting into a smile beneath her mask.

*

The restaurant's front door locked for the night, the four women talked about their plans for Chinese New Year. Liao Meixiu would let them off work in three days and all had found tickets home, no small feat at this time of year. Fatty Zhen was going to Zhejiang, Baby Zhen to Guangzhou, and

Liao Daiyu and her husband would meet their daughter, son-in-law, and granddaughter in the village. That left Meixiu.

"Where'll you go, boss?" Fatty Zhen asked, chewing on a piece of dried beef as she spoke.

"I'll stay here," Meixiu said. "You know the tradition, the son goes to his wife's family on New Years. He'll come here for Tuan Nian Fan."

The women knew that this too was tradition, but Fatty Zhen and Baby Zhen had not seen Meixiu's son home at the end of the last month to celebrate Tuan Nian Fan nor at any of the other Decembers while they had worked for her.

"You should go to Shenzhen," Daiyu said to her cousin once the other two women left.

"I have to take care of Gang and he can't go."

"Then call Ma Huan. I'm sure he misses his mother and Bao Bao misses his grandmother."

After Daiyu went home, Meixiu checked on Ma Gang who snored loudly as a war drama played on the partition's television. She filled his cup with jingjiu in case he awoke and went upstairs to the bedroom where she made a video call to her son.

"Hi mom," Huan said when he answered. "Are you ok?"

"I'm always good when I talk to you," Meixiu said, the sight of her son, however infrequent, reminding her of the past. For Huan looked exactly like Gang had at that age except for the white scar that ran down the younger man's left cheek like a solitary tear.

"Is Bao Bao awake?" Meixiu asked about her grandson.

"He's sleeping. He likes school but it wears him out."

"Keep sending his pictures. I always show him off to the ladies at work. He's a real hit with them."

"I'm sure he is. What else did you want to say, mom? I've got office things to finish up and can't talk long."

"Huan, are you going to come home for Chinese New Year?"

"We're staying with my wife's family."

"I know, but you could all come here and bring Bao Bao. It's two hours by train and you can go back the same day."

"Dad?"

Meixiu answered the question honestly, even though she knew what that meant. "He's the same."

Ma Huan shook his head. "I won't be coming. It's a bad environment for Bao Bao and I don't want him around that. I have to go. My work needs to get done."

The call ended, Meixiu put the phone in her pocket and dried her eyes with her hands. Ma Gang called for help and she dutifully walked down the stairs to the partition. He had spilled most of the plastic cup of jingjiu on his shirt which was not uncommon after too much time elapsed between his libations. Meixiu poured him another cup from the pink thermos and steadied her husband's liver-spotted hands as they carried the cure for delirium tremens to his mouth.

"We should get you drinking beer," she told Gang. "It's not as harmful to your body."

"I drink what I want."

They were the words he had spoken to Huan in anger the last time Meixiu and Gang's son had come home for the New Year. His wife and Bao Bao asleep on the second floor, Huan had been chatting with his mother in the restaurant's dining area, dimmed by the red New Year's lanterns that covered the room's lightbulbs. And like them, Huan dressed in red for the night to ward off evil spirits during his zodiac year.

Gang strode in at half-past midnight, smelling of smoke and sweat from the gambling hall. With satisfaction, he threw a pile of cash on the table. The notes were of small denominations and it could not have amounted to more than five hundred kuai.

"It's because of me you got that expensive university education," Gang said to his son, his loose jowls wimpling as he spoke. "All that money of mine you spent and you're a low-level functionary in some insurance company."

"I'll work my way up," Huan said.

"You better have my courage if you're going anywhere. Without me your mom'd still be in her home village washing dishes and taking orders from some old tiger woman. See everything here?" Gang proudly surveyed the room with his eyes. "This is all my doing."

"I never saw you work a day in the kitchen with mom and Auntie Daiyu and I never saw you serve a single customer."

Gang slapped the table. "You young kids don't show respect," he said to his son. Then to his wife, "Who saved up the money for this place?"

"You," she softly answered.

"Whose idea was it to come here?"

"Yours."

"That's right, woman. Get up and get me some jingjiu."

Huan held up a hand, signaling for his mother to stay put. His face flush with embarrassment and anger, he took a bottle of Tsing Tao from the fridge and loudly set it in front of his father. "Drink this you useless jiugui."

Astonished by words that no one dared say to him but Daiyu, Gang sat silently before warning his son never to make him lose face again.

"You have no face left to lose," Huan retorted.

Gang deliberately wrapped his fingers around the beer bottle's neck and said, "I drink jingjiu. I drink what I want." He rose from his chair and before anyone could react, he had smashed the bottle across Huan's face. Meixiu managed to pull Gang away and get him into his partition. She called Daiyu whose husband came and drove Huan to the hospital. "You were lucky," Daiyu's husband told his nephew after stitching the wound. "If the bottle had come down three centimeters farther in the other direction you would have lost your eye. This'll only leave a scar."

That had been the Year of the Dog. Three years ago and Meixiu had not seen her son or grandson in person since.

*

Ma Gang trudged into the kitchen and told Meixiu to give him money, his presence sending Fatty Zhen and Baby Zhen scurrying out with the excuse that they should clean the tables.

Meixiu wiped her hands and took off her apron. "Let's go to the bank," she said. "We're opening soon so we need to hurry."

Daiyu kept dicing peppers and gave Gang a hard look through her round glasses. "We'd have as much money as a bank if you'd quit your gambling, Hongbao. Could've bought the whole city by now with what you frittered away."

"Forget it," Meixiu said in an aside to her cousin. "If he's out gambling at least he won't bother us."

During the restaurant's afternoon dead period, Meixiu and Daiyu travelled to the wet market. Here their personalities reversed. Daiyu would stand to the side while Meixiu haggled with the vendors for what she needed. The younger of the Liao women had gained such a fearsome reputation for negotiating that when she showed up at a stall, most sellers asked Meixiu what price she would accept and then gave it to her without further debate.

Walking down a side street, the women laden with bags of vegetables, oil, rice, beef, and pork, Daiyu said she had a solution for cutting costs.

"What is it?"

"You know the story nainai told us about great auntie Liao's husband."

"He accidentally drowned in a rice paddy."

"You really think that's what happened?"

"There's more?"

"There's more. But wait here," Daiyu said in front of a bakery. "I want to get some cakes for my granddaughter."

Meixiu put down her bags. She readjusted her surgical mask and massaged her right shoulder with her hand, thinking of how Ma Gang used to carry the restaurant's supplies from the wet market.

Daiyu rejoined her cousin and, setting out again, continued her story. "Great auntie Liao's husband was popular with two ladies in the village," she said. "He was also lazy. Our great auntie did all the work and he spent what she earned. Three of her Liao brothers came to visit one day and that same day great auntie Liao's husband went out to the fields he never went out to and didn't come back. It was no coincidence."

"You mean..."

"I mean he didn't drown by accident. Nainai told it all to me the day we left home for the city."

"Why didn't she tell me?" Meixiu said, somewhat hurt, and needing another rest, she sat down on a concrete bench facing the street.

"Because we're different, elder sister. That day nainai said I needed to protect you and…and I didn't do what I promised her."

"Gang isn't the same as great auntie Liao's husband."

"He's not," Daiyu said and sat next to her cousin. "He's worse. He hits you and he's going to break us."

"What is your idea?"

"It's like this. Who is to say Gang doesn't have an accident? The kind he doesn't recover from. He could buy a sleeping potion from my husband and mistakenly take too much and pass out behind the restaurant some freezing night. Or he's drunk and trips in front of a moving car. A little accident is all, and to be honest, with how he drinks I'm surprised the natural way of things hasn't done the job already."

"I can't," Meixiu said, holding her head back to stanch her emotions. "Gang was so good to me. He would bring me gifts almost every weekend. I was the envy of all the wives."

"You know the old saying, elder sister, everything in the past died yesterday. What hasn't died is Hongbao drinking and gambling away what us women worked for. We're Liao women. With him gone it'll be like starting new again. Just think about it, elder sister. Just think about it," and Meixiu did think about it that night when Ma Gang struck her twice.

He had come home and from his disposition she could tell that his losses had been worse than normal. "How much did you lose?" she asked while pouring him jingjiu.

"San."

The answer surprised Meixiu who thought she had misread Gang. "You've had worse days than three thousand," she said.

"San wan. The cards didn't go my way."

"*Thirty thousand*? How is that possible? Where did you get that much money?"

"I borrowed it."

"You *borrowed* it?" Meixiu exclaimed, thirty thousand an amount she would have to pay for out of her savings for Ma Huan. "You *damn* fool. What rate did they–"

Gang cuffed his wife across the side of the head with his closed fist and when she started to cry he hit her again.

"*Hundan,*" Meixiu screamed and shoved her husband who stumbled over his bench. "*You ruin everything.*" With her arms she swept the television from the table as Gang looked on, cowed by a woman he had never known. "*You're bleeding us dry and you've destroyed our family, our work, our traditions. Our son won't come to see us for three years because of you. Bao Bao grows up without us because of you. It's enough. I've had enough,*" she cried and threw Gang's heavy pink thermos onto his abdomen and walked away while he gasped for air.

Meixiu returned to her sink-full of dishes to collect her thoughts. The air was cool and damp and she reached up to feel the damage done to her face which had begun to swell. She could not hide this and she thought of her cousin's words. A little accident is all.

The first New Year they shared as a married couple, Gang bought Meixiu a pair of wooly socks. They were too thick for that warm winter but she had worn them anyway as they sat together watching the fireworks illuminate the February sky. It had been another time and she could not go back to somewhere that existed only in memories. That would make easier what she needed to do and tomorrow she planned–

Meixiu felt as though she viewed the kitchen from above, Ma Gang standing over her prostate body, his pink thermos in hand. He raised it above his head like it was a pestle ready to descend on a stone mortar of glutinous rice and in an instant her mortal thoughts ceased. She saw no more.

As was usual, Daiyu arrived first in the morning. Entering through the backdoor she found her cousin lying on the floor. A pool of dried blood surrounded Meixiu's head like a rust-colored halo and flecks of it led across the floor to the partition on the other side of the wall.

"Oh elder sister," Daiyu whispered.

But she allowed herself no emotion as she removed a whetstone from the drawer and the heavy knife for cutting vegetables from the sink. In the way their nainai taught them, Daiyu drew the knife across the stone at a twenty-degree angle until it was sharpened to perfection.

In the partition, a broken television lay on the floor and a bloody thermos lay on the table. Ma Gang sat hunched forward on the bench, his chin resting on his chest, a thin strand of spittle dribbling from his lower lip. Daiyu might have even thought him dead were it not for the uneven breathing that whistled through his nose.

"Wake up, Hongbao," she hissed through barely parted lips. "Wake up."

Daiyu kicked Gang and he fell onto his back, stirring slightly. She climbed on top of him and, straddling his stomach, began slapping him until he parted his eyelids.

"Wuh-wuh..." he croaked.

"Do you see who this is, Hongbao? Wake up. You need to see who this is."

"Wuh...what are you doing Daiyu?"

"Good. I want you to know who ended this for you."

Daiyu put the point of the knife over Gang's heart and threw all of her weight down on its butt. The man below her writhed and his teeth gnashed together like someone thrown to the outer darkness, but the years of drinking had taken their toll and the knife moved faster. Then as quickly as it began, the fight evaporated from his body and nothing showed in his eyes, not even pain.

Knowing that what she had done she had done too late, Daiyu gave the impaled man a last, spiteful look before going to the kitchen. There she sat next to the woman with whom she had shared a life and took her hand in her own.

"We're Liao women," Daiyu began to say, but she could restrain her tears no longer.

On the cold floor she wept and waited with her cousin for Fatty Zhen and Baby Zhen to arrive. Then the day would begin. It would all begin anew.

Highway 29

Mike O'Driscoll

The woman shook her head and said the shoes didn't look right on her daughter. It was the fifth pair the girl had tried on and my nerves were starting to fray. I smiled at the plump little girl, said I thought they suited her and didn't she think so too? But mom jumped in before the girl could speak, saying she knew best what kind of shoes her daughter needed. If that was the case, I was tempted to say, then why couldn't she just point out that pair and stop wasting my time. I stood and followed the woman to another display stand where she picked up a red patent leather pump and asked me to get a pair of those in her daughter's size. As she thrust the shoe in my hand I noticed another, younger woman enter the store. She stood there, brushed long silver-pink hair back from her face and surveyed the racks of shoes as if there wasn't a goddamn chance in Hell we would have something she might like. Jai was already making a beeline for her. I hurried forward and intercepted him, nodding to where the woman and child were waiting and told him they needed assistance.

"You were dealing with them," he said. "I was going to take care of that lady just walked in."

We both turned to look at her. She wore a black, knee-length skirt patterned with blue, pink and orange flowers, and a pale blue blouse with the sleeves rolled up over the elbows. I guessed she was about my age, twenty-two, or younger. As we watched she wandered over to a display stand, reached into her grey shoulder bag, took out a pack of cigarettes and lit one up. I glanced at Jai. "You want to deal with that?"

A look of uncertainty flickered across his face. I pressed the shoe into his hand and told him the child was waiting. He gave me a resentful shrug and wandered off to the storeroom. I went to where the woman was studying a lemon yellow sandal.

"Excuse me, ma'am," I said. "There's no smoking in this store."

She turned, sandal in one hand. A bolo tie hung loose from her collar, the silver clip shaped into an ornately curved 'H' with a blue stone laid in to the middle bar. "How much are these?" she said, pink hair cascading over her shoulder.

"I'm sorry, ma'am," I said. "But you can't do that in here."

"Why not?" Her voice sounded older than she looked.

"Store policy."

"You ought to have a sign up," she said, taking a pull on the cigarette and blowing smoke in my face. Orange butterflies emerged from beneath her sleeve and curled around the arm to her wrist.

I pointed to a 'No Smoking' sign on the wall.

She held the cigarette up and looked at it askance. "What do you expect me to do with it?"

"Let me take it." She gave me the cigarette and I took it out behind the counter and extinguished it in the waste bin. When I returned, she had moved on to browse a section of high heels. "Anything I can help you with, ma'am?"

"Do I look like a ma'am?"

I was taken aback, but only for a second or two. "You look like a lady interested in shoes."

"Are all the staff as astute as you?"

"Nope," I said, thinking maybe she was out of my league.

"How do I know that?"

"Because I'm the one made it his business to assist you."

"Is that right?" She cocked her head to one side and raised a hand to her throat, two fingers resting on a vein like she was checking for signs of life. Her lips parted ever so slightly and she made a sound I barely heard but thought I knew the meaning of. "I need a pair of shoes."

"You come to the right place."

Her eyes narrowed and the light changed her hair from pink to gold. "We'll see."

"You want to try one of those?" I gestured to the shoe rack.

"I doubt it. You got SAS?"

"No, ma'am, we don't stock that brand."

"What about Esquivel?"

"We don't have those either."

"But this is a shoe store?"

She was trying to make me feel foolish, but I didn't mind it so much. She moved on to the next display stand and picked up an Aurora sandal. "Is this vegan?"

I shrugged and told her I wasn't sure.

"You have any Mesa shoes? They make vegan, you know."

"You want to wear them or eat them?"

"You fancy yourself a wit?"

"I wouldn't say that."

"Neither would I. So, you got a pair or what?"

"I'm sorry, we don't."

"What do you have?"

I folded one arm across my belly and raised the other hand to my chin, as if I was giving it some thought. "Why don't you let me pick out a pair?" I said.

"I don't know," she said. "I'm particular about what I put on my feet."

"I can see that." I glanced down at her left leg where more butterflies climbed up from behind her ankle. "Size seven?"

She nodded, walked to the box seat and sat. I made a show of deliberating over the display before selecting a pair of taupe Munro Abby's priced at $179.99.

"That's a nice color," she said when I showed her the shoe.

"Goes with your hair."

"You think so?"

"Yeah. You wanna try it on?"

She crossed her left leg over the right, revealing the tattoo of butterflies that swirled up her slender calf. I knelt before her and removed the blue pump from her foot. My hand shook a little as I cradled her heel. "You got nice feet," I said.

Her gaze fell on me like a benediction and her lips curled into a smile. "What's your name?"

"Travis."

"Do I make you nervous, Travis?"

You need to stop right now, I told myself. Instead, I stroked one butterfly with the tip of my forefinger. "That's quite the swarm you got there."

"You think so?" She straightened out her foot.

I slid the shoe on and tightened the heel strap. "You must really like butterflies."

"I like what they stand for."

"What's that?"

"They're a symbol for the soul."

"I didn't know that." I lowered her foot to the floor, caressing her lower calf. "This bunch look like they're on their way to heaven."

She laughed as I took her other foot and slid on the matching shoe and asked her how they felt.

She didn't say anything but stood and looked down at her feet and walked to a free standing mirror. Something hummed inside my belly as she turned one ankle and then the other. "They look good on you," I said.

"I don't know," she said, frowning.

I stood, feeling a little lightheaded. "We can try something else."

"Let's do that." She returned to the seat while I scanned more shoes, selecting a pair of Rafa sandals with chunky heels. I sat on my haunches and removed the Munros, aware that she was watching me. What the fuck are you doing, I asked myself. This is not the time or place. But I was beyond caring and I think she knew that because when I looked up she slipped me a piece of paper. The touch of her fingers lit up something inside me. It was unreal. Right then I saw myself stumbling into a dream. In the dream I put the paper in my pocket and told her how soft her skin was. My mouth was dry as a bone and I wasn't sure she understood, but a second later, when I slipped my hand up her skirt, I knew she did.

She left the store emptyhanded. I took the slip of paper from my pocket, opened it out and saw the name Holly written there and a number. I spent the next two hours in a kind of daze until it was time to close. I called the number and told her to meet me at a roadhouse out on Highway 29.

•

She arrived at the roadhouse just minutes after I got there. I asked her what she wanted to drink. She turned to look through the window at the parking lot and said she wasn't thirsty yet. I nodded, took her hand and led her outside to my Corolla. We fell into the front seat already clawing at each others' clothes. Afterwards, I held her naked in my lap and traced the line of butterflies as they climbed over her left hip, spiraled up her spine to the shoulder and down her right arm. "How long you had them?" I asked.

"First one was when I was sixteen," she said, her breath like a desert breeze in my ear. "They multiplied since then."

"How old are you now?"

"I'm twenty-four."

"I thought you were younger."

"You disappointed?"

"Let me think on it."

"Maybe this will make up for it." She pulled my face to hers and kissed me on the mouth.

We fucked again, slower this time, making it last.

When we were done we went back inside the roadhouse and ordered burgers and fries. I drank beer and she had vodka and coke. I asked her about herself and was surprised when she said there wasn't much to tell. Most girls I'd known liked to talk about themselves. Her reticence only served to sharpen my curiosity. When I pressed her she said she was from Lafayette, but hadn't lived there since she ran away from home at fifteen.

"You been on your own since then?"

"Mostly."

"Must of been tough."

"Some."

"How'd you survive?"

"Does it matter?"

"I guess not."

She stared down at her plate and sighed. "You learn to get by."

I nodded. "I can see that."

"What about you?"

"What about me?"

"You always work in a shoe store?"

"You kidding me?" I said, wanting to impress her. "That's just a stopgap."

"For what?"

"I got aspirations."

"Oh yeah?"

"My future is elsewhere."

"I never been there."

"Me neither, but I will get there."

"I got as far San Diego once."

"California. Now you're talking."

"It's not how you think it is."

I put the last of the burger into my mouth and thought about it. Ever since I left high school I'd been planning to leave this shitty town and hightail it to California one day. Yet here she was telling me it didn't live up to her expectations. "Well," I said. "I think I'll need to see it for myself."

"Everybody says that until they get there."

I was stung. "I believe I could make a go of it."

"What makes you so different?"

I felt like she was testing me in some way. I don't know why but I wanted more than anything to have her believe in me. "I don't say anything I don't mean."

She sipped her drink slowly and her eyes watched me over the rim of the glass. I felt myself drowning in her gaze but I didn't care. "So when you leaving?"

"Soon," I said. "My mind's made up."

"You got it all figured out."

"More or less. You should come with me."

"What makes you think I'd want to do that, Travis Bowers?"

"Cos you like me. You like a fella that's got ambition."

She leaned back in her seat and raised a hand to the bolo, holding it between her fingers. Her eyes roved across the crowded room before they came to rest on me. "Tell me something," she said. "Are you one of those blowhards who never live up to all their big talk?"

"I told you," I said. "That's not me. I'm the kind of fella can make things happen."

"What kind of things?"

"Anything you want."

"I'd like to see that."

"Stick around and you will."

•

I ran out the door, gun in hand, looking for the car that wasn't there. My heart pounded like crazy and the dry taste of fear was in my mouth. Bright midday sun made the air shimmer, blurring the edges of the world, and from somewhere beyond it came the sound of somebody screaming. The Corolla screeched to a halt right in front of me and the passenger door flew open. I held the holdall to my chest and fell into the seat, shouting at her to hit the gas.

"Jesus, Holly," I said, as she spun out on to the road. "Where the fuck were you?"

"What happened?" she said, wide-eyed and jittery.

I shook my head, trying to clear my thoughts. It had happened only moments ago but already it seemed unreal. Everything had happened so fast, I'd had no time to think. "It's done," I said, feeling a tightness across my chest. "We did it."

She glanced at me, her face marked by confusion and fear. "Oh fuck, Travis," she said, sounding close to panic. She was staring down at my lap, where the top of the holdall had opened. Bloodstained banknotes spilled out on the floor. The shirt beneath my jacket was turning red. A wave of nausea rose up inside me as I put a hand there and became aware of a burning sensation in my belly.

"You're shot!" Holly cried. "Didn't you know?"

I do now, I thought, as I bit down on the pain. "It's not so bad," I said. "Just keep driving."

"Drive where?"

"South," I told her. "Like we agreed." That was the plan. She couldn't have forgotten it already. We had talked about it. A small town bank, get in and out real fast and head south toward the border before any fucker could raise the alarm. We'd get fifty, maybe a hundred thousand dollars for sure. It had seemed so easy in the talking. "Not too fast," I reminded her as I wiped the bloody hand on my jeans.

"Is it bad?" Holly said. "Are you dying?"

What was she talking about? She was looking at me, lips trembling, tears rolling down her cheeks. "Watch the fucking road," I shouted. She was driving too fast. "And slow down."

"Don't shout at me," she cried, slamming on the brakes and skidding to a halt on the gravel verge. "It's not my fault."

"Jesus Christ, Holly — I never said it was."

"Then just tell me what happened."

I looked back over my shoulder. There was nobody on our tail. Not yet. "I'm sorry, but please, just drive slower is all I'm saying. Stay on the back roads. We don't want to draw attention to ourselves."

Her hand shook as she put the car in drive and pulled back out onto the highway. "It's not my fault," she repeated, as she pushed it up to fifty and held it there. I saw the effort she was making to get herself under control. Something thumped repeatedly against my right leg and when I looked I saw my hand was spasming, tapping the Hi-Point .45 against my thigh. I dropped the gun in the door pocket and winced as a sharp pain lanced through my gut. I must have made a sound because Holly looked at me again and said, "It's bad, isn't it? What the fuck are we going to do?"

"It just hurts a little," I told her. "I'll be all right."

"What happened in there, Travis?"

I shook my head. Everything was still a blur. "I had a gun," I said by way of explanation. "You know the rest."

"No, Goddammit, I don't," she said. "You said there'd be no trouble."

There wasn't supposed to be. The Evanston First Direct branch had one overweight, middle-aged security guard. Family man, looked like. They had protocols, I knew. In the event of a robbery, just go along with the demands. Compliance, that was the word. Everything was insured. No need at all for blood to be spilled. I'd wave the Hi-Point around and bark a few simple instructions and customers and staff would all fall into line, just like that. I was thirsty. There was grit in my eyes. I tried to stay focused on the way it was supposed to be. Nobody shot, nobody dead, just a half dozen people with a story to tell their friends over coffee. *You'll never guess what happened to me today. Do tell. I got caught in a real live bank heist, that's what. What do you think of that? Don't that beat all?* There'd be a report on the evening news and in the next day's papers. *Desperados get away with fifty grand*, it would say. *No casualties as victims stay calm throughout.*

"Christ," I said. "Why didn't he listen?"

"Who?"

I closed my eyes for a moment, trying to ride another wave of pain. When it passed I had difficulty remembering where I was. Through the windshield was just desert and sky, and sitting beside me was this woman I had known barely a week. I wondered why she was crying. I had bought her nice things. Things she had wanted. Things I couldn't afford. My last evening at the shoe store I had emptied the cash register, knowing I wasn't coming back. You did it for her, I told myself but I knew it wasn't true. I'd done it for myself. I drifted off for a minute or two, maybe longer. When I came to, the fog still lingered in my brain and I felt an unnatural chill in my bones. I asked her where we were going but she didn't respond. The situation had an unreal quality, like something I was imagining, or maybe it was just a dream. "I need a smoke," I managed to say. "Real bad."

She reached down into the pocket and grabbed a pack of cigarettes and her lighter, passed them to me. It took three attempts to get one lit. When I did, she asked me how I was feeling.

"I like those boots," I said. "They really show off your legs."

"What?" She looked down at the cowboy boots I had stolen from the store. "Why are you talking about boots?"

I turned my face to the window, confused. I wondered what I had done. Right up to the minute I went into the bank I had never believed I'd go through with it. I'd come to my senses, turn round and walk back to the car, get in and tell Holly this wasn't who I was. She would understand. I'm not a bad man. I must have said it out loud because she answered me.

"I know you're not. It's just ..." She left the rest of it unspoken.

"Just what?"

"You keep drifting off. We're talking and I keep asking you what happened and you keep saying you don't know or somebody didn't listen."

"It doesn't matter now."

"I don't know what we're going to do."

"Stick to the plan."

"The plan," she said, and I sensed the anger and hopelessness in the words. "There's a fucking plan?"

"Just keep driving." The sun was low on the horizon now, red streaks painting the sky.

"What about that?" She gestured at the bullet wound.

"I'll live. Right now we got to put distance between us and Evanston."

"I been driving two hours," she said.

It didn't seem that long. We passed a sign for Freer. "Where you taking us?" I asked.

"You said to avoid Laredo so I swung back east."

"We haven't crossed the border yet?"

"No. You told me to stay on the back roads."

"We're heading south?"

She nodded and sunlight glistened off the bolo on her chest.

"Okay baby."

An awful weariness came over me. I touched my shirt and my fingers came away sticky and red. I leaned back in the seat and turned my face to the window as darkness began to fall on the desert like a bruise. I thought about the impossibility of what I had done, wondering if I was still the same man. The two cashiers had almost done filling the black holdall when I saw the guard rise up on one knee, pull his sidearm from the holster and tell me to put the gun down. I could have done it. He gave me a chance, but I was not that man. If he had known he would never have told me to do it, he'd never even have pulled the gun. If he had only known the type of man he was dealing with.

The thought that flashed through my brain right before I pulled the trigger was, didn't he know the fucking protocol? Adrenalin had coursed through my veins as I blasted away, three or four shots, I wasn't sure. People began to scream. It was an awful sound they made. I stood there looking at him, laying on his back on the polished floor, blood pooling beneath his chest. I felt nothing at all as I grabbed the holdall from the cashier and ran from the bank with the echo of gunshots still ringing in my ears and the stink of gunpowder in my nose.

•

It was dark when Holly stopped at a Costco just outside Hebbronville. While she went inside I turned on the radio to listen to news and found nothing but angry preachers and country music stations. Right before I turned it off I heard an old Bruce Springsteen song that sounded familiar. But as I let it play and listened to him sing about hearts turning black and devil-filled souls, a cold fear crawled up my spine till I could stand it no more and turned it off.

Holly came out of the store carrying a large paper bag. She lit a cigarette and stuck it in my mouth. We drove on through the town and a couple miles south we saw the yellow neon sign for a Motel 9, and turned into the parking lot. When she'd checked us in she drove to the far end of the two-storey row. I opened the car door and swung my legs out. The air felt hot and clean in my lungs. A coyote yelped out beyond the parking lot. I stood and felt my head start to spin. I grabbed onto the roof of the car and wondered how the Hell I had got here. It was just bad luck, I told myself, but the lie wouldn't stick. It was something else. The words of the Springsteen song came back to me and I remembered when I was a child, being taught in catechism class how we all were tainted with some original sin, and I wondered if that was what had been smouldering inside me my whole life.

Holly came round the car and helped me into the room. I collapsed on the bed while she went back to the car to get the things she'd bought. I must have faded out for a while because when I saw her next she had opened up a first aid kit and was laying out tape and surgical dressings on the bed. She took an antiseptic wipe and began to dab at the hole in my belly.

"Jesus Christ," I gasped.

"I'm sorry."

"Is the bleeding stopped?" I said through gritted teeth.

"I think so. I can't tell for sure. You need a doctor."

"No doctor."

She frowned. "Does it hurt still?"

"Some," I told her. "You get painkillers?"

She disappeared for a moment, then returned with a pack of Tylenol and a glass of water.

She pressed two tablets from the blister pack, put them in my mouth and raised the glass to my lips. I swallowed. I asked if she'd bought alcohol. She showed me a bottle of Tito's vodka and half filled the glass, topping it up with Coke. I drank a good mouthful, just about managing to hold it down.

"I can't believe I'm shot," I said. She finished cleaning the wound and spread Sudocrem over it, covered it with a surgical dressing and taped it in place.

She put a hand on my cheek. "What happened in there?"

"I don't want to talk about it." I sat up and saw the holdall on a chair. I pointed to it and asked if she had counted it. She said she had.

"How much?"

"Six and a half thousand dollars."

I stared hard at her. "How much?"

"Six thousand, six hundred and ten dollars."

"That's all?"

"There's maybe a few more dollars in the car."

"How many more?"

"I don't know, Travis. Not a whole lot."

"I took a fucking bullet for that? Jesus Christ!"

Holly stared blankly at the bag and said nothing.

"I killed a man for six and a half thousand lousy bucks? Jesus, Holly — what the fuck."

"I guess that's all there was."

I shook my head, disgusted. "It don't make sense."

She gave a dry, bitter laugh.

"Should it have done?"

"What do you mean?"

"You expected this thing to make sense?"

"You're saying you didn't?"

Her shoulders sagged." Fuck, Travis — the only expectation I had was that it would last longer than it did."

"You mean you and me?"

"Everything."

I slumped back on the bed, unsure what she meant. She asked if I was hungry. Besides the bottle of Tito's and two bottles of Coke, she had bought a half dozen bars of Snickers, and a couple party-size packs of Zapp's voodoo flavour potato chips. I told her no and asked her to fill me another glass of vodka and coke. It was a struggle to hold it down, but by the third glass, the pain in my belly had faded to a dull ache. She tried to talk about what we were going to do, but my mind kept wandering, whether from fatigue or the vodka I couldn't tell. After a while she turned on the television. I closed my eyes and listened to the voices. I heard music too, the kind you hear in church, and for a moment I wondered if anyone was praying for my soul.

Later, I heard her say, "Are you going to be all right?"

"Probably," I said, opening my eyes. She sat beside me on the bed, hugging her knees, blue light from the television flickering over her face. Sweat glistened on her lips and her eyes were red from crying. Even so, I saw something in them that gave me hope. She leaned over and kissed me on the forehead. The bolo dangled before my eyes and that curved 'H' seemed to confirm what I thought I knew.

I drifted off again and slept the long, dreamless sleep of the dead.

•

I woke at dawn, covered in sweat and with a burning sensation in my stomach. It hurt to breath, which made me wonder if I was dying. The thought of it scared me to the core. There was still time to put a stop to it. I could call the cops and tell them to come get me. If I turned myself in they would take me to a hospital and save my life. I would tell them that Holly had no part in it. I had threatened to kill her if she didn't come along, I'd say. It was the right thing to do and thinking it made me feel kind of noble.

Pale light streamed through the blinds, throwing strips of shadow on the walls. In my mind was a picture of Holly the first time she walked in the store. For a moment I felt the same feeling I had when I saw her, that sense of being overwhelmed. I imagined driving out to meet her that night on Highway 29, my heart pounding as we walked out from the roadhouse to my car. It seemed like a lifetime ago, but also something that was happening to me right now. Disturbed by the contradiction, I left Holly sleeping and stumbled to the bathroom and filled the sink with cold water and washed my face. When I saw my reflection in the mirror above the sink I knew I wasn't going to turn myself in. There seemed no point in letting them save my life only to stick a lethal injection in my veins. Or to let me rot away what ever time I had left in a penitentiary.

Blood had seeped through the dressing. I peeled it off and looked at the swollen, discoloured flesh. I wet a towel in the sink and dabbed at the wound, flinching when I touched it. I swallowed two Tylenol, found the first aid kit and put on a fresh dressing and wrapped a bandage around my waist. Holly had cleaned my shirt and left it hanging on the towel rack. I pulled it on and returned to the bedroom and looked at Holly sleeping. If I left her now, she would have a chance. I thought about it, imagined myself hightailing it out of there, heading south across the border. But I didn't want to be without her. And she wouldn't want that either, I told myself.

She opened her eyes and smiled when she saw me watching her. "Hey, Travis," she said, before the smile wavered and became something made of sadness. She pushed herself up and asked how I was. I lied and told her I was feeling better. She got out of bed and went to the bathroom. I found the bottle of vodka and took a large slug. Some went down but I gagged and brought most of it back up on the floor.

I wiped my mouth and sat on the bed.

"You want me to change the dressing?" Holly asked when she came out of the bathroom.

"I already did it."

"It's still bleeding?"

"Not so much."

"You think it's infected?"

I ignored the question. "Listen, Holly," I said. "I been thinking. You don't have to come with me if you don't want."

"Why are you saying that?"

"I'm just trying to think things through."

"There's nothing to think about." She pulled on her skirt and boots.

"They can't pin anything on you."

"That's not how it works," she said.

"I don't want you to feel pressured."

"Is that what you think? That I got no mind of my own?"

"That's not what I mean," I said, but I didn't have the strength to argue with her. "I'm just saying I don't know how this goes."

She put her hands on her hips. "Neither do I, but my mind's made up."

I nodded. "Then we'd best get going."

Minutes later we were headed south on a dusty two-lane blacktop. She drove the first hour but I took over before we reached the border. We had no trouble crossing over into Reynosa but soon after I began to feel cold. My body started shaking and by the time I pulled into a filling station, I could hardly keep my hands on the wheel. Holly asked if I was all right. I told her I was just tired and needed to piss. I got out of the car and started to walk toward the bathroom when my knees gave way and I fell. Pain flared in my stomach and I clutched my belly, feeling something wet through my shirt.

Holly knelt beside me, calling my name. "Travis," she said. "Oh God!" She rolled me over onto my back and undid my jacket. "You said it had stopped."

I coughed and spat blood on the forecourt. "Help me up," I said.

"You'll bleed out if we don't get you to a hospital."

I grabbed her arm. "Not yet, Holly. Help me to the bathroom."

She helped me to stand. In the bathroom she changed the dressing and told me again I had to see a doctor right away. "We should've stayed at the motel."

"I told you you could have."

"And I told you I wasn't staying without you."

I couldn't remember her saying that. It seemed like something I had dreamed. "They would've got us," I said, thinking it would've been better for us if they did.

Holly stared at me. "What are we going to do?"

I didn't know what to say. I should have told her the truth then, but I couldn't find it in myself. "We keep going."

"Going where?"

"Where they can't find us."

If she knew as little about that place as I did, she didn't let on. Instead, she laughed and grabbed my arm. "Well, let's get the fuck on with it," she said as she led me out to the car.

•

I woke in the back seat, shivering and sweaty at the same time. My brain was numb. I stared out the window at the Sierra Madres on the horizon, thoughts running in slow motion, obscuring whatever meaning they might have had. I wondered if I was still dreaming, but quickly realised that no dream I'd ever had was as desolate and cold as what I felt.

"You're awake," Holly said from the front seat.

"I guess I must be."

"How you feeling?"

I tried on a smile but wasn't sure it took. "I'm not dead."

Her eyes found mine in the rearview mirror and held them. "You sure about that?"

"You can talk to ghosts?"

"I can talk to anything."

"I know that. Pull over."

She stopped on the side of the road and I got out and moved stiffly to the front of the car. I leaned against the hood, breath coming shallow and weak. The winter sun shone through the black trees like a premonition. I knew what it said but it was still hard to take. Holly got out and came to stand beside me. You did it because of something in her, I thought. You needed her to think you were someone.

"Travis?"

"What?"

"We had some fun, didn't we?"

I turned to face her and saw she was crying. She laughed softly and wiped her eyes with the heel of her thumb. "We sure did," I said. "Like I never had with anybody else."

"You don't have to lie to me no more."

"I'm not." I reached out and pulled her close and held her. The heat of her body gave me back the strength to see the way things really were, and I realised it wasn't anything in her that made me do what I did. It was something in me, something reckless and bold that sent me chasing empty dreams my whole life. It had been coming for a long long time and now at last here it was.

"Let me drive," I said.

She nodded and helped me sit in behind the wheel.

BANG!

•

The air thrummed with the beating of paper-thin wings and all the sky was suddenly filled with a vast kaleidoscope of butterflies. They chased us along the desert highway and descended upon us in a blur of color, swirled around our bodies and carried us aloft. I felt my pain slip away and saw no tears in her eyes. She was laughing just the way I remembered and I knew I was the one who made it happen.

She squeezed my hand and said she'd like to see that.

I didn't know what she meant, so I asked her to tell me again what butterflies stood for. She didn't respond. I thought maybe her mouth was full of monarchs and swallowtails but when I looked I saw it was full of blood. "Holly," I whispered. "What's wrong?"

A red butterfly bolo glistened against her breast. But she wasn't saying anything. It was just a dream.

The road was filled with broken glass and the smell of gasoline hung acrid and heavy in the air. I felt the cold wind come silent through the windshield and knew what it meant but I was long past caring. I stared at the snowcapped peaks, the sky and pines, and knew where I should be.

You're already there, I told myself as I closed my eyes and saw that I was running. I was running, then I was flying.

Contributors

Mia Dalia is an author, a lifelong reader, and a longtime reviewer of all things fantastic, thrilling, scary, and strange. Her short fiction has been published by *Night Terror Novels, 50 word stories, Flash Fiction Magazine, Pyre Magazine, Tales from the Moonlit Path*, Sunbury Press, and HellBound Press. Her fiction will be featured in the upcoming anthologies by Black Ink Fiction, Dragon Roost Press, Unsettling Reads, WMB anthology of Lunar Horror, Phobica Books, Wandering Wave Press, Off-Topic Publishing, and DraculaBeyondStoker Magazine. Mia's Noir tales have been featured by *Mystery Magazine* and her debut novel, *Estate State*, is tentatively set for 2023 release..

https://daliaverse.wixsite.com/author
https://twitter.com/Dalia_Verse

Roxanne Dent is a full-time professional writer who has sold nine novels, dozens of short stories, flash fiction, novellas, drabbles, and an E-Zine in a variety of genres including Regencies, Horror, Fantasy, Sci-Fi, Steampunk, Mystery, Westerns, and Middle Grade. She has also written screenplays. "The Pied Piper," won first prize in "Fade-in Magazine, and her three-minute movie thriller, "Valentine's Day, won the Audience Choice Award in the Bare Bones International Film Festival. She also co-authored short stories and plays with her sister, Karen Dent. At the time of publication she is completing her third short story in the Adventures of Harlow and Jack, an unusual mystery series.

Yvette Viets Flaten was born in Denver, Colorado and grew up in an US Air Force family, living in Nevada, North Dakota,

CONTRIBUTORS

and Washington State as well as England (Birchington, Kent), France, and Spain. She holds a Bachelor of Arts in Spanish ('74) and a Master of Arts in History ('82) from the University of Wisconsin—Eau Claire. Yvette writes both award-winning poetry and fiction. Her short stories have appeared in *The London Reader, Lakefly, Red Cedar, Wisconsin People* and *Ideas, Summer Bludgeon*, with another forthcoming, in *Sheila-na-gig*. Yvette lives in Eau Claire, Wisconsin, near the banks of the Chippewa River, with her husband Daniel, and Daisy, a golden cocker spaniel. She is currently working on her first full-length mystery.

Gary Fry is a semi-retired academic who lives in coastal countryside in the northeast of England. He has had published around 100 short stories, a bunch of novellas, and several novels. He was the first author in PS Publishing's Showcase range, and none other than Ramsey Campbell has described him as a "master of philosophical horror". He plays piano, loves dogs, and reads a frightening number of books each year. His web presence can be found here:

https://garyfrytalks.blogspot.com

Jamey Gallagher lives in Baltimore and teaches writing at the Community College of Baltimore County. His collection *American Animism* will be published in 2024.

Leif Hanson was born and raised in Colorado, except for the eight years he spent in the United States Marine Corps. He received a BA in Writing at the University of Colorado, Denver. Leif began creating works of fiction at a young age, intent on becoming a famous author, but discovered his love for computers in college and became a technical writer. However, he still loves to pen a few hunting and alt-fiction stories in his off time. When he's not writing, he can be found hiking the Rocky Mountains, travelling, or remodeling his home. Leif currently lives in the Denver area with his beautiful wife and three cats.

Gabriel Heller is a writer based in Brooklyn, New York. His stories have appeared in *The Best American Nonrequired Reading, Crazyhorse, Electric Literature, Tough,* and other venues. He teaches writing at New York University.

Andrew Hook has edited three previous anthologies: *The Alsiso Project* (which won the 2004 British Fantasy Society award for Best Anthology), *punkPunk!,* and *Elasticity: The Best of Elastic Press.* As writer, he has published around twenty books, the most recent being *Candescent Blooms* (Salt Publishing). In October this year a time-novel, *Secondhand Daylight,* so-written with Eugen Bacon, will be published by Cosmic Egg Books.

Brian Howell is an author and teacher living and working near Tokyo, Japan. He has published three novels and over forty short stories online and in print, including two short story collections as well as inclusion in *Best British Short Stories 2018* (edited by Nicholas Royle). His novels have often dealt with themes around Dutch genre painting, while his short stories tend towards the uncanny or speculative. He is a keen film-watcher and cyclist, and listens to many podcasts.

Rhys Hughes currently lives in India. He began writing fiction at an early age and his first book, *Worming the Harpy,* was published in 1995. Since that time he has published more than fifty other books and his work has been translated into ten languages. He recently completed an ambitious project that involved writing exactly 1000 linked narratives. *The Rhys Hughes Megapack* issued by Wildside Press is a good retrospective of his short fiction. He is currently working on a novel called *Average Assassins* and several new collections.

Andrew Humphrey is the author of two collections of short stories, both published by Elastic Press. *Open The Box* appeared in 2002 and *Other Voices,* which was one of the winners of the inaugural East Anglian Book Award, in 2008.

His debut novel, *Alison*, was published by TTA Press also in 2008. Described as East Anglia's laureate of loss and alienation, Andrew's short fiction has appeared in *Crimewave*, *Midnight Street*, *Black Static* and *The Third Alternative*. His second novel, *Debris*, and his third collection of short stories, *A Punch To The Heart* were both published by Head Shot Press in 2022. He lives and works in Norwich, UK.

Maxim Jakubowski worked as a publisher for many years alongside his writing in the fields of SF, erotica and crime, and editing over 100 anthologies. He was for over two decades the crime critic for *Time Out* and then the *Guardian* and now reviews at *Crime Time*. Under a pseudonym he has written ten volumes in a literary erotica series which reached the Top 10 of the *Sunday Times* bestseller list. His last two novels are *The Louisiana Republic* and *The Piper's Dance* and Head Shot Press have recently issued his collection *Death Has Thousand Faces*. He lives in London and is the current Chair of the CWA. Find him at www.maximjakubowski.co.uk.

Benedict J Jones is a writer from southeast London who mainly works in the crime and horror genres. His Charlie Bars series of neo-noir crime includes the novels *Pennies for Charon*, *The Devil's Brew*, and *The Gingerbread Houses*, as well as the collection *Skewered and Other London Cruelties*. His horror works have included the novellas *Slaughter Beach* and *Hell Ship* along with a collection of western-horror stories, *Ride the Dark Country* (Dark Minds Press). Together with Anthony Watson *he writes the historical horror series The DAMOCLES Files*.

Tim Lees is the author of the novel *Frankenstein's Prescription* (Brooligan press) described by *Publisher's Weekly* as "a philosophically insightful and literary tale of terror", and of the "Field Ops" series for HarperVoyager: *The God Hunter*, *Devil in the Wires* and *Steal the Lightning*. He hopes to have a new story collection out in the coming year. When not writing, he has had a wide variety of jobs, including film extra, teacher, conference organiser, lithographer, and lizard-bottler in a museum. He spent several years working on the rehab units of a psychiatric hospital, a hugely rewarding job in every way except financially. Tim is from Manchester, England, but now lives in Chicago with his wife and small dog. He always has an alibi.

Jenean McBrearty is a graduate of San Diego State University, who taught Political Science and Sociology, and received her MFA from Eastern Kentucky University. Her fiction, poetry, and photographs have been published in over two-hundred-sixty print and on-line journals. Her how-to book, *Writing Beyond the Self; How to Write Creative Non-fiction that Gets Published* was published by Vine Leaves Press in 2018. She won the Eastern Kentucky English Department Award for Graduate Creative Non-fiction in 2011, and a Silver Pen Award in 2015 for her noir short story: *Red's Not Your Color.*

Cate Moyle writes mystery stories; she's won numerous recognitions, including the latest as a Silver Falchion Award finalist. She is also an award-winning poet, having been published in literary journals from *The Southeast Review* to *Wicked Alice.* Moyle's recent works appear in *Mystery Tribune* and *Bowery Gothic,* and *Crimeucopia.* Find her on the web (and socials) at

https://catemoylepens.weebly.com/

Mike O'Driscoll's fiction has appeared in *Black Static, The Magazine of Fantasy and Science Fiction, Interzone, Crime Wave* and numerous anthologies including *Best New Horror,* and *Year's Best Fantasy & Horror.* Two collections of his stories, *Unbecoming* and *The Dream Operator,* were published by Elastic Press and Undertow Publications, and his story, *Eyepennies,* appeared as the first of TTA Press's series of stand alone novellas, in 2012. His story, *Sounds Like,* was adapted by Brad Anderson for an episode of the mid-noughties horror anthology show, *Masters of Horror*. His novella, *Pervert Blood*, appeared in *Black Static* #80/81 in 2021.

Melissa Pleckham is a Los Angeles-based writer, actor, and musician. Her work has been featured in numerous publications, including *Flame Tree Fiction*, *Tiny Frights*, *Luna Luna*, *Hello Horror*, *Under the Bed Magazine*, and FunDead Publications' *Entombed in Verse* poetry collection. She is a member of the Horror Writers Association; *Neon Graveyard* marks her first foray into crime fiction. She also plays bass and sings for the garage-goth duo Black Lullabies. You can find her online at melissapleckham.com and on social media at @mpleckham.

Song Gao Lei was raised in the upper Midwest of America. In 2005, he left the States to begin graduate studies in England before moving to mainland China in 2014. Presently, he lives with his wife in south China where he teaches at a university. He counts Yu Hua and Zhang Ailing among his favorite writers, in addition to Western authors Graham Greene, Cormac McCarthy, and Evelyn Waugh.

Variously classed as a Science Fiction, Weird, Surreal, Literary, or Historical Fiction writer, **Douglas Thompson** is a former Chair and Director of the Scottish Writers Centre and author of more than 20 short story and poetry collections and novels, including *The Brahan Seer: Scotland's Nostradamus*. He won the Herald/Grolsch Question Of Style Award in 1989, 2nd prize in the Neil Gunn Writing Competition 2007, and the Faith/Unbelief Poetry Prize in 2016.

https://douglasthompson.wordpress.com/

Grant Tracey is author of the Hayden Fuller Mystery series. He has published three Fuller novels and stories in *Tough*, Twelve Winters Journal, and *Groovy Gumshoes* edited by Michael Bracken. He is currently working on an Eddie Sands novel and is Fiction Editor at *North American Review*. In another lifetime, it seems, he wrote literary fiction, publishing four collections and over fifty short stories in little magazines.

He is an avid Toronto Maple Leafs fan.

Saira Viola is the author of *Jukebox* and *Crack, Apple & Pop*. She is a multiple Pushcart Prize and Best of The Net nominee Her fiction and poetry have appeared in *Vautrin Magazine*, *International Times, Mü Magazine,* several other publications, and the latrine walls of The Little Red Door Paris.

Charles West was born and raised as an "Army Brat," growing up in Japan, Germany, and various army bases in the U.S. He ended up in Fresno, California, becoming a teacher and writer. He has published short stories in such publications as *Ellery Queen Mystery Magazine, Isaac Asimov's Science Fiction Magazine, Hardboiled, Passager, Kings River Life,* as well as a number of anthologies. His mystery novel, *The Sacred Disc,* was published in 2001 by Salvo Press. He has also had plays produced in California, New York, Florida, Wisconsin, and Michigan. In addition, he is the dramaturg and an actor for the Woodward Shakespeare Festival in Fresno, California.